Dark Wolf

Published by Kensington Publishing Corporation

Dark Wolf

The Spirit Wild Series

KATE DOUGLAS

APHRODISIA

KENSINGTON PUBLISHING CORP.

www.kensingtonbooks.com

KENSINGTON BOOKS are published by

Kensington Publishing Corp.
119 West 40th Street
New York, NY 10018

All Kensington titles, imprints, and distributed lines are available at special quantity discounts for bulk purchases for sales promotion, premiums, fund-raising, and educational or institutional use.

Special book excerpts or customized printings can also be created to fit specific needs. For details, write or phone the office of the Kensington Special Sales Manager: Kensington Publishing Corp., 119 West 40th Street, New York, NY 10018. Attn. Special Sales Department. Phone: 1-800-221-2647.

Aphrodisia and the A logo Reg. U.S. Pat. & TM Off.

ISBN-13: 978-0-7582-8818-9
ISBN-10: 0-7582-8818-2
First Kensington Trade Paperback Printing: May 2013

eISBN-13: 978-0-7582-9006-9
eISBN-10: 0-7582-9006-3
First Kensington Electronic Edition: May 2013

10 9 8 7 6 5 4 3 2 1

Printed in the United States of America

If not for the amazing response to my original Wolf Tales series, this new series, Spirit Wild, would not exist. And so, I very humbly dedicate the first story, Dark Wolf, to you, the readers, who have made Lily's story possible.

Acknowledgments

I've wanted to write this series since the day I typed the final page of *Wolf Tales 12,* but for a long time I wasn't sure if I'd have that chance. Publishing is a fascinating and sometimes frustrating business, but it's one I've grown to love with all my heart—along with the wonderful people I've met along the way.

I want to thank my agent, Jessica Faust, of BookEnds Literary Agency, for her support, her advice, and her ability to get me pointed in the right direction. It's not an easy job, believe me! I also want to thank my editor at Kensington, Audrey La Fehr, who bought my very first Wolf Tales in 2005 and is still reading my convoluted tales of the sexy Chanku shapeshifters. She's been amazingly supportive, which is a wonderful confidence builder for an author. But most importantly, she has encouraged me to write my stories my way, and that alone is a gift beyond price. My sincere thanks also to Martin Biro, assistant editor extraordinaire—if I have a question, Martin can answer it, and if I need something, he takes care of it. He keeps me sane . . . relatively speaking.

This first book of the second generation of Chanku has truly been a labor of love, but I always need someone to read for the inconsistencies and gaffes that can so easily slip through. My wonderful beta readers read, commented, and critiqued on a tight schedule without complaint. Many thanks to Nicole Passante of sharearead.com, Rhonda Wilson, Lynne Thomas, Kerry Parker, Rose Toubbeh, Jan Takane, Ann Jacobs, Karen Woods, and Lynn Sicoli, who not only gave me a really fast turnaround, but also asked the right questions. I just hope I found the right answers.

The original idea might be the author's, but the final book goes through many hands. Thanks to the many hands who have left and will leave their fingerprints on Lily and Sebastian's story.

1

Crickets chirped. An owl hooted. A dusting of starlight shimmered faintly against granite peaks, but here at the forest's edge, all was dark. Shivering slightly in the cool night air, Sebastian Xenakis stood beneath the gnarled oak, just one more shadow among many. With great humility and as much confidence as he could muster while standing naked in the darkness, he raised his arms, drew on the magic coursing through his veins, and once more called on the spirit within the tree, one he affectionately thought of as *the lady*, humbly asking for her strength.

Nothing.

"Damn it all." He exhaled, accepting the rush of air for what it was—a huge blast of frustration at the serendipitous nature of his magic. He stared at the massive tree towering overhead and methodically emptied his mind of all thoughts, all distractions. He put aside anger and frustration, fears and hopes, leaving room for nothing but *here* and *now*. Focusing everything within, he opened his heart to possibilities, and waited.

A few long, frustrating minutes later, he felt her warmth envelop him. An unexpected frisson raced across his bare shoulders, along his arms. It caressed his naked buttocks and swirled over his belly, lifting the dark line of body hair that trailed from navel to groin. Then it slithered along his thighs, circled his calves, and tickled across his bare feet. His cock, flush with hot blood, swelled high and hard against his belly, giving homage to the gift of power.

Then, sliding away as soft as a whisper, the intimate sense of touch, of sentient communion, bled off into the damp loam and returned to its source through thickly tangled roots. Sebastian sighed, a shuddering acceptance of sensual pleasure, the gift of contact with such a powerful force.

The lady of the oak.

His erection remained, strong evidence of her touch, the visceral connection he'd made with a spirit ancient beyond recorded memory. His body thrummed with her life force, with her power, until Sebastian felt each and every one of her thick and twisted branches spreading far and wide, until he bowed beneath the age and innate wisdom of the ancient tree. This mother oak must have stood here, a silent sentinel of the forest since long before the dawn of modern history. A few heavy branches had fallen over time, but he knew her roots were strong, her branches healthy. As if challenging time itself, the graceful beauty and symmetry of the tree remained.

He remembered the first time he saw the oak, recalled the sense of life, the sure knowledge of the tree's spiritual power. It was on that day he'd learned his father wielded the kind of power Sebastian had quickly grown to crave.

Standing just beyond the reach of the great branches, unsure of his relationship with a man he barely knew, Sebastian had watched Aldo Xenakis call lightning out of a clear, star-filled sky—call it and control it with the deft hands of a master.

He'd been seduced so easily, so quickly by that flashy show of fire and magic. Of power. Immeasurable power. So thoroughly seduced he knew he might never break free of its siren call.

Might never break free of the man he'd consciously sought, despite his mother's warning. Now it was much too late. His die had been cast, commitments made, and he was almost glad his mother was dead.

Glad she couldn't see what he'd become.

Sebastian quickly shoved thoughts of his moral weakness, his failures—and his father—aside. There was no need to mar the beauty of this night. He took a deep breath and then, almost as an afterthought, cleared his mind of all obstructions and drew more power to him. Pulled it from the earth, from the sky, from the water of a nearby stream, from the mountain itself. The fire must come from within, but he called on that as well and felt the power build.

Then he buffered the swirling energy with the strength of the oak until it was entirely under his control. Until he was the one holding the power.

Unlike his father, unwilling to display or even acknowledge such arrogance, Sebastian turned and bowed his head toward the oak, giving the tree's spirit his grateful thanks for her help. Then, spreading his fingers wide, he consciously breathed deeply and opened himself to the energy flowing into him from all directions. A brilliant glow surrounded him, but it wasn't lightning that lit the dark night.

It was power. Raw power he'd pulled from the earth, from the air and water. From the spirit in the tree and the fire burning in his soul.

Within seconds, the light blinked out. Gone as if it had never existed at all.

As was the man. In his place, a wolf darker than night raised its head and sniffed the air. Then it turned away and raced into the forest.

4 / *Kate Douglas*

* * *

"Lily? Have you seen this morning's news?"

Lily Cheval fumbled with the phone and squinted at the bedside clock in the early morning darkness. Blue numbers blurred into focus. Her best buddy looked at her out of the screen on her phone. "Alex, it's six fifteen in the morning. On a Sunday. What can possibly be important enough to . . ."

"There's been another one, Lil. Just inside the entrance to the park this time."

Lily bit back a growl and sat up. The last body, discovered less than a week ago, had been found along the highway leading into Glacier National Park in Montana. Much too close to the Chanku pack's main residence. The one before that had been on the outskirts of Kalispell. "What have you got?"

Alex sighed and wiped a hand across his eyes. Poor Alex. How he'd ever ended up as the pack's liaison to the Flathead County sheriff's department was beyond understanding. He might be brilliant and charismatic—not to mention drop-dead gorgeous—but he was not cut out to deal with, much less deliver, bad news, especially early on a Sunday morning.

She wondered if he'd even made it to bed the night before. His eyes looked bloodshot, and Alex did love his social life on a Saturday night.

Even in Kalispell.

"Same as the last seven," he said, pulling her back into the conversation. "Young woman, beaten, brutally raped. Throat torn out. Just like the others, probably killed somewhere else and dumped. A park ranger found her body beside the road."

"Shit. I hope you've got an alibi." She hated having to ask, but with public sentiment the way it had been heading . . .

"I was with Jennifer last night. I got the call on the way home this morning."

Jennifer. Poor choice of woman, but at least she could account for Alex's time when the attack occurred. Frustrated,

Lily dug her fingers into her tangled hair and tugged. Anything to help focus her thoughts. "Let me know what you find out. Check with the pack. See if they've got any new leads. I'm stuck in San Francisco until after the reception, but I'll try and get up there by the weekend."

"Okay. Sorry to wake you, but I just wanted to warn you. Be careful. Whoever's behind this, they've hit the Bay Area just as hard. I'll find out what I can. Thanks, Lil."

Quietly Lily set the phone back in the charger and leaned against the headboard. Another young woman dead. Another murder with all the signs of a wild animal attack—except for the rape.

Just like the other seven.

Eight young women, dead by a combination of man and beast. Five in or near Glacier National Park. Three in the San Francisco Bay Area.

And where were the largest populations of Chanku shapeshifters?

"Glacier National Park and the San Francisco Bay Area. Shit." A chilling sense of premonition shuddered along Lily's spine. If they didn't find the one behind this, and find him soon, someone was going to be hunting Chanku.

The sharp click of Lily's heels echoed against the pale gray walls of Cheval International, one of the more profitable branches of Chanku Global Industries. She walked quickly toward her office, wishing she could ignore the tension headache pounding in sharp counterpoint to her footsteps.

Her father insisted headaches were purely psychosomatic—according to Anton Cheval, Chanku shapeshifters were impervious to human frailties. "Tell that to my head," she muttered, timing the steady throbbing between her eyes against the click of her heels.

Damn. She did not need a headache. Not on a Monday, not

with a full day of meetings ahead, including lunch with the mayor and a one-on-one with the head of security.

Resentment of the long-lived Chanku shapeshifters had been simmering for years, but the recent series of attacks against young women had brought that simmer to a boil. It didn't help that a local celebrity had taken a very public stance against the Chanku, blaming them for everything from the current downturn in the economy to the vicious rapes and murders.

Aldo Xenakis had been a thorn in Lily's side ever since she'd assumed leadership of Cheval International. Recently, his verbal attacks had taken on a frighteningly personal slant.

It didn't help that he owned a massive amount of land that abutted her father's vast holdings in Montana. It was bad enough he was stirring up resentment here in California, but Montana was home. Having longtime friends and neighbors turn against them hurt Lily and the rest of the pack on a much more personal level. They'd worked hard at being good neighbors, at integrating themselves into the community.

Now this.

"Good morning, Ms. Cheval."

"G'morning, Jean." Lily paused in front of her assistant's desk. "Have you got today's calendar?"

Jean nodded. Gray haired, round-faced, and very human, she'd been Lily's assistant since Lily'd been named CEO of the company seven years earlier. And, while Jean continued to age, Lily still looked as youthful and fresh as the day she'd walked out of UC Berkeley with her MBA.

One more reason for humans to resent shapeshifters, though she'd never noticed any resentment at all from Jean. Considering the good pay and generous benefit packages all CGI employees—including all Cheval International hires—received, she didn't expect it to become an issue.

Lily glanced over the daily calendar Jean handed to her. The morning wasn't too busy, but . . . "Why have you got a question mark by my lunch date with the mayor?"

Jean shook her head. "Her office called a few minutes ago. When the mayor's schedule went out to the media yesterday, they forgot to black out your lunch appointment. Reporters know when and where you're meeting, and the mayor said she'd understand if you decide to cancel."

The pounding between her eyes got worse. Goddess, but it had been too long since she'd shifted and run. Right now, Lily really wanted to chase down something furry and kill it. "Not necessary," she said, rubbing her temple. "We really need to talk. Maybe I'll wear a disguise."

Jean grinned as she gave her an appraising look. "Don't think that would help. You're hard to miss."

Lily raised her eyebrows and glanced at Jean. "Thank you. I think." She grabbed the mail Jean handed to her and headed toward her office, but paused at the door. "I'm expecting a call from Alex Aragat. Be sure and put him through even if I'm on something else."

"Okay." The phone rang, but before answering it, Jean added, "You'll find a list of the calls you need to return on your desk. Uhm, more than a few from your father." Lily just shook her head when Jean laughed and said, "He wanted to remind you not to forget the reception Thursday night."

"I wish," Lily muttered, but she turned and smiled at Jean. "I won't. And even if I wanted to, dear old Dad would make sure I got there on time."

Lily shut the office door as Jean took her call. She glanced at the clock over the bookcase. Seven thirty, which meant that with any luck, she'd have time to get her desk cleared before lunch. Her head was still pounding like a damned jackhammer, but she flopped down in the comfortable chair behind her desk and read through Jean's messages. All were carefully organized by importance. The stack from her father—and damn, but how many times had the man called?—was set off to one side.

Obviously, he was already awake. Might as well check in with the boss first. The phone rang as she reached for it. She glanced at the caller ID, sighed, and flipped on the video.

"Hello, Dad. I was just getting ready to call you."

"How's your headache?"

She frowned at his smug image. "How do you know I've got a headache?"

"Because I've been trying to mindspeak all morning and I know you're blocking me."

"Oh." No wonder her head hurt. She'd developed the habit of keeping her shields high and tight since she was just a child, but that never kept her father from trying. He'd rarely managed to give her a headache, though. "Well, if you knew you were giving me a headache, why'd you keep pushing?"

No answer. Typical. She was convinced he only heard what he wanted to hear.

"You've talked to Alex."

Not a question. He'd know, of course. Anton Cheval knew everything. "Yes. He called first thing yesterday morning, but he didn't have any details. I expect to hear more today. Have you learned anything else?"

"How well do you know Aldo Xenakis?"

"Not well at all," she said, used to her father's non sequiturs. Amazing . . . her headache was gone. She almost laughed. Dear old Dad had been the cause all along. "Why do you ask?"

"His son will be attending the reception Thursday night. I want you to meet him."

"He has a son? Since when? I thought Xenakis lived alone."

"The younger Xenakis has stayed in the background. From what I've learned, he didn't even know Aldo was his father until a couple of years ago. When the boy's mother died, he traced Aldo through her private papers."

"Interesting. Why do you think the son's important?"

"He's been staying at his father's home up here for the past month. You know where the house is. It's a few miles from our place, though our properties share the southern boundary. Tinker thought he smelled an unfamiliar wolf near the edge of our holdings night before last. He traced the scent to a ridge on the Xenakis property. The wolf scent disappeared, but he picked up the trail of a man and followed it to the house. The only one there was a young man who appeared to be Xenakis's son."

"He's Chanku?" Now that would be interesting, considering how xenophobic the father was.

"We don't know. The elder Xenakis has powerful magic. If the son inherited his father's gift, he could be shifting by magical means, not natural. I want you to get close enough, see if you sense anything."

"Do you think he's our murderer?"

"I don't know, Lily. But the women have been killed near Kalispell and in the San Francisco Bay Area. Xenakis has homes in both places, and his son spends time at both locations. I've got Alex looking into his schedule now, checking flight records, that sort of thing. Be very careful."

"One question. What's his name? How will I know him?"

"Sebastian. I don't know what surname he used before, but he's taken his father's name. Look for Sebastian Xenakis. Tinker says he's tall with dark hair. And really odd eyes. Teal blue, according to Tink. Not amber like most of us. And, Lily?"

"Yes?"

"I love you, sweetheart, but I have a bad feeling about this. Be very careful. We don't know a thing about this guy, but he's got my sense of premonition in high gear. No specific danger, just a strong feeling he'll have some kind of effect on our family."

Lily stared at the handset long after her father had ended the call. The pack might tease Anton Cheval about his premonitions, but invariably he'd been proven correct. She flipped on her computer and typed in Sebastian Xenakis's name.

It never hurt to be fully informed about the enemy.

"Lily. So glad you agreed to meet even after my office bungled this so badly."

"Well, hopefully the media haven't bugged the dining room." Lily smiled at the mayor and shook her hand. "It's good to see you, Jill." Then she nodded toward the group of reporters gathered just outside the restaurant. "I was hoping they were here for you, not me. It's been awhile since I've run a gauntlet like that."

Mayor Jill Bradley shook her head as she reached for the menu. "It's the killings, Lily. We're doing everything we can to keep a lid on things, but . . ."

"I know." Sighing, Lily reached for her own menu. "I heard from Alex Aragat, our pack's law enforcement liaison in Montana. People are scared, and I can't blame them. My father's got every available resource working on this from our angle."

Jill shook her head. "My gut feeling is that it's not a Chanku killing these girls. I think someone's trying to raise public anger against shifters."

Lily had to agree. "Dad feels the same way, but until this guy is stopped . . ."

"Or they. DNA is inconclusive, but I've been told it points to more than one perp. Wolves, definitely, but possibly more than one human committing the rapes."

Crap. "They've narrowed it down to wolves?"

"Yes. We're keeping a lid on that info." Jill spread her hands in a helpless gesture. "Your people are catching enough flak as it is."

"No kidding. Is it a single male? If a woman had consensual sex before the attack, it could explain more than one."

Jill nodded. "There's one consistent set, a few variables. That's the conclusion. For now."

The waitress reached their table before Lily could respond. Jill set her menu down to place her order; Lily closed hers and studied the mayor. Jill Bradley had held her post for almost five years now, and her popularity had yet to wane. She'd become a good friend and a powerful ally, a woman Lily would have liked and admired even if she hadn't been the mayor.

It never hurt to have friends in high places. Smart friends. The fact that she had already considered what Lily figured was happening was a good sign. She glanced up and realized the waitress was waiting patiently for her order.

"Hamburger. Rare." Lily smiled at the waitress, waiting for the admonition that rare beef wasn't safe. Instead, she got a saucy wink. "You got it. Be back in a minute with your wine."

"Did we order wine?"

Jill laughed. "It's on me. I figured you could use a glass about now. I know I sure can. Let's discuss the reception and your father's generous donation. The other topic is too frustrating when we don't have any answers."

"I agree. I think we're being set up, but I'm not sure it's more than one person."

Jill's dark brows drew down. "You'll let me know if you learn anything to substantiate that, won't you?"

"Of course. I mentioned Alex Aragat, our pack liaison with law enforcement in Kalispell. He's working on a couple of things, but at this point it's all supposition."

The waitress reached the table and opened a bottle of wine. She poured a taste for the mayor, who sipped and quickly agreed.

"I'll have your meals in a few minutes. Enjoy." Smiling, the young woman moved on to another table.

Lily tipped her glass in a toast to her friend. "Here's to the new wing at the museum. I saw it this weekend. It's turned out beautifully."

"Thanks to your father's generosity."

Lily dipped her head, acknowledging the mayor's comment. Anton Cheval, via Chanku Global Industries and its subsidiary, Cheval International, had become a generous benefactor over the years, and Jill Bradley's status as mayor had benefited greatly from his many gifts to the city during her administration.

"Consorting with the local fauna, Mayor Bradley?"

Lily fought the urge to spin around and glare. Instead, she sat perfectly still, outwardly calm and relaxed, though she raised one eyebrow at the mayor. Jill set her wine on the table and glowered at the man beyond Lily's shoulder.

"There's no call for such rude behavior, Aldo. You're inter-rupting a private lunch."

Lily slowly turned in her chair, at a disadvantage to the tall, elegant man standing much too close behind her for comfort. The hairs along her spine rose and she bit back a growl. She'd never met Aldo Xenakis in person, but the man was on the news often enough. Lately he'd made a point of baiting Chanku shapeshifters, and Lily Cheval in particular. She recog-nized him immediately.

Shoving her chair back, she stood while privately enjoying the satisfaction of watching him back up when he realized she met him at eye level. "Ah, Mr. Xenakis. I'd say it's a pleasure, but we both know differently." She smiled, showing a lot of teeth, and held out her hand. He stared at it a moment. Lily didn't waver. Reluctantly, he shook hands.

The frisson of awareness left her wanting to wash her hands. There was something wrong about Xenakis. Something she couldn't place. Oddly enough, it wasn't her Chanku sense that left her skin crawling.

No. It was her magic, something as much a part of her as her

Chanku heritage. Her innate power recoiled almost violently at the man's brief touch.

Lily surreptitiously wiped her palm against her slim skirt. She noticed that Jill wasn't the least bit welcoming. "Was there something you wanted, Aldo? Ms. Cheval and I are enjoying a private lunch while we discuss business."

She placed her emphasis firmly on *private.*

"No." He stepped back and nodded. "I merely saw a beautiful woman sitting here and took a chance to say hello." He kept his gaze planted firmly on Jill and blatantly ignored Lily.

Lily remained standing, purposefully invading his space until the waitress arrived with their meals. Aldo stepped out of her way and then left without another word. Lily turned, sat, and raised her eyebrow again as she glanced at Jill.

Jill shook her head. The moment the waitress was gone, she took a sip of her wine. "I do not like that man. Something about him . . ."

Lily nodded. "Makes your skin crawl?"

"Exactly. Why? He's handsome enough. Well mannered."

"Rich and powerful." Lily laughed. "I bet he's asked you out."

"He did, and like a fool, I accepted. I couldn't wait for the evening to end."

"Did he make a pass?"

Jill shook her head. "Nothing so obvious, but he makes me very uncomfortable. Just a feeling I wasn't safe with him."

Lily took a bite of her blood-rare hamburger and swallowed. "You sure you're not Chanku? You've always got good intuition."

"No. Not a drop. I was tested. Took the nutrients for two weeks. Not even a hint of the need to howl." She shrugged and turned her attention to her salad.

Lily used her French fry as a pointer. "I'm sorry. I think you could have given the guys in my pack a run for their money."

Jill sipped her wine. "I still can. I just have to do it on two legs."

They both laughed, but at the same time, the fact she'd tried the nutrients meant Jill had hoped she was Chanku. Lily was sorry for her, for the fact that her friend had wanted something badly enough to go for it, yet failed.

It was something Jill had to accept she could never have. Lily wondered what that would be like, to want something that was totally impossible, something forever out of reach.

They concentrated on their food for a bit. Then Jill set her fork down. "You know, Lily. I think the world of you, and I really love your folks. You're good people. All of you, your mom and dad especially. They give generously whenever there's a need, and they've done a lot for this city, even though they don't live here. I don't want to see these killings hurt any of you, but if we can't find the killer, I don't know how we're going to keep the anger under control. I worry about your safety."

Lily glanced toward the crowd of reporters waiting at the front door. The questions they'd thrown at her as she walked into the restaurant had been pointed and ugly. In their minds, shapeshifters were committing rapes and murders, and she was just as guilty as the ones actually doing the deed.

The sudden jackhammer inside her head had her gasping.

"Lily? Are you all right?"

Jill reached across the table and took her hand.

Lily pressed fingers to her skull. "Just a minute."

Her father's voice filled her mind.

There's been another killing, Lily. A woman's body was found about ten minutes ago in Golden Gate Park, not far from the garden your mother designed many years ago. If you're in a public place, you might want to find somewhere private to finish your lunch with the mayor.

"Shit." Lily took one more quick bite of her burger and tossed back the last of her wine, taking a moment to consider the consequences of her father's words. She focused on Jill, one of the few people aware that the Chanku were telepathic. "My father just contacted me. There's been another murder. The body was found about . . ."

The mayor's cell phone rang. She answered the call, but her gaze was glued to Lily. With a soft curse, she asked a couple of brief questions and then ended the call. "That was the chief of police. I'm needed back at City Hall." She stood up. "I'm sorry, Lily. I'll do what I can."

"I know. Thank you. Go ahead. I'll get lunch."

Jill was reaching for her handbag. "That's not . . ."

"Go. Call me later."

"I will." She slipped the strap to her purse over her shoulder and gave Lily a quick hug. "Later. And thank you."

Lily watched her walk away. A pleasant-looking woman in her early fifties, Jill Bradley looked like someone's mom, not like the head of one of the nation's largest, most diverse cities.

She walked as if she didn't have a care in the world, passing through the throng of reporters with a quick smile and a friendly greeting to the ones she knew.

Lily wished she had that kind of grace under fire. She handed her card to the waitress, signed the tab when it came after adding a sizeable tip for that perfectly prepared, almost raw burger, and walked toward the back of the restaurant.

There was no way she was going to try and get through the reporters. Nope. She'd take the coward's exit, through the kitchen and out the back.

And the first thing she'd do when she got back to the office was call Alex. The last murder had been in Montana, but this latest had happened barely a mile from her office.

She wondered where Sebastian Xenakis had been last night.

2

"Anything newsworthy?"

Sebastian glanced away from the big bay window with its unobstructed view of the sun slipping into the Pacific Ocean, something he found more attractive than anything that could possibly fill the media screen this time of day. "I have no idea. I've not been paying attention."

His father paused in front of the screen, raised the volume, and then spoke over it. "Maybe you should, son of mine. I don't understand your lack of interest in events shaping the world. How do you expect to help shape those events if you're not even aware, if you don't care, what's important?"

Sebastian merely shrugged. "I have no interest in shaping events. I'll leave that to men like you."

"That's the coward's way. No son of mine—"

Sebastian smiled as he interrupted. "Wants to compete with his father. You're obviously good at what you do, Father. There's no need for me to fight your battles. You do quite well on your own."

His father stared at him a moment, and Sebastian wished he could read the man's mind. He couldn't even read his aura, something that came naturally to him with most people. The man remained a mystery. Sometimes he wondered if the elder Xenakis wanted to send him away, if he'd rather not claim a son who was so unlike himself. Other times, Sebastian was certain his father was proud of his accomplishments, even a bit impressed by his magical abilities.

The shapeshifting had certainly gotten the old man's attention. When he'd demonstrated his ability, Sebastian's shift from man to wolf had left Aldo Xenakis speechless. Of course, with his father's avid hatred of Chanku shapeshifters, Sebastian possibly could have chosen a creature other than a wolf—one more politically correct—but that was the one that came easiest to him.

He had not wanted to risk failure, and he hadn't. In fact, he'd grown so comfortable now with the shift that it took less energy every time, but he really should work on some new creatures. He'd watched the Chanku on the neighboring property. Hiding high on the mountain on his father's land, he'd used a powerful telescope to study them as they went about their daily lives.

Even the children could shift. Fascinated, he'd watched the little ones take the shapes of various creatures, of birds and lions and leopards, always under their parents—or at least an adult's—watchful eye. And always creatures of prey, whether it be hawk or cougar, wolf, or even, on at least one occasion, a snake.

He'd not ventured beyond the wolf. His greatest fear was finding a shape and getting caught in it, but eventually he was certain his skill would allow shifts of all kinds.

"What do you know of this?"

Sebastian glanced at the digital tablet his father shoved in front of him. The evening news was updating—he read the headlines. Another body had been found, another young woman raped and murdered. Raped by a man, yet murdered by a beast. Or beasts.

He raised his eyes and stared directly at his father. "Not a damned thing. Why? Do you expect me to have inside knowledge?"

"The last murder occurred Sunday in Montana, not far from our home. This one was here in San Francisco. You were in Montana on Sunday. You're here now."

He tapped the screen, shutting down the view. Then he turned away from Sebastian and stared out the window.

Silence truly could be deafening.

Sebastian clamped down on the surge of anger. There were some topics he'd rather not argue. This was one of them, but he wasn't about to let his father's insult go entirely unanswered. "What's your point, Father?"

"Are you still shifting? Still running as a wolf?" Aldo continued to gaze out the window as he questioned his son.

"I am." Sebastian took a deep, controlling breath. "Are you insinuating that I have anything to—"

"Do you?"

The question, the fact the man would actually voice it, startled him. He stared at his father's back. Stared until the bastard slowly turned and glared right back at him. Energy sparkled in the air between them. Energy and anger unlike anything Sebastian had ever experienced. He felt his wolf stir within, an unnerving, unexpected sensation. For the first time ever he had to consciously hold back the shift. There was no magic in this—it was rage. Pure, relentless rage.

He clenched his jaw, fought for control, and won.

Still the two of them stood there, glaring at each other like two alpha wolves daring one another for control. Neither of them spoke. They didn't have to. Anger simmered, a palpable force in the room.

Sebastian was the first to lower his gaze. Seething inside, fighting the wildness reaching for release, he stared at the stone tiles that covered the floor. He didn't raise his head until he was certain his father had left the room.

Once again, he'd been judged.

Judged, and found wanting, even though he knew he had his father bested.

Sebastian could shift. The wizard couldn't.

Long moments later, he felt the wolf subside, took a deep breath, and then let it out. He inhaled again, slowly, until his thundering heart settled back to its normal cadence in his chest.

He turned to the window, breathing slow and steady as he watched the fog rolling in over the dark water, but his thoughts were far away. He wondered about the latest victim—who she was. What she had been like.

What her thoughts had been before she died.

If she had known the one who killed her.

It was a little after ten when Lily paid the cabbie near 19th and Lincoln, got out of the car, and slipped into the fog and shadows at the edge of Golden Gate Park. She wore loose sweats and sandals and carried a cloth bag, well aware she looked more like a homeless transient than the CEO of one of the largest import companies in the city.

It was exactly the look she wanted.

Slipping into the thick shrubbery that bordered this area of the park, she stripped out of her clothing and stuffed shoes and sweats into the bag. Naked, shivering in the cool night air, she bent low and shoved the bag with her stuff under a low-growing shrub.

A branch cracked nearby, sharp and loud as a gunshot. She went totally still, crouched low beneath the brush. After a moment, Lily heard laughter, a feminine giggle, and the soft tones of a masculine voice. She raised her head and sniffed, picking up the faint hint of cologne, a softer, feminine perfume, and the rich cloud of pheromones in the still night air.

She heard the sound of clothing rustling, a soft whimper, and a rough, masculine moan.

Just her luck. She wanted to run, and the dude on the other side of the bush wanted to fuck. It would be funny if she weren't so desperate to leave her human self behind tonight, though she almost laughed out loud when she thought of what Alex would make of the situation.

He had a smart-ass comment for everything, and he'd absolutely be loving this mess, which meant she'd probably tell him about it later. She could hear him now, running a riff about her hunkered down in the bushes alongside one of the busiest streets in the city, bare assed and buck naked while some bozo tried to make it with his girlfriend less than two feet away.

She waited, hoping they'd disappear, maybe find a room somewhere. Instead, she heard the snick of a zipper, a soft, "Oh, baby. That's it . . . that's . . ."

Shit. Enough already. Lily called on her wolf and felt the change sweep over her body. She paused as all her senses synced with the night around her. Within seconds she'd slipped through fog and shadows without making a sound. The soft gasps and moans faded as she silently left the couple behind.

The fog grew thicker as she ran, muting the ever-present sounds of civilization as well as the soft pads of her paws against the trail. With mouth open and tongue lolling, Lily drew great draughts of air into her lungs. Her wolven brain easily categorized the scents—alder and pine, pungent eucalyptus, and freshly mowed grass. A hint of cigar smoke and the familiar odor of marijuana. The acrid smells of many who had passed through the park earlier, scents of dogs and children, of perfumes and colognes.

Familiar smells, but not the ones she wanted. Not tonight. She missed the smells of home, the sharp tang of cedar and the clean scent of damp earth. The sounds here were lacking as well. Owls hooting in the night, the squeak of bats overhead. There were some small rustlings of mice in the weeds and the occasional slither of a snake or the crackle of voles in the leaves, but no rustle of deer in the brush, no bugling elk.

No pack members to run beside her.

No male who wanted her as his mate.

And that was the crux of it all, wasn't it? She was damned tired of living alone, though she'd never admit that to her parents. They wanted her to find love and had always hoped it would be with Alex Aragat.

Even Alex found that idea insane. They'd slept in the same crib, and played together as toddlers and beyond, until they each went off to college. Through all their years together, Lily had been the big sister, the one in charge.

She still was. That dynamic would never change.

She loved Alex, and sex with him was amazing, but it wasn't enough. Not nearly enough. He didn't challenge her, and she would always intimidate the hell out of him. They laughed about it, pretended to go along with the wishes of their parents, but both of them accepted their relationship would never go beyond what they had now: packmates—special friends with benefits.

Lily realized she was growling as she ran. Time to stop thinking about Alex and her lack of male companionship. This run was supposed to relax her, not leave her frustrated and angry.

She put in a fresh burst of speed and raced through the park. Normally she preferred to run in the Marin Headlands or through the tangled grounds of the Presidio, but her time tonight was limited and she *needed* this run.

Desperately.

She raced past the golf course and circled the soccer fields, keeping to the shadows, out of plain sight. Circling back, she found herself drawn toward the small garden her mother had designed over thirty years ago. Keisha Rialto had been a young landscape architect when her life was turned upside down by a horrible assault and an unexpected shift from woman to wolf.

In spite of everything, her design had won a contest that resulted in the beautiful memorial to Tibetan Sherpas who had lost their lives guiding climbers into the Himalayas. Her simple yet elegant design had changed so many lives—including her own.

Somehow, the woman who would one day give birth to Lily had included specific plants native to the Tibetan Steppe—plants containing nutrients Chanku shapeshifters needed to shift.

Instinct? The hand of the goddess? Whatever force had lead Keisha to those plants had also led Lily's father to search for her mother.

If not for that garden, Lily might never have been born, her parents might not have found one another, and the Chanku species could have disappeared forever.

She'd always loved the garden and felt a special connection to the peaceful memorial near Stow Lake. Now, though, as she drew closer, Lily sensed something different.

A darkness that hadn't existed before. A sense of evil so powerful that the entire area felt tarnished.

How could she have forgotten so soon? A woman had died here just a few hours ago.

Raped by a man, her throat torn out by a wolf.

Lily eased up on her ground-eating lope and slowed to a trot, moving silently among the large stones and softly clumped grasses. The scent of blood hung thick in the foggy night despite the best efforts of the cleaning crews to remove all signs of the assault and murder.

Lily's sensitive nose picked up the stale scent of fear, of sweat and blood, of semen. Overlaying it all was the powerful scent of wolf.

Not a wolf she recognized, and not just one. She crossed

back and forth, breathing in the smells. At least four different wolves. Maybe more, but there was an underlying stench of something wrong, a darkness that didn't fit with the familiar scent of Chanku.

It made no sense. Man and beast had been here, but had they been Chanku? Or had it been humans and natural wolves—wolves trained to kill?

She was certain she knew all of the Chanku capable of shifting. Over the past twenty-six years, ever since their existence had become public knowledge, they'd searched among normal-appearing humans in hope of finding more of their kind, those who carried the genes for shapeshifting.

Very few had been discovered, but each of them had been brought into the pack, taught to live as a wolf, and encouraged to stay on as part of the ever-growing family of Chanku.

A few had chosen life elsewhere—generally those who preferred solitude to life within the pack. Still, they all kept in contact with her father, and all acknowledged Anton Cheval as the über-alpha, their pack leader.

Just as every one of them looked to Keisha Rialto as the true power over all Chanku. Lily was so proud of her mom, and like everyone else, recognized the quiet strength in the woman who had easily brought über-alpha and powerful wizard Anton Cheval to his knees. Her father might act like the ruler of his own kingdom, but even he acknowledged his mate's alpha nature.

Of all the known Chanku, none of them, as far as Lily knew, were evil. As wolves they had the power to kill, but they also lived by a code of honor. Evil was a trait that would have shown up very quickly. One thing she'd learned to count on with the pack was the way they watched out for one another. They truly were a family, and if someone had problems, they were the pack's problems to be dealt with and solved before they were put aside.

But someone was raping and killing young women, and if it wasn't Chanku, it was someone intending to make it look like Chanku. Lily circled the garden once again.

Her nose wrinkled at the stench of old blood and death, and the overlying sense of something terribly wrong. She couldn't place it, knew that, if asked, she'd not be able to describe it, but she also knew she would never forget it.

Finally, satisfied there was nothing more she could learn, she turned away and trotted slowly back to the spot where she'd left her clothes.

Her joy in the night felt tarnished, just like her mother's garden. She was absolutely certain it would be a long time before she ran this way again.

Sebastian adjusted the bow tie on the black silk shirt he'd selected to wear with his tux and once again checked the time. The week had flown by, but he'd spent the hours immersed in his father's collection of books on magical theory and practice, and he felt as if he'd strengthened his own magic through knowledge. Now it was time to study another kind of magic.

Tonight's reception was his first truly public event with his father—though why the man had chosen a reception in San Francisco honoring the Montana neighbor he claimed to despise really didn't make much sense.

No matter. Aldo Xenakis had an amazing, inbred charisma. When he walked into a room, people naturally gravitated toward him and gathered about him. When he spoke, they listened. When he gave an order, no one asked why.

They merely did his bidding.

That was the thing that had stood out the first time Sebastian met his father, the trait that had impressed him the most. He'd since studied the man carefully, watching the way he moved, the words he used, the intonation of his voice.

Tonight Sebastian would do as he always had—he'd keep his

mouth shut and stand beside the man he knew he'd never fully understand, and continue to do his best to figure him out.

How else was he going to learn how to move within the same rarified social circles? His mother certainly hadn't had the opportunity. No, she'd spent her life living alone and afraid, focusing entirely on her only son. Loving him.

He sighed. She'd loved him all right, but she'd lied to him, too. He wondered what his life would be like if he'd never found her divorce papers or his original birth certificate with his mother's real name—one listing Aldo Xenakis as his father.

How different would things be if he'd never hunted for the man, if he'd listened to his mother's pleas that he leave well enough alone?

She'd asked him to promise. On her death bed she'd begged him to promise he would never search for his father.

He hadn't been able to do it. Hadn't even had the guts to lie to her. She'd gone to her grave, telling him he was making a terrible mistake.

Some days he had to agree. But then, some days . . .

"Sebastian?"

"Yes, Father?" He glanced at his father's reflection in the mirror and corralled his unsettling thoughts. Aldo stood in the doorway, still dressed in his everyday dark suit.

"I'm sorry," he said, studying Sebastian as if he was some sort of exotic bug, "but I will not be attending tonight's event after all."

Sebastian turned slowly and watched his father, wondering what the old man was up to now.

"I've had some other business come up," he said. His stare was direct, his manner as formal as always. "You will go. I understand Mr. and Mrs. Cheval will not be at the reception. Their daughter will represent them."

Interesting. Why would that matter? Well, two could play this game . . . if a game it was.

Of course, with his father, it was always a game—or a contest—of some sort. "Which one?" Sebastian checked his cuff links as he spoke. "Don't they have two daughters?"

"They do. The oldest girl, the one who runs Cheval International. Her name is Lily. Lily Cheval. She's single, very intelligent. She's also quite attractive."

That caught his attention. Sebastian raised his head. "You've met her?"

Aldo nodded. "This week."

"Why do you mention her?" He watched his father's face. As usual, the man gave away nothing.

He shrugged, as if the question meant little to him. "You're young. You're not seeing anyone. I thought you might be interested."

Sebastian raised one eyebrow. "You're playing matchmaker? With the daughter of the most powerful Chanku alpha alive? A man you openly dislike? Why do I find that so interesting, Father? So unlike you."

There was the slightest flicker of . . . what? Indecision? Discomfort? Now that was a rarity. He focused on Aldo's eyes. Dark brown. So dark they almost appeared black. Nothing like his own, but their physical resemblance was still remarkable. The same tall, lean build, the pronounced widow's peak, a certain intensity . . .

"Matchmaker?" His father chuckled. Unconvincingly. "Not at all. I merely thought you would feel more comfortable attending without me if you knew our neighbor's daughter would be there."

"I've never met her. Never had any desire to. She is, after all, the enemy, isn't she? Or at least the enemy's daughter."

His father's eyes went wide. Sebastian almost laughed. The man couldn't look innocent no matter how hard he tried.

"I've never said that. Anton Cheval and I have met on more

than one occasion. We are always quite civil to one another. I have issues with the species as a whole, but not any one shifter in particular."

"I guess I misunderstood. Still, I don't see how her presence should change things." Sebastian turned away from his father, but he watched him in the mirror as he finished adjusting his bow tie. "I hope your business goes well."

Aldo nodded and left the room. Sebastian watched him leave, aware of a faint buzzing in his head. He'd noticed it a lot lately. Almost as if someone pushed at his mind.

From the inside.

It wasn't until the bedroom door closed quietly behind his father that he remembered to breathe.

Lily stared into the vanity mirror and clipped the diamond studs first to one ear and then the other. Such a nuisance, not being able to pierce her ears, but the holes closed up after every shift, and it was hardly worth the trouble.

She smoothed her hands down over the silky fabric and wondered if this was the right dress for the CEO of the largest import business in the city to wear to an event honoring her father. Dark russet shimmered over her skin. The halter top plunged deep in front and was almost nonexistent in the back. The color shifted with reflected light. Turn this way, the gown looked black, that way, russet. Yet in the direct light it was a brilliant, almost metallic copper.

Almost an exact match to her hair and close to her caramel skin. She'd chosen to wear her hair long and loose tonight. Thank the goddess the tight ringlets of her childhood had loosened into softer waves and manageable curls after so many years of shifting.

Even so, it hung almost to her hips when it was dry, but stretched past her butt when wet. Leaving it loose when the back of the dress dipped to the upper curve of her buttocks kept her from feeling half naked, though she loved the sensual feel of her thick hair sweeping over her bare back and arms.

Arousal blossomed, and she took a deep, controlling breath. Probably not a good idea to run again this afternoon, but damn, she'd felt so trapped this week. Trapped and frustrated by too many pressures coming from too many directions.

The murders, the press hounding her for comments, this reception. Damn, she really didn't want to go to this event tonight. She'd rather be running through the tall grass on the flanks of Mount Tamalpais than forcing her feet into these damned high heels and worrying if her dress was apropos or not.

She wished Alex had been able to come. He'd have had her laughing by now, but he hadn't been able to make it down for the reception. She really needed him tonight, if only to burn off the rush of sexual need that always followed a shift.

But Alex was trapped on the investigation in Montana, and it was up to Lily to represent Cheval International tonight. She wondered what he'd discovered, if anything. After the bombshell he'd dropped on her this morning, she'd been so upset she'd walked out of her office and headed straight for Mount Tam. She'd badly needed a chance to breathe some fresh air and think.

Sebastian Xenakis had been in Montana last weekend, when that body was discovered. He was in San Francisco the night the latest victim had died. But could he shift? The only thing they had was Tinker's nose, the fact he'd followed the scent of a strange wolf and it had led directly across the Xenakis property.

Right to the staircase leading up to the huge Xenakis home.

Her father's warning floated through her mind, and she looked longingly at the beautifully designed grotto in the bathroom behind her. Natural stone with live ferns and orchids growing from carefully camouflaged pots, a series of showerheads designed to mimic falling rain, and a deep pool off to one side with the option of soaking in an inexcusable amount of hot water with lots of bubbles and all the jets going—it sounded so much more appealing than tonight's event.

It was definitely preferable to meeting someone who might be a killer and a rapist, of having to carry on polite conversation. What would she do if she recognized his scent? She knew she'd never forget the mix of wolf and man, the stench of pain and death she'd smelled on her run through Golden Gate Park a couple of nights back.

She was certain she'd be introduced to Sebastian Xenakis tonight. The fact they were both young and single, the offspring of very powerful men, made it a given that someone, somewhere, would be pushing them together.

If only for the photo op.

She really wasn't cut out for this. All the publicity, the schmoozing with people who'd stab her in the back as easily as they'd buy her a drink. Who the hell did she think she was kidding?

You can do this, sweetheart.

Dad? What are you doing in my head? Usually she knew when he was hanging around. She must be more concerned about the evening than she'd realized.

Listening to you worry. You must have inherited that trait from me. Your mother never worries.

Lily snorted. Not a very ladylike response, but her father was right. *That's because she knows you'll do it for her.*

True. Relax. Enjoy yourself tonight. Don't make a special effort to meet young Mr. Xenakis. It will happen in good time.

It's going to happen tonight.

There was a long pause. Lily heard her own heartbeat. She could practically see her father nodding as he considered his response.

Okay, he said. *How do you feel about that?*

I'll be fine. I probably won't call you until tomorrow.

Is that a hint for me to stay out of your head?

Yes. Good night. I love you, Dad. Now go. Give Mom a hug for me.

He didn't answer, but his laughter echoed in her mind.

And Lily realized her nervousness was gone. Someday she'd figure out how he did that.

She just hoped this sense of calm lasted.

She was dressed to the max and running late. Her libido was working on overtime and her imagination wasn't much better. So be it. Grabbing her handbag, Lily slipped out the door. The company limo she'd called for earlier waited in front of the house.

The driver opened the door, and she slid into the backseat. "Museum of Modern Art," she said, checking her handbag for the speech she'd prepared.

The notes were there. She'd done this sort of thing a hundred times. So why was she so uptight about tonight?

And what if Aldo Xenakis approached her with his slimy comments, the way he'd done when she'd met him on Monday? And how the hell was she going to deal with his son?

Somehow, she just couldn't drag up any good feelings about the coming evening. As they drove into town, she found herself turning in her seat, looking back in the direction of the mountain.

What kind of CEO would rather be running as a wolf across the grassy hillside? With a deep sigh, Lily turned and faced forward. Time to put on her business face and act like a grown-up, whether she wanted to or not.

·

3

Sebastian sipped an excellent champagne and paid just enough attention to the two gentlemen he was standing with to nod occasionally in the right places.

He wasn't sure what he'd expected tonight. He hadn't intended to be here by himself, but even though his father had chosen not to come, the evening had been . . . interesting. He'd actually been enjoying himself.

For the life of him, he couldn't figure out why.

Crowds and formal events had never been high on his list of things to do. He preferred the silence of the mountains, the ebb and flow of the ocean, even a hike in the foothills rather than a fancy event where the ultimate purpose seemed to be who had more, controlled more, or wanted more.

People had been pleasant enough, a bit curious when they realized he was Aldo Xenakis's son, but he'd not run into any of the attitude he'd expected.

If anything, he'd been aware of a growing sense of expectation. It wasn't just him. Those around him kept glancing toward the entrance to the room, as if awaiting royalty. He knew the honoree wasn't expected to attend. Had he missed something? The mayor was already here. Was the governor coming?

He decided to relax and see what happened. Whoever was keeping everyone busy casting surreptitious glances toward the door would eventually arrive and the mystery would be solved.

A soft sigh spread across the huge room, as if everyone exhaled at once. Sebastian realized that he turned in absolute synchronization with every other person in the room.

Silence fell, and a few people pushed to get a better look. At times like this, he appreciated his above average height because it was a simple thing merely to peer over the heads of those between him and the entry.

There was a small cluster of people blocking the wide doorway into the ballroom, but they moved aside as if clearing way for royalty. Sebastian realized he'd lifted a bit to his toes in order to see who or what everyone was looking at.

The final person moved out of his line of vision.

Sebastian's breath caught in his throat.

She was taller than average, as slim and graceful as any woodland creature, and yet when she turned and gazed in his direction, he sensed pure predator beneath the tawny waves that cascaded in wild disarray over her shoulders and curled around her slim hips.

Without a doubt, he'd never seen anyone as lovely or as mesmerizing in his entire life. The woman, smiling and greeting those who met her like subjects bowing to a queen, moved within an aura of light and color that jolted his psychic senses on a level never before touched.

He'd always seen auras—they were a normal part of his vision, and he rarely thought much of them. They were a part of the whole, just as important in his perception of each individual as the color of their hair or the shade of their eyes.

He'd never seen anyone like this woman. She moved in a shimmer of russet and gold, but the brilliance of her aura actually reflected in the physical plane, shimmering over her gown in a scarlet wave of light and life. So many shades of red, from the deepest bloodred to a shade bordering on orange.

She wore her will, her power, and her energy like a crimson cloak, radiating life and courage, and enough blatant sensuality that he felt the connection clear across the room.

His body reacted on a level totally separate from his brain, though he wondered how many other men in the room were suddenly as aroused as he was. He sensed a thread of desire drawing all of them closer, but he fought the pull. Fought the need that pulsed deep and steady on a level he'd never once experienced.

He planted his feet, even though they wanted to move. He felt his wolf rise and forced that creature back as well.

Who was she?

What was she?

He stared at her as she raised her eyes and glanced in his direction. Then she quickly turned away, and once again appeared to focus on the small crowd that pushed closer. He recognized the mayor and a few city officials, but they were nothing. No one of interest. Only the woman.

His heart thundered in his chest with the certainty that she was every bit as aware of him as he was of her. He pushed, sending a soft yet powerful mental command, calling her to him.

She fought him. Smiling, shaking hands, and sharing air kisses with one person after another, she slowly worked her way across the room. Her aura spiked, the red growing brighter, stronger, and he knew she drew on her own psychic power as she continued to ignore him.

Look at me. Now. Raise your head and look at me.

I think not. You're much too pushy.

Stunned, Sebastian took a step backward. She'd heard him. Heard him and answered him telepathically. She'd not raised her head, not looked his way, but she'd still managed to put him in his place.

Damn. She was absolutely magnificent.

He started slowly across the room, working his way through the throng that continued moving in her direction, as if they merely needed a chance to be close, to touch her hand, to speak to her.

The same way he did. He might have felt like a fool, except she was so obviously enjoying herself, so entirely involved in the people pressing all around that he couldn't deny the joy he felt in her pleasure.

It was as if she took the goodwill of those around her and sent it back tenfold. His father had charisma, but he couldn't touch this young woman. She was charisma personified, a veritable magnet, drawing everyone to her. Who in the hell was she?

He turned to a matronly woman standing beside him. She, too, was trying to get close. "I don't know who she is. That woman who just came in. Do you?"

She looked at him as if he'd just stepped out of a cave. "Why, that's Lily Cheval. Her father is the one being honored tonight. He couldn't be here, so Lily's attending in his place."

Lily Cheval. He should have known. "Thank you," he said, but the woman had managed to move a few steps ahead and wasn't paying him any attention at all. Her focus, hell, the focus of every person in the room, was entirely on Ms. Cheval.

Sebastian turned his head and studied her again. His father had lied. She wasn't merely attractive, she was absolutely breathtaking, from her long, tawny curls to her caramel skin barely covered in some sort of fabric that flashed like dark fire.

With the crimson flame of her aura all around, she was a burning torch of pure sensual energy. The crowd had moved closer now, and Sebastian was no more than ten or twelve feet from her.

She raised her head, and he was drowning. Drowning in eyes of deepest amber, eyes so pure, yet filled with so many secrets, he didn't care if he never found the surface again.

A sharp pain pierced his skull, a sense of intrusion, of foul air and darkness.

Sebastian blinked. Lily stared at him for a brief moment. Her aura spiked a brilliant lavender, then faded to a muddy brown. Her eyes went wide, and her hand went to her temple. Slowly, gracefully, she crumpled to the floor.

Someone screamed. A man called for calm. A woman was on her phone dialing 911. Sebastian shoved his way through the few people still separating him from Lily Cheval. He knelt beside her. Her aura was shifting color again, from gray and brown to a brilliant gold.

Someone or something watched over her. He wasn't certain, but he placed his fingertips against her throat and felt for her pulse, then brushed her hair away from her face. It slipped like silk through his fingers, but she was breathing on her own and, other than being unconscious, seemed perfectly okay.

He used his mind. They'd communicated a moment ago. Would it work again?

Lily? Can you hear me?

Who are you? What did you do to me?

I didn't do anything. My name is Sebastian. Sebastian Xenakis.

Why am I not surprised?

Now what did she mean by that? He gazed at her and realized anyone watching them would think he was merely staring at an unconscious woman. *I was looking at you and then . . .*

It felt as if you shot something into my head.

A sharp pain?

Exactly. What was it?

I don't know, but I felt it, too. Can you sit up? People are staring. I'm afraid they're beginning to wonder what's going on. A slight shudder went through her. He wrapped his hand around her lax fingers.

I am so embarrassed. Do I have to?

Biting his lips to keep from grinning, Sebastian glanced up and realized one of the waitstaff was standing close by. "I think she's coming 'round. Is there a quiet room somewhere?"

The man nodded. "Follow me. Are you sure it's safe to move her?"

"Yes. She's almost conscious. I'd like to get her somewhere private." He slipped his hands beneath her slim body and lifted her easily. She was tall—almost six feet—but so slim she barely weighed anything. She felt fragile in his arms, but he knew differently. She was a wolf, and powerful muscles rippled beneath her skin.

Her dress was slick and slippery in his hands, and he clutched her tightly against his chest. Dropping her wouldn't be the best move about now, but it was more about feeling her body close against his than actually keeping her safe.

Peripherally aware of the anxious undercurrents in the room, of the bright flashes from cameras and cell phones, he moved quickly through the crowd, but he didn't feel Lily's body relax until he'd slipped through the doors and out of the ballroom. As the big double doors closed behind them, Lily opened her eyes and winked at him.

Sebastian felt it all the way to his toes.

Holding her close, he followed the waiter down a short hallway and slipped through a door the man unlocked and held open to a private office. Along with the desk and bookcases, a leather couch stretched along one wall.

Sebastian nodded to the waiter. "Thank you. I'll bring her out as soon as she feels up to it. I think we'll be just a few minutes more, okay?"

The man sighed. "That's good. I hope she'll be okay. You're

sure we don't need a paramedic? Shouldn't she be awake by now if she merely fainted? We wouldn't want her to miss this reception. Her parents have done an awful lot for the museum and the folks who work here. This is our chance to thank her family."

"That's good to hear." Sebastian gave the man a gentle mental push.

The waiter frowned, glanced about him nervously, and then left the office.

"That wasn't very nice."

"Excuse me?" Sebastian glanced down at Lily. She was still lying in his arms, but her beautiful amber eyes were wide open and she was smiling.

She was even more beautiful up close, and her aura was back to that amazing red. So much power in her. And enough sensual energy to destroy whatever shreds of Sebastian's control remained.

Somehow he found what scraps were left and helped her sit.

"Shoving that poor man out of here like that. That really wasn't very nice of you, was it?"

How the hell had she known he was . . . well, shit. Obviously his mind was an open page to her. Now that was rather disconcerting. "It was only a little nudge."

"You took away his free will."

His eyes snapped to hers. When he saw the sparkle in their amber depths, the spikes of yellow in her crimson aura, he knew she was teasing him.

"I'll grant you that, but it gave you the privacy to quit pretending to be unconscious. How long do you think you could have run with that, figuratively speaking, of course?" When she merely rolled her eyes at him, he sat back against the arm of the couch so he could study her. "What happened in there, anyway?"

She shook her head as she carefully rearranged her gown. "You tell me. I raised my head and caught you looking at me. The moment our gazes connected, it felt like you shot me through the brain with a laser."

Shaking his head in denial, Sebastian practically stumbled over the words. "I felt something, but the power didn't originate with me. I think someone used me as a conduit."

Lily frowned. "Any idea who?"

"No. Do you?"

But he did, and he found himself wondering what his father's other business tonight had been. How strong the man's powers really were.

"No. But I will." She stood up, brushed the short hem of her skirt down, and shoved the thick curls back from her face.

Sebastian stood and placed his hand lightly on her back, just above the draped fabric that hugged her perfectly rounded bottom. The moment he connected with her warm skin, he felt a slight frisson, a sensation as if energy flew over the surface, from her smooth back to his calloused fingers.

It was slightly unnerving.

It was horribly exciting.

He wanted more of the same.

"You're sure you're okay?"

She slowly turned her head and glanced over her shoulder. Her full lips curved in a wide smile. "Oh, yeah. C'mon. I'll buy you a drink."

He laughed and guided her toward the door. "The champagne's included. You're making me feel like a cheap date."

She stopped in the doorway and touched the back of his hand with her fingertips. "I really do appreciate your getting me out of there. I'm sure my picture will be in all the tabloids tomorrow, and my father will have a fit, but it could have been much worse. Thank you."

He grinned. "I understand fathers like that. Have one of my

own." Then he shrugged. "You don't have to thank me, especially if whatever happened was my fault to begin with."

She gazed at him, a slow, steady, painless yet thorough unpeeling of his soul. He fought the impulse to lower his eyes. Instead, he faced her directly.

"I don't believe it was your fault." She smiled, but she stepped away from him.

Sebastian shook his head. "I felt something, which means whatever attacked you probably used me."

"If that's the case, you're as much a victim as I am."

He hadn't thought of it that way. The idea made him shudder inside.

"No matter," she said, shrugging those perfect shoulders. "Still, I'd like to know what happened."

Sebastian opened the door and then followed her out of the office. "So would I, Ms. Cheval. So would I."

She'd never been so aware of a man in her life. Lily kept her spine straight and her pace steady as she walked ahead of Sebastian Xenakis, leading him back to the reception. Her head pounded in time with each step, and she knew her father was trying to reach her, but she couldn't relax enough to let him in.

Not while Sebastian followed mere steps behind. His scent tickled her nostrils. She'd almost given herself away as he leaned over her when she went down. Had almost wrapped her fingers around his neck, pulled him closer, and kissed him.

She'd never felt so aroused—not with any man. Her skin prickled with the passage of air as she walked. Her breasts ached, and her nipples had tightened into sensitive peaks against the slick fabric of her gown.

She'd almost skipped wearing panties tonight, with the dress fabric so sheer and clinging so close, but she was thankful now for the tiny scrap of silk and lace she'd chosen. At least they absorbed the moisture of her arousal.

She'd never lost control this way. Lily Cheval epitomized control, even with sex.

Yeah, and if I repeat that a thousand times, I just might make myself believe it.

She really had to get herself together. Pausing just outside the door, she turned to Sebastian. "Do you mind going in ahead of me? I really don't want to make an entrance that will draw even more attention, and if the two of us walk through that door . . ."

"I understand." He smiled and her heart thudded even harder in her chest. That smile changed his looks from drop-dead gorgeous to absolutely devastating. "If anyone asks," he said, "I'll tell them you wanted to freshen up."

She nodded. "Thank you. That's exactly what I'll do."

She watched him walk away, mesmerized by the smooth flow of dark fabric over muscular thighs, the way his tuxedo jacket curved over his slim butt.

He was beyond beautiful, and it felt as if she'd gone without for far too long. He went into the ballroom while Lily turned away and found a quiet corner. She needed to connect with her father. He would have sensed whatever it was that knocked her flat. It might have felt intrusive, except she knew he would always worry about her.

She was, after all, his favorite. *I'm okay, Dad, but you're giving me a headache.*

I'm sorry, but I've been worried sick. Are you all right? What happened?

I was hoping you could tell me. What did you notice?

You disappeared from my thoughts. I can feel when you block me, and it reassures me of your presence. I could not feel you at all. Do you have any idea what . . . ?

Not really. I'd just arrived at the reception, felt a sharp pain in my head, and the next thing I knew, I was on the floor. Are you okay?

*I'm fine. A very kind man helped me to a quiet office. I'm
ready to go back to the reception.*

Do you have any idea what caused it?

She did, but Lily wasn't ready to discuss her suspicions. And
she definitely didn't want to talk about Sebastian Xenakis. Not
until she'd spent more time with him, had a better chance to see
what he was really like.

There was something about him. Something not entirely
human, but she needed to know more. Wanted to know more.

*Not yet. I'll let you know as soon as I have some ideas. Now
let me do the job you sent me to do, all right?*

She heard his soft chuckle. Then there was only silence.

Miraculously, her headache was gone.

Though she'd lived with the amazing link to her father since
before her birth, Lily had never questioned it. She'd learned to
block him at an early age, but she really didn't mind the link.
He'd never obsessively interfered with her life, and he'd been a
powerful source of strength as she'd grown and matured.

When they were physically closer, his contact never made
her head hurt. Something about throwing his thoughts all the
way from Montana to San Francisco and having them bounce
off her natural shields appeared to cause the pain.

It was better than being totally open with him, and he really
did respect her privacy. She only shared what she wanted, and
she'd learned to hide things from him. There were some things
no daughter wanted to share with her father.

The surging arousal she felt for Sebastian Xenakis most definitely made him one of those things.

Smoothing her dress over her thighs, Lily went back to the
ballroom.

Every eye in the room seemed to focus on her. Conversa-
tions halted. Smiling, she simply held her hands out in a helpless gesture. "I'm fine," she said, speaking to the room at large.
"I've had a busy day and must have skipped one too many

meals. Please, enjoy yourselves. I'm going to attack the hors d'oeuvres."

She walked toward the long buffet table, but Sebastian was there ahead of her, filling a plate with a selection of meats and chilled sushi rolls. He held it out to her.

Lily took it from him. "Thank you. How did you know?"

He glanced at the items he'd chosen. "I figured any wolf worth her salt would prefer rare beef and raw fish over broccoli and tomatoes."

Lily had no control over her laughter. "You figured right," she said. She took a small slice of crisp sourdough topped with rare tenderloin and nipped the meat neatly off the piece of bread. "Delicious."

Sebastian's eyes practically glowed. Such an unusual shade of blue—deep teal like the purest tropical lagoon. He focused them on her until she thought she might drown in those blue-green depths.

"Open."

Lily blinked and opened her mouth, like a baby bird waiting to be fed. He slipped a bite of raw salmon between her lips. She bit down on the clean, fresh taste of the fish, barely aware that she actually chewed.

Her entire focus was on Sebastian. Never had a man filled her senses the way he filled them now. His hair was crisp and dark, almost black, with a noticeable widow's peak. He wore a neatly trimmed beard that perfectly framed a mouth she wanted to savor. His skin was tan—not as dark as hers, but definitely not the pale shade of a man who spent his days indoors.

No, Sebastian Xenakis was a creature of nature. She sensed that in him. Sensed his wildness, his love of freedom, his strength.

And something more. Something she'd not expected.

She sensed his magic. It was as much a part of him as Lily's was of her. He *was* magic. He wore it like a second skin, the in-born magic of a true wizard.

Unlike her father's magic, or her own, though, Sebastian's carried a darker edge. A sense of night, of starlit skies, and deep, dark, caverns. It wasn't unpleasant, just different.

Very, very different.

Not like his father's, either. When she shook Aldo Xenakis's hand at the restaurant on Monday, she'd felt his dark magic like a layer of slime over his skin. It repelled her, a force both ugly and unclean and more than a little bit dangerous.

There was nothing at all repellant about Sebastian. He carried that same sense of danger, of darkness—but not.

Why was his different?

Why was he so different?

And why, she wondered, did it matter to her so much?

There was no way to avoid the obvious. Lily Cheval fasci-nated him every bit as much as she aroused him. Sebastian couldn't take his eyes off her. When she stood at the podium and thanked the organizers for the event, he felt as if she spoke directly to him. When she talked about the link between the art museum and the community and the importance of the preser-vation of works both great and small, he was ready to pull out his wallet.

It was obvious that Lily Cheval was beloved by the people here, every bit as much as her absent father. The Chevals had become strong pillars of this dynamic city, supporters of im-portant causes, and popular for their altruism and good works.

He couldn't help but draw a comparison to his own father, one that was so embarrassingly lacking that he quickly shut down that line of thought.

At the moment, Lily was speaking to a group of women who'd cornered her near the podium. Sebastian watched her, wondering if she would search him out when the conversation ended as she'd done a couple of times this evening.

Already he felt a sense of ownership. She wasn't his. He barely knew her, and yet he felt as if he'd known her all his life. Felt a connection that had no explanation, but knew it was one he wanted time to explore.

She broke away from the group with smiles and a few soft-spoken comments. Then she was there, beside him, looking up with those beautiful amber eyes, and once again he was lost.

Lost, and loving every second of the mystery.

"It's been a long day, Sebastian. I'm ready to leave, but I wanted to thank you for your rescue."

"You're going home?" He hadn't thought of the evening ending. Had somehow pictured himself leaving with her, but one didn't barge in on the life of a princess, and Lily Cheval was the closest he'd ever come to royalty.

She shrugged and glanced to both sides. "Actually, I'm headed across the bridge to Mount Tam. I really need to run tonight."

"Would you care for company?" He took her empty glass from her hand and set it on the table beside him.

She smiled. "I wish, but I plan to shift. My wolf hasn't had nearly enough freedom this week."

"That works for me." *There,* he thought. *Let's see what she makes of that.*

Lily frowned. "Are you Chanku? I don't sense it in you."

He shook his head. "Not Chanku, but I have other skills. I've mastered a trick or two."

Her eyes went wide for a moment. "I see." Narrowed, as if she judged him more carefully than she had earlier. "Then yes. I would love to have company. Please. Will you join me?"

His heart thundered in his chest, but he merely nodded. "Did you bring a car?"

She shook her head. "No. I came in the company limo. We can take that, or . . ."

"I brought my car. Do you have a wrap?"

She nodded, and he wondered if she regretted accepting his invitation. They waited while one of the staff retrieved a dark, glistening shawl that wrapped her in russet and gold fire.

Her aura spiked. The reds were back. Darker, deeper, flashing true crimson, more brilliant than before. Did she have any idea how openly she broadcast her own arousal?

Then he wondered if she saw auras as well. If she knew he was hanging on to polite behavior by a thread.

He touched her back lightly with his fingers, guiding her toward the door. More than a few noted the fact they left together, and he wondered how long it would be before his father got word.

Wondered if he already knew.

They waited in front of the museum while the valet retrieved his vehicle from the large lot. Lily dismissed her car and driver, but her thoughts were hidden behind strong shields. Sebastian wondered what Lily was thinking, why the easy communication between them had ended so suddenly.

He opened her door, and she climbed in, every move graceful and composed. Had she been born with grace or did she have to learn it? Had she always known her place in the world or, like him, had she ever wondered where she belonged?

No. Not Lily. She knew who she was. Why she was.

He tipped the valet, got behind the wheel, and headed north toward the Golden Gate Bridge. They traveled in silence through light traffic. This late at night, the bridge was almost empty of vehicles. A gibbous moon, almost full, cast a soft glow across the water flowing beneath the bridge on the incoming tide.

Mount Tamalpais was a dark shadow against a glimmering sky when Sebastian pulled into the lot overlooking the Golden

Gate. He shut off the engine and glanced toward Lily. She studied him with eyes gone dark in the night.

"Do you shift magically?"

He nodded. "I do. I'm still learning. At home, in Montana, I pull energy from an ancient oak. Sometimes I think the damned oak is sentient, it has such rich power. I'm hoping I can do it here without my favorite tree." Chuckling softly, he added, "I've got this terrible fear I'll be left standing in the dark, bare assed and buck naked, unable to shift."

She laughed and grabbed his hand. Squeezed it like an old friend. "That would totally ruin your image, wouldn't it? C'mon. I've had enough of fancy clothes and high heels. Let's hunt."

The parking lot was empty when they both got out of the car. He'd parked toward the back of the lot, in shadows cast by a windblown cypress. This was nothing like the tree he called on at home, but he sensed a similar power in the tree, in the air, in the mountain behind him.

It would have to do. Turning his back to give Lily privacy, he quickly shed his jacket, tie, and shirt. Kicked off his shoes and stripped out of his pants. Almost laughed as he realized this was one of the oddest first dates he'd ever been on.

Then he sobered, as he thought of what lay ahead. Fear of failing lay like a lump of stone in his chest. He hoped like hell he'd be able to shift. Hoped Lily wouldn't stand witness to an embarrassing failure.

His father's critical words filled his head, the man's absolute inability to accept his son's occasional mistakes. Then Sebastian forced his mind in more pleasant directions. He thought of the evening ahead, of the chance to run beside the most beautiful woman he'd ever seen.

He wondered if her wolf was as beautiful as the woman. His

heartbeat thundered in his ears as his body tightened, giving him yet another thing to worry about.

He hoped like hell Lily wouldn't turn and look, wouldn't see how painfully aroused he was, because then she'd know.

How very much he wanted her. And how fragile was his control, hanging by little more than a tiny thread of humanity.

4

Lily stepped out of her thong panties and shoes and put them next to her wrap on the front seat of Sebastian's car. Then she slipped her dress over her head and tossed the small handful of silk on top of her shoes and panties. Cool air swept over her bare back, lifted the tendrils of her long hair, and gave her a perfect excuse for her taut nipples and aching breasts.

She leaned over the hood of the car, watching with unabashed desire while Sebastian removed his clothing. Need that had simmered slow and steady deep inside throughout the evening blossomed into an all-consuming ache. She wanted him, and she'd not even shifted. Generally this level of arousal came after a run, not before, but she'd gone without for much too long.

Even that wasn't the whole truth. It wasn't merely the fact she'd had no opportunity for sex. No, Sebastian was beautiful beyond belief. His body was strong and hard, his mind sharp, his sense of humor unabashedly fun. Everything about him attracted her. For the first time, she looked at a man and wanted the whole package.

She found it hard to believe he wasn't Chanku. He had the tall, lean build she associated with their kind, the broad shoulders, strong thighs, and, now that he'd slipped his pants off, the most perfect ass she'd ever seen on any man.

He turned to throw his clothes in the car, and she caught her breath. He was fully erect, his long, thick penis rising high against his perfectly muscled belly. Again, graphic proof of his similarities to the Chanku males she'd known.

Lily realized she was licking her lips, but damn. This was even better than that perfect butt.

He caught her staring. Again, that smile—that absolutely devastating smile—and it was all for her.

"Oh." He honestly sounded surprised. "I thought maybe you'd already shifted."

Lily straightened, aware she was giving him a visual feast with her bare breasts showing above the roof of the low-slung car. "I was waiting for you."

She walked around the front of the vehicle and stood close. Most of the Chanku women she knew were dominant alphas. She felt no shame in wanting this man, and even less in showing him how she felt. He didn't seem to mind her attention a bit. Heat radiated off his perfect body, and he made no attempt to hide his interest. The visual of him, hard and ready for her, had her licking her lips, fighting an urge to touch.

She imagined him taking her here, now, over the hood of his car or against the wind-worn boulders at the side of the lot. Erotic visuals cascaded through her mind, a slide show of images, each one hotter than the last, until she consciously shut them down. What if he saw them? It could be embarrassing, showing him so graphically how she lusted. Later. She would know him better after the run, after she got to know his feral side.

He held her gaze for a long, breathless moment. Then he took a deep breath that expanded his chest in a most enticing manner. She wondered if he might kiss her, touch her somehow to let her know he was interested. Then she felt like an idiot. Evidence of his interest couldn't be more blatant.

He grabbed the keys he'd left on the hood of the car, clicked to lock the doors, and then walked to the edge of the parking lot. She watched as he stuck the keys in the crotch of a small tree to hide them. Then, standing in the cold moonlight, he raised his arms and faced the looming mountain and the moon hanging overhead.

Lily felt the rush of energy as he called the power to him. Whatever spell he invoked was silent, but energy was growing, gathering around him. She felt the power rising from the ground beneath her feet, from the mountain before them, from the air itself. Tiny hairs stood up on her arms and along her spine.

She tried to read the energy, to figure out what sort of spell he used, what entity aided him, but there was a sudden shimmer of light, a soft glow that seemed to come from within the man. Fascinated, Lily watched as the light grew until it covered him with a golden aura so bright it cast a shadow. The light swelled and then burst.

She blinked, and blinked again. In the place of the man stood a beautiful black wolf. It turned and gazed pointedly at Lily. Smiling, she called on her wolf, felt the frisson of her own power, and shifted.

Not nearly as dramatic, though definitely effective. Trotting across the asphalt, she met Sebastian nose to nose. Sniffing, growling softly, the two of them went through the typical routine of two feral creatures meeting for the first time. His scent was rich with the power of magic and something else. Something familiar.

He'd said he wasn't Chanku, but his wolf told her otherwise. Yet he'd called magic to change.

So many questions when her wolf wanted to run. Questions

could wait, and the night was waning. She yipped and spun about, nipped his flank, and took off.

Sebastian was right behind her. Jaws gaping, ears forward, and her tale waving like a flag behind her, Lily led him up the rugged slope of the mountain. Her senses hadn't felt this alive in ages. All of her senses—both wolf and woman.

Alert to the world around her, she raced the night and the alpha male that ran close behind.

Her scent drew him on, the rich, musky scent of female arousal, of wolf, of woman. He'd always run alone. Not once had he run with another wolf, never with a female, and the intensity, the pure exhilaration of the chase thrilled him.

He'd never acknowledged this side of his beast, this sensual, sexual creature that wanted the female. Blood pounded in his veins, and arousal powered the wolven creature he'd become. Running behind Lily enthralled him. His focus narrowed until all he saw was the plume of her tail and the welcoming gash of her sex. His nostrils filled with her scent and his arousal deepened.

Lily spun to the left. Alert to the night, Sebastian scented the jackrabbit before he saw it. Lily took off after their prey, body low and sleek, her ears laid back, all four feet kicking up dust and pebbles as she ran.

The rabbit slipped into a thick tangle of old blackberry vines. Lily skidded to a stop before tumbling into the briars, turned and looked at Sebastian with absolute disgust, and then yipped her challenge.

He had no time to think, to consider the fact he was running as a wolf, thinking like a wolf before they were off again, racing through thick grasses and over rocky trails. Lily Cheval was beautiful. So sensual, so alluring that his body thrummed with need. He ran faster, closing the gap between them.

Something buzzed in his mind. He sensed a presence, a familiar *other*, but he brushed it aside. Nothing would come between him and the glorious bitch he followed.

She was his. Not prey. No, she was so much more. She was destined to be his mate, and he would have her. His gaze narrowed until all he saw was Lily, all he wanted was Lily. His sensitive nostrils filled with her scent, and he drew closer, crowding her now along the narrow trail.

His wolf was larger than hers. More powerful. More commanding. His focus narrowed further until the world around him disappeared. She ran in moonlight, this female he hunted, but the light couldn't penetrate his darkness.

The female glanced over her shoulder without breaking step, but there was no fear in her eyes.

She should fear him.

He sensed her confusion. She wondered why he pursued her in deadly earnest. Wondered what he wanted.

It was so simple really. He wanted Lily Cheval.

They ran through the night, and he harried her. Nipped at her flanks, bumped his shoulder against hers, forced her to race toward a narrow canyon that had trapped him once. She thought she'd escape him, but he knew this place.

He knew better.

She was his, and he would have her.

If he'd been human he would have laughed when she raced through the opening to the canyon, heading in exactly the direction he wanted her to go. He knew there were tumbled rocks and a sheer wall at the end.

Knew she wouldn't be able to escape him now.

He cornered her against a fallen tree, brushed her shoulder with his front paw, and pressed close with jaws open wide, going for the thick skin at the back of her neck.

If he could hold her, restrain her, he could have her. He growled deep in his chest as he closed in, as his strong jaws clamped down on the loose folds of skin around her neck. Blood coursed through his veins, hot and powerful. Arousal grew until the need was a thick, all-consuming shroud covering him, filling him with strength. Images and sensations battered his feral mind—the soft welcome of her body, the slick slide of his wolven cock, the clasp of her warm sheath. Wanting, needing, he tightened his hold.

Growling, she twisted her entire body and snapped at his face. One sharp fang slashed his sensitive nose. Surprised by her strength, he yipped and released his hold on her neck. She twisted away, snarling as she broke free.

She slipped into the shadows, and her dark coat helped her disappear as she scrambled through a narrow crevice between two large boulders. It didn't matter. Her scent told him exactly where she hid.

He stopped at the entrance to her refuge. Blood dripped from his slashed nose, but it was nothing. A small price to pay to be this close. She was trapped here, surrounded by blocks of stone on both sides, the mountain at her back.

He heard her low growl, edging into a vicious snarl. Felt her thoughts pounding at his mind, but he refused to lower his shields. There was no need to listen. No, the darkness was all about, and he had her now. His cock swelled beyond the tight lupine sheath; his muscles tensed.

He saw her eyes shining amber-bright in the darkness. She faced him without fear and snarled again. Deeper, angrier. This was no longer a game, now that she realized the serious nature of his chase. Good. She should know. Know, acknowledge, and accept his superior strength.

The deep timbre of her growl raised his hackles. He lowered his head, faced her in the shadows, and waited. Her angry voice pounded against his brain, but words meant nothing.

Humanity meant nothing. He was bigger, stronger, faster.

He would wait.

And then he would have her.

Sebastian! Listen to me. What in the fuck do you think you're doing? She wasn't sure when she'd first noticed the change in him, but something was radically wrong. This wolf was not the same as the man, unless Sebastian Xenakis had a seriously split personality.

She thought of Alex's warning, the fact that the vicious murders had occurred in both Montana and San Francisco on the days when Sebastian had been in those places.

This was not looking good, except that none of the victims were Chanku. And she'd been certain that more than one wolf had been at the site of the last killing.

None of them had smelled like this wolf, but she sensed a similar darkness.

She thought of calling out for her father, but there wasn't a damned thing Anton Cheval could do for her now. She'd gotten herself into this mess, and it was up to her to figure a way out.

She stared at the wolf crouched just outside her refuge. He growled deep in his chest. There was no sense of humanity in him. Was it the magic? The fact his change was forced through a spell and not by his own inherent genetic ability to shift?

He was bigger than her. Stronger, but she was faster. Much faster, and she knew her wolf. Knew this body as her own, while she had the feeling Sebastian was still learning how his worked.

How the wolf thought.

Not very well, as far as Lily could tell. *Sebastian? Listen to me. Drop your shields, damn it, and listen.*

He didn't respond. Not even a glimmer of response. She crouched, ready to spring, to defend herself. Did he think to force a mating on her? A true mating only occurred when Chanku mated as wolves, but the female had to be receptive. It couldn't be forced, though she'd heard the older generation talk about that, how in the beginning they didn't know it was all up to the female.

She'd heard the story of how her uncle Jake had tried to force a mating on her aunt Tia, and just about ended up getting his throat torn out by Uncle Luc.

He hadn't realized it didn't work that way, but they'd known so little about their birthright in those early days. Maybe this guy believed the old stories. Maybe he just didn't know.

He said he wasn't Chanku, though she was almost positive he either lied or didn't know what he was talking about. Whatever. This was wrong. Entirely wrong.

Sebastian growled, snapping her back to the present. Damn him. She'd so hoped he was someone special. Someone she might actually have a relationship with, maybe learn to love.

That lost potential was absolutely infuriating!

Sebastian! Listen to me, you bastard!

Obviously, things were not working out the way she'd hoped.

A new scent tickled her nostrils. Lily sniffed, opened her senses. A shiver raced along her spine and raised her hackles. Wolves. Unfamiliar wolves, and definitely more than one.

Unfamiliar to her, though she recognized their scent.

It was the same stench she'd smelled near the garden in Golden Gate Park. The same sense of something terribly wrong.

And it was coming closer.

She pushed, mentally. Could she at least force Sebastian to acknowledge the newcomers? Something moved in the shadows, behind him and to his right, slipped closer, and disappeared once again.

She heard gravel shift. On the left, this time, but it was so damned dark here in the narrow canyon, and Sebastian's crouching form blocked much of her view through the narrow crevice between the rocks.

The scent was stronger; the wolves obviously closer. She was certain there were two, but could there be more?

Sebastian! Pay attention. They're going to attack, damn it!

This time he blinked. Shook his head and gazed at her as if he were just waking up.

She snarled at him. *What the hell is going on with you? There are at least two wolves out there. Behind you. Are they your friends? Because if they are, buddy, you are in deep shit, because I'm gonna put you there.*

Lily? What . . . ?

The nearest wolf charged out of the shadows. It was huge—almost a third again larger than any Chanku or natural wolf Lily had ever seen. Sebastian turned at the last moment and countered the attack. He was large, but the pale gray wolf that attacked was even bigger than Sebastian. And he had surprise on his side.

It missed the killing bite on Sebastian's throat but managed to clamp down on the loose skin above his shoulders. Sebastian yipped, twisted, and bit down on the wolf's front leg.

Lily heard the bone snap and winced at the gray's sharp howl of pain, but she didn't wait to see the results. Instead, she charged out of her refuge, leapt over the two wolves rolling in the dirt, and hit the second wolf as it raced to help the gray.

Her attack seemed to surprise the beast. He pulled back, but she hit him hard, slashing his muzzle with sharp fangs, rolling him off his feet, and clamping her jaws down on his throat.

He clawed at her with his hind feet, ripping dark fur out of her soft belly as he twisted and turned, struggling to break free. Then Sebastian was beside her. Lily almost lost her grip. Who would he side with—the other males or the female he'd somehow decided to claim as his own?

He bit down hard on one of the wolf's flailing hind legs. Again, that sickening snap, a howl of pain, and the animal's attack turned to a mad scramble for escape.

Lily turned the beast loose and backed off. The gray and his darker companion limped away snarling with ears back and tails tucked. They paused in a shaft of moonlight just at the entrance to the canyon, heads down, sides heaving. Blood speckled the muzzle of the gray, but Lily couldn't tell if the other one bled or not. He did, however, hold his left rear paw off the ground.

The gray favored his right front leg, but he stared at Lily and Sebastian through eyes filled with rage. After a moment, Sebastian snarled and charged the two.

They turned and raced away, each on three legs and limping badly, but still managing a fair burst of speed.

Sebastian slowly turned and walked stiff-legged back to Lily. His eyes were narrow slits, his ears back. Would he attack? Even now, after they'd fought together, after he'd helped her defeat her assailant?

He went flat to the ground, belly pressed to the dirt, and bared his throat. A totally submissive gesture. She'd not expected this, but she'd be damned if she wasted the opportunity. She closed her jaws over his throat, clamped down hard enough to make her point, and then turned him loose.

Lily, I'm sorry. I don't know what happened. Did I hurt you?

What do you mean, you don't know? You son of a bitch! You tried to mount me. You chased me here and wouldn't let me out. Not the best first date I've ever been on, that's for sure.

Oh. But . . . shit.

He looked honestly perplexed. That didn't make sense. He shook his head, a terribly human act that looked almost comical in the big black wolf. *Who were those guys? I've never seen them before. Why would they attack us? Were they after you?*

I've never seen them, either. But I recognize their scent.

How?

I smelled it a couple of days ago in Golden Gate Park. At the scene of the latest murder attributed to wolves.

Crap.

Exactly. Now, are you going to tell me what happened tonight?

He sat back and stared at the ground between his paws. *I have no idea. My last memory is running behind you. You scared up a rabbit. I remember losing the rabbit in the brambles, racing after you . . . and then nothing.*

She stared at him, searching his mind for any sense that he lied, but all she felt was his confusion. What the hell had happened? *We need to get back.* Breaking their mental connection, Lily trotted a few steps, looked over her shoulder, and waited. Sebastian sat in front of the tumbled boulders where he'd held her captive. She sensed his confusion, his need to understand what had happened to him. What he'd almost done to her.

She turned and followed the trail that would lead them to the parking lot. After a moment, she sensed Sebastian following.

This time she recognized the Sebastian she thought she knew.

But there was another side to him, a dark and dangerous side. She had no idea where it was hiding, or when or if it would break free again.

Trotting along behind Lily, Sebastian couldn't recall ever feeling as much shame as he felt at this moment. Shame and fear, and an overwhelming sense of confusion. What the fuck happened back there? He'd never before lost himself in the wolf, never once had his sentient human mind disappear during a shift.

Until tonight. Tonight there was nothing but a huge black hole in his memory. Tonight, when he'd finally met a woman who could matter to him, who might understand him, he'd totally fucked up any chance with her. He'd be lucky if she'd let him give her a ride home after this.

The parking lot was as empty as when they'd left it over an hour ago. The moon had settled a bit lower over the ocean, but the shadows were as dark and the night as still. Sebastian trotted over to the tree where he'd hidden the car keys, rose up on his hind legs, and snagged them with his teeth.

Lily waited for him beside the car. She hadn't shifted yet, and he searched her mind, expecting anger. Disgust, maybe, though he hoped there was no fear. He hated to think he'd frightened her, but there was none of that. No, the only thing he felt was her arousal, strong and rich, drawing him close. Teasing him with her ripe scent, her beautiful dark eyes.

It was too much. He drew inside himself and called on the magic. After an interminable wait, he felt the shift take hold and he stood in the darkness, a tall, naked man staring at a wolf bathed in crimson with strong shafts of iridescent pink.

All colors of sexual desire. A powerful, driving need to mate. His breath caught, stuttered in his chest. Her aura hadn't been visible to eyes seeing with the wolf's visual spectrum, but his human eyes now registered the colors, the beautiful aura he would always associate with Lily Cheval.

Damn.

He unlocked the car and reached for his clothing, turned his back, and pulled his knit boxers on, then his slacks. He almost laughed. He'd been hard and aroused when they'd first started out. Shame had left his dick entirely flaccid. He wanted to howl his disappointment, but his wolf had gone silent.

The night was warm, and his body hot from the run. He picked up his shirt and stared at it a moment, debating whether to put it on.

"Leave it off."

He jerked his head up at Lily's soft comment. He hadn't even been aware of her shift, and jealousy spiked through him, that she could do this so easily. She'd slipped that beautiful dress over her head, and somehow she actually looked more naked wearing it than when he'd seen her earlier, unclothed.

Then her words hit him. "This?" He clutched the black shirt in his hand. "You want me to leave it off?"

"Oh, yeah."

She winked. Lily actually winked at him? She should be furious. Disgusted. She . . .

"Less to take off when we get to my place."

With that, she slipped into the seat on the passenger side. Sebastian just stood there, feeling like an idiot. Then he leaned over, grabbed his shoes and socks, his tuxedo coat, and his shirt, and threw them all into the back.

He wished he had a clue what she was thinking, but she'd blindsided him with her invitation. Did her body clamor for sex after a shift the way his always did? Imagining Lily Cheval hot and naked and willing was almost more than his libido could handle. What the hell was going on? His thoughts spun and his hands shook as he started the engine and pulled back onto the highway.

They were only a short drive from Lily's home in the Marina District. He hoped like hell she wouldn't change her mind before they got there.

The slick fabric sliding across her nipples sent an electric pulse directly to her clit. Lily tightened her shields to keep her traitorous thoughts away from the man beside her, well aware she had to consciously force herself not to look at Sebastian. Not at his gorgeous chest with its perfect dusting of dark hair, an insidious lure that made her want to bury her fingers in its crisp texture. And she knew she'd be caught like a mouse in a trap the moment she focused on the rhythmic bunch and stretch of his powerful arms.

And, of course, like that stupid mouse drawn to the cheese, she realized she was staring, and yes, she was caught. There wasn't an ounce of fat, not a blemish anywhere beyond a small cut across his very fine nose where she'd marked him when he tried to mount her. No flaw in that coal black widow's peak over his forehead, or the darkly defined trail of crisp hair disappearing beneath the flat waistband of his black slacks.

Her vaginal walls tightened, clenching against emptiness, flooding the car with the ripe scent of her need. She wondered if Sebastian was sensitive enough to pick up a scent that was embarrassingly strong to her, one she knew a human man wouldn't even notice.

She clenched her fists and let out a deep breath. Damn it! She had no reason to feel embarrassed. She could no more deny her needs than she could refuse her wolf. She was Lily Milina Cheval, an alpha Chanku bitch, and her libido was part and parcel of the whole package.

If she were mated, if sexual release wasn't something she only prayed for, it would be different, but she hadn't had sex in much too long. The last time had been with Alex, and it had been wonderful as always, but it would never be enough because Alex wasn't enough. She loved Alex Aragat, but he was little more than a precocious child when compared to Sebastian Xenakis.

Lily had always been a stronger wolf than her lifelong buddy and best friend since birth, and both of them knew it.

She needed a man. One who challenged her.

A man like Sebastian, with all his quirks and his strange aura of darkness, with the mysteries she itched to unravel. She wanted his arousal, his sharp edge of danger, and his powerful hunger.

Hunger focused solely on her.

She studied his strong profile, and a shiver ran along her spine. There was something about him that might have frightened her had she been a little less sure of herself, but Lily knew and trusted her strengths. Where her magic might not be enough against a wizard as powerful as Sebastian, her wolf would always protect her.

She turned away and stared out the window as the massive struts of the Golden Gate Bridge flashed by, thinking of Alex, the one constant lover in her life. Where Alex was home and safety, unconditional love and acceptance along with a certain amount of hero worship, Sebastian was dark shadows and danger. Mystery clung to him, a subtle sense of peril that Lily found as arousing as the man's body.

No, there was nothing safe about Sebastian Xenakis. He'd tried to mount her tonight, but then he'd turned and fought wolves much larger than himself to protect her. He had her so twisted up inside she wasn't sure what she wanted or what she really believed about him, but one thing was certain.

She wanted him in her bed. Not as a wolf, at least not until she trusted him, but as a man. And she wanted him tonight. Her gaze was drawn once again to his strong profile just as he shifted his eyes in her direction. Even in the reflected lights from the dash, she could tell they were an inhuman shade of teal blue. Nothing of the wolf about them at all, but the slight crinkle at the corners as he smiled at her dissolved the danger, chased the mystery aside.

Was the mystery all in her mind? Was he merely a very sexy, very nice man who just happened to use magic to become a wolf? But, what if . . . ?

"Have you ever been tested?" she asked.

He frowned, but his concentration was on the bridge and the traffic slowing for the automatic tollbooth. "Tested? For what?"

"To see if you're Chanku."

He shook his head. "No. No reason. How's that work?"

Lily shrugged. "You take a capsule that's filled with specific nutrients for a couple of weeks. Either you shift or you don't. If you have the right DNA, you can become another creature.

The first shift is generally a wolf, but some people do other predators."

He laughed. "I can already shift, in case you hadn't noticed."

She punched his arm. "I noticed. Trust me on that, but I also think you could shift without the magic. Just a feeling. If I give you the capsules, would you take them?"

"I guess. No reason not to."

He took the exit that led to her home before Lily even thought to give him directions. "You know where I live."

"Busted," he said. He glanced her way. "I've wanted to meet you. I've heard of you. We're neighbors in Montana, but you're never there."

"Rarely. The job keeps me tied here more than I like. I prefer Montana." She stared out the window as he followed the road to her house. Her mom's uncle Ulrich had owned the place for many years, but all the family had settled on the compound in Montana years ago, when the world of man first learned that shapeshifters lived among them.

Luckily, the expected backlash hadn't been nearly as bad as they'd feared, but Tia and Luc, along with the rest of the pack, had decided they preferred living a communal life. It meant the kids could grow up with others like themselves, but it also meant the parents weren't alone raising children with powers even the adults didn't always understand.

It was almost funny, now, to think of everyone's shock when she and Alex and then the others had shifted while they were still so young, but they'd been exposed to the nutrients since conception, and then through breast milk. Unlike the older generation who hadn't discovered their Chanku heritage until they were already adults, Lily's was a generation born Chanku.

Precocious didn't come close to describing them, and they hadn't necessarily chosen wolves as their creature of choice, though Lily would always prefer that form.

She glanced again at Sebastian and wondered if he'd tried other creatures, and then she tried to imagine him shifting as easily as she did. None of them truly understood how the shift occurred, though Lily had been the one to discover that it entailed manipulating time in another dimension.

Which led to thoughts of what she was going to say to Sebastian as he pulled the car into her driveway. Her thoughts were still shielded, as were his, but she turned to him.

"Thank you, Sebastian."

He raised his eyebrows and then slowly shook his head. "For what? For trying to rape you? For losing control? I only hope you'll accept my apology, Lily. I am so sorry. I don't know what happened, but I swear it won't happen again."

His look was direct, his apology heartfelt, but then he turned away and stepped out of the car, walked around, and opened Lily's door. He took her right hand and helped her out of the car. She hung on and lightly touched his cheek with her left hand, cupping his jaw in her palm. "Will you come inside?"

He went very still. She caught the flare of his nostrils, the slight widening of his eyes and knew that he was well aware what she was asking.

"Are you sure? After what happened?"

She shrugged. "We ran as wolves. You chased me. I got away, and then you protected me from two wolves intent on doing harm." She laughed, as much at the surprise in his eyes as the fact it felt so damned good to stand here in her driveway, flirting with a sexy, mysterious man. "Don't look so surprised. As far as I'm concerned, it was one hell of a first date. I'm a wolf, Sebastian. I always enjoy a good fight." She winked. "A pretty good time was had by all, don't you think? Well, except for the two who will probably be limping for a few more days."

When he stared at her as if she'd sprouted horns or something worse, she laughed, clasped his other hand, and drew both of them close against her breasts. "I am Chanku, Sebastian. After a run, I really want to fuck. No strings. No ties. I just really, really want sex. Are you up for that?"

He shook himself, and she thought of a big dog coming out of the rain. But then he glanced down at the front of his slacks and raised his head and one eyebrow. "I guess I am."

This time, when she tugged his hands, he followed her into the house.

5

This was absolutely the last thing Sebastian had expected. Hell, he wouldn't have been surprised if she'd called the cops after the stunt he'd pulled during their run, but she didn't appear upset or angry.

Just the opposite—she'd invited him inside.

It was almost two in the morning. She said she wanted sex. So did he, in that overwhelming manner he'd learned to associate with running as the wolf, only tonight it was tempered by Lily's presence. Stronger, because her exotic beauty had grabbed him by the balls from the very beginning, but also caution.

He did not want to screw things up. As much as he wanted the physical connection with Lily, the pure, unabashed relief of need, he wanted more. He wanted to know her, to explore feelings that had slammed into him the moment she'd walked into that reception tonight.

Lily Cheval was special.

He wanted to know why. How. What it was that made her so different. Her aura remained as clear and bright as it had been when he first saw her. She wasn't angry. She was sexually aroused and had made it very clear she wanted him. No games. No pretense, but it made no sense. None at all. She wasn't anything like any other woman he'd known.

She was better. A million times better.

He took the key from her hand and unlocked the front door. Held it open for her. Lily turned and smiled as she stepped inside. Her shawl trailed over one shoulder in a shimmer of copper and crimson, the colors slipping in and out of her aura.

He barely noticed the tastefully decorated entry, the large living room, or the subtle lighting that gave everything a soft yet welcoming glow. No, there was only Lily, glowing brighter than everything else.

She filled his senses.

"I always feel like I need a shower after a run," she said.

How the hell could she sound so carefree? So entirely relaxed and casual? He blinked like an idiot. Shower?

"Would you care to join me?"

It wasn't often that a woman got the better of him, but Sebastian stopped in his tracks and stared at her. "Lily?" He sighed and shook his head. She was so far ahead of him, he wasn't even in the race, but at least his soft chuckle made her grin. "Please tell me, in simple words, what the fuck's going on?"

She grabbed his hands and leaned close, pressed her mouth against his, and surprised him with a sharp nip of his lower lip. "You must not read the gossip rags," she whispered. Her mouth stayed so close, he felt her lips moving against his. "Chanku are not human. We are creatures ruled by our strong sex drive. Our *very strong* sex drive. After a run, arousal peaks, and believe me, it's especially powerful tonight. I promise you, the sex will be incredible."

She stood back and sighed. "I could masturbate, but it's not nearly as much fun, not when I've got a gorgeous man I find terribly appealing standing in my foyer. I won't get pregnant. I'm immune to human disease, and I want you. From the look in your eyes and the obvious erection in your trousers, I'm guessing you want me, too. It will be fun, Sebastian." She grinned. "C'mon, big guy. Let your hair down."

He laughed and wrapped his arms around her. She slipped into his embrace as if they'd been lovers forever. "Let my hair down? That sounds like something my father might say, only he's much too uptight."

"It is something my father says. In fact, give me a minute." She slipped out of his embrace and closed her eyes. He couldn't take his eyes off her. She'd clasped her hands over her flat belly and raised her head, but he felt a buzzing in his mind and wondered if she communicated with someone.

He was trying to figure out how to read her thoughts when she wasn't actually projecting, but then her eyes flashed open and she smiled. "I had to let Dad know I'm okay. He tends to hover, and he'd caught my distress earlier. I suggested that if he continued hovering, he might see more than he wants."

Sebastian ignored her reference to his behavior—they'd have to talk about that later—but he wanted to know more about her link with her father. "His mind is that strong? He's in Montana, right?" That made no sense at all. Sebastian and his father could barely communicate across a room.

"He uses a combination of his Chanku abilities and his skills as a wizard, but we've always had a very close connection. He worries about me." She laughed. "He's an excellent worrier. But no more about my father, especially when he's promised to leave me alone. Knowing him, he won't hold his promise for long." She grabbed Sebastian's hand and tugged.

She didn't have to pull very hard, though he planted his feet at the doorway to the master bedroom. What an ass! Any other guy would be all over her, but he couldn't get past what had happened tonight, how he'd lost control. How he'd lost the memories of the entire event.

It scared the crap out of him. What if he did the same thing during sex? What if he hurt her?

What if he really was the one killing those girls?

"Lily." He tugged his hands free of her grasp. "I'm afraid. I know you think I'm nuts, but what if I hurt you? What if . . ." He shook his head, a short, sharp jerk as much to clear his thoughts as to deny his fears. He couldn't be the one killing those girls. He wasn't a killer, damn it.

Lily stood there a moment with her hands on her hips, just smiling at him like he was a complete idiot. "If I'm not worried, you don't need to be, either." Then she winked, reached down, grabbed the hem of her dress, and slowly pulled it up her body, over her head.

His mouth went dry. She wore nothing but a tiny scrap of lace that might be considered panties. No bra, but with perfect breasts like hers, she certainly didn't need one.

"I'm going to take a shower, Sebastian. If you want to join me, it's through that door." She cocked her head toward the far side of the bedroom, turned around, and still wearing her high heels and those tiny panties, walked away.

His feet might as well have been locked to the floor. Any remaining blood in his circulatory system immediately left his brain and went straight to his cock. Each soft footfall she made echoed in the heavy pulse engorging his shaft.

He was practically panting by the time she paused in the open doorway, bent at the waist with her back to him, and carefully removed first one shoe and then the other. Then, with a slight shimmy of her hips, she slid the tiny lace panties over her hips, down her long, long legs, and stepped out of them.

Sebastian's hands were shaking so hard he could barely get his pants off. He was thankful he'd not put his shoes back on after shifting, because he doubted he'd be able to manage laces, the condition he was in. He kicked his pants off his feet and almost tripped when the left one hung up on his foot, but his gaze never left Lily.

She was breathtaking, a vision in shimmering light. Her aura spiked in brilliant shards of pink, the flashes so bright, so iridescent, he wondered if she were ready to orgasm without him.

He was practically running when he hit the bathroom door, but he skidded to a halt the moment he caught up to her. The bathroom was a sybarite's fantasy—huge and completely open on one side to windows looking out onto a softly lit walled garden. The shower was nothing more than a natural stone enclosure with walls a little over three feet high that reminded Sebastian of a woodland grotto. Ferns and orchids grew in small niches inside the shower proper, and indirect lighting lent the effect of moonlight in a dark forest.

A skylight overhead would give natural light during daytime, but now it was a fantasy of shadows and falling water, dark stone and soft lights with Lily standing in the middle, a forest nymph beneath a shower of rain. Wet, her hair hung well past her hips, a dark, sleek mantle rather than the tangle of loose tawny, coppery curls she'd worn earlier. Her skin glimmered like warm honey in the low lighting, her burnt umber nipples ruched now into taut points of arousal.

Sebastian stared at her, lost in her beauty, in the sleek muscles, long legs, and slightly rounded hips. She ignored him, which was probably better than he deserved. What an ass he'd been, but self-recrimination solved nothing, and after a moment, he let out a deep breath and stepped beneath the warm water.

Still she ignored him.

He pressed close against Lily's back and wrapped her in a loose embrace. Water fell gently over his head and shoulders. Her breasts rested softly against his forearms. She leaned against him, tucking her head beneath his chin and her sleek bottom against his groin, sighing as she ran her long fingers over the tops of his thighs.

He kissed his way down her neck, over her shoulder, and across the curve of her jaw. Then he bent and placed kisses along her spine, over the rounded curve of her bottom. Finally, kneeling, he gently turned her toward him, lifted her left leg, and draped it over his shoulder.

She tangled her fingers in his hair for balance. Chuckling when she lightly tugged, he pressed his cheek against her inner thigh and inhaled the musky scent of aroused woman. Impatiently, Lily tilted her hips forward. Sebastian wrapped his hands around her hips, clutching her buttocks and holding her still as he nuzzled the soft curls between her thighs.

"Now, damn it!"

He lifted his head and laughed. "She speaks!" He sighed dramatically. "But only to give me orders. So demanding." Then he leaned close and ran his tongue across her clit.

Lily groaned and laughed at the same time as he teased her with tiny licks and nips. If he was reading her right, this woman liked control. He imagined she was a voracious lover, used to getting her way, used to directing her men.

He really didn't want to think of Lily with other men. For some reason, the wolven side, the one he usually worked so hard to call, rose up now and made his presence known.

Sebastian hadn't realized he was such a possessive creature.

But it had to be the wolf telling him the best approach with this woman would be to take away her control. Sebastian agreed. He stroked her with his tongue and thought of shifting to lick deeper, but he'd already screwed things up as a wolf. It was enough to follow his creature's suggestions without actually shifting. Tonight he'd make a point of not pushing her. Of giving her what she wanted.

Within reason.

Lily's hands tightened in his hair as he licked and sucked between her legs. Water fell like warm rain against his back as he nipped at her labia and drew each sleek petal between his lips. He used his tongue to tease and lick her clitoris and the tiny hood surrounding it.

She must have been right on the edge. With just a couple of licks, her hands tightened in his wet hair and she arched her hips close against his mouth. Her body shuddered, and she cried out with her climax. Fighting his own powerful arousal, Sebastian licked faster, deeper, and she came again, harder this time, until she curled her lithe body around him, tugging almost frantically at his hair. Her taste filled his mouth, a flavor unique to Lily, an aphrodisiac like nothing he'd ever experienced. She was panting when, with a final lick, he stood, grabbed her around the waist, and forcefully bent her over the stone wall surrounding the shower.

The water stopped falling as they stepped away from whatever sensor must be controlling it, and now the silence was broken by the harsh sound of his breathing and Lily's soft whimper as he positioned her on the smooth stones.

High enough to keep her feet off the ground, her bottom in the air, and her long hair lying in tangles on the polished stone floor below her head, it was the perfect height for sex. He wondered if she'd designed it that way, with this in mind. Wondered how many men had taken her this same way, but then he shoved that thought out of his head.

He had no right to such thoughts. He was the one here now, and she honored him with her generosity and giving nature. It was just the two of them, and that was more than he'd hoped.

He'd read more than enough of the polyamorous nature of the Chanku. Alternately disgusted and aroused by the thought of multiple partners, he'd held the images close. Images of men with men, women with women, all of them aroused, all of them together.

He didn't need those visuals now. He had Lily, and he ran his palms over her sleek flanks, leaned close, and nipped the rounded curve of her buttock. Lily groaned, and the last of his fantasies fled. Lily Cheval was fantasy itself as she slapped the rock wall with both hands for balance, as he parted her legs and, without foreplay, rested the thick head of his cock against her.

Her gasps for air blended with his harsh breaths. The sounds of the last drops of water draining into the pipe beneath the shower and dripping from the stones, Lily's soft whimpers, his thundering heart—all coming together in a powerful crescendo.

Lily's hands slid across the stone wall, and he heard her fingers scrabbling for purchase on the rocks to hold herself steady. Her long, lean body writhed beneath him, and he wondered for a brief moment if he was being too rough, if he might be hurting her.

Almost as if Lily answered his brief thought, she raised her hips and pressed back against him, forcing his entry. Sebastian pushed forward, slowly, relentlessly working his way deep into her tight channel. She was sleek and hot, her muscles quivering and clenching along his full length.

And then, as if she'd turned on a switch, Lily's thoughts entered his mind. Not words so much, but sensations as she shared the thick intrusion of his cock, forcing her vaginal walls to stretch and give way. Her nipples tightened and he sensed the sweet pain as if it were his own. Her arousal became his.

Her desire ruled his needs. Opening his mind, he shared his feelings, the way it felt when his balls brushed against her as he seated himself deep, the pulsing, clenching rhythm of her feminine muscles, the cool brush of air along his damp shaft when he slowly withdrew.

Again he drove deep, and again he retreated, his mind caught in an ever-escalating loop of sensation. A sweet yet musky scent filled his nostrils—Lily's arousal and his own. Sounds, their small grunts and groans and harsh breaths magnified until his mind spun on overload. His muscles clenched, his body tightened, and he sank deep inside Lily, but there was no relief. She was all grasping muscles and sleek heat, holding him inside.

He needed more, wanted more. He thrust harder, faster, his hips a powerful piston slapping against her sleek buttocks, hands grasping her waist, holding her in place. Desire blossomed as her images melded with his until Sebastian and Lily were one entity, one thrusting, twisting, sweating, gasping entity of lust, their bodies no longer under conscious control, directed by passion, ruled by need and a deep, overwhelming hunger.

He'd never felt so powerful before, had never wanted so much, never given as much or taken so completely, and yet Lily was taking as well, finding her pleasure, giving back and sharing the amazing sense of completion, the knowledge that she'd been missing this for far too long.

He had given her that gift, just as she'd shared that same gift with him. It had been too long. *Forever,* he thought, as her body arched, her inner muscles clamped down hard and held him close. Lily's cry echoed with Sebastian's harsh curse, as he gave up what little control he'd tried to hang on to since she'd invited him to her home. He surged into her, blood pulsing in his veins, his ejaculate filling her clenching sheath. His hips moved with their own rhythm, his thighs flexing as he thrust once, twice, and then he buried his cock deep inside while his rigid muscles spasmed.

His climax lasted forever; it was over much too soon, and when his legs gave out, he slumped over her back, arms quivering and lungs heaving with each deep breath.

They lay there for a moment, both of them locked away in their own thoughts. He missed the sharing, the mental joining that had felt as important as the physical link they'd achieved.

Lily was the first to move, the one to raise her head and turn enough to look him in the eye. "Well, it's good, I think, that at least we're still in the shower. I need to hose off again." She winked.

His emotions were in turmoil, and Lily wanted a shower? His head was still spinning, but uppermost was the thought that this amazing joining on so many levels hadn't had the same emotional impact for Lily that it had for him.

Feeling curiously flat, Sebastian grunted and lifted away from her, took her hand, and tugged her upright, easily lifting her away from the smooth stone. He steadied her, taking notice of the way her legs trembled and the red marks across her torso where she'd lain across the wall. "I'm sorry. I hope I didn't hurt you."

She didn't answer. Instead, Lily wrapped her arms around his waist and pressed her face against his chest. "No," she said. "Far from it. That was . . ." She looked up at him. "Pretty spectacular. I'm glad you let me talk you into it."

Unexpected anger surged when she pushed gently away from him and stepped beneath the shower. The water flowed immediately, falling as a warm and gentle rain. Obviously unaware of his roiling emotions, she shrugged and glanced away. "I don't usually have to work so hard to get laid."

His body went rigid as he stared at her, forcing Lily to meet his gaze. "Is that all that was, Lily? Getting laid?"

She blinked. "Of course," she said. "What else can it be?"

"I don't know." He grabbed the soap and a washcloth, leaned over, and planted a short, hard kiss on her mouth. "But at least I'm man enough to want to find out."

He was right, and she was wrong, damn it! Lily turned away and reached for her own cloth. Her inner muscles continued their rhythmic clench and release, and her body still thrummed with the power of her orgasm, but that was normal after sex, wasn't it? At least with good sex. Hell, exquisite sex—sex unlike anything she'd ever experienced in her life.

He claimed he wasn't Chanku, but they'd linked so easily, as if they'd already mated. She knew her parents experienced this kind of connection during sex, but Lily hadn't. Never. Not even with Alex, a man she knew as well as she knew herself.

Now, having experienced it, she didn't know if she was terrified or thrilled. She had to give Sebastian the capsules, see if he changed. He had to, or there could be no future for them. Not if he wasn't Chanku.

She'd heard too many horror stories of Chanku living with humans, none of them good. After a while, the frustration and emotional isolation eventually destroyed whatever love had brought them together. Chanku were pack animals. Lily had always been part of the pack. Not even love could make her give it up.

And then there was the aging thing. Humans got old. Chanku didn't. End of story. Good way to kill a relationship.

She ran the cloth over her arms, preternaturally aware of Sebastian bathing behind her, but she kept her back to him. The intimacy in and of itself wasn't a bad thing. She had no shame being naked with either man or woman, but the intimacy she'd experienced with Sebastian had left her shaken and vulnerable.

She had so many questions about him—hell, he had questions. He'd lost almost half an hour tonight. Half an hour when he'd pursued her as if she'd been prey. He'd tried to mount her—the wolven version of rape—but she didn't blame him entirely.

Something had happened. Just as something had happened at the reception, when he'd turned and looked at her. The pain that knocked her flat had come from him. No doubt there, but she didn't think he'd been the instigator. No, he'd been a conduit.

But for whom? And why?

She turned to find him watching her, and she reached up to

smooth away the frown between his amazing teal blue eyes. "What's the matter? You look worried."

"I am worried. I'm not a man who likes mysteries, and yet I have more questions than answers. Why did you collapse tonight? I felt pain at the moment you went down, but it came from somewhere else. And later, when we were running. I remember shifting, and I remember chasing after a rabbit, then nothing. I don't recall anything else until those two wolves attacked us."

She glanced away, remembering the look in his wolf's eyes. There'd been no sense of the man behind those eyes. He'd been nothing but a feral beast, pursuing a female. "We need to talk." She leaned close and kissed his chest. Ran her finger down his breastbone and felt his skin shiver beneath her touch. "But I can't do it when we're standing here naked."

He laughed while she rinsed off. When she stepped out of the shower, she handed him a soft robe that was hanging beside another identical robe.

He dried off and slipped the robe over his shoulders. She noticed the frown was back.

"What?"

He shrugged. "You live here alone, but you have two robes by the shower. Is there someone in your life?"

She smiled and thought of all the snarky things she could say to tweak his male possessiveness, but finally decided honesty was best. "I'm Chanku. We're pack animals. I often have packmates here overnight, especially when they're in town on business. CGI, Chanku Global Industries, is huge. I run Cheval International, which is merely a small part of the entire conglomerate. Though most of us live in Montana, all the main offices of the company are headquartered in the Bay Area."

He glanced away and then focused on her. "Thank you. I really have no business asking you something like that, do I?"

She smiled to take away the sting. "Not really, but I don't mind. Better to get that sort of thing out of the way. There is a lot about the way we live that's different from humans, and most of the differences are tied to our sexuality. You should know what you're getting into with me." She laughed and tugged his hand. "C'mon. It's late, and I actually do need to go to the office in the morning."

"I should go home."

But he didn't look as if that's what he wanted. "No, you should stay. We need to talk." She ran her finger over the small scratch on his nose. "You're healing quickly. That's good." Then she yawned, stretched her arms up over her head, and smiled at him. "We need to talk, but we need sleep, too. I'm exhausted and I know you have to be as well. Stay with me tonight, Sebastian. We can talk over breakfast. I make a mouthwatering omelet."

She wasn't sure where the invitation came from, but it felt right. And no matter what was going on in Sebastian Xenakis's life, it felt right.

And he was definitely smiling back at her.

Lily dropped the terrycloth robe on the chair by her dresser and crawled into the big bed, between crisp, clean sheets. A pale swath of moonlight illuminated the dark coverlet. Sebastian got in beside her, as naked as she was, but his long, lean body was hard where hers was soft.

Masculine to her feminine. He scooted close and wrapped his arms around her, tucked her head beneath his chin, and enveloped her in heat and warmth.

She felt his soft sigh of contentment as much as she heard it. It was an echo of her own feelings—feelings she couldn't put a name to. Not yet.

They made love again. Soft, sweet love that brought tears to Lily's eyes and made her heart ache in her chest. He was so perfect. So damnably perfect.

So why did that make her heart hurt so much? Maybe they'd find the answers in the morning. For now, she merely wanted to enjoy the unique thrill of falling asleep in the arms of a man who might just have what she'd always looked for.

He filled an emptiness she'd known for far too long. One she'd suspected might forever stay the same. Snuggling close to him, she fell quickly into a deep, dreamless sleep.

Except, when she awoke in the morning, the bed beside her was cold, and Sebastian was gone. She stared at the place where he'd slept and blinked back tears. Men never left her without a good-bye kiss at the very least.

This was a first. She hadn't even heard him go. No, she'd fallen asleep with the secure knowledge he'd be here this morning.

The phone rang. Numb, wondering if he might be calling to explain, she fumbled for the phone.

"Thank the goddess you're okay. There's been another one."

"Alex? What?" She shook her foggy head and tried to focus on his image on the small screen. "What are you talking about?"

"Another murder. A young woman getting off the late shift at one of those all-night delis near Market Street. Raped by a man and mauled by wolves. Happened around five this morning."

Lily shoved herself upright against the headboard. "Where?"

"Not far from your house. Her body was found on the green at Fort Mason."

"Oh, shit."

"What's that supposed to mean?"

"Sebastian Xenakis spent the night. He was gone when I woke up."

" 'Oh, shit,' is right, Lil. Damn it. You need to contact your dad. Let him know what's going on. According to my records, Xenakis has been in the general vicinity of every single death. He flies commercial, first class, so he's easy to track. Be careful, sweetheart. This guy's dangerous."

"We don't know for sure, Alex."

There was a long silence. She was sure Alex was trying to control his temper. "You like him, don't you?"

His gentle question almost undid her, but damn it, she did like Sebastian. A lot. But she could never lie to Alex. "Yeah," she said. "I do. He was so open with me, Alex. I can't imagine him hiding something as huge as murder. Multiple murders. And his isn't the same scent I picked up at the scene."

"Which scene? When?"

She probably should have told him. "I went to the site of the last killing, the one near Mom's garden in Golden Gate Park. I picked up the scent of strange wolves but no human scent beyond the ones that belonged there. I think the victim was raped somewhere else, but mauled to death by wolves at the park. Last night, when Sebastian and I ran . . ."

"He shifted? He's Chanku?"

She let out a huge sigh. "I don't know. He used magic to shift. A lot of magic. Drew it from the mountain and the trees around us, enough that he glowed with magefire before he turned into a wolf, but he's definitely a wolf. Stuff happened last night, Alex. I need to wake up better, think about it, before I lay it all out. Later, okay?"

"Lily. Be careful. Please. I can't get down there right away. Too much going on, but I hate to think of you dealing with this guy on your own."

"Thanks, Alex. And don't worry. I'll talk to Dad. He's good at helping me get my thoughts organized. I need to take a shower, wake myself up a little more." She glanced at the clock. It was already after seven. She had a meeting at nine. "I do miss you."

"I miss you, too, sweetheart. Just be careful, okay? Whoever this guy is, whether it's Sebastian or someone else, he's dangerous, and his kills are coming more often."

She stared at the bed, at the indentation of Sebastian's head in the pillow beside hers, and sighed. He couldn't be the killer. She had to believe that. He'd been too open, too concerned. Too perfect.

"I know. I'll be careful."

"You'd better be. You know how much I love you, Lily. If anything ever happens to you, I swear I'll haunt you forever. And I'm not kidding, because Eve'll be right there beside me."

She laughed as the image of Alex and their goddess hovering overhead popped into her mind. "Just try it. Eve always liked me better."

They ended the call on uneasy laughter, but Lily sat there a moment, staring at the phone. Why hadn't she thought of Eve? Goddess she might be, but she was also Lily's closest friend and confident. It had been much too long since she'd walked the astral and visited Eve in her own perfect world.

A bit of astral perfection sounded really good, because her own world was obviously way too fucked up.

She inhaled and caught Sebastian's scent, and her body reacted immediately. Her nipples ached. Her breasts felt heavy, and she was suddenly wet and aching between her legs. Damn. Her wolf should have better sense than this—how could it let her be turned on by a guy who might be a rapist and a murderer?

She took another deep breath, remembering. His scent was not what she'd picked up at the last murder scene, but damn it all, she figured she really needed to check out this newest one.

After she took a shower. And after she talked to her father. Lily felt the dull ache in her head and recognized it for what it was. Well, dear old Dad was just going to have to wait until she washed away Sebastian Xenakis's seductive scent.

No matter how much she wanted to carry it with her the rest of the day.

6

Sebastian sat in the kitchen, sipping bad coffee and staring out the window. Fog lay low over the ocean, turning the water the same dark pewter as the sky.

The monochromatic view fit his mood.

He should have stayed in Lily's bed. He could be enjoying fresh ground coffee in her beautiful, sunlit kitchen right now, watching her make that promised omelet for his breakfast, just soaking up the pure joy of being in her presence.

Instead, he was drinking instant coffee because he'd been too pissed off to make a fresh pot, waiting for a showdown with his father that was sure to be unpleasant.

He rubbed his finger across the bridge of his nose. The scratch where Lily nipped him had completely healed. He almost wished it had lasted longer, proof of a most amazing yet frustrating night.

A reminder he needed answers. Lots of answers.

He sensed his father before he saw him. Felt his presence with the sense of something unclean entering his consciousness.

He'd never noticed it before Lily, but Aldo Xenakis carried an almost oily feel about him.

Where Lily was fresh and clean, a shining ray of magical energy and life, his father left the psychic taint of a sewage spill. Why hadn't he sensed this before?

"Ah. So the social butterfly has flown home."

Sebastian turned slowly, frowning. "Excuse me?"

His father was practically chortling. "How was it? Sex with the princess?" Before Sebastian could respond, Aldo slapped both hands on the table and leaned close, until they were eye to eye. "I know you nailed the bitch. How'd it go?"

Rage flashed. Sharp, burning rage, striking hard and hot as lightning. He reacted. His hand clamped around his father's throat before the man finished speaking.

Aldo's eyes went wide. He gasped unintelligible words, but they were enough to call the power to throw Sebastian across the room. He slammed up against a wall of cabinets and slid to the floor, stunned. Remnants of mage energy sparked and danced over his skin, but he shook it off and shoved himself to his feet, shaking from anger, not fear. He spoke his own words of power, and the remnants of Aldo's spell slid away.

At least the old bastard looked rattled. He raised his head and glared at Sebastian. "Don't ever lay your hands on me again."

Drawing deep breaths, Sebastian stood tall and ground out his own threat. "Then watch your mouth, old man. Do not speak of her that way."

"I could kill you, you know." Aldo folded his arms across his chest and studied Sebastian as if he were some sort of insect. Power radiated from him, shimmering about the room.

Power but no aura.

Sebastian clenched his jaw. His father probably could kill him. He wished he had a better idea of the man's basic nature, though he knew his magic was strong. How the hell the old bastard managed to hide a feature so intrinsic to a soul as an aura was frustrating as hell.

"You probably could kill me. But you won't." Probably not the smartest thing he could say.

"You're right." Aldo smiled. "I have plans for you. You are my sole heir, after all. Heir to more than mere wealth."

Shivers raced along Sebastian's spine.

Aldo walked over to the counter and pulled out the coffee grinder and fresh beans. "So, how did the reception go? Did you have a good time?"

Just like that, he switched off the wizardly display of power and was suddenly Sebastian's loving and concerned father, interested in his son's night out.

Sebastian refused to react. Instead, he brushed off his tuxedo slacks and walked across the kitchen to stand in front of the large window. He'd had enough coffee, and he really wanted to put some space between the two of them. "You already seem to know all the details," he said, staring at the pewter sky. "In fact, I have a few questions for you."

Aldo was suddenly standing beside him at the window. Sebastian hadn't heard the man move.

"I always loved this view," Aldo said. "San Francisco has its own kind of energy, but it's stronger near the water. Do you feel the magic?"

"I always feel the magic." Sebastian turned and stared at his father. "I felt something else last night. A sharp blast of power using my brain as a conduit. It would take a powerful mage to wield that kind of energy."

"What kind is that?"

"The kind that can do harm. The kind that went straight for Lily Cheval and knocked her unconscious." Sebastian watched for a sign, any flicker of emotion that would tell him his father was connected.

"Interesting. And who do you think was responsible?"

Bastard. "The same one who did something to my mind later so that I lost at least half an hour while running as a wolf. Lost all sense of who I was, who Lily was. My lack of attention almost got us killed."

That seemed to set the old man back a bit. "What do you mean? What happened?"

"You tell me. Lily and I were hunting as wolves. Next thing I know, I've got her cornered in a cavern on Mount Tam, trying to rape her."

Aldo's eyebrows lifted. Then he frowned. "You mean you didn't?"

Sebastian took a step back, an instinctual need to put space between himself and the man. "You sound disappointed. Of course I didn't. I don't rape women, but two other wolves showed up, intent on fighting. Or rape. I'm not really sure. We didn't stand around and chat. They must have been rogue Chanku, because they were obviously intelligent, but the threat of the two males snapped me out of whatever had taken control."

Nodding, Aldo glanced away. "I see."

"No, father dear. I think I finally see." And why hadn't he, before now? How in the hell could he have been so stupid? "It was you. You somehow got past my shields at the reception. You're the one who hurt her. And later, when I thought the wolf had taken over, it wasn't my wolf nature at all. Again, it was you, wasn't it?"

"Oh, Sebastian." He sighed, and his condescending tone made Seb's jaw ache from clenching. "You give me far too much credit. I'm strong, but controlling your mind from a distance? That's impossible. Not that I wouldn't embrace power like that, but I fear you're mistaken."

Sebastian glared at his father, realized he was clenching his fists as well as his jaw, and forced himself to relax. "You have no aura," he said, which wasn't what he'd intended to say at all. Hell, he didn't know what he wanted to say. What he believed.

Aldo raised his eyebrows. "No aura? What are you talking about? Auras don't exist. They're pseudo magic. Auras have as much validity as palmistry."

"So you say." Sebastian slowly raked his gaze over his father. Nothing. No hint of an aura, no sense of anything about the man, though the oily, evil stench felt stronger. He turned away. He really had to get out of here.

"There was another one, you know. Early this morning."

Sebastian stopped, turned slowly, and stared at Aldo's bland expression. "Another what?" But he knew. Damn it all, he knew exactly what the bastard was talking about.

"Another young woman murdered." He shrugged. "Depending on when you left Ms. Cheval's home on Marina, you probably just missed it. Her body was found on the grounds at Fort Mason. Raped, mauled by animals. Wolves. Or wolf. One very strong wolf might have managed the kill. One who could shift could have raped her as well."

"Don't just prance around it, Dad. What exactly are you implying?"

"What time did you leave Ms. Cheval's?"

"A little after four." Damn. Why did he automatically answer the bastard? It was none of his business.

His father smiled. Sebastian clenched his fists to keep from punching that smile off his face. "Reporter said she died between four and six this morning. I hope you have a good alibi." He paused. Raised one expressive eyebrow. "Should you need one."

There was nothing to say. Not a damned thing. Sebastian spun around and left the room. Alibi, hell. Like anyone would believe him if he told the truth. When he left Lily's bed, he'd driven straight home and then walked back to Ocean Beach to watch the sun rise.

Except it had been foggy and the beach was empty, and he'd sat there feeling like shit, knowing he had to face his father.

Knowing he had to find out if the man was using some sort of mind control, but as always, Aldo had turned everything around.

Turned it around until Sebastian was left wondering if he'd done as he thought. Had he really spent the early morning hours sitting alone on a beach, freezing his ass off? He'd lost almost half an hour last night while running with Lily. Behaved in a manner that was the opposite of the man he thought himself to be, and yet he remembered none of it.

Had he somehow shifted and murdered a young woman? Was he capable of living an alternate life, one entirely separate from what he knew as his own reality?

In the past, when he'd run as a wolf, he'd retained his sentient thought processes. His senses had been enhanced, his ability to see and hear and smell so much stronger that it was intoxicating. Even so, he'd never lost time during a shift.

Or had he? Had he murdered and raped that young woman?

And if he had, she wasn't the first. Hell, he didn't know anything anymore. His life was spinning out of control, and the one person he'd found, the only one he'd felt any sort of connection to in all his thirty-nine years could be in danger because of him.

He'd already shown her he couldn't be trusted.

But neither could he trust his father. The man was much too smug, too pleased with himself. Sebastian had sensed something familiar in his mind just before Lily collapsed. But what? The memory was lost in fog.

He tried to recall that blank period from last night. Something had happened. Something he'd recognized at the time, a trigger of some kind, though that sense of recognition, of familiarity, was gone as well. But something had affected his behavior. Something that teased the edges of his memory.

Sebastian raised his head. He caught his father studying him with an expression that could only be described as a self-satisfied smirk. Aldo wiped his expression clear the moment Sebastian caught his gaze, but there was no doubt Aldo Xenakis was terribly pleased about something.

Destroying his son's life, perhaps?

But why? And to what purpose?

What if Sebastian's suspicions were groundless—rooted in nothing more than paranoia?

No. This was too real, too deadly to be mere imagination. The answers were out there. He merely had to find them.

But until he had answers, he would stay away from Lily. She already meant too much to him. He wasn't about to put her at risk again.

"Lily? Are you all right?"

Lily stared at the screen on her phone, at her father's frantic expression, the way he rubbed his fingers over a heavy silver spoon he held in his right hand. He'd developed the habit of holding something to keep his hands occupied when they talked. She was convinced it was his way of reminding himself she was an adult and he could no longer run her life, so she schooled her features to present a mature, adult appearance. "I'm fine, Dad. I told you not to worry. I said I'd call as soon as I showered."

"I feel something you're not telling me. What's wrong, sweetheart?"

"Nothing." Well, almost nothing, but her dad was the ultimate worrier and "nothing" was her standard answer to the question he always asked. The last thing she wanted to do was give him something to worry about that might actually be an issue.

Like Sebastian Xenakis.

"But I do have a few things I'd like you to check."

"About Aldo or his son?"

Someday, she might actually surprise him. "Both. Here's the

deal. I'm not going to hide anything from you and Mom. Sebastian is . . ." She shrugged and figured her father would read all sorts of things into that. Sometimes she wished phones lacked such good video. "I think he could be the one, Dad. I remember how you said when you met Mom, you just knew. When I saw Sebastian last night, I don't know how to explain it, but there was a connection."

"Was that before or after you passed out?"

His dry comment actually let her know he wasn't totally going nuts worrying about her.

"Thanks for reminding me." She chuckled softly. "That's part of what I want you to check. See if you can find out the extent of Aldo Xenakis's power. I'm convinced he's a practitioner of the dark arts. There's something wrong about him, as if the residue of evil clings to his skin. When he interrupted my lunch with Jill Bradley on Monday, I forced him to shake hands, even though my first instinct was to run far and fast." She laughed softly. "I should have listened to my instincts. I felt like I needed to disinfect my entire body."

"Obviously you sensed nothing foul about his son."

She almost laughed at his dry comment, but then she thought about it. Sebastian's energy wasn't like hers. "No. Not anything offensive like I did with his father, but definitely something dark. Especially when he shifted last night. Something weird happened. I'm still trying to work through that."

"Will you tell me?"

"I will, but I don't want you to judge Sebastian by what happened. I have a strong feeling someone was controlling him. And yes, I'm convinced his father was involved." She noticed her father's subtle nod, as if he considered her comments and then filed them for later perusal.

"We started out running, playing tag, just goofing around, and then something changed. He got this feral look in his eyes, and when I tried to mindspeak, he didn't respond."

Anton's look went from fatherly concern to feral wolf in a heartbeat. Her alpha questioned her now, not her father. "What did he do, Lily? Did he hurt you?"

"Boy, do I remember that look," she said, hoping to lighten the moment. "No, he didn't, though I think he would have mounted me if he could have caught me. That's not the man I know. It's like Sebastian wasn't in there, if you get my drift."

"You don't know him well enough to say that."

"Possibly true. But I've never doubted my instincts, and my original response was to trust him. And, Dad, he didn't mount me."

Anton nodded. "I'll accept that. What stopped him?"

She was pretty impressed. Anton Cheval could be rather hotheaded at times, and he was controlling himself admirably, though she wondered if she should mention that he'd just bent one of her mom's best sterling serving spoons into a perfect *U*.

"That's another thing I want you to check on. Remember those tests the army was doing, trying to find Chanku among the troops to create a shapeshifting force?"

"Of course I remember. It was an abject failure. Chanku are killers by nature, but they won't follow a leader merely because of his rank. The military couldn't seem to understand that the number of stars on a helmet doesn't always equate with pack alpha standing. They had no control over the few troops they found."

"Exactly. But what happened to those Chanku the military discovered? Were they assimilated back into the general military population?"

The silence was telling. Frowning, Anton finally said, "I don't know. I think a few of them have registered with the pack, but I have no idea how many eventually were turned and what became of them. I should. I generally don't let things like that slip."

"You've had a few other things on your mind." Like the expansion of Cheval International and the various other companies within Chanku Global Industries including Pack Dynamics, their search and rescue team. And the pack, which had grown slowly but steadily over the years. It was almost as if her father had taken on the role as monarch of his small country of Chanku, with the vast majority of his subjects living on the extensive holdings he had in Montana, not far from the town of Kalispell.

He hadn't asked for the role, but it had found him.

And of course, the deadly attacks on so many young women, presumably by wolves and men . . . or wolves who became men.

"Dad, what saved me last night, when Sebastian was chasing me across the flank of Mount Tam with sex controlling his wolven brain, was an attack by more wolves. Big wolves. A third again larger than Tinker."

Anton stared at her for a long, silent moment. Then he nodded and carefully set the bent spoon on his desk. "What happened?"

Now he sounded way too calm. "When I first realized that Sebastian was chasing me with more than a romp across the mountains on his mind, I took off and found a bolt hole in a small cave between tumbled boulders. He caught up to me; we were facing off, and I was trying to get him to respond to me as a thinking creature when I scented strange wolves."

"You didn't recognize them?"

"Actually, Dad, I did. There were two of them, and I recognized their scent from the place where that girl was killed last week, the one near Mom's garden in Golden Gate Park."

"How did Sebastian react?"

"My first thought was that the whole evening was a setup, that he was with them, but it didn't fit with the way my wolf had so quickly responded to his. Mindspeaking, I told him we were about to be attacked. Finally, something broke through, and he responded to me. I honestly didn't know if they were friends of his or not. I mean, what a perfect way to kill me—get me cornered in the boonies and call in his buddies, but he turned on them. Snapped the closest one's front leg while I went after the second wolf. I nailed his nose and then got him by the throat. He was big, but I'm faster. Still, I'm not sure what would have happened, except Sebastian finished with the first one and took out the second one as well. His jaws are powerful. Broke the bastard's hind leg."

"Good. That's good that he recognized the difference between right and wrong. Did he realize what happened?"

"Yeah. Later, he was embarrassed. Devastated, really." She chuckled. "When he took me home and I invited him in, he was honestly shocked."

"I don't think I need any more of the details." Anton's dry comment was pure father.

"Good." She laughed. " 'Cause you're not getting them. The thing is, we both knew we needed to talk about everything, and I thought he'd be there when I woke up. He was gone."

"Have you spoken with him since?"

"No. I called you first."

"I should hope so." He laughed. "I'm glad you're still keeping your priorities straight."

"There's more, Dad. I hope you're taking notes."

"I'm assuming you're referring to the murder this morning. It was just a few blocks from your house."

"I know. And Sebastian wasn't with me when it happened. I'm worried, Dad. What if he's involved? What if he really is guilty? I didn't pick up his scent at the other murder site, but maybe I just missed it. He doesn't strike me as a killer, but there's darkness in him. It doesn't fit with his actions or his personality or even his aura."

"What, exactly, do you want me to do?"

So simple, really, to ask her father for help. She knew he was worried, knew he had a million questions, but he focused on what she wanted, what she needed.

Not on his own needs or wants, which, she imagined, included shooting Sebastian Xenakis between the eyes. Or maybe just ripping out his throat. She almost laughed, imagining what Anton Cheval was thinking behind that placid exterior.

Even though her father trusted her intelligence and her ability to think logically, he would always be her father, and it was his very nature to protect her. She laid out her requests as succinctly as she could. "I want to know if Aldo Xenakis is working magic beyond what's considered normal for practitioners, even those who touch the dark arts. Is he delving into something we're missing, doing something that would give him enough power to affect his son's actions?"

"That's a pretty big stretch, sweetheart. He's not Chanku. Telepathy and some minor mind control is natural for us."

Lily chuckled. "It's a good thing the humans haven't figured that out yet."

"Here's hoping they don't. We've already got enough trouble. Besides, Aldo would have to be working death magic for the kind of power it would take to control his son. Sebastian's not weak."

"No. Sebastian is definitely not weak. And he is telepathic. We linked at the reception. Clearly." Lily focused on her father's eyes. "As far as Aldo's power, there have been a lot of dead women, and their numbers are growing. Plus, the killings are coming closer together now."

Anton's silence was telling. Then, as if speaking to himself, he said, "Aldo Xenakis is awfully high profile for murder."

"I know. But he's also one of our staunchest detractors. He'd like to see all of us reclassified as animals, not humans. He has an agenda, and he's been very open about it. He wants all Chanku banned from commerce, from voting, from all rights as citizens. He maintains a respectable public demeanor, but the man is a complete fanatic. I wonder if he might be insane."

Her father nodded. "I'll find out what I can. What else?"

"See what you can learn about the military program to create a Chanku army. I want to know what happened to those Chanku that were discovered. For all we know, the military could still be using them, but under top secret conditions. Or they could have destroyed them, or maybe they just went back into the general population. Battle trained wolves could create a lot of trouble set loose on society. Or with the wrong alpha."

"You're really making me nervous now, Lily." He scribbled something on a tablet she'd not noticed. "Anything else?"

"Sebastian's mother. She died a couple of years ago, but he claims he's not Chanku. I'd bet good money that he is. My wolf says he is. Maybe she just never found out. I told you he shifts using magic. He draws it from the trees, from the mountain. Draws it out, but gives nothing back. Could this be the source of his darkness? I don't know, but I think his mother is the key."

"He hasn't taken the nutrients?"

"I asked him, and he said he hadn't, but he also said if I gave them to him, he'd give it a shot. But he was gone this morning, before I could give him any."

She had plenty of the capsules with her. Every once in a while she'd sense her own need for the nutrients or someone would ask for them. So many people wanted to be Chanku, but so far they'd found very few. Not nearly as many as they'd expected.

The Tibetan grasses their race had once relied on were the one way to guarantee whether someone was Chanku. Ingesting the right combination of nutrients was usually all anyone needed if they had the right genetics.

Lily was almost positive Sebastian fit the profile.

"Another thing, Dad. I need to visit Eve. I haven't been on the astral in ages, and I've missed her. Maybe she'll know something about Sebastian's mother. Plus, I want to ask her if she's sensed the military Chanku. Have you spoken with her?"

"Not recently, but Alex has. Last week."

"Alex?" Alex never walked the astral. At least not if he could avoid it. "Whatever for?"

"He's frantic, Lily. The killings are getting to him. He's catching flak from a few locals who are trying to stir up trouble in town, and he's worried about the young women he knows."

"And goddess knows, Alex knows more young women than most."

He slanted a rare, disapproving glare her way. "So true, but it's not a joking matter. Kalispell has always been very open to us, very welcoming, but the killings have all the hallmarks of a wolf and human combination, plus they're occurring in areas where Chanku populations are largest, in the Bay Area and here in Montana. People are scared. They have a right to be, but it's affecting our relationship with people we've known and trusted for years. People who have trusted us."

Before Lily could apologize for her flip comment, her dad paused and glanced over his shoulder. Lily saw her mom in the background and waved. Keisha moved close to the screen. "Hi, sweetheart. I hope you don't mind. I've been listening to your conversation. Be careful, but trust your instincts and listen to what your wolf says about your man."

"I will, Mom. But he's not my man. Yet."

Her mother's soft laughter had Lily grinning. "Why do I hear a very loud *but* at the end of that?"

"Probably because he's what I want. But not until I'm sure. There is so much circumstantial crap pointing toward him, that it's almost too much."

"What do you mean? What do you suspect?" Her dad studied her in that way he had, forcing her to work through various scenarios in her head to learn what her instincts were trying to tell her.

"Flat out? I think Aldo Xenakis is involved. I think he's somehow controlling his son, and I also believe he's setting him up to take the blame for the murders. I have no idea why, but I fully intend to find out."

She heard a knock on her parents' door. Keisha blew a kiss at the phone. "Bye, sweetie. I love you, but that's Xandi, and grocery shopping awaits. I gotta go."

"Bye, Mom." She blinked back unexpected tears. "I love you, too. And thanks."

"You okay, sweetheart?"

She grinned at her father. "You I can talk to all day and I'm fine. I see Mom, and I immediately want to come home so she can hug me and make cookies for me."

"Your mother spoils you outrageously."

"Not nearly as much as she spoils you."

Her father didn't even attempt to deny it, which made Lily even more homesick. She wanted what her mother and father had, the connection that only mated Chanku could ever feel. That sense of homecoming whether the two of them were together or apart.

She'd sensed that with Sebastian. Just a hint of the potential, and it had been so seductive. Damn it all, she wanted him to be innocent. She didn't want to think she'd fallen for a killer, but even more important, she wanted him to be the man he seemed to be. The Sebastian Xenakis she'd made love with last night had been special. He'd been honorable and brave, and he'd shown her the stars. For that alone she would fight to prove his innocence, to know his true character.

She chatted with her dad a while longer. She missed her twin brothers and younger sister, and she really missed Alex and Uncle Stefan and Aunt Xandi. She was a pack animal. Most of the time there was no pack close by. The ones living and working in the Bay Area had lives as busy as hers—it was rare for them to get together.

She really needed to see Eve. If nothing else, connecting with the goddess who had once walked among them would ground her. It always had.

And dear goddess, but Lily needed grounding now. She looked into her father's eyes—eyes so much like her own—and realized what she really wanted. The decision was a no-brainer. She could access the astral from just about anywhere, but it was easiest through the gateway in the cavern beneath her parents' home.

Montana was only a short flight away. The company jet was available any time she wanted. "Dad? Are you and Mom going to be home this weekend?"

Anton's eyes lit up. "Are you thinking of a trip home? I realize you never take vacations, but this is business, right?" He chuckled softly.

"Yeah. I need a personal chat with the chairman of the board." She laughed, suddenly feeling freer, more grounded than she had in days. "I've got some things to take care of at the office, but I'll call and have them get the small jet ready. I should be out of here before lunch."

"I've missed you, Lily."

"I miss you, too, Dad. Tell Mom I expect cookies at some point during the weekend."

They closed the connection. Lily threw a few things in her overnight bag. She kept plenty of clothes at the house in Montana—clothing much more comfortable than the designer suits she wore each day to the office.

Throwing on a pair of jeans and a knit top, and choosing hiking boots rather than heels, she dressed for home. Her driver was waiting as she stepped through the door, but her mind wasn't on the few things she needed to do before she could leave. No, she was already caught up in thoughts of heading home.

7

Sebastian took a last glance at the website, added a few final comments to his notebook, turned off his tablet, and glanced at the media screen on the wall. He'd left the large monitor running while he hunted for information on his tablet, though he'd turned the volume off some time earlier.

He stared at the images on the big screen a moment, but at first he couldn't place what he saw. Enlarging the picture, he recognized the face of a local newscaster in the corner of the screen as an overhead camera focused on a large, raucous crowd gathered downtown. Familiar landmarks placed the action near the Civic Center.

The camera zoomed in on a striking silver-haired man on a raised dais surrounded by what appeared to be half a dozen large bodyguards. Sebastian turned up the volume just as his father raised his arm and the crowd fell silent.

There was nothing Aldo Xenakis loved more than an attentive crowd. The microphone amplified his already mesmerizing baritone voice, carrying his words out to the spellbound group gathered about him like fans at a rock concert.

Except his father's form of entertainment was spewing hate, railing against the Chanku shapeshifters, blaming them for yet another death. The man was nothing if not consistent.

Staring at the screen, at the hatred on the faces of so many idiots standing in the crowd, hanging on to their exalted leader's every word, Sebastian thought of Lily. Lily and her flashing aura and her beautiful spirit.

He thought of Lily with his father's filthy diatribe in the background. At that moment he realized how much he hated the man. Hated him for his arrogance and sense of superiority that apparently made him think he had the right to incite a crowd of mindless fools to violence against a people who meant them no harm.

Without any proof beyond his own xenophobia, Xenakis encouraged bloodshed. With that mesmerizing, almost poetic cadence to his voice, he blamed the Chanku for the rapes and murders, pumping his fist in the air as he threatened revenge for the deaths of innocent young women.

"You bastard." Disgusted, Sebastian reached for the controls to turn off the flat screen, when one of the bodyguards in the background shifted his weight. It was more than obvious the man was injured. Sebastian zoomed in for a closer look. The man was huge—heavily muscled and quite tall, but he wore a walking cast on his left leg. Curious now, Sebastian used the controls to move across the row of bodyguards until he saw what he was looking for.

The one on the far left had his right arm in a sling. Sebastian skipped back to the first bodyguard, the one with the cast, and zoomed in on his face. A deep cut ran across the bridge of his nose. It was mostly healed, but he'd heard that Chanku healed faster when they shifted.

The same nose Lily had slashed with wolven teeth? The leg he'd snapped with powerful jaws? And the other one's arm. It couldn't be mere coincidence, but what were Chanku doing with his father, a man who hated the species? And why would the same ones who had attacked him and Lily the night before be part of the half dozen men guarding Aldo Xenakis?

He had to call Lily and tell her what he suspected. She'd said last night that she didn't know the wolves, but she'd recognized their scent. A scent associated with one of the murders.

Was his father aware of the fact his employees were behind the rash of killings? Could he be directing them? No. Sebastian shoved that thought aside, but it didn't disappear. Not entirely.

Damn, but he needed to talk to Lily. She was smart and levelheaded, and she knew more about shapeshifters than anyone else possibly could.

He wished he'd stayed for that talk they'd promised each other. Wished he'd done a lot of things differently, but it was too late for misgivings. He needed to call her, but an idea had taken hold and wouldn't turn him loose, so he shut down the monitor, grabbed his tablet computer, and headed for his room at the back of the house.

At least he knew he'd have a few hours before his father returned home. Time enough to try a spell he'd come across that might take him to the astral plane. He was certain his answers lay in that mysterious space out of place, but he'd never managed to access it before. His father drew a lot of his power from the astral. Not all—Aldo claimed he had other sources as well.

Sources he wouldn't discuss with his son.

Damn, he really needed to talk to Lily.

Reaching for the phone, Sebastian thought of the sense of unclean magic clinging to his father. He had no proof, so he wasn't in a position to accuse him of the murders, but he needed to find some answers, and damn it, as much as he needed to talk to her, he didn't want to involve Lily.

Not yet.

He stared at the phone in his hand. Slowly, he put it down. He'd try once again to access the astral. See what he could find on his own.

Then he'd call Lily.

The flight had been smooth, the trip from the airport to the Chanku estate with her mom giving her a chance to talk privately about her feelings for a guy who might or might not be *the one.*

With her parents' curiosity appeased for now, it was time to visit Eve. Hopefully, she'd find answers with the goddess, but even if Eve didn't know a thing, Lily could kick back and relax.

Besides, Eve always had the best food and wine, though where it came from remained a mystery. No matter what, it felt so good to be home. The air was fresh and clean, and the big Montana sky an absolutely perfect shade of blue. Lily drew in a deep breath as she closed the door on her small cottage at the edge of the woods. Walking quickly, she crossed her mother's beautifully landscaped gardens that set her parents' quarters apart from some of their packmates' houses.

Damn, but she'd missed coming home. Missed her own kind. No matter where she was, Lily knew she always had the pack, but it was so much better when they were close by. She drew on them, on their strength, their strong sense of family.

Since birth, she'd been surrounded by people who loved her, who wanted only the best for her. Family. Always here. Always looking out for her.

Sebastian had never known anything like that. No wonder the guy had issues, but issues or not, she missed him. She hardly knew the man, and yet . . . she missed him.

That made no sense. None at all.

It was quiet this afternoon. Babies must be napping. Not everyone lived within the main compound, though all the original families now had homes on the same huge piece of property her father had purchased years ago. Many of their children remained, and some had their own homes on site. Others, like Lily, kept small cottages where they could come and go at will.

She sometimes wished things were still the way they'd been when she was small, when so many of them lived in the main house, except for her adopted older brother Oliver and his mate, Mei Chen. She'd loved their little cottage, just across the driveway, but all of that changed after the fire.

None of them would forget the terrible fire that burned much of the forest almost three decades ago. The original house and Oliver's cottage had burned to the ground. That fire had been a defining point for the entire pack. The fire and the fact their existence—a closely held secret until then—had suddenly become public knowledge.

In one single, unexpected event, in less than a heartbeat, they'd gone from legend to reality when one of their own shifted from man to wolf in front of dozens of network news cameras. The fact he'd shifted publicly to prevent a terrorist attack on a group of young people—including the president's daughters— outed the Chanku in a totally positive manner, but once their secret was caught on film, there was no turning back.

That event had forced a decision they'd been vacillating over for ages—to live closer to one another, to become a single, united pack rather than continue on as separate family groups scattered about the country. There was safety in numbers and a chance for the children to develop in a society where they never felt alien, were never alone. Unlike their parents who had grown up isolated and unaware of their Chanku birthright, this new generation had been raised with pride in their amazing heritage, surrounded by others just like them.

They'd been free to explore their shapeshifting nature, to know their roots. From the very beginning, they had existed as they were meant to exist—shifting from human form to animal whenever they wished, with thousands upon thousands of acres of forest and meadowland set aside for their use.

Lily appreciated the beauty of her upbringing, the freedom she'd known, and the opportunities she'd been given. She'd blossomed in freedom, and her magic had grown as a natural part of her development.

Magic that had nothing to do with being a shapeshifting Chanku. No, according to her mom, Lily's magic was all her father's fault, a gift from his Romanian ancestors, though in Lily, the innate power of her magic was nothing short of miraculous. Still, it meant that, like her father, Lily was of the pack and yet separate. She was special and she knew it—Chanku, and more.

So much more, even Lily realized she'd not tested her full potential. That alone set her apart. And maybe that was why she couldn't get Sebastian out of her mind.

He was the first man she'd known with magic as strong, if not stronger than her own. He challenged her in every way, but the connection she'd felt with Sebastian reinforced the fact that there was no future for her with Alex Aragat, no matter what their parents wanted.

She grinned as she thought of Alex. Who wouldn't? He was adorable, but no matter how cute and sexy and smart he might be, Alex lacked the strength to stand up to her, the will to challenge her. He was a strong alpha male in his own right, but not where Lily was concerned. He'd deferred to her his entire life. That wasn't going to change. She'd run right over the poor guy, just as she'd done all their lives, and they both knew it.

Sebastian, on the other hand, would stand toe to toe with her, and she'd be lucky to come out unscathed.

Did she really want that?

The shiver along her spine and the sudden coil of heat centered in her womb confirmed that, yes, she really did.

"Hey, Lil. Your folks said you were home. I've missed you."

She jerked to a stop and laughed. "Alex! Me too."

He wrapped his arms around her shoulders and kissed her hard and fast. "You ready for 'the talk'?"

"Hell, no." She rolled her eyes. "Why? Did you just get nailed?"

He nodded. "You, Lily Cheval, are a paragon of all things Chanku, and I'm a bloody fool to let you slip away."

Laughing, she flipped him off. "Sorry, big guy. I can't help it if I'm a paragon. I am what I am."

"Well, it would help if you'd screw up a little. Do you think you could work on that?"

Lily glanced at the house, knew her dad still wanted to talk to her, but she really needed Alex right now. "I think I already have, Al. You got a minute?"

"What's the matter, sweetie?"

"C'mon." She grabbed his hand and drew him across the yard to a small pond built of native stone, shaded by twisted aspen trees. She sat on a stone bench and patted the spot beside her.

"Okay," he said, still holding her hand. "Spill."

"I think the days of the talk are coming to an end." She glanced down at his long fingers wrapped around hers and wondered how Sebastian would deal with another man in their bed. She'd never give Alex up altogether. She loved him. She just didn't see herself mated to him.

"You've met someone, haven't you?"

Why in the hell did she feel so guilty? Lily nodded. "I have, but I don't know if there's a future for us."

"He's not Chanku?"

"Actually, I think he is. He shifts, but by magical means. Even so, my wolf recognizes a kindred spirit."

There was a long silence. "Please tell me it's not Aldo Xenakis."

She burst into laughter. "Oh goddess, no. That man's an ass." Then she sighed. "Not Aldo. His son. Sebastian Xenakis."

Alex's harsh intake of breath told her more than she wanted to hear. "Lil, he's on our radar. The guy could be our killer. Are you . . . ?"

"I know." She squeezed his hand. "Last night I ran with him and some really weird stuff happened. I'll give you the details later, but we were attacked by two strange wolves. I'm sure they were Chanku, but they're huge. Even bigger than Uncle Tink—and I recognized their scent. They were present at one, at least, of the murder sites."

Alex grabbed her hand. "Goddess, Lily. Do you realize that's the first lead we've gotten?"

She nodded. "I know. I hope to have more to give you later, when I've got more time, but right now I'm on my way to check in with Dad and then go and talk to Eve."

Alex squeezed her hand as she continued. "Sebastian helped me fight them off. I told you when you called this morning that I invited him home with me. He spent most of the night."

"You said he was gone when you woke up."

She nodded. "I really thought he'd be there in the morning. I wanted him there. I've never . . ." She sighed. "We had a pretty amazing night. Really amazing, but I haven't talked to him since we fell asleep. Shit, Alex, he was gone before that girl was murdered at Fort Mason. I realize I hardly know him, but I just can't see Sebastian Xenakis committing rape and murder."

Alex slipped his arm around her shoulders and hugged her close. "I'm sorry, sweetie, but you said it. You hardly know him."

"Yeah, but I don't think it's Sebastian. I wish I knew, but I can't be sure. I do, however, believe his father is somehow involved." She kicked at some loose gravel with the toe of her boot. "I also have a really bad feeling that it's too late, as far as my heart is concerned."

"One night with the guy?" Alex's laughter had an unfamiliar bite to it. "He must be damned good in bed."

"Oh, Alex. That's not it at all. It was the connection, the mental connection we fell into so naturally. As much as you and I love each other and as often as we've made love, that's never happened. Not the way I felt it last night. I want that. I want it for you, too."

Alex leaned close and kissed her, wrapped his arms around her and deepened the kiss. Lily went with it, tasted his familiar flavors, and felt the same wonderful arousal that always built when she and Alex kissed.

But it wasn't the same. Not even close.

He broke the kiss and pressed his forehead to hers. "I love you, Lily, but you're right. We both deserve more. I just wish I could find the right woman." He laughed. "One as smart and sexy as you who won't beat the crap out of me."

"Alex!"

"Teasing. Really!" He kissed her again. "I hope like hell you've found the right man. I don't want you hurt."

"Me either. But I wanted to tell you about him first, and I want you to let me know if you hear anything at all that can help me either exonerate him or prove he's guilty. I need to know for sure if there's a chance for us, or if he's someone to stay far away from."

"I promise." He stood, held out his hand, and pulled her to her feet. "But for now, I need to get going. I've got a date in town and don't want to be late." He waggled his eyebrows. "She's really hot, and she loves my body."

Laughing, Lily covered her ears with both hands. Alex was never going to change. "I really don't need to hear that, dear boy. And just because I can't get pregnant by a human doesn't mean you can't impregnate a short-timer."

Alex rolled his eyes in disgust. "Trust me. I've spent the last half hour hearing a detailed lesson in basic Chanku sex from both parents. Again. My head hurts." He spun away, then glanced back. "We'll talk later, okay?"

"Promise."

He tipped her a quick salute. "Wish me luck. Maybe I'll actually get laid tonight."

"Alex, you are totally hopeless."

"I know. And you love me for it."

Lily watched him walk away. She did love him. She loved all kinds of things about Alex, from that sexy saunter in his walk to the way his jeans fit his perfectly shaped butt to the amazing man she knew him to be.

But she didn't love Alex in the way of mates.

She never would.

The way she felt wasn't even close.

And as that thought flitted through her mind, Sebastian's dark features and teal blue eyes filled her thoughts.

Alex sauntered across the main street of old town Kalispell, thinking of Lily but checking out the girls. It was Friday night, and he knew just about every young woman in town. They were pretty interchangeable, as far as he was concerned, but tonight he was supposed to meet up with Jennifer Martin. She was hot, and she liked sex, but if it didn't work out, he knew he could always go back and spend the night with Lily.

It really would make life so much simpler if he and Lily loved each other romantically, but it just wasn't going to happen. Sex with Lily was always good, but it was more fun and laughs and the need to scratch the constant itch that was part of Chanku physiology than a love match. It worked for both of them, but it was going nowhere.

Just like his serial relationships with the human women he'd dated. As much as he hated it, he had to agree with his folks. A Chanku-human pairing wasn't going to work.

Short-timers couldn't offer what he needed, not when he wanted to run with his woman through the dark woods and hunt as a wolf, or fly when he took his eagle form. No can do when your date's as earthbound as dirt.

"Hey, Alex."

He glanced toward the front of the movie theater. Jenn was right where she'd said she'd be. "Hi, Jenn. Hope I'm not late. Ran into an old friend."

She shrugged. "Nah. You're okay. I'm early."

"Good." He wrapped an arm around her waist and leaned close for the expected kiss, but before their lips met, voices from the alley around the side of the coffee shop intruded.

"Leave me alone."

"What's the matter, sweet thing? You think you're too good for us?"

"I didn't say that. I merely told you jerks to leave me alone. Get out of my way."

"Jerks? Now, honey, you don't mean that, do you?"

Alex tilted his head. Whoever those idiots were hassling was obviously outnumbered. "Jenn, stay here."

She grabbed his arm. "Stay out of it, Alex. I know those guys. They won't hurt her. They're just teasing, but they'll beat the crap out of you if you get in their way."

"They're scaring her. Wait here."

Jenn hung on, but the sharp sound of a slap had him tearing free and racing around the building. Three huge men had a small, dark woman trapped against the side of the building. Her blouse was torn, but her eyes glittered. A palm print marred her left cheek. The sense of Chanku was strong, and from the fear in her amber eyes, he knew she was right on the edge of shifting.

Alex had to reach up to grab the closest man by the collar,

and he hoped he wasn't making the biggest mistake in his life. This idiot was massive. Jerking him back, Alex planted a fist in the guy's face and he went down with blood spurting from his nose. The two others spun away from the girl with fists raised. Cursing, they both flew at Alex. He caught the larger of the two with a quick chop to the throat with his right hand and came up with his left fist to plant a solid punch in the second one's belly. Both men folded, but then the one Alex had punched in the nose tried to stand. The girl he'd been hassling kicked him in the head, and he fell back, groaning.

Alex flashed her a grin, but he kept his eye on the three men. As big as they were, if they came after him together, he was toast, but instead, as soon as they rallied enough to get to their feet, they slunk around the back of the building. Alex watched them leave to make sure they were definitely gone before he turned his attention to the young woman.

"Thank you, Alex." She pulled her torn blouse up to better cover herself, shivered, and wrapped her hands around her waist.

Frowning, Alex stared at her a moment before recognition finally dawned. "Annie? Annie McClintock? Damn. I didn't even recognize you. You've cut off all your hair. You look totally different with it short." Stepping closer, he said, "I like it."

He took his jacket off and wrapped it around her shoulders as he talked, hoping his aimless chatter would help calm her down. The poor kid looked rattled, but she had every right to be upset. "I haven't seen you in years," he said, as if nothing had happened here, as if she wouldn't have a huge bruise on her face by morning. "I thought you were still in England."

He smoothed his jacket over her arms, patted her shoulders. When he felt her trembling beneath his coat, his heart clenched. He wished he could chase down the bastards who'd hurt her and hit them again. Instead, he took a deep breath and looked directly into her beautiful amber eyes. "Are you okay, Annie? Did they hurt you?"

She shook her head and touched her fingertips to her bruised cheek. "I'm okay now." She let out a deep breath. "The big guy grabbed my arm and dragged me into the alley. The other two were already here, waiting. I didn't know what to do. I was afraid to shift." She grimaced. "Not with public sentiment so against us."

Alex chuckled. "Yeah. Ripping out their throats probably wouldn't make good press, but I bet it would have made you feel a hell of a lot better."

She flashed him a quick, shy smile that hit him right in the gut. Damn, she was absolutely beautiful. He didn't remember Annie as anything special. She'd been a tiny, shy little sprite with too much hair and not enough chest, but it wasn't just growing boobs and getting a haircut that had worked wonders. He certainly didn't remember thinking she was at all sexy, but damn. There was no denying the impact she had on him.

"Alex? Aren't you going to introduce us?"

Jenn stood close beside him with her arms folded tightly across her chest. He'd completely forgotten her.

"Uh, yeah. Jennifer Martin, this is Annie McClintock. Annie's folks are good friends of my parents'. We've known each other forever, but Annie's been studying in England for, what? About four years now?"

Annie nodded. "Six. I graduated from Oxford a couple of years ago, but I stayed on to finish up my masters in interspecies social dynamics."

"I'm glad you're back." Alex glanced at Jenn. She glared at Annie. In fact, jealousy poured off her in waves. That made no sense at all. It wasn't like he and Jenn were in a relationship or anything. They'd gone out a few times, but nothing serious. Even the sex had been her idea.

Even so, there was no way Alex wanted to deal with her now. Didn't she care those guys had just scared the crap out of Annie? Had assaulted her? He returned his attention to the one who needed him.

"Annie, do you have a car nearby?"

She shook her head. "I haven't been home long enough to renew my American license. I'm supposed to call Mom to come get me when I'm through. I had some errands to run and then wanted to see a movie, but I think I'd rather just go home."

"I'll take you." He glanced at Jenn. "After what happened, I don't feel comfortable leaving Annie here alone."

Annie shook her head. "Alex, you don't have to—"

Jenn interrupted. "I thought you wanted to go to the movie."

"Considering the circumstances, Jenn, I think getting Annie home safely is more important than a movie." He turned to Annie. "And no, Annie. No arguing. Your dad would have my head if he knew I'd left you alone after what happened."

"If that's how you want it, Alex." Jennifer swept a dismissive look over Annie and turned away. "Another time, maybe."

"Yeah. Right." Alex watched her as she stalked out of the alley and disappeared around the corner. It felt as if a huge weight lifted off his chest.

"I'm sorry, Alex." Annie was looking at the ground, shaking her head. "I don't want to come between you and your girlfriend."

He slung an arm over Annie's narrow shoulders. "She's not my girlfriend. Just a friend, and obviously not a very good one. It's really not a problem, squirt," he said. "C'mon. I'm parked at the end of the block."

Annie's soft laugh stopped him. "I don't know that the name still fits. You used to drive me nuts, calling me squirt. I'm hoping I've outgrown it by now."

He smiled at her. Damn, she was something, but he wasn't going to let her know what he was thinking. No way. "I don't know about that. You're not very big. As huge as your dad is, I'm amazed at how tiny you are. I think you still qualify as a squirt." Annie fit perfectly beneath his arm. He held her closer than he probably needed to, but it felt right. She felt right, and he wondered why he'd never noticed before just how cute she really was. Cute and sexy and so feminine she made his chest feel tight. Not to mention his jeans.

"Please, not when we're at the compound." She poked him in the side. "I was hoping everyone had forgotten that horrible nickname."

"I promise." He leaned close and sealed his promise with a kiss. Her lips were full and soft against his, and he found himself lingering longer than he'd intended. When Alex raised his head, Annie stared at him with her brows wrinkled in a tight, confused little frown.

He hugged her close and took off walking. Annie fell into step beside him. His heart thundered in his chest, and his sensitive nostrils picked up the scent of her arousal.

He'd had sex with most of the other young Chanku women of his generation at one time or another, but never with Annie. She'd been so shy and quiet, he'd pretty much ignored her when they were kids, and everyone held her father in such total awe, that it hadn't been worth the risk of making Tinker mad.

Alex was sorry, now, that he'd been such a coward, because, well, damn. Who'd have thought little Annie McClintock would grow up to look like this? To smell like this. To have a killer smile and perfect breasts and a body he wanted to taste. All over.

But damn it all, he'd have to tell Lily, and she was going to give him hell. He'd totally forgotten what she'd said years ago, that Annie was his perfect match. All he'd seen was the bratty little kid with the flat chest and frizzy hair who always had her nose stuck in a book.

Goddess, how he hated it when Lily was right. Unfortunately, it wasn't just most of the time.

It was all of the time.

He grinned. For some reason, this time he actually looked forward to telling her she'd won another one.

8

Counting her blessings and thankful she'd managed to duck her father's inevitable interrogation, Lily walked quickly through her parents' huge kitchen, down the stairs into the pantry, and from there through the narrow tunnel to the massive cavern beneath the house.

She really owed her mom on this one. Keisha had managed to interrupt Anton before he really had a chance to get started, and the moment Lily realized she'd had an escape handed to her, she'd taken it. Damn. What she wouldn't give for a mate like her mom—one who understood the way she worked and loved her enough to put up with all her idiosyncrasies.

The way her mother managed her father's. Laughter spilled out as she stepped into the cavern and paused. Moist, warm air washed over her. This had always been one of her favorite places, this massive cave that had provided sanctuary to the entire pack during the terrible fire so many years ago. All of them had remained safe down here while the entire house above them burned to the ground.

It had been a favorite place to play when she was a kid. Where she'd experienced her first sexual exploration with Alex when they were little more than children. Where she'd realized he wasn't meant to be her mate, but someone just as important.

He was her friend. He would always be the man she could count on for complete honesty, the one to let her know when she was wrong, to encourage her when she was right.

Now, if only there were a man with all of Alex's attributes—and more. A man who would love her in spite of herself, who would always be at her side. One with the strength of character to be alpha male to her alpha bitch.

Sebastian could be that man. She'd felt it from the beginning, but she had to know more about him. Had to know if he was as good as she wanted to believe, or if he were somehow tainted by his father's darkness.

There was only one way to find out. Eve should have the answers she needed. Eve always had the answers.

Taking a deep breath, Lily cut to the left and walked around the large pool that filled part of the cavern floor. Low lights powered by solar panels high on the surface of the mountain illuminated the walls, the water, and the various tunnels leading away from this centrally located cave. The caverns were an important safety feature known only to members of the pack, with the extensive system of caves and tunnels spreading for miles beneath the rugged mountains. Solar panels provided power, the many artesian springs meant drinking water was always available, and her father maintained a huge stash of emergency supplies that could keep the entire pack fed for as long as might be needed.

Over the years they'd explored much of the system, but even more of the network remained untouched. However, it wasn't the miles of tunnels and caverns that called to Lily on most of her trips home. No, it was the series of hieroglyphics carved into the wall beyond the pool—specifically a pair of handprints that were this cavern's most intriguing feature—the key to a portal leading directly to the astral plane.

She still remembered the first time she'd discovered the doorway and scared the crap out of her parents. What felt like a long, busy day to her six-year-old self had actually been weeks for her mother and father. Weeks when they knew she was safely in the hands of first the goddess and then a small surviving group of ancient Chanku elders who taught Lily the history of their kind—but much too long for parents worried about their child.

That had certainly been a wild summer. Nick Barden, one of the younger members of the pack, had managed to out the Chanku to the world at large when he got caught shifting in front of cameras at a gathering in Washington DC, a forest fire burned her mom and dad's house to the ground while the entire pack huddled here in the caverns for safety, and Adam's mate, Liana, had given birth to tiny Phoenix Olivia while the fire raged overhead.

The pack had merely grown stronger, more united than ever after all that happened. But now, the attacks on young women threatened all they held dear. Threatened their peaceful relationship with the human population. Threatened everything.

Lily had sensed Eve for most of the afternoon, and the goddess filled her thoughts as she traced her fingers over the ancient marks carved in stone. She remembered when she'd looked at them the very first time and realized they weren't just pretty pictures—they were words she understood.

What everyone had thought of as artful carvings, six-year-old Lily had been able to read. And what she read were directions to enter the astral. The markings hadn't been left by Native Americans as the grown-ups had believed, but by some of the earliest Chanku.

Had they known what was to come? Was Eve expecting her now? Placing her hands on the palm prints she'd once had to stretch to reach, Lily pictured the goddess. She'd thought of her as Sparkly Eve when she was little, but over the years, as Lily grew up and their friendship grew stronger, she'd become just Eve.

Friend, confidant, sister of her heart.

The stone shimmered as Lily held her hands against the prints and visualized Eve's perfect *where* and *when.* A patch of brilliant light poured through the portal, growing broader and brighter, filling the dark cavern with a shimmering glow. Without any hesitation, Lily stepped from the cavern in northern Montana through what had been solid stone and into the perfect dimension that contained Eve's world on the astral plane.

There was no sense of the portal or the caverns behind her. Lily gazed in all directions, surrounded by Eve's world. She'd always wondered if her blood pressure really dropped, if her heart rate slowed when she was here, though today, for some reason, there was an edge to the usual sense of peace she felt.

A mist hovered just ahead, a small cloud glimmering with its own inner light, filled with tiny sparkles that seemed to dance like dust motes in sunlight. Misgivings slipped away as Lily held out her arms. "Eve! It's been too long. I've missed you."

Forming fully from mist and sparkles to corporeal woman, the goddess shook her head slowly and sighed. Instead of the brilliant smile Lily expected from her friend, Eve hung her head.

Lily's arms fell to her side. "Eve? Is something wrong?"

"Oh, Lily. Yes. I fear something is terribly wrong." Then the goddess stepped close and enveloped Lily in a warm and very human hug.

Lily smoothed the soft white robe around her ankles as she and Eve sat together in the bright glow of what passed for day on the astral. They'd gone for a soothing dip in the magical waters of the pond that had fascinated Lily as a child.

It had bubbles. Lots of sparkly bubbles, and when they'd climbed out of the water, she'd wrapped herself in the soft robe Eve had conjured out of the air.

The grass might be a little too green, the trees much too perfectly formed, and the sky a robin's egg blue that existed only in fairy tales—or here in what was truly Eve's very own here and now—but it was familiar and comforting to Lily.

Most of the time.

Not so much right now. Eve, always so calm, was obviously anxious. All was not right in what should be paradise. Lily took Eve's hand and felt the tension in her slim fingers. "Eve? Enough small talk. Tell me what's wrong."

Instead of answering, Eve stretched out her hand and pulled a glass of sparkling white wine out of thin air. She handed the chilled goblet to Lily and then grabbed one for herself. Any other time, Lily would have teased her about such a blatant display of power, but Eve seemed so disconnected from the process, Lily kept her mouth shut.

Once they both had their glasses, Eve took a sip of her wine and sighed. "Over the years, I've learned to sense when you're troubled, Lily, and I know you are tonight, but I have a selfish reason for wanting you here. I'm so glad you've come. I need your help."

Lily stared at her friend over the lip of the glass. "Anything, Eve. You don't even have to ask. I am troubled, but obviously so are you." She smiled. "Your turn. I'm listening."

Eve stared beyond Lily. Her eyes swirled in their familiar but disconcerting pattern from green, to gold, to blue. Finally, she seemed to shake herself out of whatever thoughts held her, and focused on Lily.

"When I became the goddess, I knew such unbelievable power. For the first time in my life, I could choose my own way. I could help those I loved, experience the love each of you felt for one another. There was very little beyond my abilities.

Nothing, I believed, could ever hurt me again. Or hurt the ones I love."

She turned her swirling gaze on Lily and sighed. "I was wrong, Lily. So terribly wrong."

She glanced about, as if searching for something just out of sight. "There's trouble on the astral plane. I sense it, but I'm unable to determine its source. All I know for certain is that it's based on magic, but not a magic I've ever experienced. I'm afraid it's dark magic. You're sensitive to magic in its many forms. I'm hoping you'll be able to trace the dissonance to its source, find out who or what is causing the rift in my world."

"Have you gone to the Mother? Asked her?" Lily sipped her wine, but her mind was spinning. Eve could do anything. She knew everything. How could Lily know something Eve didn't?

"I've tried, but she doesn't answer me, and that's part of my worry. Something is disturbing the normal flow here. It's interrupting my ability to communicate with the Mother." Her chin dropped; she bowed her head. "I'm unable, at times, to connect with any of you. When I knew you were coming to me, I wasn't sure we'd be able to meet. It's as if the dimensions are sliding along beside one another, not linked as they should be, as if the fibers of time are disrupted."

Staring into her glass of wine, she sighed. "I can't watch over you when that happens. I worry, especially now, when humans are growing concerned about your place in the world. I don't want any of you to come to harm."

Lily tossed back the last swallow of her wine and handed the glass to the goddess. Eve threw it into the air, and the glass winked and disappeared.

Lily blinked and squeezed Eve's hand. "Now that beats washing dishes all to hell."

Eve smiled, stood, and tugged Lily to her feet. "It would

have been handy when I was still part of the pack. I washed a lot of dishes."

She'd once been as mortal as Lily, mated to the pack's healer. But because their first goddess had screwed up, Eve died before her time. As punishment, the goddess Liana was sentenced to life on earth while Eve took on the role of goddess and protector of the Chanku.

Liana's punishment had worked beautifully for everyone. She was now happily bound to Eve's mate and mother to Adam's children, while Eve had blossomed as the perfect goddess for a growing group of shapeshifters.

She'd also taken on the job as Lily's guardian angel long ago, something that gave Lily the courage now to follow Eve across the meadow and take a seat beneath an impossibly huge tree with gnarled branches and thick moss growing over the thick trunk. Protected beneath its branches, Lily opened her senses to the ebb and flow of power within the astral plane. No matter what she found, she knew Eve would watch over her.

Sitting with legs akimbo, Lily searched for any anomaly, for the slightest touch of magic that could be causing trouble.

She loved taking mental journeys while on the astral plane. She'd traveled it in reality when she'd been nothing but a child, and now, as an adult, relished the rich sense of power, the ebb and flow of life and time, of energy linked to forces both negative and positive.

There was balance on the astral—for every light, a shadow, for every spike, a depression. Floating, her mind moving free of her body, Lily spread her questing thoughts wider, opened her heart to the bits of consciousness caught within the flowing bands of energy and life.

She had no idea how long she sat, arms spread wide to capture the slightest sensation, when a ripple passed through her. The fragile wave of energy was slightly out of sync, not part of the ethereal rhythm of the astral plane. The anomaly was so slight that Lily had to consciously reach for it. She concentrated all her senses on the dissonance, that tiny bulge of energy moving across the astral bands, rather than with the flow.

The bulge paused, almost as if it were aware of Lily's perusal. Without any defined form, it still managed to project a sense of curiosity, as if it wondered who or what she was, why she was here, what she searched for. Then, as Lily opened to the energy, something changed. She sensed darker emotions, hate and malevolence growing and expanding, taking shape as the bulge of energy slowly spun. Caught in the swirling strands of power, Lily stared at the thing, at the way the energy swirled and clumped and slowly morphed into . . . *oh, shit.*

A pair of shimmering teal blue eyes—familiar teal blue eyes—blinked slowly and locked on Lily. Sebastian? But how? Why?

She gasped, covered her lips with icy fingertips. It had to be him, and yet she saw only the eyes. The color was magical, as true as the brightest tropical lagoon with dark, liquid pupils, perfectly human-looking eyes framed in thick lashes, staring at her out of swirling darkness. No face, no sense of gender, though she had no doubt she looked into the eyes of the man who had been her lover just last night.

Only now, there was a sense of evil surrounding him, an ugly nature the beauty of his eyes couldn't disguise. Not merely the darkness she'd felt in him, but a truly evil nature that was every bit as wrong as his father's.

Yet even so, Lily's body reacted in pulsing need, a tightening of womb and nipples alike, a flowering of moisture between her legs—sensual heat unlike anything she'd experienced with any other man. Only with him.

Physically captured in a power she couldn't explain—something as sensual as it was terrifying—Lily struggled, but her muscles wouldn't obey. She tried to scream a warning, but her lips formed only the sound of his name.

"Sebastian?" Barely a whisper before her voice was silenced. Those gorgeous blue eyes seemed to widen in surprise even as Lily sensed Eve's desperate attempt to pull her free. She wanted to go to her friend, to her goddess, but the power in those mesmerizing eyes sucked her down, deeper into a shimmering pool of power, until she was nothing more than a wisp of energy. A tiny breath of life clinging to a mere shred of reality.

A scream. Far, far away, she heard an angry scream.

"No. You can't have her. Go! I command it!"

Lily sensed a small pop, as if a tiny bubble had burst. Then all was darkness and silence as she tumbled bonelessly into utter emptiness.

Blinking rapidly, shaking his head in confusion, Sebastian pushed himself up from the wood floor in his bedroom and leaned against the edge of the bed. As his head slowly cleared, the pain set in. Every muscle, every joint, every bit of him inside and out ached. His stomach lurched, and he thought he was going to throw up. A few deep breaths brought the nausea under control.

For now. He gazed about, wondering how he'd ended up here. He'd been lying spread eagle in the midst of the pentagram, his body naked, his wrist bleeding when he'd cast the spell.

The last thing he recalled was staring through heavy mist and seeing Lily. On the astral? Only his spirit should have moved from the place of magic he'd created, but somehow, he'd either been tossed out of the pentagram or he'd made it here, entirely across the big room, on his own. He couldn't remember.

Blood dripped slowly from the shallow cut he'd made across his wrist, pooling on his naked belly, but otherwise he didn't think he'd hurt himself. He was erect. Now that was weird, but he was hard as a post, his cock and balls aching. No matter. He turned slowly. Clutching the frame of the bed for balance, he managed to stand and take the few shaky steps to the bathroom.

He turned on the faucet and thrust his wrist beneath the cold running water, holding it there, staring blankly at the blood dripping into the sink until the wound looked clean. Wrapping a soft white towel around his wrist, he held a wash-cloth under the running water, squeezed it out one-handed, and wiped the blood off his belly and groin.

Damn, for a small cut, it bled like crazy. He rinsed the cloth and watched the red-tinted water swirl down the drain.

He shut off the tap and turned away from the sink. His cock bobbed against his belly. He often grew aroused when casting spells, but generally returned to his flaccid state once the spell ended. Obviously that wasn't the case today.

He still felt light-headed. The room slowly spun. He grabbed at the door frame with his uninjured right hand and stared at the mess he'd left in his bedroom. Smears of blood from the self-inflicted slash on his wrist left garish streaks on the pale oak flooring. The bloodstained lancet he'd used to cut himself still lay safely locked within the pentagram he'd etched in charcoal in the middle of his bedroom floor.

The stink from the burning candle sitting beside the bloody blade almost made him gag.

Carefully, he pushed himself away from the door and stumbled to the edge of the pentagram. Kneeling just outside the carefully drawn design, he leaned across without touching it and blew out the sputtering candle. His nose wrinkled against the stench of burned blood, and he swallowed convulsively, once again fighting the urge to puke.

He'd followed the instructions perfectly, but where had he actually gone? He'd not stayed long enough to determine whether or not he'd really been on the astral. And what the hell was Lily doing wherever he'd ended up? She'd seen him, recognized him. He'd heard her whisper his name, but were they on the astral? It felt right, but she was here in San Francisco, wasn't she?

Well, hell. So was he. Did Lily travel the astral? But how? Was she that much stronger than he?

Head still reeling, his gut churning with nausea, he sat back on his bare butt on the cold floor and stared at the red seeping slowly through the towel.

The blood fascinated him, even as it repelled him. Was this what was meant by a step too far? As the thought entered his mind, his erection quickly deflated.

Fear did that to a man.

He wanted power like his father's, but all of the man's spells, his dark brand of magic, demanded sacrifice. Sebastian had sworn never to cross that line. Nothing justified taking any kind of life for the sole purpose of making his magic stronger.

This time, he'd skirted the edge. He'd tried something new, but had he gone too far? Blood magic merely required blood. Nothing he'd read in any of his research defined the source of the blood needed for the spell to walk the astral, beyond the fact it must come from a living, warm-blooded creature.

Nothing said he couldn't use his own. Even so, the moment he felt the sharp bite of the lancet slicing across his wrist, Sebastian knew he'd gone beyond anything he'd ever attempted. Everything had changed when those few drops of blood dripped into the flame.

The small candle hadn't sputtered at all—no, it had flared brighter and higher until its brilliant flame lit the entire room. He'd lay there, bare back flat to the cold floor and watched as a gateway *somewhere* had opened like the aperture in an old camera, slowly at first, then bursting wide in brilliant color as if inviting him to come inside.

An entire dimension had opened up to him.

Along with Lily Cheval. Rubbing his hand over his eyes, he

tried to remember exactly what he'd felt when he saw her. What he'd thought. And he realized his first thought was, *What the fuck is Lily doing there?*

He hadn't noticed the one beside her until she'd shouted at him, blasted him with her power.

Lily was strong, but the one who remained hidden in the shadows was at least as powerful as his father, if not stronger. Her shout still vibrated through his body like a physical blow. Her words had rattled him so badly, he hadn't been strong enough to hold on to his magic.

Had she been strong enough to throw his physical body out of the pentagram? He doubted even his father had that much power.

He felt dirty from the blood magic, as if he were shrouded in some sort of evil filth. He needed a shower, though he wondered if he'd ever wash away the feeling that he'd stepped into something foul. Something wrong.

Damn it, he hadn't done anything wrong. It was his own blood. Nothing died, and the cut barely hurt. No sacrifice at all. So why was he so sure that using blood had tainted the spell?

Because he knew. He'd felt the evil, the sense of malevolence that seemed to shadow his every move from the moment he'd dripped his blood onto the flame. Blood had fouled the spell even as it strengthened it. He couldn't explain it, but he could still feel it. And for whatever reason, it felt very much like his father's energy. Almost as if his father had been with him, a silent passenger as he accessed the astral.

Impossible, wasn't it? His stomach roiled.

What the hell had he just done?

"Lily? Lily, are you all right?"

Blinking slowly, Lily struggled back to consciousness, feeling as if she pulled herself out of a deep, viscous pool. Rubbing a hand across her eyes, she slowly sat up. "Eve? What happened?"

"I was going to ask you the same thing. Who was that person? You said a name. Sebastian?"

Lily nodded as memories surfaced. "Sebastian Xenakis. I'm sure it was him." She shook her head, hard, in an attempt to clear her thoughts. "Yeah. It was him. His eyes are so unusual, and the sense of him was strong. There's no doubt in my mind, but the feel of him was all wrong. Eve, he's the reason I wanted to talk to you, but now . . ." She shuddered. "Now, I'm afraid."

Eve clutched Lily's hands in both of hers. "You think you love him? I can feel the need in you. You see him as your mate, don't you? They're strong, Lily, the feelings you have for this man, but he's evil. Didn't you sense it? That malevolence?"

Lily shook her head. "No . . . I mean yes, I did sense it, but I don't think that whatever feels so wrong is really him. I would have noticed it last night. We were completely intimate, our minds every bit as synchronized as our bodies. He was wonderful. Open and good, not this. Not this sense of evil. I can't explain it." She squeezed Eve's hands. "I need to see him. Need to talk to him and find out what's going on."

Eve began shaking her head long before Lily finished her thought. "Lily, I've got to caution you against that. There's something terribly wrong about him. You have to stay away from that one. I recognize the taint clinging to his magic. It's the same as what's causing the disruption here. I'm almost positive he's the one destroying my world."

"Are you absolutely sure?" Lily forced Eve to meet her steady gaze.

After a moment, the goddess lowered her eyes. "I believe he is the one. I hope I'm wrong. You know I can't force you to my will. Even if I could, I wouldn't. Promise me, Lily. Promise me you won't take any chances. I think he's very dangerous."

"There's definitely danger, Eve, but I'm not so sure it's coming from Sebastian. I'm convinced it has something to do with his father and with the murders of all those young women, but I have no way of proving it. Not yet, but I do have some questions for you. Things I'm hoping you can find out for me."

Eve smiled. "Things you hope will clear your young man?"

Lily couldn't smile in return. Not with so much evidence against him. "I hope so, Eve. I really do. I hardly know him, but . . ." She shrugged. "I'll be careful."

When she finally returned to her parents' home in Montana, Lily had Eve's promise to learn what she could about the huge wolves that had attacked them on Mount Tam. She'd asked about Sebastian's mother, too, but Eve's answer was less than satisfactory.

Unless the Chanku blood ran hot and strong in his mother's veins, since she hadn't taken the nutrients and allowed her wolven nature to manifest itself before her death, there was no way for Eve to know if the woman might have been Chanku.

Lily would have to give the nutrients to Sebastian.

And that would mean seeing him again. Getting close to him, gaining his trust.

Eve hadn't been at all happy about that. Lily, however, silently thanked the goddess for giving her just the excuse she needed.

She left the astral plane, slipping through the portal and into the cavern where she'd begun her journey. Movement caught her eye, a ripple in the pond, and Lily went perfectly still, scanning the surface of the water while staying in the shadows.

She heard a soft laugh, a familiar voice, and she relaxed. "Hey, Alex. What're you doing down here?"

Alex laughed and said, "Hiding from Tinker."

"What? But why?" She walked around the pool to the far side. Alex stood in water that lapped around his thighs, his nude body so perfectly sculpted, his obvious arousal creating its usual havoc with her senses. Maybe this was what she needed to settle her rattled nerves. Sex with Alex always calmed things down.

Then she realized he wasn't alone. She caught a glimpse of a slim arm snaking around his waist and realized a woman stood behind him. If he'd brought that bitch Jennifer into the caverns, her dad was going to be furious. It was an unwritten but closely held rule: no one was allowed unless they were pack. "Alex, please tell me you didn't bring . . ."

A small, dark sprite dressed in wet cutoffs and a tank top slipped around Alex. "Hi, Lily. It's okay. It's me. Annie."

"Annie? I would never have recognized you! When did you get back? Oh my god! You cut all your hair!" How many years had it been since they'd seen each other? Lily burst out laughing. "Goddess, girl! Last time I saw you, you were still a little twerp with long frizzy hair and skinny legs."

"Thanks loads. I really needed to hear that. Again." Annie punched Alex's shoulder, laughing as she stepped out of the pool with Alex right behind her. She threw herself into Lily's arms for a hug. Her slim arms and surprisingly long legs left wet splotches on Lily's jeans. Lily stepped back, but then she got a better look at Annie.

Gently she traced the dark bruise on Annie's left cheek. "Sweetie, what happened?"

Annie shot a quick glance at Alex and sighed. "A couple of jerks cornered me in town. Alex rescued me." She gazed at him with a look of absolute hero worship.

Lily tried to catch Alex's eye, expecting his usual twinkle, but he was staring at Annie as if the sun rose and set with her smile. Lily felt an unwelcome twist of something in her chest.

Jealousy? No, at least not of Annie. Maybe of what Annie and Alex seemed to have discovered. And of course, her thoughts chose that moment to drift to Sebastian. Damn.

"I'm just thankful I showed up when I did," Alex said. He wrapped an arm around Annie's slim waist. "Three big guys had her cornered." He ran his fingers over her unharmed cheek, and when he glanced at Lily, she almost sighed.

It looked as if Alex might have found the one. Only his true love wasn't working dark magic and fucking with the astral plane, blast it. She shoved Sebastian Xenakis out of her head. "Me too," she said. "Any idea who they were?"

Annie shook her head. "Alex's girlfriend Jennifer acted like she knew them, but I've never seen them before. Of course, I've been away for so long that I've lost touch with a lot of people I might have recognized before."

"I told you, Jennifer isn't my girlfriend." Alex focused entirely on Annie. "And after tonight, I don't think she's even my friend. Not after the way she acted." He glanced at Lily before looking at Annie again. "Jennifer showed absolutely no compassion for what happened. It's like she thought it was all a big joke. Friends like that I don't want or need."

Lily nodded. She knew how that was. Humans were often fascinated by Chanku, but so jealous that they seemed to relish bad things happening to shapeshifters.

Another reason why they needed to solve the murders. "So why are you hiding from Tinker? You afraid your dad won't want to see you with Alex?" She laughed. "Of course, I couldn't blame him."

"Watch it." Alex growled. "You're supposed to be on my side."

"Since when?" Laughter bubbled up before she could stop it, but it was so much fun, seeing that absolutely besotted expression on Alex Aragat's face. He didn't do besotted, and she clearly remembered telling him years ago that Annie would be his perfect match. This was gonna be so much fun!

"Since we were toddlers and you used to cover for me. That set a precedent. I'm sure it'd stand up in court."

"Yeah, right." Lily was still laughing, but Annie leaned against his side and Alex tightened his arm around her waist.

"I don't want Dad to see the bruise. He's so overprotective that he'll never let me out."

"He let you go to Europe for what, six years?"

"I know. Can you believe it? Mom convinced him that since I was on another continent, he couldn't worry about me, that Eve would watch over me."

Alex's eyebrow shot up, just like his father. "And he bought that?"

"Alex!" Lily jabbed him in the ribs with her elbow. "You know Eve watches over all of her Chanku, no matter where they are." She glanced at Annie. "I see your point. Why don't you shift? That always helps heal stuff faster."

Annie's eyes practically glowed. "It's been such a long time since I've shifted. Alex? Do you want to run?"

"Whatever you want."

His studied disinterest was such a tell. The boy definitely had it bad. Lily glanced from Alex to Annie. "Do you mind if I come with you? I was planning to go by myself, but . . ."

"I'd love it." Annie squeezed her hand. "It's been so long since I've had anyone to run with."

Lily opened her thoughts, checked in with her father, and let him know they'd be out for the next few hours. She could hardly contain her relief when he merely said he and her mom were going out for the evening and they could discuss her visit with Eve in the morning.

She wasn't ready to talk to her dad. Not yet. Not until she had more time to figure out how she planned to approach Sebastian. Not until she knew for sure if his magic was the source of the malevolence tainting the astral, or if Aldo Xenakis had somehow commandeered his son's abilities.

She barely knew Sebastian Xenakis, but she'd sensed goodness in him. Even when he'd chased her on Mount Tam, she'd not been able to accept that he was scaring her on purpose.

Somehow, once she got back to San Francisco, she needed to get him on the nutrients. Once he shifted naturally, without magic, she should be able to read him better, see what made him tick.

And hopefully discover what force was using him, working through him, to harm her. Lily had no doubt someone wanted her either too badly frightened to function, or maybe just plain dead. But it wasn't Sebastian. It couldn't be Sebastian.

9

Alex shifted. Lily had always loved the way his wolf looked. She thought the glossy black fur with silver tips on his rough outer coat made him look very much like his father. When she was little, she'd had a horrible crush on Stefan Aragat. Like his son, he was handsome and smart and too funny for his own good.

Alex glanced toward both girls before trotting out of the big cavern, following a long, winding tunnel that would eventually lead them up and out of the caves higher on the mountain.

Annie and Lily quickly undressed and shoved their clothes in a corner. Lily completed her shift, but she stopped in her tracks and stared at Annie's wolf. *I never would have recognized you. Your coat used to be almost as dark as mine.*

Now Annie was a pale gray with black tips, an almost perfect mirror image of Alex's black and silver. *It changed while I was in England. Dad blames it on the lack of sunlight.*

Lily's snort was pure wolven humor. Padding on big paws, she led Annie away from the artificial light in the main cavern, along twisted tunnels and through huge caverns, so familiar with the various routes that the utter darkness didn't slow her down. It was dark outside by the time they took the narrow tunnel that led to an opening high on the mountain above the valley where most of the pack lived.

Alex waited for them, his eyes glimmering in the moonlight. Lily felt Annie's excitement practically bursting out of her as the gray wolf scampered through a narrow crevice between two huge boulders and took the lead. With Alex close behind on her right and Lily on the left, she led them down the steep hillside, away from the caverns, and into the forest. The moon wouldn't be full until tomorrow night, but it glowed so brightly in the big Montana sky that light shimmered between the huge pines and cedars and filled the open meadows with an ethereal silvery glow.

Lily followed easily, holding the steady pace Annie set, head high, ears pricked forward, with her tail waving behind her. The air was fresher here, the scent of cedar and pine, of bay and damp, mushroomy humus, and the drying needles crackling beneath their feet an almost overwhelming cry of home.

She missed this. Missed the freedom to run without fear, to breathe air unpolluted by the stench of so many humans living so close together.

Wolves were not meant to live in cities.

Wolves aren't meant to live alone, either.

She refused to think of Sebastian. Not tonight. Tonight she was with friends she knew she could trust.

They paused on a hilltop beneath a towering oak. Lily raised her head and sniffed the air. Faint, so fragile a scent she could barely catch it, but she knew Sebastian had run this way. Not recently. No, it could have been as much as a week ago or longer, but he'd been here, on Chanku property.

But why? His father owned thousands of acres. Not as much as Anton Cheval, but more than enough to give him room to run. He didn't need to come on their land.

Unless this was the oak he'd mentioned, the one he used to shift. Lily had long sensed the spirit that resided here, the strength inherent in the tree that had dominated this promontory for hundreds of years. She knew it was somehow linked to the same huge tree she'd sat beneath on the astral, though how she understood that was a complete mystery to her.

Still, there was a sense of familiarity about the oak. A feeling that she knew the entity that lived within. A dryad, perhaps? A wood nymph? Sebastian drew on the natural energy of the world around him to power his magic. Had he called on the spirit of this particular tree? Would she ever know for sure?

Damn. The man confused the hell out of her. Confused her and at the same time, fascinated her. Somehow, she had to find the answers she sought. But not tonight.

She gazed out over the valley below. Lights from her parents' house twinkled brightly in the distance, lighting up the meadow and surrounding forest. More homes, some nearby, others scattered farther out from the center glowed with their own light. Others were dark. Her own tiny cottage was lost in shadows, but she hadn't left any lights on. She'd not expected to be away this late.

Nothing about today had gone as planned.

Annie spun and kicked up loose dirt as she took off again. It was impossible to ignore her high spirits. Just as impossible to ignore the pheromones arcing between Annie and Alex. Lily followed the two of them, almost drowning in the scents and sense of need and want, of desire that raised her arousal right along with theirs.

She tried to concentrate on the night around them, on the almost soundless flitter of bats overhead, the soft hoot of an owl, the scream of a panther off in the distance.

Igmutaka, maybe? She wouldn't be surprised, as surly as the big cat sounded. The spirit guide had taken to spending most of his time in his puma form since his charge, Star Fuentes, had gone off to Yale without him. None of the pack really knew the details, but apparently Star had grown weary of the Ig's over-enthusiastic guardianship as she'd reached adulthood. He'd watched over her father and all the males of his line going back beyond memory, but Star had been his first female charge.

She'd left for college almost fourteen years ago after leaving Ig with explicit instructions that he wasn't welcome to come along. Lily wondered if Star was ever coming back. Probably not, as long as Igmutaka insisted on protecting her from every-thing under the sun—especially any young men she might meet.

Anton Cheval might be an overprotective father, but Igmu-taka, spirit guide, was a whole lot worse. Lily really did feel sorry for Star. Having a gorgeous spirit guide getting in the way of every potential relationship had to be beyond frustrating.

Annie's sharp yip pulled Lily out of her thoughts. The gray wolf veered off the trail. She'd found a narrow path through a patch of wild blackberry vines and raced beneath the tangle with Alex close on her heels. Lily followed, leaving a few tufts of thick fur in the brambles before bursting out into a moonlit meadow. A steaming pool glimmered at one end.

She'd not been here for years—one of the more isolated hot springs on the huge piece of property—but it had always been one of her favorite places. The water was always warm, even when snowdrifts made the trail hard to follow, and the smell of minerals lay heavy on the still night air.

Annie shifted first and Lily was right behind her. The night was still, the thick grass damp beneath their feet. Small patches of snow lingered in the dark corners of the forest even in June, but here, near the warmth of the spring, the air was warm and humid. Lily glanced at Alex—he'd been quiet throughout the run, which wasn't at all like him. He hadn't shifted. In fact, he crouched as if to run, his body tense, hackles slightly raised. His sharp gaze was fixed on Annie.

Alex? What's going on?

Look at her, Lily. Just look.

Okay, that was definitely not typical Alex behavior, but she tried to see Annie as Alex might.

She was absolutely breathtaking, small for Chanku, just under five and a half feet tall, with slim shoulders, small breasts with dark nipples, slightly rounded hips, a tiny waist, and long, long legs. She stood with one foot in the warm water and gazed at Alex with painful longing.

Lily glanced at Alex. His eyes glowed like amber jewels in the moonlight, and his body was so filled with tension he quivered. He jerked his head around and stared frantically at Lily. His thoughts punched into her like a fist.

I'll be back. I promise, but I can't stay right now. I can't, Lil. I'm sorry! He'd barely completed the thought before he spun about and raced back through the brambles.

"Where'd he go?"

Annie looked so crestfallen, Lily moved closer and wrapped an arm around her waist. "I don't know," she said. "He'll be back. The pond was a great idea. C'mon."

She took Annie's hand and led her out into the water and over to the far side beneath a cliff of solid granite. There was a natural ledge along this end where the two of them sat. Even sitting up straight, the water lapped at Annie's chin while barely covering Lily's breasts.

"It's a good thing you're not any shorter." Lily tightened her arm around Annie and pulled her close. "I just don't get it. Your mom is tall, and your dad's a moose. How come you're so petite?"

Annie snorted. "I think they saved all the tall genes for my brothers. Have you seen Mike and Ricky lately?"

"How can you miss them? They're huge! Bigger than Tinker."

"Exactly." Annie shivered.

"Are you cold?"

She shook her head and hugged herself. "No. Just really aroused. I haven't run in ages. I forgot what it feels like, that all-consuming *fuck-me-now-before-I-scream* need to get laid." She gazed wistfully in the direction Alex had run. "I wonder how long Alex will be gone?"

Lily's laughter echoed against the stone walls of the grotto. "Hang on for a few minutes. He shouldn't be gone long, wherever he's off to. You and I used to have a pretty good time together, before you left. Let's wait. It'll be more fun with Alex. Three's always better."

"Lily, I can't." Annie scooted away from her. "I've never . . . I mean. I just can't."

"What? You can't what? Have sex?"

Annie glanced off to the side. "Have sex with Alex."

"Why the hell not?"

"I've . . . it's complicated." Annie's cheeks flushed dark, and she shook her head, then shrugged and looked away.

Bemused, Lily just stared at her for a minute. When Annie didn't say anything more, she asked, "How complicated? Spill, Annie. What's going on?"

"You'll laugh at me."

"I won't. I promise." It was so quiet, Annie's breaths, even her heartbeat seemed to echo in Lily's head.

"I've never been with a man. I wouldn't know what to do."

The silence hung in the air. Annie stared down at the dark water. Lily stared at Annie.

Finally she took a deep breath. Annie was Chanku. They were ruled by a libido so powerful it took a lifetime to learn to control the needs they felt. Their parents hadn't known of their own Chanku heritage until much later in life, and they'd all fought their own sexual demons without understanding how their Chanku genetics affected them even before they'd ever shifted.

They'd learned the hard way, the effect shifting had on the

Chanku libido. Arousal took on an entirely new level of meaning, so powerful, so demanding that abstinence wasn't an option.

Lily didn't know a single Chanku capable of abstaining after shifting. Even her father, with his brilliant mind, his magical powers, and all his strengths admitted that fighting the need for sexual release after a shift was the closest thing to hell he could imagine, if such a place existed.

"Annie, you and I've had sex. I mean, it was years ago, but you were certainly no blushing virgin. But you're thirty years old. You're saying no guys? Ever?" Lily couldn't believe they were having this conversation.

Annie nodded. "With girls, sure. I mean, we all learned how to bring each other off when we were teens, when we felt the first stirrings after shifting." She raised her head and grinned at Lily. "Thank goodness we didn't get aroused when we were real little. That could have been awkward."

"No kidding. I don't get it, though. Pregnancy's not an issue. Human diseases don't affect us so we're not limited to Chanku males. You could have slept with a human. Why no guys?" She laughed. "Hell, all men are interested even if they haven't shifted. They don't have to be Chanku for the sex to be good."

Annie stared off in the direction Alex had gone. Lily waited, tempted to look at Annie's thoughts.

She was glad she hadn't snooped when Annie sighed softly and said, "I didn't want you to hate me, Lil." She turned and looked directly into Lily's eyes. "I've never wanted any man but Alex. I've always loved him. Since I was a little girl and he used to protect me from the bigger kids."

She bit her lip and looked away. "I was always small for my age and such a serious kid, but he made me laugh. I've loved Alex for as long as I can remember, but he was yours. We all knew that." She turned and smiled at Lily. "It was like the two of you were mated in the crib, or at least betrothed by your parents, which put him firmly out of bounds. I didn't want casual sex with Alex. I wanted Alex. Unfortunately, no other man ever appealed to me. I figured if I couldn't have the one I loved, I didn't really care about sex with any other guy. Why do you think I chose to study in England?"

Lily hugged her close. "Oh, Annie. I'm so sorry you felt like you had to go away, that you couldn't see what was right in front of your eyes. Alex and I were never meant to be mated. Besides, I think every girl in the pack has loved him, but he's never looked at any of them the way he looks at you. He's always loved women, and he's more tomcat than wolf, but I have a feeling Alexander Aragat's days of chasing around have come to an end."

Annie's eyes glowed like two amber saucers in the moonlight. "Do you really think that? And you don't mind?"

Laughing softly, Lily leaned against the slick granite wall behind her. "Everyone, including our parents, have had us in love and bonded since we shared the same crib. I do love Alex, but not in the way of mates, and he doesn't love me that way, either."

She turned and cupped both hands on Annie's shoulders. "He needs a woman like you, Annie. Someone who will love him, who appreciates his manic side, who knows what a brilliant, amazing man he is under all the silly jokes and laughter. He's tender and sweet and very brave. I think he's very much like his dad."

Tears sparkled in Annie's eyes. "I've always adored Uncle Stefan. He's a lot like your dad, but without the scary vibe."

"Scary vibe?" Laughing so hard she could barely get the words out, Lily hugged Annie close. "What's that?"

"That look he's got. He can stop anyone in their tracks with that look. Except you, of course."

"I don't think anyone's ever stopped me," she said. But a

shiver raced down her spine. One man had that power. Only one.

Sebastian's image filled her mind. Firmly, she pushed him aside.

Goddess, he was such a fucking idiot, but he'd run like a scared rabbit the moment the girls shifted. Lily was beautiful, a truly striking woman, especially naked, but when he saw Annie McClintock naked for the first time, it hit him like a speeding locomotive. She stood there beside Lily, looking so petite and perfect, and he'd realized that whatever he'd ever felt for Lily Cheval paled beside the feelings he had for Annie.

He'd wanted to beg her to shift back to her wolf form so he could mate with her right then and there with Lily as their witness, and wasn't that just the dumbest thing ever.

They hardly knew each other. She'd been gone for six years. He'd not seen her once, not on any of her visits home, and why was that? Had she been avoiding him? Had he somehow known this was going to happen and stayed away?

He raced as if an army hunted him, ran until his sides were heaving and foam covered his lips and realized he'd made a huge circle and was almost back to the hot spring where the girls waited. What the hell was he going to say? What should he do?

He'd never imagined this feeling. He'd heard his parents and the other elders talk about meeting one another, how they'd known from the beginning when they'd found their one true mate, or two as the case may be. Star's parents, Tala, AJ, and Mik, certainly made their relationship work.

How did he court Annie? He didn't have a clue. His relationships weren't relationships at all. They were serial one-night stands with human women, or hot, no-holds-barred sex with Lily whenever they got together.

He'd avoided most of the girls in the pack as they'd grown older because he didn't want to get entangled with anyone in particular. Now he couldn't imagine not being tangled with Annie.

He slowed to a trot. Wished he could get Lily off by herself and ask her for advice. Of course, he'd have to put up with her snarky "I told you so." He'd just have to man up and handle it.

A rabbit jumped up under his feet and took off across the meadow, and suddenly it all came very clear. Alex leapt after the foolish creature. He knew exactly how to win Annie's heart.

"What am I going to say when he comes back?" Annie hugged herself, terrified and thrilled, apprehensive and anxious, and so tied in knots she thought she might throw up.

Lily thought Alex loved her? Impossible, but what if it was true? She shivered and her stomach lurched.

Lily wrapped an arm around her waist and pulled her close. "I've got an idea how to take your mind off Alex until he gets back. One that requires sharing body heat. Among other things."

A frisson of awareness raced across her skin and settled right between her legs. "I think that's a marvelous idea. I'm a wreck." Talk about your understatements. Before she could talk herself out of it, Annie wrapped her arms around Lily's shoulders and pulled her close for a kiss.

Warm, firm lips, the tip of a tongue, the taste of her own kind, of Chanku. "It's been so long," she breathed, opening to Lily's searching lips. This was comfort. Familiar ground, a woman she'd been with before. One she had known intimately when they were teens, admired greatly as an adult, and would always love.

The one she'd thought would stand between her and Alex. She felt so stupid now, thinking of all the wasted years, time when she might have been with him.

"Not wasted." Lily smiled against her mouth before running kisses across her jaw, along her throat. "I'm not snooping. You're broadcasting your thoughts, sweetie. Don't feel as if you wasted time. Those were the years Alex needed to grow up, to mature enough to be the man who could possibly love you back. And it was a chance for you to explore life without the pack to fall back on. That's huge."

Annie's lips were busy, but she had so much to say. She slipped into mindspeak, connecting easily with Lily. *I was so lonely at school. I wanted to come home, but I couldn't bear to see him. I didn't want to see him with you.*

And you would have seen us together. We've been each other's safety net all our lives. I hope that if you and Alex end up as a mated pair, you'll include me on occasion. He's been my closest friend since we were babies.

I doubt he'd want it any other way. Look at the relationship your parents and his have had over the years.

Laughing, Lily slid off the stone shelf, dipped down into the warm water, and grinned up at Annie. "Which is exactly why they've wanted Alex and me mated. Ain't gonna happen."

She wrapped her hands around Annie's thighs and easily lifted her to sit on the smooth stone edge of the pool with her feet dangling in the warm water. Shoulders deep, Lily leaned forward between Annie's knees.

Shivering, as much from anticipation as from Lily's sensual touch, Annie closed her eyes as her arousal blossomed. Lily left soft, sucking kisses along her inner thighs and then bathed those sensitive spots with her tongue. Moaning, Annie's nipples ruched into tight peaks, and it was hard to catch her breath. Biting back a sob, she lay back against rock still warm from the sun. When Lily's tongue stroked a line of fire over her labia, her entire body jerked. Arousal once blossoming now exploded.

She whimpered and ached. So long. It had been so damned long since she'd felt this perfect touch, this molten fire racing through her veins, sizzling along her skin, and stoking a climax that kept building, building higher and hotter. Lily clutched her thighs with strong, long fingers, lifting her hips, tonguing her clit. She slipped her fingers deep inside Annie's clenching sheath, curling forward against the sensitive inner walls, until the fire raced from clit to womb and back again.

Too good. Over the top good. The damp sweep of Lily's beautiful hair, the perfect pressure of her lips, her teasing tongue and long fingers touching and stroking. On the edge, gasping for air, Annie raised her head and glared at Lily. "What about you? I don't want to come without you."

"Good. Me either." Laughing, Lily lunged out of the water as Annie quickly turned and scrambled into the thick grass beside the pool. She was so much shorter than Lily, but somehow, laughing and giggling, they made it work with Annie on her back in the soft but chilly grass while Lily knelt above her, caging her in warm arms and strong legs.

The grass warmed quickly beneath her body. Annie sighed. This was something familiar. Comfortable, this touch and taste between women. Between herself and someone she'd known so well, so long. She used her tongue and her fingers, teeth, and lips to nibble and suck, to penetrate and caress.

Lily responded, her senses obviously as tightly wound as Annie's, and she whimpered when Annie clasped her sensitive clit between her lips and used her tongue and even her teeth to tease the sensitive bud.

Yet even as the pleasure between them grew, Annie wondered vaguely when Alex would return. If he would return. Then Lily was touching and tasting, quickly bringing her back to her peak, and Annie lost herself in taking and giving pleasure with one of her dearest friends.

Even dearer, now that she knew Lily held no claim to Alex.

Opening her thoughts, she found Lily waiting to connect. Mind to mind, she promised. *I'm never leaving again, Lily. Whether or not Alex loves me, I'm not walking away from the pack.*

Good. The pack needs you. Your mom and dad have missed you. I've missed you.

She answered Lily with laughter. *I've missed this!* She felt the swipe of Lily's tongue running from her butt to her clit, swirling a tight circle around that sensitive nub. Whimpering, Annie arched closer to Lily's mouth. *And dear goddess, Lily, but you do this so well.*

Gasping, hanging on to Lily's slim hips, Annie opened to the boiling need, the familiar sense of overwhelming arousal and soul-deep yearning that was both the blessing and the curse of shifting, of running as the wolf. She'd forgotten what it was like to satisfy that need with one of her own kind.

With someone she loved. And with that thought in mind, with Lily's taste on her lips and tongue, Annie gave in to the rush, the heat, the amazing climax she shared with Lily Cheval.

Lily had sensed Alex's presence just before she and Annie reached their shared peak, and she'd wondered what his reaction would be.

He'd done nothing. No, he'd just stood there beside the pond, not five feet away from them, his ears forward, eyes bright, holding a freshly killed rabbit in his mouth. Now he sat motionless, still holding the rabbit, still watching Annie, his amber eyes glittering in the last shimmering rays of moonlight as it passed behind the mountain.

Substitute that damned dead rabbit with a duck or pheasant, add a shotgun next to his feet, and he'd look like one of those old paintings: faithful hunting dog bringing in the kill.

She wouldn't laugh. She couldn't. Not when she could sense how deeply Alex had been affected by Annie. She had the distinct feeling he hadn't expected this at all.

Lily touched Annie's shoulder and nodded in Alex's direction, heard the catch in Annie's breath, and realized she'd been totally unaware of his presence. As far as Alex was concerned, Lily wasn't even in the picture. She quietly slipped away from Annie and back into the pool, leaving Alex and Annie to work this out on their own.

Her body still thrummed with the force of her orgasm. The warm water should have soothed her, but she was so sensitive that the small current abraded her sensitive nipples instead.

Gliding through the water, she swam to the far side and found an outcropping where she could sit and yet remain almost entirely submerged. She wanted them to forget she was here, but she didn't want to miss this, either.

It didn't appear that would be a problem. Alex waited until Annie regained her composure. Then he stood and walked over to her and gently laid the dead rabbit down in front of her.

Annie's eyes went wide. She shot a quick glance toward Lily as if looking for confirmation. Lily didn't say a word. This was for Annie to figure out.

Annie's eyes were shining with what could only be tears. She knelt and ran her fingers over the rabbit's soft fur. Then she raised her head, looked directly into Alex's eyes, and shifted.

Now in her wolven form, she sniffed at the offering Alex had brought.

Lily watched and wondered. Did Annie understand the significance? For a Chanku male, sharing a fresh kill went way beyond a corsage for the prom. Lily relaxed as soon as Annie took a bite, holding the body down with her front paw, tearing through fur and skin while Alex watched. She swallowed it down, licking blood from her muzzle before sitting back.

Lily grinned. *Good girl,* she thought, but the words stayed behind her shields. Annie was doing exactly as she should, offering the rest of the kill to Alex. He stared at her for a moment. Then he finished the rabbit in a couple of bites.

When he'd cleaned his bloody muzzle on the grass, Alex shifted. There was no way to ignore his blatant arousal, and

Lily realized she was enjoying this chance to sit back and admire him. He really was a beautiful man.

What did Annie see when she looked at Alex? Nudity was nothing unusual, but Lily realized she couldn't remember much about Annie when they ran as a pack. She'd usually arrived in whatever form she was taking and would head back to her parents' house, still in her animal form.

Their few sexual encounters had been fun and open, but now that she thought of it, none of the guys had ever been around when she'd had sex with Annie. How could she have missed that? But it explained Annie's hesitation as she gazed up at Alex.

Then she shifted, sooner than Lily expected. Another good sign. Lily had no intention of interfering or even reminding them she was here. At least, not this first time, but she wasn't about to leave, either. She felt Annie's need, her insecurities, and even some fear.

Not of sex with Alex, but that he would be disappointed, that he'd expect her to know more, to be more experienced.

Okay. A little interference was warranted.

Tell him, Lily said. *He needs to know.*

Annie nodded and stepped into Alex's embrace.

She was warm and sleek and absolutely perfect. Her hesitancy only made him want her more. She trembled, and he wondered if she was as nervous about this as he was.

Sex was as natural as breathing. Sex with Annie? Goddess, but he'd never felt nervous about sex with any woman. Right now he was actually shaking.

He sensed Lily, knew she waited nearby, close enough for Annie, yet far enough to give them at least a sense of privacy. He'd always loved Lily. Loving her was just a part of who he was, how he saw himself, but watching her make love with Annie had hit him like a blow to the heart. He'd stared at the two women, both so beautiful yet so unique. He'd watched them reach their climax together, and it was then that he realized his attention hadn't been on Lily at all.

No. His focus had been entirely on Annie McClintock. He'd often wondered if this day would ever come, if he could look at another woman and feel something, anything remotely as powerful as the feelings he had for Lily.

It had finally happened.

He felt more than *something* for Annie. Emotions so powerful he didn't even mind the fact he'd have to admit, once again, that Lily was right. He nuzzled his chin in Annie's tousled hair, and kissed her temple and the fading bruise over her cheek. A couple more shifts, and it should be gone by the time she returned home.

Running his hands along her back, he cupped her bottom and lifted her, pulling her close against his erect cock. She smelled so damned good, like the forest at night and clear, fresh water, in spite of the minerals in the pool. Her skin against his was dark silk, but as he held her close, she shuddered.

He felt the tension in her body, thrumming like the string on a guitar. Opening his thoughts, he tried to read her, but her shields felt like a brick wall between them.

"Annie? Sweetheart, what's the matter?"

She tilted her head and turned her face against his chest. He wanted to ask Lily, but she'd moved away for a reason, a reminder that this was something he needed to figure out on his own.

He really hated when she did that, but this wasn't about teasing or playing games. This was about Annie, and a future that had opened itself to him so unexpectedly, so perfectly, that he really didn't want to screw it up.

He lifted Annie higher, and she wrapped her legs around his waist as he carried her to a fallen log worn smooth by time. Almost hyperaware of her damp sex against his belly, of the fullness of her small but perfect breasts pressing against his chest, he sat down with her in his lap, his hands linked at the small of her back, hers behind his neck.

Her buttocks, so round and firm, rested upon his thighs, and his sinfully erect cock pressed tightly in the crease between her buttocks, throbbing in time with his racing pulse. He took a deep breath and searched for control. For focus.

He wanted to look into her eyes, but she'd pressed the side of her face too close against his chest to see them. Her entire body trembled. What was she so afraid of? "Tell me. Please, Annie. Whatever has you upset needs to be fixed before we go any further."

She nodded, but she still wouldn't look at him. "I know. Lily said to be honest with you, but it's hard to say the words."

"Then open your thoughts. Let me in."

She didn't speak, but he felt her shields drop, sensed the turmoil in her mind. And when he finally heard her mental voice, he realized he hadn't expected anything like this.

I've never been with a man. She tucked her head even closer against his chest, and he wondered if she'd noticed that his heart skipped a beat. Or more. It took him a minute to digest the magnitude of what she admitted. She was Chanku. They'd all had sex with one another throughout their teen years. All but Annie?

He hadn't really thought about it, but he realized now she'd never fully been a part of their closely knit group.

He stroked her short curls and then lifted her chin, forcing her to face him. *And that's bad, why?*

She pulled back and finally looked him in the eye, but her confidence had returned. Sort of. *You'll think I'm a freak.*

He shrugged, doing his best to keep his voice level. Goddess, but he wanted her so much. Wanted to bury himself deep in her welcoming heat. Wanted to claim her, both as woman and as wolf. But not yet. Not until she was sure she wanted to take this step.

Is the reason you've not had sex with any guys freaky?
She shook her head. *I dunno. Maybe. You might think so.*

He realized he was smiling in spite of the odd situation. She was absolutely precious to him, her confidence coming and going with each thought. *I want the truth, Annie. I want to know you, without secrets. Definitely without any fear. Why have you chosen to wait? And don't try and tell me it wasn't a choice. You're Chanku. Your drives are as strong as the rest of ours. Your needs just as powerful.*

She took a deep breath and faced him again. Licked her lips, took a long, slow breath. *There was no one else I wanted. Only you. Never anyone else. Since I was a kid, it's always been you.*

That definitely sucked all the air out of his lungs. He looked into those gorgeous amber eyes and wanted to shout. A rousing cheer, maybe? At least a few cartwheels should be in order, but he kept his voice calm and softly said, "Oh, Annie. Why didn't you say anything? Why didn't you let me know? Guys can be pretty clueless." He chuckled softly. "According to Lily, I'm one of the worst."

Shaking her head slowly from side to side, Annie finally looked up at him and said, "I couldn't. You were Lily's. At least that's what I thought."

He'd sort of figured the same thing for most of his teen years. He'd been Lily's, though she'd never really been his. It was easier than thinking for himself. Easier than going against what the pack appeared to have agreed upon. "That's what everyone thought, because that's what our parents wanted. Lily and I do love each other, but we figured out a long time ago that it's the love of very dear friends. We're not meant to be mated." He laughed. "Trust me, we both know it would never work."

"That's what Lily said." She shrugged. "I don't think I really believed her, but if you're agreeing . . ."

"Sweetie, Lily and I will never lie to you. What she said is the truth. Another truth? I want to make love with you, Annie.

Tonight, not just because our need is strong after the shift, but because you're finally opening to me. We've got a connection like I never imagined. I want to keep it. Hold it close. Build on it."

"I want that, too. I want you." She looped her arms loosely over his shoulders. "I never thought you'd be interested." She kissed him, and it was sweet and perfect, just an innocent kiss, but it left his blood boiling and his cock rising to press even harder against that hot and secret place between her thighs.

He stood up, still holding Annie close but feeling pretty stupid when he realized he was blinking away tears. "Believe me, Annie. I'm interested. Way more than interested."

Then he carried her to the same soft, grassy spot where she and Lily had made love. Kneeling on the flattened patch of grass, he waited while she unfolded her legs from around his waist and sat. He knelt in front of her. Held her hands in both of his, and the solemnity of the moment had him pausing, thinking of what they were about to do. In more ways than he could possibly imagine, this was a first time for him, too. "I'll do my best to make it good for you. I promise."

Her fingers squeezed his, and she took a long, deep breath. "Alex, I've loved you since I was little. I never thought I'd have the chance to say that. Never expected we'd ever be able to do this. It's already good."

He leaned close, and kissed her hard and fast. "Wonderful. Then let's make it better."

10

Sebastian stood on the well-lit front porch of the huge Cheval home and wondered if he was making the most foolish mistake in his life. He'd come here without invitation, without a plan of any kind, but when he'd finally called Lily's office, when her circumspect assistant working late on a Friday night would only admit Lily was visiting family, Sebastian knew he had no choice.

It had been easier than he'd expected to get a flight out of the city, and the closer he'd gotten to Lily's Montana home, the better he'd felt about his decision. The rental car had been waiting and the front gates to the Cheval estate wide open, almost as if he were expected. He'd parked behind a large garage, out of sight of the house.

He wasn't hiding on purpose. He wasn't going to hide from anyone, especially from Lily's mother and father. He knew they were home because he'd watched them drive in just a short while ago. Another couple had been with them, but they'd entered the huge, sprawling house through separate doorways, and he imagined they must all live here together.

One of his father's favorite rants was about the blatant immorality of Chanku, the fact that they swapped mates and had indiscriminate sexual encounters, that they were nothing more than animals.

It was hard to deny they were animals—beautiful creatures of the wild, choosing their forms at will, and as far as Sebastian was concerned, what consenting adults did behind closed doors was their own damned business. No matter their morality, Lily's parents had raised a pretty amazing daughter.

With that thought foremost in mind, he raised his hand to knock on the door. It swung open before his fist connected with the intricately carved wood.

Startled, he stepped back. Lily's father, the very famous and yet somewhat reclusive Anton Cheval, stood in the doorway. One hand supported his weight against the door frame, the other grasped the heavy brass handle. His shoulder-length dark hair was tousled, half out of its queue as if he'd just crawled out of bed, though Sebastian knew he'd arrived home mere minutes ago. His long-sleeved white shirt was unbuttoned over a lean but muscular chest. His shirt sleeves were rolled back along his forearms exposing narrow, graceful wrists with a dusting of dark hair, and his shirt tail hung loose from his dark gray slacks. Sebastian had the horrible sense he'd interrupted something intimate, something between man and wife.

But all that was noted in a heartbeat, and it was nothing compared to the man's aura. Red and maroon flames shimmered all around him, cascading arcs of pure power at least as strong as, if not stronger than Lily's.

Sebastian sucked in a breath. He should have expected this, but he forced himself to look at the man's face. He was immediately caught in the brilliant gleam of the most amazing amber eyes he'd ever seen. There was so much power here, power beyond his own, beyond his father's. No wonder Lily's magic was so strong.

Her father was flat out terrifying.

He buried his fear and stuck out his hand. "Mr. Cheval? My name is Sebastian Xenakis. I hope I'm not interrupting anything. I've come to see Lily."

Her father grasped his hand, holding it a fraction longer than a handshake should require. Sebastian wondered if his entire life had just been read like an open book.

As Cheval released Sebastian's hand, one corner of his lips lifted in a feral grin. "It's good to meet you, Mr. Xenakis. Lily has spoken of you. We all owe you our thanks for watching over her at the reception last night."

Hadn't she told him what happened after? He maintained eye contact, even though an unfamiliar instinct had him wanting to press his belly to the floor and bare his throat. "It was definitely a unique way to meet a beautiful woman. Is Lily home?"

Cheval shook his head. "She's running with friends tonight. I expect her back in a few hours." He held the door wide. "Would you care to come in?"

"I don't want to disturb you." Sebastian shrugged and gazed toward the mountains, and wondered if he'd be able to find her, if he should shift and go after her.

If she'd even want to see him.

"I believe she wants very much to see you."

Mind reading? Sebastian turned slowly and stared at Cheval. He wondered what he was thinking.

The man smiled, looking every bit the wolf. He stepped back and held the door open wider. "You probably don't want to know that. I really think you should step inside, Mr. Xenakis."

Like he had a choice? "Sebastian, please. Mr. Xenakis is my father."

Cheval nodded. "As you wish, Sebastian."

Holding his head high and struggling not to take the submissive pose his body cried out for, Sebastian stepped through the doorway and entered Anton Cheval's home.

An absolutely beautiful dark-skinned woman stood in the foyer. She wore a bright blue, silky gown wrapped around her full-figured body, color that created a stunning contrast against her bittersweet chocolate skin. With her black hair flowing in long, smooth waves past her waist, her full breasts, and her rounded hips, she looked like an artist's rendition of a fertility goddess ready for a pagan ritual. So beautiful, so sensual, she took his breath.

He recognized Lily in her mother's beauty, though Lily's lean height and tensile strength was a direct gift from her father. Her mother's aura pulsed in soft shades of green and blue, and he read her as healer, caretaker, and empathetic lover.

And it was more than obvious she was adored by her husband. Cheval stood before her and took her hands in both of his. Focusing entirely on his woman, he said, "Sebastian, this is my wife. Keisha is the better part of me, the iron strength and the heart of our pack. My love, this is Sebastian Xenakis, the young man who assisted Lily at the reception last night."

She tugged her hands free of her husband's and moved forward with a welcoming smile and her arms held wide. "Sebastian! I'm so glad you've come. It's a pleasure to meet you, to thank you in person. Please, come in. You are welcome in our home." She hugged him, enveloping him in strong arms and a sense of such peace, such overwhelming acceptance, that his eyes welled with tears.

So not like him, but before he had time to wonder at his sudden rush of emotion, she quickly stepped back, took his arm in both hands, and led him down a broad hallway. "Would you care for a drink? We just got home, and Anton and I were going to have a glass of cognac. Come. Join us."

Cheval's soft voice, surprisingly humorous, filled Sebastian's mind. *My mate is a force of nature, Sebastian. I suggest you just go with the flow.*

As if he had any choice. With a quick glance over his shoulder and a raised eyebrow at the man's barely controlled smile, Sebastian allowed Lily's mother to guide him toward a large, oddly shaped den. With five rather than four walls, richly paneled in wood inlay, it was filled comfortably with dark oak and leather furniture. Colorful rugs overlay floors of natural stone. A flat video screen covered most of one wall and a massive oak desk filled the corner.

A mottled green and black granite bar ran the full length of the wall opposite the screen. Anton stepped behind the bar and set out three heavy crystal goblets without stems, then reached beneath for an expensive-looking bottle of cognac. He glanced at Sebastian, who nodded. As Anton poured, he gestured toward one of the leather bar stools.

Sebastian sat. Keisha patted his shoulder, leaned across the bar, and kissed her husband. "I'll see you later, my love." Then she winked. "Be kind."

As she turned to go, she brushed her fingers along the side of Sebastian's face. The gentle, loving gesture was so much like one his mother had made when she still lived, that he felt the sting of tears once again. What the hell was going on?

And what were Lily's parents up to? No one was this nice, not to a guy who'd had sex with their daughter and then bailed out like a damned coward before she woke up.

Of course, they wouldn't know that. He watched intently as Keisha took a half-filled glass from her husband. She gave Sebastian one last smile as she left the room. He wanted to follow her, wanted to spend more time near her, absorbing the sense of peace that seemed so much a part of Lily's beautiful mother.

He realized he was still staring at the empty doorway. Damn, what an idiot. Lily's father was going to think he was nuts. He turned. Cheval had remained behind the bar, but the affable smile was gone. Sebastian had a feeling he was getting a glimpse of the real man behind the handsome face.

Cheval's voice had an edge to it as he held his glass without actually taking a drink. "Actually, Sebastian, I do know that you left our daughter's bed without telling her why. I also know another young woman died shortly after you left, but if I believed you were the killer, you wouldn't be sitting in my home, drinking my best spirits, or accepting kindness and hugs from my beloved wife. I do, however, have grave misgivings about your dealings with my daughter."

This was more along the lines of what he'd expected. Sebastian thought of taking a sip of the cognac for courage, but decided there wasn't enough alcohol in the world to give him the courage he needed. He cupped the glass in his hands and faced Lily's father. "First of all, Mr. Cheval, I would never harm Lily. I understand and respect your misgivings." He took a deep breath and searched for an elusive sense of balance. "The reason I'm looking for Lily is that I want to apologize."

"For sneaking away in the middle of the night?"

Sebastian stared at the amber liquid in his glass. "That, and for frightening her today on the astral. I didn't mean to. I had no idea she was there."

Cheval went dead still. Sebastian felt the tiny hairs on the back of his neck stand up. He really didn't want to meet the man's gaze, but he raised his head and looked directly into narrowed eyes and the face of a feral creature barely under control.

There was an edge as fine as sharpened steel to his voice. "You were on the astral? Why? And how? How did you gain access?"

Slowly, Sebastian shook his head. Hell, even he wasn't quite sure how he'd gotten there or if that was where he'd actually gone. He took a sip of the cognac. Smooth as silk and yet it still burned going down. He'd never been much of a drinker. "I used a spell I found among my father's papers."

"Blood magic?"

He nodded, not totally surprised that a wizard as powerful as Cheval would know.

"That requires a sacrifice. What did you kill and how?"

He shook his head. "No. Never. I won't kill to empower my spells. I used my own blood." He sighed, still slowly shaking his head. "I won't do that again. The blood tainted the spell. It felt wrong the minute the drops hit the flame."

Cheval merely nodded. "Do your father's spells, the ones he casts, require the death of living creatures?"

Sebastian stared at the granite bar, grounding himself in the natural patterns running through the stone. "I believe so, though I've not witnessed any sacrifice. My father is very secretive with his magic." He should have felt like a traitor, divulging his father's methods, but something about Cheval made Sebastian comfortable trusting the man. There was a sense of honor here that was sorely lacking in his father.

"Possibly the deaths of young women?"

Sebastian raised his head and once again looked directly into the man's eyes. He consciously dropped his shields, should Cheval want to see his innermost thoughts. "I hope not. I wish I knew for certain, but I've a growing suspicion they might be his source of power."

Again, there was no reaction. Cheval turned as he took a sip of his cognac and stared at the big window. From the position of the house, Sebastian imagined that during daylight it would look out on a huge meadow with the granite peaks of the Rocky Mountains rising majestically behind. Tonight, with the lights shining inside, Sebastian saw only the reflections of two men, lost in thought while searching carefully for answers.

He wondered what Lily's father saw.

Anton glanced over his shoulder. "I just reached Lily. She'll be here in about half an hour."

Seb's gaze flashed from the window to the man. So calm, and yet so very powerful. It wasn't common knowledge that Chanku were telepathic, but from what he'd learned, most of them were limited to a fairly short distance. Cheval appeared to have no limits.

Was it the magic, or merely his personal set of Chanku genetics? Did Chanku gain power with age? Anton Cheval was no kid. Sebastian had done his research, knew he'd been born in the twentieth century, in 1955. That meant he was eighty-four years old, and yet in both appearance and action, he was a man in the prime of his life. Chanku were said to be nearly immortal. Seeing him, Sebastian had no doubts the rumors were true.

By appearance alone, Anton Cheval could be one of Sebastian's contemporaries. It was unnerving, knowing Cheval was older than his own father and yet looked half Aldo's age.

Almost as unnerving to feel the power that was so much a part of him. At least Cheval's aura had settled. It no longer spiked and flamed, though it continued to glow with bursts of red and magenta.

When he spoke of Lily, though, soft pale pink wove in among the red. He truly loved his daughter with a pure and enduring love that Sebastian couldn't even begin to imagine. What would it be like, to be loved so completely?

His mother had loved him, but she'd also lied to him. He'd grown up believing his father was dead.

Maybe he'd have been better off if Aldo *had* died. Or, at the very least, if he'd never learned his father lived. In hindsight, it had been a rash decision to search for Aldo after discovering his name on the birth certificate. Even more foolish to take that name as his own, but it had pleased the old man.

In the beginning.

Cheval stepped out from behind the bar and faced the big window. He glanced over his shoulder at Sebastian. "What makes you think your father is involved with the murders?"

Sebastian slipped off the stool and walked across the room to stand next to Lily's father. They were of equal height, and seeing their reflections together like this, Sebastian realized he'd been right—they appeared the same age.

Standing here beside the man, it was easier to think of Cheval as a peer, not as the father of the woman he might be falling in love with. He shoved his fingers through his hair in frustration and looked at Cheval's reflection in the glass.

"Please realize, I don't know Aldo Xenakis very well. I only discovered he was my father a couple of years ago, when my mother was dying and I was helping organize her papers. I found my birth certificate, their divorce papers. She warned me to stay away from him, but my curiosity won out. After she died. I contacted him. He knew nothing about me, but when I sent him copies of the paperwork, he asked me to come. I did. I'm still not sure if it was the smartest or stupidest thing I've ever done, but there is something different, almost mesmerizing about . . ."

His voice trailed off. What was there to say about the man? Aldo was fascinating in the same manner as a cobra. Sebastian glanced at Cheval and realized he had his full attention. "Anyway, when I first saw Lily at the reception . . ." He shrugged. "She's beautiful. Charismatic. I've never felt a connection like I felt with her. I was trying to influence her to look my way."

Cheval chuckled. "Did it work?"

Sebastian laughed outright. "Hell, no. She said I was much too pushy."

"That sounds just like Lily."

"I'd never really communicated telepathically before. My

father can push at my mind, and occasionally I understand what he wants, but we don't actually speak. Not the way Lily and I can. To say she grabbed my attention is an understatement. She was working her way through the crowd, talking to people greeting her, and at the same time, we were tossing telepathic comments back and forth."

He remembered how she'd looked, like royalty acknowledging her subjects, and his heart sped up. "We made eye contact, and suddenly a sharp pain spiked through my head. Lily collapsed. Just went down like someone had coldcocked her. I was aware of a sense of evil, of darkness, but there was a subtle familiarity. I pushed it all away and ran to Lily."

He chuckled. "She was awake but pretending to be unconscious because she was embarrassed. She asked me—telepathically, again—to get her away from everyone, so I carried her to a private office. She recovered quickly, we went back to the reception, and all was well."

He glanced at Lily's father. Cheval stood motionless, listening carefully to everything Sebastian was saying, but watching him in the way of a predator studying his prey.

What did he see? Facial expressions or something more? Did he see auras the way Sebastian did? Was he searching Sebastian's thoughts, looking for words he wasn't speaking aloud? He'd often thought his father could read his mind, and he already knew Cheval was capable. So be it. He had no intention of lying. The man could turn his brain inside out for all he cared. All he'd find was just how very much Sebastian already cared for his daughter.

"After the reception, Lily said she was going to run on Mount Tam. I asked if I could go with her, and she said she'd be running as a wolf. I'm not Chanku, but I can shift by magical means. She was okay with that. But something happened that's never happened to me before. Shortly after we shifted, I lost almost half an hour. I have no real explanation, but Lily says I chased her as if I intended to mount her."

He shook his head, still ashamed of what had happened. "I vaguely recall a sense of evil, as if something foul had entered my mind, similar to what happened at the reception, but it's not clear enough for me to be sure. Whatever it was, I can only assume I was mentally compromised until we were attacked by two huge wolves. Lily was able to get through to me then, thank goodness, because they were bigger than anything I've ever seen. They were smart, obviously working together, but Lily wasn't sure if they were Chanku. She and I fought them off."

He shot a quick glance at Cheval. "Your daughter is amazing. She doesn't give an inch in a fight, and together, we were able to overpower them. One left with a broken right front leg. The other one had a broken left hind leg, and a slashed nose."

"There's more to this. Something Lily doesn't know, right?" Cheval's focus was laser sharp, aimed directly at Sebastian.

"Yes, sir. Early this morning, my father made a couple of comments that let me know he was aware of what had happened last night. When I admitted to losing myself in the wolf, he seemed disappointed I'd not raped Lily. He was rather crude about it."

Anger surged, fresh and hot with the memory. He realized he was clenching his hands into such tight fists he'd cut off circulation, and he stared at his hands a moment, flexing his fingers, getting the circulation back. After a moment, he raised his head and faced Lily's father. "His comments infuriated me. We had strong words; it got ugly. Later, before I did the spell to access the astral, he held one of his big public rallies against Chanku rights of citizenship. I watched the remote feed and noticed he had at least six large bodyguards up on the stage with him. Men I'd never seen before, but he likes to flaunt his power, so their presence wasn't unusual. Except one bodyguard had his right arm in a sling. Another had a slashed nose and a walking cast on his left leg."

"Coincidence?" Cheval raised an eyebrow.

"If you say so." Sebastian met his steady gaze.

Cheval studied him for what felt like a very long time. Then he nodded, as if answering his own questions. "I have a condition if you want to continue seeing my daughter. Now, obviously I can't prevent you and Lily from being together if that's what she wants, but I hope you'll humor me on this."

Sebastian merely waited while Cheval walked across the room to his desk, reached into a bottom drawer, and grabbed a small plastic jar. Sebastian walked over to stand beside the desk, and Cheval dropped the jar into his hand.

It was filled with large brownish-green capsules.

"These are the nutrients I want you to take. I believe you are Chanku, but I want to know for sure. Once you take these, if you are Chanku, you can't go back. You will no longer be human. The changes are at a cellular level, and they are permanent."

Sebastian held up the plastic container and looked at the capsules. "Lily asked me to take them. I told her I would."

"And then you left."

Sebastian nodded. "And then I left." He glanced at Cheval. "Not a very bright move on my part. I knew it the moment I shut the door behind me I'd made a stupid mistake."

"Good. There's hope for you yet." Cheval glanced at the jar. "They go well with cognac."

Sebastian removed the lid and dumped one of the capsules into his palm. He retrieved his glass from the bar, swallowed the capsule down with too big a gulp of cognac and almost choked.

Cheval ignored his coughing and checked his wristwatch. "Do you play chess?"

"I do."

"Good. We can play while we wait for Lily. And when she arrives, I would like to hear more of your walk on the astral."

None of this felt real. Annie gazed into Alex's eyes and wondered if she should pinch herself. He was usually so funny, teasing and playing jokes, acting like a clown. Making her laugh.

Not now. Not here. His hands slid down her arms, but his fingers trembled against her skin. His lips parted when he cupped her breasts, and he sort of gnawed on his lower lip as if he was totally lost in touching her.

She was quickly losing herself. Losing any sense of who or what she was beyond what she could be for Alex. What they could be together. Was this love, this terrifying sense of free fall, the feeling that if he didn't do more now, make love to her *now,* she'd burst into flames?

She'd had sex with a lot of women—girlfriends both human and Chanku. None of them, not even Lily tonight, had affected her the way Alex did, merely by looking at her as he ran his big hands over her body.

She reveled in the rough scrape of calloused palms, his strength, and the flex of muscles barely visible in the darkness. Even with her Chanku eyesight, he was all line and shadow, shape and form without truly defined edges, but he was every inch an alpha male.

What was he thinking? She wondered if he'd open his thoughts to her, and when she dropped her shields, just like that he was in her head.

And firmly entrenched within her heart.

Beautiful. So beautiful, and I don't know if I'm good enough, if I'll ever be good enough. Beautiful, perfect Annie.

Her breath caught in her throat. He had no idea she was listening, that he was broadcasting, and as much as she wanted to hear more, it wasn't fair to him. Not when she could answer his questions so easily.

Since I was little, you were always the best thing in my world. The boy I looked up to, and then the man. The one who made me laugh, even when you didn't realize I was in the room. The one who always kept the bigger kids, including my brothers, from teasing me. You've always protected me. Make love to me. I'm thirty years old, and I've waited almost all of those years for you. You know how this is supposed to work, but I don't. Please don't make me wait any longer.

He groaned and kissed her, but there was nothing practiced in the press of his firm lips, the click of teeth bumping, the sensual tingle of tongues touching, stroking, searching deeper. Annie sensed that Alex was every bit as nervous as she was, and his sweet anxiety gave her courage.

She loved his taste and the way it felt when they were skin to skin. She twisted beneath him to bring their bodies closer together. She wanted him inside where no man had touched her, where she'd kept that one small bit of herself inviolate, just for him.

Did he care? Did it matter?

It matters, sweetheart. You have no idea. Matters so much, and yet I'm afraid of hurting you. Afraid I'll screw up and you'll hate me, hate what should be wonderful. He laughed, breaking their kiss and looking at her with so much tenderness that a lump grew in her throat and his image wavered through tears. He kissed her again, a short quick taste of her lips. "I'm not kidding, you know. Believe me, if anyone's going to screw something up, it'll be me."

"Only if you don't shut up and make love to me."

He chuckled, a sound from deep in his chest, almost as if he groaned at the same time. "See? What did I tell you?"

But then he leaned close and clamped her right nipple between his lips, worried the sensitive peak gently with his teeth. Her body writhed and twisted beneath him, and she wondered if a woman could come merely from having her breasts licked and nipped, but then he brushed the curls between her legs, and she knew this intimate touch would definitely make her come.

"No." She moaned the words. "Please, not with your hands. Not with your mouth. I want you inside me. All of you, as deep inside as you can be. Please?"

Her body trembled and his was shaking, and she wondered what it was like for him, a man who'd been with so many women, making love with someone so inexperienced, but he followed her plea, lifted her hips beneath his hands, and nudged at her needy sex. He was gentle, parting her slickened labia with his fingertips, pressing forward until he'd seated the broad head of his cock just inside.

She wanted more. Wanted him now, and she raised her hips and thrust against him, impaling herself on his thick length, thrilling with the burn and stretch as he filled her. She'd used sex toys to ease the pressure of unmet needs, but they were nothing like Alex's thick, hot erection. She lifted her hips, pushing against him until the solid pressure of his cock against the mouth of her womb, the soft slap of his balls against her bottom, signaled she'd taken all she could, that she'd taken all of him.

He held still for a moment, giving her time to adjust to his size, and both of them a chance to savor the feeling. When he finally withdrew, the wet, sucking sounds as he pulled free made her shiver. He paused with the thick head of his cock resting against her entrance, and then he drove home again. And almost as if it were an afterthought, he opened his thoughts to her, shared the sensation of her inner muscles rippling along the fullness of his cock, the way her skin felt to him, like silk. He shared his sense of surprise and amazing joy, that since Annie had suddenly reappeared in his life, he knew his life would never be the same.

Annie returned the sensations, magnified through her sense of wonder, that the man she'd loved for so long truly cared about her, maybe even loved her. This was what she'd waited for. So many times she'd dreamed of just this moment, this wonderful sense of fulfillment, but only with Alex Aragat. Never any other, and now that it was happening, it was more than she'd hoped. So much more, so much deeper, more meaningful than anything she could have imagined.

It wasn't just sex. No, this was so much more. This was Alex making a commitment unlike any he'd ever made. She felt the strength of it in every move he made, in every touch.

It was a commitment to her, to Anne Marie McClintock. Not even Lily, a woman he'd loved all his life, had affected him this way. There was no doubt in her mind. He was telling her with his eyes, with his body, with the soft words he whispered in her ear, that he hoped this was worth the wait for her.

That she was definitely worth the wait for him.

His words of love heated her mind as his touch heated her body. Her climax grew closer. His thrusts went from long and slow to short and fast, and she saw the shimmer in his eyes, the sweat on his forehead and across his broad chest making his muscles gleam in the faint reflective moonlight that lingered.

She opened to him, found him waiting, balanced on the precipice. Waiting for her. *I love you,* she said, unashamed to tell him what she'd imagined saying for so long.

Oh, Annie. Sweet, sweet Annie. I never thought I'd know this feeling, but I love you, too. I think you were made for me to love. Be mine, Annie. Forever mine.

Forever, Alex.

Climax caught them, lifted them together, tossed them to the stars, and then settled them, gently intertwined, connected in a way neither one had ever felt. They lay there in the cool grass, and she was lost in the harsh rasps of his breathing, the thundering beat of her heart pounding in time with his. Even the rush of blood in his veins turned her on, completed her. Her body clenched and pulsed around him, holding him deep inside, and she dreamed of the day they would mate as wolves. When they would bare all to one another and complete a link that had always been nothing more than a lonely young woman's fantasy.

Except it wasn't merely a dream anymore. No, not when she held the reality of Alex in her arms.

Lily felt like such a voyeur, but they'd known she was here all along, at least until they totally forgot about everything but each other. She brushed tears away from her cheeks and thought of sneaking away, but then she realized she wanted them to have her cottage tonight.

Alex still lived in the big house with his parents and hers, and Annie hadn't been home long enough to think of where she might want to live, so Lily knew she must still be at home.

The idea of Alex spending the night there with Annie, under the same roof with her wonderful but intimidating father almost made her giggle. Almost.

She'd give them a minute to come down from their high, and then let them know her place was theirs, at least for tonight.

Lily?

Dad? What's up?

I want you to come home. You have a visitor.

A visitor? Who the hell would come all the way to Montana to see her, especially this late at night? It must be close to ten by now. *Who?*

Sebastian Xenakis.

Holy shit. *Sebastian's here? But . . . I'm a good half hour from home. Do you think he'll wait?*

She heard her father's soft laughter. *Oh, I think he'll wait. But hurry. We have much to discuss.*

She glanced at Alex and Annie. They lay together in the tall grass, totally immersed in one another, but she had to leave, and she wanted them to know about the cottage. She glided across the pond, crawled out, and shook the water out of her long hair over Alex's butt. It seemed only fair.

He whipped his head around and glared at her, but Lily just laughed. "Be nice to me, big guy. I'm here to do you a favor."

"What?" He sounded surly, but she caught his private aside when he added, *You've already done me the greatest favor in the world.*

She just grinned. "I thought you and Annie might like the use of my cottage tonight. The sheets are clean, and the fridge is stocked. I'll stay in one of the guest rooms at the big house. Wish I could stay and play with you, but Dad's summoned me."

Alex sat up and brought Annie with him. She snuggled against his chest with a sigh of contentment, oblivious to Alex and Lily's conversation. "Anything wrong?"

Lily shook her head. "I hope not. Sebastian Xenakis showed up on the doorstep tonight, looking for me. Dad hasn't killed him yet, so that's got to be a good sign."

Alex frowned. "Xenakis is here?"

"He is, and if you meet him, you will play nice."

Alex growled. Lily merely leaned over and kissed his nose. Then she turned away, shifted, and took off at a steady lope.

She wondered how her father and Sebastian were getting along. Wondered if the poor guy would be in one piece by the time she arrived. She certainly hoped so. She had to hand it to him, though. It took a brave man to meet Anton Cheval on his own turf, especially a man who was sleeping with his daughter.

Excitement simmered in her veins. This could be interesting.

It could also be an absolute fiasco.

Stretching out, Lily put on an added burst of speed as she raced down the mountain toward home.

Home and Sebastian Xenakis.

Now why did those two things sound just perfect together?

11

Questions. So many questions. Why had he left her bed during the night? What was he doing on the astral? Where had that horrible taint of evil come from?

Why is he here? What does he want? What will I say to him? Does he truly care about me?

She thought of stopping at her cottage to clean up, to rinse away the earthy scent of the forest and sex and everything that made her exactly who she was, but that wasn't her way.

No. She was Lily Cheval, and she would play no games. Not for any man. Especially not for Sebastian Xenakis, though she did stop her headlong rush as she neared her father and mother's home. If, by chance, Sebastian was watching for her, she'd rather he first saw her trotting casually across the meadow rather than running like a lovesick fool.

She was really glad she'd slowed down as she crossed the meadow. The back lights went on, which meant her father was watching for her. He'd not communicated a word since his first call for her to return. She wondered what had happened, what he thought of Sebastian. She tried to imagine what the two men had talked about. On second thought, no. She'd rather not go there.

The brilliant deck lights illuminated the entire back of the house and much of the meadow. Nothing like a spotlight when a girl had to shift. She leapt easily to the deck, clearing the railing with room to spare. Pausing to sniff the air, she picked up the scents of both her father and Sebastian, so close they must be out here on the deck.

She swung her head to the left and spotted the two men almost lost in shadow, sitting next to each other on top of the picnic table, feet resting on the bench seat below. Each of them held a glass of what she was certain had to be her father's favorite Hennessy cognac. Another good sign. He didn't share that with just anyone. Both men looked relaxed, shirt sleeves rolled back. No blood, no bruises.

Still looking good. Her dad's shirt was unbuttoned and untucked, and he was barefoot, but he rarely wore shoes at home. She'd always thought her father was a beautiful man, but sitting beside him, Sebastian looked even better, so darkly handsome he took her breath. Her wolf definitely approved. She padded across the deck and rested her chin on her father's knee.

I'm glad to see you haven't tried to kill each other.

Anton glanced at Sebastian, who was obviously fighting a grin. "I have strict orders from your mother to behave."

Good. I'll have to thank her. Hello, Sebastian. I'm surprised to see you.

He hadn't taken his eyes off her. "I'm glad to see you. I've missed you. I never should have left."

No, you shouldn't have.

She shifted, standing tall and proudly naked. Her father handed a brilliant red sarong to her. She quickly wrapped the silky fabric around herself and expertly knotted the ends so they lay in the valley between her breasts.

She knew her hair was probably a tangled, windblown mess and that the scent of wolf would be strong, but from the look in Sebastian's eyes, none of that was an issue.

"I'm going inside, gentlemen. It's chilly out here without my fur. Care to join me?" She walked inside without looking back, went straight to the bar, and poured herself a healthy shot of the same cognac the men were drinking.

Taking a seat on one of the bar stools, she waited. Her dad took his usual spot behind the bar, but Sebastian sat on the stool beside hers.

And still he watched her.

But it was her father who spoke. "Your mother's waiting for me to join her, and I imagine you two have a lot to discuss, but I wanted to find out what happened today on the astral." He glanced at Sebastian but focused his gaze on Lily. "I've spoken with Eve. She said there's something dark and unnatural affecting the normal flow of power, something she associated with Sebastian after she saw him today."

"Eve?" Sebastian glanced at Lily. "Was that the really powerful mage beside you?"

"Not a mage," Lily said. "Eve is our goddess, the entity who watches over us. She resides as spirit on the astral plane, but when I visited with her today, she told me that there's something wrong, a dissonance that she believes is based in dark magic. It's affecting the patterns on the astral, her ability to follow us and protect us. It's also interfering with her communication with the Mother who watches over all creatures."

Sebastian stared at her as if she'd grown a third eye, before looking at her father. "You communicate with a goddess? One who lives on the astral?"

Smiling, Anton nodded, but Lily answered.

"That's who you saw today." Lily sighed. "Sebastian, I have to know this. Do you practice dark magic? Blood magic? That's why she shouted at you and forced you out. She said your magic was tainted with evil. That it felt the same as what's been causing the trouble."

He looked stricken. She didn't think he could fake that expression of absolute horror if he'd tried. "Good gods, Lily. I had no idea. That was my first time. I wasn't even sure if I'd ended up in the right place, and I was absolutely shocked to see you. When she yelled at me, I lost my grasp on the spell. Got tossed back into my room in San Francisco."

Lily stared at him, sickened. Blood magic? The taint of evil she'd thought was his father was actually Sebastian? Using sacrifice to power his spells? She swung around and glared at her father. Did he know this already? It changed everything!

Anton quickly covered her hand with his. "Lily, it was blood magic, but he used his own blood. He didn't use a live sacrifice. Stupid, but not an unusual thing for an apprentice wizard to do. We're always testing limits. Learning." His eyes actually twinkled, and Lily felt the tension melt away.

He squeezed her fingers. "Trust me, sweetie. I tried the same thing in my early days when I was still learning the craft, and my results were just about as disastrous."

She glanced at Sebastian and nodded. "Okay." If her dad wasn't concerned, she wouldn't be, either. She trusted his instincts. She'd never known him to steer her falsely.

Anton focused on Sebastian. "Actually, I think my experience might have been worse. You said you were nauseous? I puked all over myself. It was not a pretty sight." He studied Sebastian for a moment, and Lily was surprised that Sebastian didn't even flinch. Her father's close scrutiny could be more than a little bit intimidating.

Then he did something even more surprising. He rested his hand on Sebastian's shoulder and gave him a comforting squeeze. "Sebastian, I'm not positive, but I suspect your father might be linking to your magic. Piggybacking on your power, so to speak. I've met Aldo, and he's a very strong wizard, but I sense more power in you. Untapped and untrained, but still very much a part of your basic nature; more than Aldo Xenakis will ever wield. I can only imagine his envy, because he's not a man who wants to be second to anyone."

Sebastian was obviously turning that over in his mind when Anton added, "I think that might be what Eve sensed on the astral today. Not you and your spell, but your father's spirit tagging along for the ride. He's probably curious as to what skills you have, how powerful you are. I'd like to help you work on your shields. It's a different method of blocking when you're trying to keep another mage out of your mind, but I think it's something you need to consider. And if you're interested—and I'm not trying to force you into anything—but I'd like to work with you, help you learn to use your magic. Learn to find power in other methods than blood and sacrifice."

Sebastian shot a quick glance at Lily. She merely raised one eyebrow, but she really wanted to do a handstand or two. She'd never known her father to make such an offer.

"Thank you. Yes. Definitely yes. There's so much I don't know, so many things I've tried to learn, but my father's ways aren't mine."

"His is dark magic, worked with blood and the energy gained from stealing a life force. Ours is a little different." He caught Lily's eye and winked. *You might want to explain the source of our power to him. I'm sure he'll be interested.*

Then he took Lily's hand and held it tightly, and there was something in his eyes that gave her pause. She tried reading him, but her father's shields were powerful. Right now they were stronger than she'd ever sensed. "Lily? I think your mother and I learned our lesson with Alex. This must be your decision. Do you want Sebastian to stay? He's taken the first capsule. I've told him I would like for him to remain among us until we know for sure he's Chanku, but it's really up to you."

She gazed directly at Sebastian. "Actually, it's up to you. I think the question is, Sebastian, do you want to stay here?"

He reached for her hand and wrapped his long fingers around hers. "Try and make me leave."

"Good." Now, this could get awkward. "Dad, I've given my cottage to Alex and Annie for the night. Are any of the guest rooms here at the house made up?"

He raised one very expressive eyebrow. "Alex and Annie?"

"Yep."

"Interesting. And you don't mind?"

"No, Dad. I don't mind. Guest rooms? Available?"

Both eyebrows this time. "How many?"

She raised her own, right back at him. "One."

He cast an appraising glance over Sebastian and then leaned across the bar and kissed Lily's cheek. "Take your pick, sweetheart. I'll see you two in the morning. Sebastian?"

"Yes, sir?"

"Be sure and tell her about the bodyguards. And, Lily? Explain to Sebastian the power behind our magic." Then with a final glance her way, he left the two of them alone.

Lily tossed back the rest of her cognac, stood, and took Sebastian's hand. "You can tell me once we get to our room. Do you have any bags?"

"I wasn't intending to stay." He laughed. "I didn't plan well at all. All I could think of was getting to you, apologizing to you, and hoping like hell you'd see me. I just caught a plane, didn't even pack a toothbrush, and flew into Kalispell. Picked up a rental and came straight here." He stood and took both her hands in his. "I had to see you, Lily. I wasn't sure if you'd even speak to me, but I was wrong to leave when I did." He sighed. "Hell, I'm not even sure why I left."

She tugged and he followed, out of the den and down the hall to her favorite of the guest rooms. It was almost dead cen-

ter in the house, farthest from both her parents' rooms and
Alex's mom and dad. And far from Alex, when he stayed here,
though he often used her cottage when she was in the city. She
wondered if he and Annie were there now.

She opened the door and led Sebastian inside. The room was
large, more a suite than a bedroom, with a small kitchenette and
a beautiful bathroom with a tub large enough for two.

She stopped beside the bed, aware that her heart was pounding and her body aching. She'd shifted and run, and had just
enough sex with Annie to take off the edge until watching
Annie and Alex had aroused her again. But first she needed to
ask Sebastian a question that had been haunting her.

A question linked very much to her father's concerns. "How
close are you and your father tied? How much control does he
have over you?"

"What do you mean?"

"Can he access your mind?" She sighed and took his hands
in hers. Warm and strong, with long fingers and a dusting of
dark hair at his wrists. A girl could feel safe holding hands such
as these. Being held by these hands. His fingers laced in hers as
she asked him the rest of the questions that had plagued her.

"These are the things I've been wondering. Was he the one
who sent that sharp pain through my head at the reception?
Could he have forced your feral side to dominate when we ran
last night?" She paused, but her eyes never moved, and her gaze
remained fixed on his. "Could he have made you leave my bed
at precisely the time you did, just before that girl's murder? I
guess, Sebastian, what I want to know is whether or not your
father is setting you up. Does he want you to be accused of the
attacks on all those young women? Because it's the only explanation I can come up with that makes any sense."

*   *   *

He didn't want to admit that he'd had a lot of the same thoughts. No son wanted to accuse his own parent of such horrible things, but he was beyond protecting his father, and he'd never lie to Lily. She meant too much to him. Somehow she'd gotten under his skin the first time he saw her, and the feelings weren't going away.

Instead they grew stronger with every minute he spent with her. "I've wondered the same things for the past few weeks. There's often a pressure in my skull that makes me think he's either in my mind or pressing against my shields. The timing of the murders—they've happened up here when I'm in Montana, in the Bay Area when I'm in San Francisco. It's too much to be mere coincidence. Then there's the incident your dad wanted me to mention to you, about his bodyguards."

Lily tilted her head and frowned. "Bodyguards? I didn't realize your father needed them. Is his life at risk? The only cause he's had lately is against Chanku, and we're not violent. Well, killers by nature, but not when we're acting civilized."

She flashed him a grin as she sat on the edge of the bed. He loved the way she watched him. Her focus was absolute, but he could sense her mind spinning, coming up with an interpretation of everything he said. Open to him, but unwilling to be led; she thought for herself.

Even her father didn't intimidate her, and Anton Cheval was not a man to be trifled with. He loved that about her. Admired her strength, the fact her personal integrity appeared to be absolute. There was damned little integrity in his father's life.

Not nearly enough in his own, but that was going to change.

He shoved his hands in his pants pockets and rocked back on his heels. "Civilized killers? Now that's an interesting concept. The truth is, my father has a lot of enemies. When you crave power the way he does, people who get in the way get hurt. Not always physically, but he doesn't have any problem destroying reputations. He's good at finding ways to control people, and I don't think he hesitates going outside the law to do it, though I have no proof of that. Right now, he's got at least half a dozen big guys working for him who look like they'd take your head off without provocation. Two of the men with him this morning caught my attention. One had his right arm in a sling. The other had an ugly slash across his nose and needed a walking cast. Left leg."

Lily grimaced as she nodded in agreement. "There's our link. The one I've been looking for. I told you I recognized the scent of the wolves that attacked us. They were definitely at the site of that murder in Golden Gate Park. They must be shape-shifters, which means they're Chanku. No other beings shift naturally, and I can't imagine your father is powerful enough to change them by magical means. He can't shift himself, can he?"

"No. He seemed surprised when I shifted."

"Eve's not in contact with any others beyond the known members of the pack, though we do know of a set of experi-ments, using the nutrients to find Chanku in the military, but that was years ago. It was deemed a failure and ended abruptly. We don't know how many Chanku might have been discovered or where they ended up."

"Then maybe that's where we need to start looking. I'm positive my father's bodyguards are the ones who went after us, and we can tie them to at least one murder scene. You said you've got a guy up here working on the Montana cases. Has he picked up any Chanku scent?" Damn, he wanted answers. He wanted all this behind them, because he really wanted Lily.

"Alex's nose isn't as good as mine. The difference between wild wolves and Chanku is really subtle, so no, he's not noticed anything. I did tell him that I recognized the scent from the murder scene when those wolves attacked us, and he said that was the first really good lead. Now that we can link them to your father through his bodyguards, the evidence is even stronger."

She looked at him with that wonderfully direct gaze of hers.

"It's not looking good for your father. Are you going to be okay with this, even if it results in him going to prison?"

He shook his head. "Absolutely. If he's guilty of organizing these horrific crimes, he belongs there." Actually, if Aldo was guilty, Sebastian knew it wouldn't be easy to keep from killing the man himself. The murders had haunted him for weeks now. He couldn't imagine what the women's families were going through.

"Okay." Lily squeezed his hand. "I just need to be sure. Eve's checking on the military Chanku to see if there are any in the civilian population. We need to tell her what you've discovered and the scent link between the bodyguards and the murders. If your father is working with rogue Chanku, we really need to tell Eve. Tomorrow we'll visit her on the astral." She shot him a quick grin. "Without a blood sacrifice—yours or mine."

"What about tonight?"

She smiled and ran her fingers across the front of his slacks. He'd been aroused all evening, but her touch immediately took him beyond mere arousal, straight to demanding need. She cupped him, holding his testicles through the soft fabric of his jeans, and smiled up at him in all innocence when he groaned.

"I'm exhausted. Tonight I need sleep, a shower, and a man. Not necessarily in that order."

He struggled for breath. "How about we start with the shower and the man?" Leaning forward, he planted his hands on either side of her hips, caging her within his arms.

She glanced over her shoulder at the door to the bathroom and then tilted her head and looked up at Sebastian. "Works for me, but you're wearing way too many clothes."

He reached for the knot on her sarong. "So are you."

Alex followed Annie as she trotted through the dark forest, taking the long way back to Lily's cottage rather than using the shortcut through the caverns. He felt drunk on feelings, his mind so overwhelmed by Annie, by her love, her trust, her absolute faith in him, that he found it hard to concentrate.

He wanted her. Wanted her as his mate, as his wife, as his partner for all time. They'd linked closely during sex, but he knew it could be more.

Would be more, once they mated as wolves. He'd never felt this way around a woman, this sense of completion, as if the man he wanted to be had finally come into existence because of her.

His parents had said he would know, but they'd always hoped he'd know with Lily. Thank goodness she'd understood even before he had that they weren't meant to be together. He loved her and would always need her friendship, but something about Annie was just . . . right. Such a simple concept, but so true.

She paused, one foot lifted, ears pricked forward as she gazed at him over her shoulder. They were close to the valley where most of the pack had their homes. Not far from Lily's, but he knew immediately why Annie had paused.

She'd only been home a few days after so long away. He knew her parents must be worried. *Do you need to let your parents know where you'll be tonight?*

I should. My father worries.

Would he stop worrying if you were my bonded mate?

She sat. *Alex?*

His heart twisted in his chest, as if it were growing too big to fit. So much emotion, and damn, but he actually loved the feeling, the sense that this was bigger than him.

Bigger than both of them. He'd never imagined himself saying those words, meaning them with every beat of his heart. When he spoke, it wasn't his conscious mind coming up with the words. It was something more. Something deeper. Something totally beyond his control. *I love you, Annie. I want you*

*for all time. I think I knew as soon as I saw you today. You are
so brave, so strong. You are the woman I want as my mate. The
one I want to bear my children. To love me, if you can, for all
time.*

She stared at him as if she'd never seen him before. Almost
as if she didn't know him. *You haven't seen me for six years.
How can you know?*

He had no idea, but he knew. There was no doubt in his
mind. *I've never felt this way. Not this soul-deep certainty that
you are mine. That we're meant to be together. You said you
loved me, Annie. Do you?*

I do.

*I won't pressure you. It doesn't have to be tonight, but I
don't want to wait. I want the link that allows us always to be
connected. I want you to know what's in my heart so there's no
doubt how I feel.*

He'd moved closer to her until their noses touched. Her
thoughts blossomed, stronger, even more intimate than before.
It's hard for me to accept, she said. *You've always been Lily's.*

*I've been Lily's friend, her lover, and her excuse, just as she's
been mine. As long as we've stayed together, we didn't have to
pretend with anyone else. I'm through pretending. Let your
parents know you're staying with me tonight. When you're
ready, we'll take that next step.*

*When I'm ready? How do I know when? I've always known
I loved you, but there was never a resolution to that love. I
never . . .*

Now you will. With me.

She was silent for what seemed like a very long time. He
didn't pry, didn't intrude on her conversation with her parents,
but when she turned to him, her beautiful eyes sparkled.

My father says as long as I'm with you, he's not worried.

Tinker said that? Martin McClintock, known to one and all
as Tinker, was big and scary and loved by everyone in the pack.

He was the one who generally kept the young men in line. A glance from Tinker was usually enough to settle any disagreement.

He'd saved Alex from himself more than once.

Yeah. He did. Pretty amazing, don't you think?

You have no idea. He'd been one of those young men always pushing the edge. There were times he was convinced his own father wanted to strangle him, but Alex had survived his teen years without becoming a statistic—much to everyone's surprise—and due in part to the mentoring he'd gotten from Annie's father.

Even more surprising had been his choice as the pack's liaison to the Flathead County sheriff's department, but he'd discovered a talent for working with people, for calming situations before they blew out of control.

Right now, he was the one on the edge of control. He wanted Annie now, wanted her as his mate. He didn't want to wait, but it appeared that she did.

So he'd wait.

Annie turned and raced down the hill toward Lily's cabin. He loved following her, watching her beautiful tail waving like a flag behind her. He filled his head with her scent, oblivious to everything around him. Only Annie existed. She was beautiful. She was perfect. She was everything he wanted—and she was his.

Without warning, something big and hard hit him from the side. Rolled him off his feet. He cried out a warning to Annie, but she was down with a massive wolf at her throat.

He sent out a cry for help, a cry to the first name that came to mind, even as he twisted frantically, trying to break the grip of the wolf that clamped down with sharp teeth and powerful jaws on the thick fur at his neck.

* * *

Lily preened like a cat, sitting on the floor as Sebastian knelt at her back and dried her with a big, fluffy towel. She wondered if she'd ever get enough of him. He'd made love to her in the oversized tub, again as they'd showered to rinse off the soap, and now he was erect again, his cock rising high against his belly. His body was so big and hard and powerful, yet his hands held her and dried her, as gently as if he handled a child.

She tilted her head back and looked at him upside down. His eyes really were teal blue, the color of a tropical lagoon. His irises were ringed in black, his eyes framed in long, thick black lashes. "You have gorgeous eyes."

"The better to see you with."

She laughed. "Old, old line. Were your mother's eyes that color?"

He leaned close and kissed the end of her nose. "No, her eyes were gold, like yours."

Even better. "Not gold. Amber. I bet she had amber-colored eyes. Typical of Chanku. Most of us have eyes that color."

He shook his head. "There's no proof she was Chanku. I know you think I might be, but there was nothing about her that fits any of the descriptions I've read. That thing about the libido? As far as I know, she had none. No interest in men. She never dated. I didn't know she'd actually been married to my father until I found the divorce papers."

"Did she ever talk about him?"

He shook his head. "No. She was afraid of him. She divorced him before I was born; didn't tell him she was pregnant. She changed her name and hid from him, kept my birth secret. I grew up in Hannibal, Missouri, a place she figured he'd never look for her. She never told me anything, only that my father was a dangerous man and she wanted to keep me safe. I was Sebastian Roberts, not Xenakis, though she did put his name on the birth certificate. That and the fact he was my father. Everything else was fictitious. My whole life was fiction."

How sad, she thought. Her own childhood had been so amazing. Filled with love, with minds totally open and honest to each other. "Was Roberts her real name?"

"No. I think she was Romanian. Her real surname was Lupei. Angela Lupei. I found it in her records. I knew her as Angie Roberts."

Lupei? That name sounded so familiar. She parted her lips to speak.

Alex's frantic cry slammed into her mind.

Lily! Help. We're being attacked!

"Something's after Alex and Annie! C'mon." Lily shoved to her feet, opened the sliding door to the deck, and shifted the minute she was outside. She could hear growling on the hill above and Annie's frightened yips. She linked to her dad, but he'd already shifted and was leaping from the far end of the deck even as she hit the thick grass beneath.

Energy around her shifted, and she knew Sebastian had called magic for his wolf and then Tinker came flying out of his house with Annie's mom Lisa right behind.

Others raced to join them, Annie's brothers, Ricky and Mike, Luc and Tia Stone—all the members of the pack who lived here in the valley coming from all directions; Stefan and Xandi charged off the deck together, and two of their healers, Adam and Liana, ran out of the woods, all of them headed toward the fight taking place on the low hill just above their valley.

Lily and Anton raced ahead of the pack, and it took them less than a minute to cross the meadow and reach the fight. A massive wolf had Annie cornered against a fallen pine, but he bled from a ragged gash across his muzzle and another across his throat.

Alex was bleeding from a wound to his neck, but the wolf he faced was favoring his front leg, and one ear was torn almost completely away. Lily sensed more strange wolves in the forest, but she couldn't be sure how many were out there or why they hadn't joined their packmates in the attack.

Anton reached the fight first, but the two rogue wolves must have realized they were outnumbered. Spinning away, they raced into the forest with Anton chasing.

Lily shifted and went straight to Annie, who'd collapsed in a heap and lay on the torn ground. Alex limped a few steps closer and stood there, breathing heavily, head down, blood running from the deep tear at the back of his neck. Stefan and Xandi arrived and paused to converse silently with their son. Then they spun away and followed Anton in pursuit of the rogues.

Adam and Liana, both healers, arrived together and shifted to help Annie and Alex. Annie's parents, Tinker and Lisa, skidded to a stop beside their daughter, but Adam already knelt at her head, his hands against her bloody shoulder.

Tinker and Lisa paced, both of them agitated and growling. Then Tinker's hackles went up, and his growl sounded like thunder as Sebastian raced into the meadow. Lily shook her head. "He's okay, Tink. He's with me."

Tinker's hackles went down, but he glared at Sebastian with his ears flat to his skull, wary of an unknown among the pack in a time of danger. Alex stood alone, panting, his head down, his wounds still bleeding. His thoughts were a cauldron of anger and fear, worry about Annie, and frustration that they should have been attacked here on private property.

Mostly, Lily sensed his anger at himself for failing to protect her.

Adam's mate Liana left Annie's side and took over with Alex, settling him with her hands, pushing him gently to the ground. He lay down, but his gaze never left Annie, and he stretched his muzzle across the torn grass as if trying to reach her. Lily glanced at Sebastian, who stood off to one side, still in wolf form watching the activity. "Adam and Liana are healers," she said to him. "They go inside and repair injuries at the cellular level."

Sebastian moved closer to Lily and sat beside her, but he remained alert, watching the woods. Guarding them. Lily felt warmth blossom in her chest. He had to be wondering how it was that Adam did his healing, sitting as he was, silently beside Annie's wolf, his hands pressed to her shoulders, his face blank of all expression. Sebastian didn't question anything. He followed Lily's lead and watched for danger.

Lily ran her fingers through Annie's thick pelt, searching for more injuries.

I'm okay. How is Alex?

"Good. You had me worried when I saw you go down. I'll check on Alex. Lie still and let Adam decide how okay you are, okay? Your mom and dad are here." Tinker sniffed his daughter's wounds while Lily moved aside and went to sit with Alex.

"What happened?" she asked him. "Where did they come from?"

No idea. Annie and I were heading down to your cottage when the two of them shot out of the woods on the right. There might be more. I sensed others holding back, but those two hit us without any warning at all. The big one bowled Annie over, and the other one got me by the neck. Annie's tough, though. And really fast. She got away from him and managed to do some damage.

"That she did." Lily smiled as she stroked Alex's shoulder. Liana's hands were pressed to either side of the gaping tear on his neck, holding the skin together as she worked from the inside to rebuild the torn flesh. Alex was so proud of Annie, he didn't even seem to notice his own injuries.

She sensed the change in energy as Sebastian shifted and sat beside her. "So this is your Alex," he said. He gently placed his hand on Alex's shoulder, as if to comfort him. "His aura is strong, even as an injured wolf. I can see why you love him."

She turned and studied Sebastian. There was no sense of jealousy, none of the typical guy reaction to the other man in a woman's life. "I do," she said. "I've loved Alex since we were children. Even when he's not all that lovable." The wolf growled and she laughed.

Be nice to me. I'm bleeding.

"Not anymore. Liana's got you just about put back together."

How's Annie? She says she's okay, but . . .

"She's going to be fine. I have a feeling though that her mom and dad might want to take her home with them tonight. You okay with that?"

No, but I can handle it. She just said the same thing. She feels badly about scaring them like this. I understand, even though I'd rather she stay with me.

"I bet. I'm guessing things went well tonight?"

Oh, yeah.

She chuckled. "I don't want you to be alone tonight. Do you mind if Sebastian and I stay with you?"

I'll be okay. But thanks. I don't want to mess up your date.

I don't think that's a problem. She glanced at Sebastian who followed their interchange with avid interest. What would he say if she asked him to stay with Alex? If she asked him to share their bed? For Chanku, it was nothing unusual, but what if he wasn't one of them? What if he was just what he said he was, a human with magical ability?

Sebastian? She narrowed her thoughts so that only he could read them. *I really don't want to leave Alex alone tonight. Do you mind if we stay with him?*

He glanced at Alex and then at Lily and slowly shook his

head. His hand still rested on Alex's shoulder. *Of course not. As long as he doesn't mind a strange man in his bed.*

She hadn't expected that. Not at all. But she smiled and leaned against his side, while her fingers tangled in Alex's fur and Liana finished putting the torn wolf back together.

12

Tinker shifted before the rest of the pack had returned and lifted Annie, still in wolf form, in his powerful arms. Lily had told him about Tinker, but Sebastian hadn't truly imagined the guy's massive size and amazing presence.

He was, without a doubt, the largest African American man he'd ever seen, and when he'd made that lightning fast shift from massive wolf to huge naked man, Sebastian had almost gasped aloud. Tinker's mate stayed in wolf form, but Sebastian caught her thoughts as she raced down the hill, that she was going home to make Annie's room ready.

Tinker cast a quick glance at Alex, but he didn't say a word, and Sebastian sensed Alex's dismay. Was it guilt over Annie's injuries? Did Tinker blame Alex? He hoped not. That didn't seem fair. He'd been the object of speculation and accusation often enough to know how painful it could be.

Liana sat back on her heels, and Alex blinked, shook his head, and slowly struggled to a sitting position. He leaned close to Liana and ran his tongue across her cheek. She laughed and batted him away.

"Thanks, but no thanks, Alex. Now take it easy. Don't overdo it, and you should feel fine tomorrow. Adam said Annie's going to need some rest, too. You know how it works—we can put stuff back together, but it needs time to settle and stick where we put it."

She kissed his nose, hugged Lily, and then turned to Sebastian and stuck out her hand. "I'm Liana. It's nice to meet you, Sebastian. Even though we're both starkers." She laughed, and it was such a wonderful sound he found himself grinning in response, not feeling quite as naked as he had. "We'll talk tomorrow, preferably with clothes on, but Adam is calling." She smiled, and suddenly he was staring at a beautiful gray wolf. Then she was gone, racing after her mate.

Sebastian watched her go before turning to Lily. Alex lay curled up beside her, still a wolf, but Lily was every inch a beautiful woman. A beautiful *naked* woman.

Trying not to laugh, Sebastian wrapped his fingers around the back of Lily's head and pulled her close for a kiss. "I think that's the first time I've ever been introduced to a naked woman before. Interesting, especially since I haven't got clothes on, either."

Lily kissed him quickly. "Get used to it. Unlike the werewolves of fiction, our clothing doesn't shift with us. We essentially ignore nudity, unless we really want to see it."

She raised an eyebrow and looked him over. "And I have to say, I love what I'm seeing."

"That works both ways. Are you ready to go back?"

"Not yet." Lily glanced toward the woods. "I want to give Alex a few more minutes to recover, and I'm waiting for the others to get back. I just heard from Dad. They lost the trail. It appears the rogue wolves must have gone into the caverns at some point. There are any number of tunnels connecting your father's property and ours. If they've learned the tunnel system in these mountains, it could be really bad. They're all connected, and it will make it almost impossible to guard against attack."

"I had no idea there were caverns around here."

"Their existence isn't well known, but we've used them for years, as kids to play in, as adults for safety. The whole pack once took refuge in them when a forest fire ripped through this valley and burned my parents' house to the ground. That was almost twenty-six years ago."

He didn't hear a sound, but before he could ask for details, the small hilltop was suddenly filled with wolves, slipping out of the forest like dark ghosts and gathering close around the three of them. Sebastian had no idea who they were, though he was almost certain the large black wolf in the lead was Lily's father. Another wolf, similar in markings to Alex, stood beside the black one, but all obviously deferred to the black wolf. Lily had referred to her father as their *über-alpha*.

The alpha shifted, as did the three wolves standing closest to him. Lily's mother and father and two people he assumed were Alex's parents quickly knelt beside Alex. Sebastian realized he still had his left hand on Alex's shoulder, but the wolf was asleep and he didn't want to disturb him. He left it there.

"Sebastian, you've met my parents, but these are Alex's. Stefan, Xandi, this is Sebastian Xenakis." She smiled at them. "He's with me. His father owns the property next to this one."

Stefan held out his hand, and Sebastian took it. He'd not seen Alex in his human form and wondered if he looked like his father. It was strange, realizing the people he was meeting were probably in their seventies or eighties. They all looked his age.

Keisha touched his shoulder. "This probably isn't what you imagined when you came to see our daughter. I'm sorry this happened. Especially to Alex and Annie." She glanced at the wolf. "Poor baby. Xandi? Do you need help getting him home?"

Before Alex's mother could speak, Sebastian interrupted. "Lily and I were planning to take him to Lily's cottage." He glanced at Lily, caught her smile, and relaxed. Even though they'd talked about it, he hadn't been entirely certain. "Liana said he's healed, but he needs to rest. I can carry him down."

"Good. That's good. We won't worry, then." Stefan glanced at Anton and nodded, and he wondered what Lily's father had said. It must have been all right, since the four of them stood and stepped away from Alex. Lily stood beside her father.

Xandi kissed Lily's cheek. "I want to talk to you tomorrow. What's going on between Alex and Annie?"

Lily flashed a big grin. "Excellent things. I'll let Alex tell you all about it."

Laughing, Stefan hugged Lily. "I'd rather hear it from you. He leaves out all the good stuff."

"Not this time." She glanced at Alex, who still appeared to be soundly asleep. "We'll make sure he's okay. If you need us, we'll be at the cottage."

Anton stared toward the forest and nodded. "Lily? I've asked Mei and Oliver to escort you back to your place. The wolves weren't alone. We picked up some human scent back there, too, though they might have shifted to escape. Until we know what the hell is going on, I think you should have a couple of guards along, at least until you reach your place. Just in case the rogues reappear. I doubt they'll bother you once you're home."

"Thanks, Dad. They'll definitely think twice about bothering us with those two for backup." The four parents shifted and headed down the hill with the rest of the pack following. Lily sat again and grinned at Alex. "They're gone. You can quit pretending and wake up now."

The wolf opened his eyes. He sat up, but swayed and quickly adjusted his feet to keep from falling. Lily grabbed his shoulder to steady him. "Blood loss," she said. "That was too damned close, Alex. Sebastian, he's awfully heavy. Are you sure you can carry him?"

"I think so." He glanced at the big wolf who glared at him as if he'd like to take a big bite.

Lily tapped the wolf on the nose. "Quit arguing, Alex. You're too weak to make it off the hill on your own, and I don't want to sit up here all night and wait on you to feel stronger."

The wolf sighed and slowly collapsed onto the trampled grass. Without another word, Sebastian slipped his arms beneath the huge creature and lifted him close against his chest before standing. Alex was heavy, but he didn't struggle. Just the opposite, in fact, as he settled close against Sebastian's chest and hooked his right front leg over his shoulder to hang on.

Slowly, picking his way along a well-worn trail in his bare feet, Sebastian followed Lily down to her cottage. He sensed the two who protected them, but never once saw the pair of wolves.

It wasn't until they reached Lily's tiny cottage, tucked in beneath a huge cedar, that he realized they hadn't been flanked by wolves at all.

A beautiful pair of snow leopards drifted out of the thick undergrowth, stopped to take a look at Alex, sniffed Sebastian's legs, and then silently headed toward the main house.

"Mei and Oliver," Lily said. "Beautiful, aren't they?"

Stunned, Sebastian stared after the two until they disappeared in the shadows.

Sebastian carefully laid the wolf on the big bed while Lily dug through the closet. A moment later she emerged with a pair of loose shorts for Sebastian to wear and a teal blue sarong for herself. Watching Lily as she checked over Alex's injury, he slipped into the shorts, though he realized he'd not been at all uncomfortable with his nudity.

That was something new. Something he needed to think about.

Lily ran her fingers through the wolf's bloodstained coat,

and Alex opened his eyes. "I know you're not that badly hurt, at least not anymore, so when you shift, do it outside, okay? I don't want blood flaking all over the bed."

Grumbling, the wolf looked over the edge of the bed and then made sad eyes at Sebastian. No words were necessary. Sebastian lifted the big animal to the floor and opened the front door of the cottage. Alex walked slowly outside and down the steps to a large tree, lifted his leg, and peed. Then he walked back to the house, stood on the grass just beyond the front porch, and shifted. Tall and beautifully naked, he stalked back inside the house and glared at Lily.

"There. Are you happy?"

"Deliriously so." She kissed him and then looped her hand through Sebastian's elbow. "Where are your manners, Alex? The least you can do is say thank you. Sebastian and I were just getting to the good part when we had to break it up to go rescue you and your ladylove. And then he carried your sorry ass all the way down the hill."

Alex grumbled at her, but he turned to Sebastian and held out his hand. "She's right, I guess." He glared at Lily. "I hate it when you're right. You were right about Annie, too." Then he smiled at Sebastian as they shook hands. "My apologies, and my thanks. I really do appreciate everything you've done, but if I can't pick on Lily, my life's incomplete."

"No wonder you two aren't mated." Sebastian grinned, shot a quick glance at Lily, and then laughed at Alex. "It would be incest. You two bicker like you're brother and sister."

Lily drawled, "Well, not entirely," and Alex just laughed. She tossed a pair of pants at him. He caught them against his chest, shook them out, and put them on.

"Alex and I were born just three weeks apart. We shared a crib as babies and grew up together, but I was always well aware he wasn't a blood relation." She jabbed him with her elbow. "We were each other's first sexual partners."

"Long before our parents had a clue," Alex added. "In fact, they still don't know when we started—quite literally—screwing around, but we were . . . what's the word, Lil?"

"Precocious. Highly precocious. Unfortunately, our parents have been lovers for years, and expected us to take our relationship to the next level and make it a permanent bond."

"But we don't love each other like that," Alex added. "Not that I don't love Lily, because I do and I always will, even when I want to strangle her."

"Or vice versa," she added.

While Alex continued as if she hadn't interrupted, "But the dynamic between us wouldn't make for a good mating bond. We'd end up hating each other."

"Or dead," Lily said. "It would never work, which is why I'm so glad you've found Annie. You and I are not meant to be mates."

"You have no idea how thankful I am for that." Sebastian's dry comment had Lily giggling, so he wrapped an arm around her and planted a big kiss on her very kissable mouth. He knew he was a bit too obvious and it probably wasn't necessary, but he had to stake his claim, needed to tell Alex in the best way he knew how that Lily was most definitely his.

Obviously agreeing, she turned in his embrace, wrapped her arms around his neck, and held him close, kissing him back with all the enthusiasm he could have wished for.

Alex cleared his throat. "Uh, wounded guy here? You're not supposed to be ignoring me."

Lily broke the kiss and stared over her shoulder. "That's because you smell like a rank combination of wolf and just-got-laid male. Go take a shower. Then we'll pay attention."

Grumbling, Alex headed into the bathroom. Lily took Sebastian's hand and led him out on the deck. They sat close beside one another on the top step. Lily leaned against his side while he wrapped his arm around her shoulders. "Thank you," she said. "I really do appreciate your carting his ornery carcass off the hill."

"Any time. I'm just glad it wasn't you who was injured. Alex and Annie were pretty torn up."

"They'll be fine. Thankfully we had Liana and Adam close by." She sighed, still playing with his fingers. "Sebastian, I'm not sure how much you know about us, though you've probably figured out that we are extremely open, sexually. Are you okay, sharing a bed with Alex and me? Sharing sex with the two of us? Because that's where tonight is heading. He's hurting, and he's going to be missing Annie something fierce. We've all been through a hugely emotional evening, and for Chanku, anything like that really ramps up the libido."

Sebastian took a deep breath, let it out, and stared into the dark sky. "I don't know." He laughed softly, embarrassed by the wealth of feelings storming through him when he thought of sex with Alex. "There's one way to find out. I've never been with a man. Never even thought of it before. Your dad talked about that tonight, about the open sexuality of your kind."

He shrugged. Maybe they were his kind, too. Hard to know. He'd only had the one capsule, but Anton seemed to think that since he'd been shifting by magical means, it might only take a few days for his Chanku nature to appear.

"How do you feel about it?"

Her eyes were dark pools, but her aura glowed like a multicolored halo around her, so many different splashes of color she reminded him of the aurora borealis. She was all light and magic, and her aura excited him, but everything about Lily Cheval was exciting. "If you're there," he said, "I imagine I'll feel perfectly fine about anything."

Her smile lit her entire face. "Good. And here's something else for you to think about, what Dad wanted me to tell you."

"About your magic?"

She nodded. "About where we find the energy to power our

magic. It's such a simple thing, really. It's all about love. Love and the sexual energy we produce. Years ago, when my father and Stefan were in the very early days of building the pack, they discovered that sexual energy could give my dad almost unlimited magical power. One of our pack was kidnapped, and with the combined energy from the pack members gathered here in Montana, Dad was able to possess a raven on the east coast and use the bird to find the missing packmate."

He tried to imagine that kind of power, but it was totally beyond him. "That's really hard to believe." He looked into her sparkling eyes and believed. "You've learned to share energy?"

She nodded. "We're all telepathic, and it's a simple thing to create the energy, either through fantasy or actual sex, and then share it. Dad takes it into himself and then works it."

"It's that simple?"

"Yeah, though not without risk. Years ago, when I was just a toddler, there was a plot against the president . . ."

"Of the United States?"

She laughed. "That's the one, and the entire pack was supposed to share energy at precisely the same time so that Dad would have the power to create a blackout in San Francisco where the president was scheduled to speak. At the time, the packs were scattered all around the country, but they all worked really hard at building up as much as they could." She laughed. "We're really good at producing vast amounts of sexual energy."

"And it worked?"

"Oh, yeah. Much too well. Dad blew out power over the entire Bay Area, but the energy surge left his brain fried for weeks. He couldn't connect telepathically with anyone, couldn't concentrate or carry on a conversation. It was really horrible. The president was saved, but we were sure we'd lost my father. Personally, I thought it was a crappy trade-off."

"What happened next?" He ran his fingers through her hair.

It was so beautiful, gleaming the color of dark copper beneath the low porch light, soft as silk falling in long waves and curls.

"I don't remember the details, but I somehow knew that part of my dad's consciousness had essentially gone into hiding to escape the blast of power. I found it and put it back."

"You what?" He really couldn't stop laughing. "How?"

She actually looked embarrassed. "I recognized part of Dad was in my uncle AJ. I was about nineteen months old, barely talking, and I guess I kept jabbering about 'Dada's smile.' "

"His smile?"

Shrugging, she picked up his hand again and played with his fingers. "That's what I called it, the part of him I loved so much. It was hiding out in AJ's brain. I somehow knew how to take it from AJ and return it to my father."

"Wow. Precocious doesn't even come close, does it?"

Shaking her head, she gazed across the dark meadow. "I've been blessed by our goddess in so many ways." She sighed, and then as she so often did, changed the subject. "Did you know that Adam's mate, Liana, the one who helped Alex tonight, was once our goddess? I mean, she's thousands of years old, but she screwed up and got kicked off the astral, and Eve, who was Adam's first bonded mate, took over Liana's job. What's cool is they're both happy with the way things turned out. Personally, if I'd been Eve I would have been pissed, ending up dead before my time because of Liana's screwup, but she's much nicer than I am. Definitely goddess material."

He knew he was looking at her like she had two heads, but that was just a little over the top. "I think that's a bit too much for tonight. It makes my head hurt." He laughed and hugged her close. "I do like the idea of using love and sexual energy to power magic, though." He affected a smarmy voice and said, "Blood sacrifices are just so messy."

Lily snorted. Then she clasped both his hands and tugged

until he looked into her beautiful eyes. He saw his reflection in their amber depths, and suddenly, it was as if his life opened up. Things he'd never thought of before because they'd brought him nothing but pain, but now, looking into Lily's eyes, he knew exactly how terribly lost he'd been. He just hadn't understood how lost. Not until Lily found him.

She cupped his cheek in her palm, and her look was so direct, so honest, it felt as if she sliced him open with her gaze, as if she spread his life out in front of her for observation.

"Sebastian, something my father said to me a long time ago finally makes perfect sense. The power of blood magic, power that comes from the sacrifice of a living thing, is finite. Once the life is gone and the power is used up, it's gone forever. Along with an innocent life.

"Not so with magic powered by love. Love endures. It grows stronger with time, and its power is never ending. Once you learn to work magic with love behind it, you'll discover there's no limit to what you can do. Love is infinite. You don't need to control it. You merely accept its strength, use it for good, and it will never fail you."

Caught in her words, her honesty, and her gentle touch, he slowly became aware of Alex moving around inside, knew he had to get up, had to move away from Lily before he did something stupid. Why did her words make him want to weep? Why did it feel as if he'd just heard an epiphany he'd needed his entire life?

He stood and tugged. Lily rose gracefully before him, and he knew he couldn't let the moment pass. Cupping her face in his hands, he lightly kissed her lips. "I promise you, I will never fail you, Lily Cheval. I love you, and that is my vow. I will not fail you."

She blinked, but tears spilled from the corners of her eyes. Her lips parted, and he waited to see what she would say. She didn't speak the words. No, they were much more intimate. Inside his head, winding around his heart.

I love you, Sebastian Xenakis. I don't know how it happened so fast, but it's real and I can't walk away. I don't want to walk away. I'd rather jump right into the middle of it.

"Works for me," he said. Then he took her hand and led her back inside the cabin. Back to Alex and the night awaiting them.

Alex was sitting at the kitchen table with a cold beer and a roasted deli chicken in front of him. He looked up. "I missed dinner," he said. Then he took another bite.

"So did I." Sebastian sat across from him and pulled a leg off the bird. "Lily?"

Laughing, she shook her head and wandered over to the cupboard. "Cognac or cold beer?"

"That's quite a selection. What are you having?"

"A glass of white wine, but Alex tells me that's not manly."

Sebastian shrugged. "Manly enough for me." He raised an eyebrow at Alex. "I don't doubt my masculinity, but you never know about some guys."

Lily patted Alex on the head. He rolled his eyes and continued eating. Sebastian noticed a red slash across his bare shoulders. "Wow . . . that's what Liana healed?"

Alex nodded. "Yeah. It's still sore, but it feels more like bruising. That wolf was a big sucker, and way too strong." He glanced toward Lily, who was setting a glass of white wine in front of Sebastian. "Any idea who the hell those bastards were? I've never seen wolves that big, or that ferocious. Even Tinker's smaller than the one that went after Annie."

Lily sat next to Sebastian. "You want to tell him what we think is going on?"

"Yeah." He took a swallow of the wine first. "Lily said you're aware of the experiments the military did, trying to find

Chanku among the troops to train as super warriors? She said no one knows how many were found or whatever became of them because the program got canceled shortly after it started."

"We think we know where at least six of them are," Lily added. She gazed at Sebastian. "They're bodyguards for Sebastian's father. Sebastian recognized two of them as the ones that attacked us the other night. The same wolves whose scent I recognized from the site of that murder in Golden Gate Park."

"Holy shit." Alex's gaze flashed from Lily to Sebastian and back to Lily. "You're sure?"

She nodded. "Have there been any more murders since this morning?"

"Not that I know of, but I've been with Annie since this afternoon. But why? What purpose would Aldo Xenakis have for harboring killers?"

Sebastian glanced at Lily. "Maybe because my father is a powerful wizard, one who pursues dark magic. Blood magic. I think he's using the life force of the young women to give him power for whatever magic he's doing."

Frowning, Alex stared for a long moment at Sebastian, before letting out a pent-up breath. "That's sick. Really sick. But to what end? What kind of spell would require the deaths of so many young women? And rape? How do the rapes fit in? What is he hoping to gain by all of this?"

"I don't know." Sebastian squeezed Lily's hand. "He wanted me to get to know Lily, though I'm not sure why. When I told him I'd lost it when she and I were running on Mount Tam and had almost raped her, he seemed disappointed, as if my not hurting her went against his plans."

Lily stared at him. "You didn't tell me that."

"I know. I told your father about it, and I'm sorry but I didn't know how to say anything to you. It's just so damned wrong. At first I wanted to think I was misinterpreting what he said. He's my father." He shrugged and looked away. "It was really hard to admit he's a murderer, but I'm convinced he's got some kind of plan that includes you and me. I just don't know what it is. The man's dangerous. He's got to be stopped."

"Where is he? Here or in San Francisco?" Alex pushed the half-eaten plate of chicken aside.

"He was in San Francisco when I left, but if his wolves are here, he could have followed me. Unless he's got more of them up here that I don't know about."

"Does he know you came to Montana?"

Alex's questions reminded him of a cop show, only he was the suspect being questioned. "I don't know. I didn't hide my trail, if that's what you mean, but I didn't leave him a note, either. It was a spur of the moment decision. I took a cab to the airport and caught the first plane up here that had a vacant seat."

"If he had you followed, he could know you're here, which means that attack on Annie and me could have been aimed at you and Lily."

Sebastian frowned. "Why would you think that?"

"Look at us, you and me. We're like my dad and Anton. People always think they're brothers, even though they're not related. You and I are both tall and lean, both have dark hair. Even similar features. Someone doesn't know either of us, they could get us confused. Hell, we look enough alike we could be related. Same with the girls. Lily and Annie are dark skinned, obviously mixed race. Annie's smaller and she's got short hair, but if they were looking for a tall, dark-haired guy and a mixed-race woman, she and I could be you and Lily."

"But why would my father want to kill us? He could have done that at any time. Hell, I live with the man, here and in San Francisco. He's had plenty of opportunities."

"I don't think he wants to kill you. I imagine he wants to capture you. Probably wants both of you to power some spell he's got planned. Those wolves that attacked us today could easily have killed Annie and me without any help at all, but they didn't go for the kill, and they weren't alone. I'm positive there were more in the woods, waiting. I heard Anton say he recognized human scent. So maybe they hadn't shifted. Maybe they were ready with restraints, but help showed up too quickly and they bailed."

"That's putting a whole new spin on things."

Lily yawned. "It is, and like you said earlier, Sebastian, it's making my head hurt." She stood and planted both hands on the table. "Gentlemen. I am exhausted. It has been a very long, emotionally trying day, and I am going to bed. You may join me, or you can stay here and gorge yourselves on whatever Mom left in the fridge and talk rings around each other until morning."

She kissed Alex and then planted a long, lazy one on Sebastian. He glanced at Alex, who merely shrugged.

"Your loss, boys." Lily headed for the bedroom.

Alex grinned at Sebastian and then batted his eyelashes. "Actually, before we go in and fuck, I'd really prefer to get to know you better."

Laughing, Sebastian grabbed the wine bottle and refilled his glass. "I agree. I'm not that kind of guy. Besides, I want to hear more about Lily." He glanced toward the doorway. "She's absolutely amazing. I've never felt like this about any woman before, and I have a feeling that's not going to change."

Alex smiled at him and laughed softly. "It's not. And believe it or not, I know how you feel about her. Part of me is jealous as hell that the two of you fit so well because I always wanted that with Lily, but I didn't really understand what she and I lacked until Annie came back into my life."

"Lily truly loves you."

Alex cocked an eyebrow. "And that doesn't bother you?"

Sebastian laughed. "Hell no, because as much as she loves you, half the time she's thinking about killing you."

"Unfortunately, you're right." Alex got up and grabbed another beer. "Let's go outside. The cottage is small, and I don't want to keep her awake. She's had a damned long day."

"Me too." Sebastian grabbed the wine bottle and his glass. "But I'm too keyed up to sleep."

"Who's talking about sleep?" Alex grinned as he opened the door. The two of them walked out on the deck, but Alex continued on down the steps, into the darkness.

The night didn't seem as dark as it usually was. Could Anton's pills already be working? No way. Not this soon. Sebastian followed Alex along a stone path that led to a small pond in the meadow. Alex took a seat on a stone bench and patted the spot beside him. Sebastian sat.

"So Anton's given you the first of the nutrients. Notice anything yet?"

Sebastian glanced about, but dark was dark. "What's to notice? It's only been a few hours. Did you ever take them?"

"Didn't have to." Alex took a swallow of his beer. "I was born to Chanku parents, and since my mother took them during her pregnancy, I was fully Chanku at birth. I've never needed them, though on occasion my body will crave the grasses and I find myself nibbling on them. Keisha, Lily's mom, is a landscape architect, which explains the gorgeous gardens here, but she's got the Tibetan grasses scattered all over the property."

"You'll have to show me which ones."

"That's the odd thing." Alex's teeth glinted in the darkness. "If you're Chanku, you'll recognize them. It's like our bodies are geared to know what they are and how much we need to get the full benefit."

"I'll have to remember that." All this talk of grasses, and yet Sebastian wasn't thinking of them at all. He was thinking of Alex close beside him, the way his bare chest was so finely cut, his sharply defined muscles a pattern of dark and light.

He'd never been so aware of a man before.

So aware, or so curious. And for some reason, the fact that Lily loved this man, that she and Alex had made love throughout their lives, made Alex even more attractive to him.

He stared at the empty wineglass in his hand.

"More?" Alex held the bottle.

Sebastian shook his head. "No. I don't think so. I've had two glasses; not enough to feel it." He raised his head and stared into Alex's amber eyes. "I know what you and I are going to do, and I don't want to blame it on the wine. I don't want to dull the experience." He glanced away, embarrassed.

"Look at me, Sebastian."

He slowly turned at Alex's soft command. "Why?"

"Because you're a pretty amazing guy. I don't want you to think you can't look me in the eye. You're too good a man to look away. It's a wolf thing."

"Shit, Alex. How can you say that? My father may be a murderer, he may be trying to use me to get at your people. How can you stand to be near me?"

"You're obviously not your father. Damn it, Sebastian, even in the very short time I've known you, I can tell that. You know nothing of our kind beyond what you've learned from Lily. Only what the media says and what you've heard from your father, who is obviously a bigot. You don't know if you're one of us or not, but you've already aligned yourself with the pack. You put yourself in danger to protect the pack. That takes courage. I admire courage. It's a rare quality in this day and age. Besides, for all you know, we're your people, too."

"What am I, Alex? Am I Chanku? Am I one of you, or just a half-baked mage who's at risk of being seduced by dark magic? Believe me, the lure of dark power is strong. I see my father do things, and I absolutely lust for that kind of power. What if I can't fight it? What if it takes me?"

"It won't."

"How do you know?"

Alex smiled and put his hands on Sebastian's shoulders. "Because Lily and I won't let it. We've got your back, Sebastian. I think you're one of us. Even if you're not, you're definitely worth saving."

His throat clogged with tears, and it was hard to catch his breath. "How can you say that?"

Alex grabbed Sebastian's hand and pressed his palm against his own chest, just over his heart. Sebastian's fingers spread out over Alex's hot skin, absorbing the feel of him, the solid beat of his heart and the soft tickle from the dusting of dark hair sliding between his fingers.

He didn't breathe. He wasn't even certain he could, but Alex held his hand there, tight up against warm, male flesh, and he gazed steadily into Sebastian's eyes. "Because I feel you here, Sebastian. Inside, where it counts. Because Lily loves you, and she could never love any man less than her father. Just keep taking the capsules. Trust me. The man I see in you is every bit Anton Cheval's equal."

13
─────────

The night was perfectly still, the air cool but not yet cold. Not a breath of air, not a sound. No owls or frogs, bats, or even the ever present coyotes. Even the crickets seemed to have toned down their clamor—either that, or he was so totally caught up in the spell that was Alex Aragat, nothing else registered.

Sebastian curled his fingers against Alex's chest and struggled for control, but there was none to be found. He struggled to breathe, and it felt as if huge, jagged splinters tore at his lungs. Something clogged his throat and burned his sinuses, and unexpected tears rolled silently from beneath closed eyelids. The first ragged sob tore out of his chest, a sound so alien to him, he wasn't certain at first what it was.

It was followed by another, and yet another, and then Alex pulled Sebastian close and wrapped strong, loving arms around him. That offer of comfort, that freely given masculine strength was all it took. Sebastian gave in to the overwhelming rush of pain and grief, to the demons battering at his soul.

He'd not cried for as long as he could remember. Not when his mother died, not even on the dark day he'd buried her in that small cemetery on the outskirts of Hannibal, Missouri, but he cried now as a lifetime of grief overfilled his heart and soul.

He cried, and it was ugly and embarrassing because he had no control over these foreign emotions. How did a guy deal with something he didn't understand? But he remembered standing there at his mother's grave, realizing he was totally alone, knowing he would search for the father his mother had risked everything to be free of. Determination had kept his tears away.

She hadn't understood how much he'd hoped to find family, a place where he might finally belong. He should have listened to her. Should never have gone looking for a man without a soul.

Without an aura.

Now Alex's words, Anton Cheval's acceptance, Lily's love. This was the family he'd always wanted. This was what called to him, what he'd yearned for.

What he wanted more than anything he'd ever wanted before. Wanted, but couldn't have. He wasn't worthy and he didn't deserve it. He was the son of a killer. His father's blood ran in his veins. His father's magic was his magic. He could never be what Lily needed, what Anton wanted. What Alex thought he was. His failure poured out of him, bathing him in horrible, unendurable grief. There was no end to it and he couldn't stop himself.

Then Alex whispered something. Words of comfort, soft, meaningless words that somehow did it for him. Comforted him, helped him find the balance and the strength to slowly pull himself together without feeling like a fool.

He was almost forty years old—a man grown, and yet his emotions had left him feeling like a lost boy, totally wiped out. When Alex stood, grabbed his hand, and tugged, Sebastian didn't question him. He merely followed blindly, clutching Alex's hand as if it were his lifeline. He stumbled on the bottom step to the cottage, grabbed the railing for support, and wondered how they'd gotten here so quickly.

The kitchen first, where Alex handed him a clean, damp towel so he could wipe his face and regain at least a bit of composure. Then Alex led him to the bedroom and pulled back the covers as if Sebastian were still a child, and like a child, he took off his cotton shorts and crawled into the big bed without a word.

Lily rolled over, and he sensed her concern, but she made room for him without saying a word. He lay down beside her, inhaling her scent, breathing in the sense of peace he felt when she was near.

Sebastian figured Alex would get into bed on Lily's other side, but he scooted in close behind Sebastian and threw an arm over him, holding him close, breathing deeply, slowly. Lily snuggled against his chest. Alex had his back.

So many emotions, pouring through him, almost strangling him until he felt Lily relax in sleep, until Alex ran his hand gently over Sebastian's hip and across his groin before finally wrapping his fingers around his flaccid cock.

He stayed soft, too enervated from all the emotion to feel any arousal, no matter how arousing the touch. He felt Alex rise against him, the gentle pressure of his semierect penis settling into the valley between Sebastian's buttocks. Vaguely, as if he thought of himself from afar, he wondered what was coming next.

But nothing happened. Alex merely turned a bit as if finding a more comfortable position. His fingers stayed where they were, holding Sebastian in a gentle caress. Sebastian thought about the way Alex's hand felt holding his cock and decided it felt right. Lily's breath tickled his chest, and he seemed to have his tears under control.

It was all good, for now. That's all that mattered, and it was the last thing he knew before drifting off to sleep.

* * *

Sebastian came out of a deep, sound sleep as Alex crawled quietly out of bed and headed down the hall in the direction of the bathroom. Lily snuggled against his chest, all warm woman and tangled hair, but he was awake now and nature called.

Still drowsy and dopey with sleep, Sebastian finally extricated himself from Lily's arms and headed for the bathroom. He passed Alex going back to bed and grunted as they stumbled past one another. Alex was still half asleep and didn't reply.

It didn't really matter. What mattered was the sense of contentment, the knowledge he wasn't alone. Whether he and Alex ever had sex or not wasn't what counted. What counted was the fact that Alex had been there for him when he'd needed a friend.

He'd never had a friend he could count on. Not one who would hold him when he needed holding, tease him when he needed to laugh. It was early—still dark out—and his mind wasn't all that clear, but the sense he was no longer alone filled his heart and mind with peace unlike anything he'd ever known.

When Sebastian got back to the bed, Alex was lying next to Lily and had her tucked close against his chest, probably the way they'd spent a lot of their nights. He was already asleep.

Sebastian crawled in behind Alex. It was cold this early in the morning, and Alex was warm. Sebastian snuggled up close behind him, wrapped an arm around Alex's waist, and drifted, not quite awake, not really asleep.

His thoughts drifted as well, and he thought of how he'd fallen apart the night before, how Alex hadn't said a word but had just let him get it out. He'd figured he'd wake up with at least a headache, but he actually felt pretty good, considering.

That was something a lot of friends might not have done for a guy. So what did that make Alex? He'd have to think about that.

He stroked Alex's flank, running his hands along his muscular thigh, down his leg. Arousal was more a simmering heat than full blown desire, though he had to admit it was pretty arousing to be pressed up against Alex's back with his cock riding in the crease between his buttocks.

Just the way Alex had been when he'd drifted off last night. Sebastian's hand brushed against what had to be morning wood, but it was right there, practically begging for attention, so he wrapped his fingers around the thick, hot length and slowly stroked Alex from base to tip and back again.

Alex moaned, a soft, sleepy sound that made Sebastian smile. He kissed his shoulder and then trailed small kisses along the rapidly healing injury that crossed Alex's neck and shoulders.

He almost stopped when he realized he was kissing a man. Then he thought about it—how it made him feel—and kept kissing.

So amazing. He'd never known any Chanku before Lily, but they were truly fascinating creatures. The healing itself was unreal, but so was that impossible life span. He wondered at the possibilities.

What if Alex was right? If Lily and Anton knew what they were talking about, and he really was Chanku? The question floated away as Alex pressed back against him, against Sebastian's rigid cock, and he tightened his grip around Alex.

Lube. Top drawer. Table beside the bed.

Obviously Alex was more awake than Sebastian had realized. He thought of what Alex offered. His cock was suddenly hard and goose bumps covered his skin. *You're sure?*

Soft laughter filled Sebastian's head. *Of course I'm sure. I do this all the time. The question is, are you sure?*

Part of me certainly is. He thrust his hips, pressing harder against Alex's ass.

Lube. Now.

I really don't want to let go. He stroked Alex's cock. Up, down, and up again to sweep his palm over the broad crown. It was damp, already slick with pre-cum.

I don't want you to let go, either, but ya gotta do it if you're gonna do it. You're sure as hell not getting in without it. Alex projected laughter, and the sound sort of bounced around inside Sebastian's head.

He let go and rolled over, found the drawer, slipped it open, and the lube was right where Alex said it would be. He rolled back and covered his fingertips with a thick dollop of gel.

Alex lay on his belly with his face turned toward Lily.

Sebastian shoved the covers down and knelt beside Alex. For a long time he just stared at Alex's butt and thought about what they were going to do, and the oddest thing was, the longer he stared, the hornier he got. His cock had been hard, but now it was rising up against his belly.

He'd never touched a guy's butt before, not with the intent of doing more than just a slap on the ass during sports. He rubbed his left hand over the smooth globes, trailing a line from the lower part of Alex's back to the dimple just above the cleft between his cheeks.

Alex pressed his hips against the bed and groaned. Just a low, soft sound, but one that registered as pure need. Sebastian ran his fingers down the warm cleft, pausing just over his sphincter and rubbing soft little circles around Alex's puckered anal ring. He tried to visualize shoving his cock in that tiny opening, and decided he'd rather do the shoving than have Alex trying it on him.

The gel had warmed on his fingers, so he parted Alex's cheeks and wiped it off against his anus. Obviously, there was more to do, though he wasn't sure. He felt stupid asking, but he figured that any guy who could hold another guy—a perfectly strange other guy—while he cried like a freaking baby, probably wouldn't mind answering intimate questions.

"What now?" He kept rubbing over that puckered ring, and he could have sworn it felt softer.

Stretch it. One finger, then two, then three. Slow is best. It doesn't hurt that way.

That made sense. He pressed with one fingertip, and the gel eased his way enough that his finger slipped right through. Alex's inner muscles tightened around his finger, and the visual of those same muscles around his cock added another level of arousal. He wasn't sure how deep to press, but since his cock would go in a good eight or nine inches, he pressed all the way to his knuckle.

Alex pushed back, so he added another finger, scissoring them back and forth, stretching the way Alex had told him to. Then a third, and again he felt the tight clench of muscle around his fingers.

His cock jerked and he got even harder, so he slipped his fingers out of Alex and lifted him up on his knees, rubbed more of the gel over the crown of his cock, and pressed against that fluttering little ring, which, of course, had closed right up again.

His hand was still slick from the gel, so he spread what was left along his shaft, lined himself up with his target, and slowly pushed forward.

It wasn't all that easy, not with Alex's involuntary tightening, but then Alex took a deep breath, pushed back, and relaxed, and Sebastian watched as the tip of his cock seemed to reshape and squeeze down from the pressure of his thrust against Alex's butt, until it somehow fit through that little opening.

Fascinated, he watched the way the puckered ring of muscle stretched, gave way, and then tightened and wrapped around his shaft, just behind the crown. He kept pushing and then resting, pushing and resting until he was all the way in.

Alex let out a deep breath as Sebastian sucked one in, and it seemed to work that way as he pushed forward and Alex pressed back, breathing in, breathing out until they'd found a perfect rhythm. So caught up in the logistics of trying something for the first time, Sebastian didn't really think about the fact he was fucking a guy.

No, that barely entered the equation. He thought more about how fantastic it felt. How unexpected the pleasure. The channel he filled was hot and slick, tighter than a woman's vagina, but it rippled and pulsed along his cock, clinging as he pressed forward. Besides, this wasn't just any guy. This was Alex, the man Lily loved, the one who'd said he wanted to get to know Sebastian before they had sex.

He probably hadn't expected Sebastian to cry all over him, but now as the power of their budding friendship took on an entirely new focus, as Sebastian realized that yes, he did like this, and it wasn't at all awkward or uncomfortable—though he couldn't really say much for what Alex was feeling—he began to accept that maybe he did belong with these people.

That just maybe, he was Chanku. Part of an amazing family of fascinating creatures.

Maybe he really was part of the pack.

Lily wasn't certain what woke her, whether it was the slow and steady rocking as the mattress dipped and swayed beneath two men caught in the bliss of morning sex, or maybe it was the thick wash of pheromones that had her coming awake with her senses twitching and her fingers between her legs, slowly stroking herself to orgasm.

Whatever the reason, she opened her eyes to the amazing sight of Sebastian kneeling behind Alex and slowly but methodically screwing him senseless.

Alex had his face turned toward her, but his eyes were closed and his face twisted in a rictus of such supreme pleasure that he was almost painful to watch.

She knew Sebastian hadn't done this before, but she never would have guessed by watching him. He topped Alex as if he'd fucked guys for years, the muscles in his taut buttocks and powerful thighs easing and contracting with each deep thrust, his right hand planted possessively on Alex's hip.

She glanced lower and watched, mesmerized as Sebastian slowly stroked Alex's thick cock with his left hand. Then she turned and realized she was staring directly into Alex's wide open eyes.

Hey, guy. She brushed the hair out of his eyes. *You okay? You usually top. This can't be easy for you.*

It's all good. So's your man. He's a good guy, Lil.

Thank you. I think so, too. She motioned to Alex to come up on his knees. When he did, she slipped beneath him, brushed Sebastian's hand out of the way, and tongued the bead of creamy fluid from the tip of Alex's cock, laughing when his entire shaft twitched in reaction.

Then she opened her mouth and swallowed him down, taking him fully into her mouth. With a little adjustment, Alex managed to get her aligned beneath him, and she felt the first bold strokes of his tongue, separating her labia and dipping into her sex.

She wondered if Sebastian was even aware she'd joined them. When she'd looked, his eyes were closed, his focus entirely contained in the moment. In Alex.

Smiling around her mouthful, she slipped both hands between Alex's legs and, without warning, cupped Sebastian's sac in her palms.

What the fuck? Lily? He jerked hard, driving forcefully into Alex, who groaned against her clit and licked harder. Deeper. Faster.

Yep. Just me, sweetie.

Sebastian groaned. Lily lightly squeezed him again and then grabbed Alex's sac in one hand while holding Sebastian's with the other. There was something almost mystical about filling her hands with their testicles, cupping the solid orbs, holding them close against one another so that she knew Alex could feel Sebastian, while Sebastian had to be even more aware of Alex.

She opened her thoughts, not certain what to expect, but what she found left her stunned. Alex, reveling in Sebastian's mastery, in the fact that he'd taken control and yet was fulfilling every desire Alex had.

And Sebastian, so many things swirling through his mind. Accepting he might have found the home he'd always wanted, the family he'd never had. Accepting as well, Lily's brilliant mind and alpha spirit. Acknowledging her father as a man of honor and integrity, one he could admire while breaking away entirely from the biological donor who had done no more than offer up sperm to create a life.

Whatever the dark nature that was Aldo Xenakis, Sebastian swore to fight it. If he was Chanku, he owed his heritage to his mother.

He owed his father nothing. Not anymore.

Hearing this, Lily wanted to cheer. Instead, she loved Alex with her mouth and hands, loved Sebastian with her heart and soul, opening her mind to both men, linking with them in the way of their kind, sharing the sensations, the very sense of what both Alex and Sebastian meant to her.

And in turn, she felt their love, the wonderful open link that united them. And then, the only thing missing, the one part that would make them whole, opened the door to the cottage, walked straight through the front room, and into Lily's bedroom.

Annie stood in the doorway and watched the three of them in the dusky morning light, their bodies all tangled in the bedding, the air redolent with the rich wash of pheromones and sex, and thought seriously about strangling her father.

Tinker was going to have to get used to the idea that his little girl was all grown up, that she happened to be an adult and she didn't need him manhandling her to keep her away from the man she loved.

If he'd let her come with Alex last night the way she'd wanted, she'd be right in the middle of what looked like an absolutely delicious time. Instead, he'd insisted she needed to be with her parents. Which meant that, as always, she stood on the outside, a serious victim of wanting what she couldn't have.

You can have it, Annie. Alex doesn't even know you're here. Take off your clothes and join us. I'll move over and make room. You can surprise him. He misses you so badly!

Really? She was already slipping out of her pants and ripping her shirt over her head. The cuts and bruises from last night's battle had already faded, and aside from a few sore spots, she felt as good as new.

Both men jerked in surprise, losing their rhythm as Lily slipped out from under Alex and Annie scrambled in to take her place. Alex's shock was worth the whole night spent missing him, especially when she took his cock in her mouth and he actually whimpered.

This was a first. An absolutely wonderful first, and the view was nothing short of amazing. Sebastian's sac was right there, pressing up against Alex on each forward thrust, and she slipped her hand around the heavy pouch and stroked him with her fingers, running her nails lightly over the soft skin.

Shit. Shit. Shit.

Hey, Sebastian. Nice to meet you. I'm Annie.

Oh, shit. Don't come. Don't come. Don't . . .

She giggled and squeezed his balls a little harder, sucked Alex a little deeper.

Hold on. Hold on. Not now. Not yet . . .

That had to be Alex, which meant she must be doing something right. His lips settled around her clit, taking her from aroused to climax in a heartbeat. She whimpered and sucked him deeper, anchoring herself on his cock as she flew from the highest precipice, her body rigid, her vaginal muscles all rippling and pulsing with the power of her release.

Alex tried to pull out of her mouth, but she wrapped her fingers around his back, holding him down, holding him close, sucking and licking through her own climax until he cried out and his cock jerked in her mouth. She felt the heavy pulse of blood along his shaft as his orgasm hit, and then she was swallowing thick bursts of ejaculate as it hit the back of her throat.

It was the taste of his seed even more than his mouth on her sex that took her over the top again, the fact he'd come in her mouth, that the fantasies and dreams she'd harbored for years were happening now, even better than all the gritty, earthy, messy, wonderful ways she'd imagined.

He tasted good. Better than good—it was wonderful sucking him, holding him in her mouth, sliding her tongue over his shaft, and tasting the intimate flavors of a man she'd loved from afar for so long.

Sebastian's strokes suddenly went from long and deep to short and fast, and without considering the consequences, she wrapped her fingers around his sac and lightly squeezed.

He cursed; his thighs slapped against Alex as he drove deep, and his muscles froze him in place, with Annie right there, watching from an angle she'd never imagined. She hoped like hell she hadn't hurt him, but it was hard to tell. She'd noticed that with Alex last night, that when he came, he looked as if he were in the most excruciating pain imaginable.

She wondered if that was how Sebastian looked now, but it didn't really matter. None of it mattered as her body slowly came down from orgasm, as her muscles clenched and released and her heart pounded in her chest.

Sebastian was the first to move, pulling out of Alex without a word and heading down the hallway to the bathroom. Alex collapsed to one side and curled his body around Annie, hugging her close. She wondered where Lily had gone, and then realized she was beside them on the bed with her fingers between her legs.

Annie stared at her a moment, not really comprehending. Then it hit her. "Oh, Lily. I'm sorry." Then she giggled, totally blowing her apology. "It looks like I got your orgasm."

"That you did. You owe me, little girl." She leaned over and kissed Annie. "But trust me, I got off. You guys looked so damned hot." She gazed down the hallway in the direction Sebastian had gone and sighed. "Is he something else, or what?"

Annie just lay there in the bed, grinning. It appeared she was going to have to have a long talk with her father. Mom was great about this new chapter in her life, but Dad needed to understand that a woman of thirty wouldn't tolerate being treated like a child.

Not when she had a man who saw her as a woman and treated her like a queen.

Sebastian stumbled into the bathroom and stared at himself in the mirror, totally shocked to see that he looked exactly like he usually did when he first got out of bed.

He cleaned up, thought longingly of a shower but decided washing his crotch and his face would have to do. As he ran the washcloth over his balls, it suddenly hit him.

Last night, he'd met Liana while they were both naked. Just now, he'd met Annie when she grabbed his balls during sex while he was busy fucking a guy in the ass he'd just met yesterday. He still didn't really know what Annie looked like—she'd been a wolf last night. An injured wolf.

He planted his hands on the counter and leaned forward. Nope. He still looked like the same guy.

Impossible. "Holy shit, Xenakis. Your social life has definitely gotten an upgrade."

He was still chuckling when he wandered back to the bedroom. Lily had gone into the kitchen to put on a pot of coffee, but Annie and Alex lay in the bed together, curled up and talking quietly. He started to do an about-face to give them some privacy, but Alex stopped him.

"Seb? C'mon in." He laughed and hugged Annie against his chest. "You haven't been properly introduced."

"Hi, Sebastian." Annie turned just enough to peek out from between Alex's arms. "It's nice to meet you."

"Hi, Annie." He flopped down on the foot of the bed. "For what it's worth, this has officially become the most surreal morning of my life. And you, Annie, are the pièce de résistance."

Alex chuckled. "See, Annie? I told you he wasn't mad."

"Mad?" Sebastian surprised even himself when he crawled across the bed and kissed Annie full on the mouth. "Sweetie, you made my morning very special."

Then he turned to Alex, but not with laughter. "You, too, Alex. Thank you. Not just for this morning. For last night. I needed what you offered more than you can ever know."

It's all good, man. That's what friends are for.

He stared into Alex's amber eyes and worked with the great surge of emotion that threatened to swamp him. Finally, he got it under control and nodded slowly. "Yeah, well maybe it's something that most guys would understand, but for me that was a first."

He got off the bed and knelt beside it, fished around underneath, and finally came up with the wrinkled shorts Lily had given him last night. He slipped into them, moving calmly while his mind was a swirling mass of thoughts and memories, emotions he barely recognized. He flashed Annie a smile and glanced once more at Alex. "Another first, for what it's worth. Beyond a couple of kids I played with in my neighborhood, you're also the first friend I've ever had."

He didn't say any more. He couldn't. Instead he left the bedroom and headed for the kitchen, and the peace and sanity that was Lily Cheval.

She glanced up as he entered the room. "G'morning."

He leaned over and kissed her, grabbed a cup off the counter, and filled it with the freshly brewed coffee. "I left my capsules in the big house. Don't let me forget to go back and get them. I had one last night."

"No problem." She reached into a cabinet over her head and pulled out an identical jar to the one her dad had given him. "Here. These are the same. Take one this morning. It's not like you can overdose on them. They're just a grass native to Tibet."

"Alex told me about that." He took the capsule and swallowed it with the coffee.

Lily turned and leaned against the kitchen counter with her cup in her hand and smiled at him. "I like this, by the way. Waking up with you in my bed, seeing you here in my kitchen. Thank you for everything you did last night. For taking on our fight as your own."

He glanced away, almost afraid to agree with her. There was so much not settled. His father was still out there. The rogue wolves had gotten away last night, which meant the entire pack was still at risk.

It made him nervous, this sense of homecoming he felt with Lily. "I like it, too. Too much. It scares me to find this kind of happiness when there's so much crap we still have to deal with. I'm afraid it could all end in a heartbeat."

Lily's smile was laced with sadness. "Sebastian, for Chanku, there's always a chance it could end. We're not the dominant race on this planet. We tread a fine line between accepted citizen and hunted beast. We've all learned to take what joy we can, when we can. We're always on guard, always alert, but always . . ." She paused, and the look in her eyes filled him with a sense of purpose, a desire to promise that he would give her *always*.

"Always, we revel in the joy. In our love for each other, in our sense of family. It's all about the pack. Do you feel that? The sense of communion, that you're no longer alone?"

He thought about that, the way he'd awakened in a bed with Lily and Alex and how the sense of family had been so powerful. As if it were a new truth for him to hold on to. Something to give him strength. "I do. I feel it with every one of you I've met." He shot a quick glance toward the bedroom, where the sounds of the bedsprings told their own tale, and smiled. "Definitely with Alex, though I'm not sure why. He's a pretty amazing guy."

"Do you know he says the same thing about you?" She walked across the kitchen and sat across from him at the small table. "He's always been my other half. The one who makes me laugh, sometimes when it's totally inappropriate. The one who's there to hold me when I cry."

A short bark of laughter burst out of him before he could stop it. "I tested that side of him last night." Amazing. He'd actually admitted falling apart without blushing, but there it was. "He passed, by the way. With flying colors."

"I'm glad he was there for you." She took a sip of coffee and her eyes twinkled. "So, tell me. What did you think of this morning? That was a first for you, wasn't it?"

"It was." He took a swallow. Set the cup down. "Hopefully not the last. It was actually wonderful, though I'm not sure I'll be able to convince Alex to let me top all the time."

She laughed, and he realized he didn't get to hear her laughter nearly enough. "Probably not. As long as you know what to expect."

"I didn't expect Annie. Definitely didn't expect Annie." This time he was the one laughing. Sunbeams swept across the room as the sun popped up over the mountains. Lily got up to fix breakfast, and a little while later, Alex and Annie wandered into the kitchen, looking for coffee.

They all sat at the little kitchen table, talking and laughing, eating the big breakfast Lily had prepared, and planning the rest of the day. Alex had to meet with members of the local sheriff's department, Annie was going shopping with her mom and a couple of other women from the pack, and Lily and Sebastian would be visiting the astral plane.

He was going to meet a goddess. One who really didn't like him very much. Sebastian glanced out the window at the mountains to the east and thought about that. This morning might have been the most surreal in his life, but he had a feeling the rest of the day just might top it.

14

It was a little after eight by the time Alex left with Annie to walk her back home. Lily knew he wasn't looking forward to seeing Tinker, but she'd suggested before he left that the two men were going to have to establish a working arrangement where Annie was concerned.

Alex had agreed. Poor Annie had just wrapped her hands around her waist and stared off in the distance, toward her parents' house. It really wasn't going to be easy, but if Alex really loved Annie, he'd figure out a way to make it work.

Lily watched through the kitchen window as the two of them walked away, hand in hand. Alex leaned close, obviously listening intently to whatever Annie was saying. She'd never seen him like this with any woman, and definitely not with her. More proof, as far as Lily was concerned, that she and Alex were not meant to be mates.

Thinking of mates had her glancing to her left where Sebastian stood in front of the sink washing breakfast dishes. He looked really good standing bare chested in her kitchen, wearing nothing but a pair of Alex's old jogging shorts, his hands in soapy water, and bubbles glistening in the dark hairs on his wrists. Damn, she really had it bad, but she turned the thought around and said, "Alex has it so bad."

She took the plate Sebastian handed to her and added, "But it's not going to be easy. Annie's dad really is wonderful." She finished drying the plate, then took the next one Sebastian handed to her and carefully dried it. She thought it was pretty cool that he'd cleared the table and started rinsing dishes while she put leftovers away. Obviously he didn't mind helping out around the house.

Score more points in his favor.

"Why do I hear an obvious *but* at the end of that sentence?" He waited while she put the plates away and then handed her a well-scrubbed frying pan.

"Do I even have to say it?" Laughing as she dried the pan, Lily couldn't help but think of how much she loved Annie's father, but the reality of the man made her sigh in frustration. Poor Annie. "Tinker is big and he's very strong, and Annie is such a little thing that he's always been protective. Way too protective. And just wait until you meet her brothers. They were the really huge dark gray wolves who left with Annie's mom last night. All the McClintock men are big and strong and extremely protective, and it's not easy for Annie. Everyone treats her like she's such a fragile little girl because she's petite, but she's thirty years old. She's got a will of iron, and she's had a lot of self-defense training. She was good enough to compete in the sport while in college, and she won competitions all around Europe, but Tinker's having a hard time accepting that she's a grown woman."

"It can't be easy for any father who loves his daughter." He chuckled. "I'm surprised your father has been so nice to me. I can't imagine how I'd deal with some strange guy showing up to court my daughter."

She tilted her head and studied him for a moment. "Is that what you're doing? Courting me?"

"You mean you haven't figured that out yet?" He leaned over, kissed her cheek, and went back to washing dishes.

Lily watched him, amazed by how calm he seemed about taking their relationship to a new level. She was still getting used to the idea she'd actually met a guy with most of the right stuff.

If only she could be sure about the rest of it.

They finished up. Sebastian wiped down the stove, and Lily put the rest of the dishes away, but there was no more talk of courtship. She leaned over to grab a napkin that had fallen to the floor. Sebastian planted his hands on her hips and rubbed against her bottom.

"Sorry, darlin'." His voice held a low, sexy timbre that sent shivers along her spine. "You can't tease a man like this and expect to get away with it."

She glanced over her shoulder. "Tease?" Her voice sounded like it belonged to someone else. "All I did was bend over."

"That's all it takes when I'm around you." The feral gleam in his eyes had her hot and ready within seconds. His hand sliding inside the waistband of her loose knit yoga pants found slick, wet heat between her thighs.

The cottage was bright with morning sun, the day would be filled with their visit to Eve and worry about the rogue wolves, but right now it was just Lily and Sebastian in her sun-warmed kitchen, with the scent of bacon and fried potatoes in the air.

And Sebastian. His masculine scent filled her nostrils and teased her senses like nothing else. She gave him a knowing glance and then grabbed the slick granite counter and hung on while he shoved her pants down to her knees.

He dropped to his knees behind her and his big hands clasped her thighs. She'd expected the thick head of his cock, but the first slick swipe of his tongue had her whimpering. Her hips jerked involuntarily, but he held her still. His grasp was firm and definitely the hold of an alpha as he licked and nibbled his way across her buttocks, along her perineum, and after shoving her pants to the floor and scooting her legs farther apart, her clit and the softly engorged lips of her sex. Deep, slow sweeps of his tongue, and soft little nips with his teeth and lips.

Teasing, tantalizing, torturing her with his slow, steady restraint, and a low, soft hum that added a shivery vibration to every inch he covered. The bruising strength of his fingers holding her in place added to the sense of control, quickly reminding her with his powerful grasp that he was physically so much stronger, so much bigger.

Just that quickly, Lily was close to the edge. So damned close to flying off the precipice that when he abruptly let go of her thighs and stood, she cried out her loss. He didn't say a word, merely pressed his hand against her back to hold her still. He surged forward, driving his thick cock between her legs, finding her wet and ready, filling her completely on his very first thrust.

She almost lost it, and she cried out, shocked into a harsh scream that swiftly morphed into a moan and then a soft whimper of pure pleasure. He thrust hard and his cock bumped against her cervix on each deep penetration, and she knew she couldn't take any more of him, couldn't take him any deeper.

But he grew larger, thicker, and her body stretched to take him. Deep, so deep, until her world narrowed down to nothing but Sebastian and the heavy weight of his shaft filling her, the bulbous tip sliding over her cervix, moving beyond the hard mouth, stretching her beyond anything she'd ever known.

What would it be like, to mate with him as a wolf? To have him fill her and then tie to her so that she couldn't escape, until she was linked to him and he to her for all time?

But only if he were Chanku. Only if she could discover the

truth behind the darkness in Sebastian Xenakis. There were some principles she could never disregard, and this was one.

She'd not mate with one who wasn't her kind, even if he could become a wolf through magical means. The thought chilled her, because it wouldn't matter if she loved him. If he loved her. It had nothing to do with whether or not he was right for her or good enough, but because it was something she'd promised the ancient ones so long ago.

And she'd learned from her father that promises were not made to be broken, that honor and integrity were more important than immediate pleasure—even if holding true cost her more than she'd ever dreamed having to pay.

As a six-year-old child, she'd journeyed on the astral plane and learned the history of her people. How the first Chanku had come to Earth as refugees from a dying planet millennia ago, how they'd found refuge on the world that would one day be host to humankind. A young world that offered shelter amid ancient forests ruled by prehistoric creatures—a world still shuddering in the cataclysm of creation.

There were so few of them left now. So very few, and she had promised. She'd been their hope, those ancient Chanku who had remained for millions of years, existing, yet not living, merely waiting for one to come along who could carry on their history.

Lily—six-year-old Lily Cheval—had been the one charged with remembering the past for a people verging on extinction. She'd held their history, their memories, and all their hopes for the future in her heart and mind.

Then she'd returned to her pack and shared those memories and hopes with all the known Chanku in existence.

And because of that, she knew it was not her lot to find happiness with any man not of her kind. She could have sex with a human male, but there would be no children from their joining. A woman with Chanku genes who had never had the nutrients could produce offspring with a human, but once she'd become fully Chanku, the egg and seed were no longer compatible. Lily had been fully Chanku from birth—she could mate only with another Chanku. The ancients had told her she would find true happiness only with a Chanku male.

Dear Goddess, she wanted Sebastian to be that male, because she already loved him. Loved him without any other reservation beyond that most important one.

What was he? Human or Chanku?

He had to be Chanku. She couldn't bear to give him up.

But she would have to, eventually. Her life span was almost immortal. As a human, Sebastian would die in sixty or seventy years. She would remain forever young, while he grew old.

He thrust harder. Faster. He clutched her hips, and his fingers dug into her muscles, holding her in place. She knew she'd have bruises. Welcomed them as marks of his taking.

Chanku males were such physical, dominant creatures. She saw his power as one more hint he might be the one. He swore softly, a steady litany of whispered curses. The rhythm of his powerful strokes changed—deeper, harder, faster. Caught in the rhythm of his loving, Lily found her own pinnacle of pleasure.

But she wasn't there alone.

He stood beside her, held her close, and their minds linked as Sebastian leapt from the edge with Lily in his arms. She cried out, overwhelmed by their shared orgasm. Not merely her own experience but Sebastian's as well. Her vaginal muscles clutching his thick erection, the rush and the sweet burn of his ejaculate streaming from balls to cock to bathe her inner channel.

His surprise looped back on her when Lily's sensations washed through him—the powerful throbbing pleasure in her womb, the sweet pain of taut nipples rubbing against the loose weave of her cotton top, the soft press of his balls against her sex.

Her legs trembled and she feared they'd collapse, but Sebastian had anchored both of them atop the granite counter. His forearms protected her from the hard surface while his chest covered her back like a warm, living blanket. The staccato thunder of his pounding heart and the warm exhalations against her ear matched her own racing heart, her own deep breaths. He planted soft kisses along the sensitive nape of her neck until all she wanted was to slide slowly to the floor and lie there until she felt strong enough to move again.

His cock still pulsed within her sheath, her vaginal muscles rippled around him with long, flowing contractions. The sound of their harsh breaths filled her ears. The pounding thunder of his heart soothed her. Enveloped in his heat and power, she could stay there forever.

Which was exactly why she should have known it was too good to last. *Lily? I want you and Sebastian at the house as soon as you can get here. We have to work on his shields as well as yours. Aldo Xenakis is in town.*

Well, damn. *Give us a few minutes, Dad.* She wondered if her father was aware what they'd been doing and almost laughed. Talk about rotten timing. Though she figured it could have been worse. Like before they'd shared such an amazing climax. She glanced over her shoulder and caught Sebastian's questioning glance. *We'll be there as soon as we can.*

Sebastian slowly pulled away from her, and she felt a moment's regret when his penis slid free of muscles still rippling and clenching, doing their best to hold him in place.

And she thought again of what it would be like, to mate as wolves. He wouldn't come free so easily if he were a wolf. Not when he'd swollen and knotted deep inside, when he'd tied with her in the way of the wolf.

She rather liked that idea. Let her father try and demand their presence then!

In the act of pulling his cotton shorts back on, he glanced up at her. "What are you laughing about?"

"Didn't you hear my father's orders?"

He shook his head. "No. He must have spoken privately. When did you hear from him? What did he say?"

She couldn't stop laughing. "Right in the middle of our climax, and he wants us at the house, ASAP."

Sebastian glanced at Lily with one eyebrow raised and his pants around his thighs. She laughed even harder when he drily said, "I guess I'm glad I wasn't included in the conversation. Talk about blowing the moment. Any idea what he wants?"

"You're not kidding, and yeah. He wants to help us work on our shields. Your father's in town."

"Crap." He tugged his pants up over his slim hips, stretching the elastic wide enough to carefully tuck himself in. Lily almost sighed when he hid all those delicious parts from her view.

"Your father's right. We both need to work on our shields. In fact, I hope I can practice blocking your father before moving on to mine."

Lily laughed and hugged him around the waist. "That's an excellent idea. I can block him, but it's from years of practice. I was leaving myself open in case he needed to reach us." Then she sighed as something her father said fully registered. "I wonder if your father was in Montana when Alex and Annie were attacked last night."

"I don't know." He kissed her, just a quick little kiss that reminded her how much she really liked this guy. How much she risked by already loving him so much. "But I imagine your father does. I have a feeling very little gets by him."

"Didn't take you long to figure that out, did it?" She didn't laugh, though. Not with the specter of Aldo Xenakis once again hovering between them.

He glanced down at his naked chest. "Is there an extra shirt in that closet of yours?"

"Not necessary. Dad may want us to shift for him, so the less you're wearing, the easier it is."

He wondered if he'd ever get used to the Chanku concept of relaxed dress, but then Lily grabbed his hand and the two of them left her cottage. Half naked or not, he held on tight as they headed across the meadow to her father's house.

Anton was in the den with a cup of coffee and the news playing softly on the big wall screen, but he turned it off as soon as they entered. "Coffee's fresh and hot on the bar. And yes, Lily, I made it myself."

Sebastian flashed Lily a quick look and caught her trying not to giggle. "Good," she said. "It's nice to know that even über-alphas can be taught a thing or two."

Anton grunted and gave Sebastian a look that could only be described as *long-suffering*. "My daughter thinks I depend too much on my lovely wife for creature comforts. She insists I make my own coffee when her mother wants to sleep in."

"Hey, it's only fair." Lily grabbed the pot and filled two big mugs. Sebastian laughed as he took the cup she handed to him. "What's so funny?"

"Nothing. Except you just poured my coffee."

She cocked one perfectly slim hip and planted her hand on it. "That's different. I only poured one for you because you voluntarily helped me clean up the kitchen."

"You cooked. As you said, it's only fair. But thank you." He leaned close and kissed her. She blinked, surprised, he imagined, that he would kiss her in front of her father, but there was no better time than the present to establish his place in her life.

And he would have a place in her life. He took his cup and sat on the couch across from her father.

Anton glanced over the rim of his mug as he took a sip. "I hope you realize that by voluntarily doing housework, you're giving the male of the species a bad name."

Sebastian glanced at Lily, and as so often happened, he couldn't look away from her. She wore a crop top and loose yoga pants and her long hair was twisted up on top of her head, held in place with what looked like a couple of chopsticks.

He'd never seen a more beautiful woman in his life.

"Sorry, Mr. Cheval. I can't seem to help myself."

Her dad let out a long, dramatic sigh. "I think you can drop the 'Mr. Cheval' and go with my given name. I have a feeling we've moved beyond formalities."

Lily glanced at Sebastian, and he knew she expected some kind of teasing comment, but he was looking at her, not at Anton. "Thank you. I certainly hope so."

Did she have any idea how he felt about her? How much he hated the fact that his father stood between them? Somehow, Aldo Xenakis had to be stopped, but the first thing they had to do was figure out how to keep him out of their heads.

The memory—or lack of memory—of his time running with Lily haunted him. That couldn't happen again. He wouldn't allow it to happen again.

He turned abruptly away from Lily and focused on her father. "Okay, Anton. Where do we start?"

They broke for lunch around two, only because Lily's mother swept into the den with a tray of sandwiches and insisted her husband take time to eat. "He gets grumpy when he misses a meal," she said in a rather loud whispered aside to Sebastian.

Lily hugged her mom, Anton kept his mouth shut, and Sebastian wanted to bless the woman for feeding him before he keeled over. Breakfast had been hours ago, and the work Anton had them doing, though it was mental, not physical, was exhausting, drawing on whatever reserves he might have had.

They ate, cleared away the mess, and Sebastian carried the empty tray to the kitchen. Keisha stood at the big restaurant-sized range, checking the temperature on a roast that looked like it could feed an army.

"We do feed an army," she said when he commented. "It's my night to cook. You'll see Stefan and Xandi Aragat, Alex's parents—you met them last night. Possibly Oliver and Mei. You might have seen them as snow leopards last night. I know Lisa and Tinker McClintock will be here. There might even be more than usual, as I imagine they'll be curious about you."

He didn't ask, but she answered, anyway. "You're the first young man our daughter has ever brought home. The pack is already buzzing about your presence, so be ready to answer a lot of questions, some not at all subtle." She slid the roast back into the oven, stood, and leaned against the counter beside the stove.

"I hope Alex and Annie come. Lily always said those two were meant for each other, but I never could see them as a pair. I was wrong. It's a lesson well learned." She smiled at him. "I need to pay heed to what our daughter says. Anyway, Sebastian, our doors are always open to members of the pack. To you, as well, since you obviously have our daughter's blessing."

She was so warm, so accepting that he stood there a moment, speechless. He felt as if something inside broke free, and he wondered if it was the darkness he'd carried in his soul. Then he sensed Anton's call. It was time to go back. "Thank you," he said. And for some reason, he, who was never comfortable with people he didn't know well, leaned over and kissed Keisha's cheek. "You've made me feel very welcome. It means more than you can possibly imagine."

She took both his hands in hers. "You are welcome, Sebastian. I feel the good in you, and I feel my daughter's love for you." She smiled. "Like I said, I've learned to trust Lily. In case you hadn't noticed, she's an amazing young woman. Now hurry. I sense my impatient spouse growing anxious."

It was after five before he and Lily escaped, with plans to return for dinner by eight, but Anton's parting words stayed with him. Lily had gone ahead when her father stopped him at the door and put both his hands on Sebastian's shoulders.

"You're a good man," he'd said. "A worthy man. Aldo Xenakis may have provided the sperm that gave you life, but you are not your father's son. You are your mother's, and I believe she was Chanku." Then he'd laughed and dropped a bombshell on Sebastian.

"You said your mother's name was Angela Lupei. We have a packmate whose name is Daciana Lupei. I'm going to see what I can find out. You might be related."

His mind was still reeling from that bit of information when he caught up to Lily and grabbed her hand. He needed her to hold on to him, to ground him. She squeezed his fingers, then led him down the hallway and through the big kitchen. The rich scent of the rib roast cooking had him salivating, but Lily tugged him past the stove. At the far end of the huge kitchen, she opened a door to stairs going down into a basement he hadn't expected.

Lily closed the heavy door behind him. Thick and made of metal, it was obviously fireproof. "Where are we going?"

"Someplace very special. I had to get permission from Dad to bring you down here. Since he didn't hesitate, it tells me you've passed inspection. Here." She stopped by a doorway with hooks beside it and grabbed a white cotton T-shirt. "You'll need this."

Curious, he put it on. It was snug and stretched over his wide shoulders, but at least it covered him, though suddenly needing clothing was an interesting thing. He hadn't told her what her father had said to him about his mother's name, but even Anton's comments couldn't compete with where Lily took him—down a tunnel that led them to a wonderland that defied description. They stepped out into a huge cavern with a large, shallow pool set in worn rock along one side. Slowly swirling tendrils of steam rose from the spring-fed pond, and the air in the cavern was warm and somewhat humid. He tried to imagine the entire pack hiding out down here during the forest fire Lily had told him about. The one that burned the original house to the ground.

It certainly explained the fireproof door.

They walked around the pool, and Lily pointed out hieroglyphs along the cave wall. She ran her hands over them as if they were old friends, before finally stopping at a point where the writing ended. She glanced at him, and he figured his amazement was written all over his face. "These are the symbols you said you could read when you were just a little girl? But how?"

She shrugged. "I never really found out. Either the goddess or the Mother, or maybe even the ancients who called me, but they're still as clear as the printed page to me. When we have time, I'll read them to you. They're the history of our kind. At least part of it. I got the details from the ancient ones on the astral, which is where we're headed now."

He had so many questions he couldn't narrow them down to the ones he wanted to ask, so he merely waited for Lily to show him. She put her hands against prints carved into the stone and stared at the rough wall in front of her. He sensed a change, a shimmer, and then a brighter glow until he was blinking against the light.

Stunned, he watched as the rock dissolved in front of Lily, opening up into the most beautiful place he'd ever seen—blue skies, green grass, and greener trees. Lily merely grabbed his hand and dragged him through the portal she'd opened. He stepped into a world he'd barely glimpsed the day before, a world too perfect to be real.

And yet it was. He turned, expecting to see the cave behind him, but it was more of the same—green, green grass, a beautiful forest filled with trees and flowers of every description—perfection so complete it was totally disconcerting.

"Look. Eve's here."

He spun around and stared as a subtle shimmer in the meadow in front of them grew brighter, sparkling beneath a brilliant sky without a sun, taking on form and shape until a beautiful woman stood not ten feet away.

Her aura shimmered like silver fire with streaks of gold and red leaping within the silver, more flames covering the full color spectrum, a woman of power. Unimaginable power, tempered by love. She raised her head and smiled. "Lily! You've come back."

He was caught in the unusual swirling color of her eyes, constantly changing from green to gold to blue until he felt dizzy. She focused on Sebastian, and he blinked as she recognized him. "It was you. You are the one bringing darkness to my world."

He glanced at Lily, but she was shaking her head. "No, Eve. This is Sebastian Xenakis. I don't think he's the one. We believe his father is the source of the darkness, but touch him. See what you sense." She glanced at him. "Is that okay?"

He nodded. "Of course."

Eve stepped closer and gazed up at him. She was tall and beautiful, similar to the Chanku he'd met so far, but there was such power in her aura that he felt as if he should kneel before her. A goddess. She really was a goddess. His knees actually trembled, but when she placed her hands on his forearms, a great well of calm filled him.

"Please?" She looked up at him out of those odd eyes.

And Sebastian realized he would give her anything. No matter what she asked. "Whatever you need."

She smiled and placed her hands beneath his shirt so that they touched, skin to skin. Her touch was warm—sensual without feeling sexual—yet he felt as if his heart might beat right through his rib cage. She smiled, slowly shaking her head as if she'd discovered something unexpected.

"You're right, Lily. The darkness is there, but it's from association, not nature." She stepped back and he pulled his shirt back down, but his skin felt all prickly, as if energy sparked over the areas where she'd touched him.

"Come. We need to talk. I have learned things, and you have experienced even more."

Lily grabbed his hand again, and they followed Eve through a meadow that was too perfect, through a small forest much too lush to be real, and then to a grassy knoll beside a perfect stream.

Eve found a spot in the shade of a huge tree and sat. Sebastian hadn't really paid close attention to his surroundings. As beautiful, as ethereal as was this part of the astral, nothing could compare with Lily. When she folded her long legs and sat beneath the tree beside Eve, Sebastian watched each graceful movement, losing himself once again in her beauty. Once she settled herself, though, she glanced up at him with one eyebrow artfully cocked, as if asking what he thought of the place.

He didn't know. He'd not really looked, but now he took a moment to glance at the wonders around him, and the mystery of where he was, who he was with, washed over him with a sense of wonder, of indescribable joy.

He was really, truly here. Not as a spirit but as a man. He, Sebastian Xenakis, a man who so often felt totally inept and out of his league, was actually on the astral plane, the guest of a goddess and a woman who seemed to love him in spite of himself.

His skin prickled with a frisson of awareness, a familiar rush of power that caught his attention and dragged his avid glance to the tree sheltering this beautiful spot of ground.

It wasn't the same tree. Not his oak, the one where he'd first drawn the power to shift, but he knew, without any doubt, that it held the same spirit.

His lady was here. Not a dryad. No, this was no simple wood spirit. Here, on the astral, she was more than spirit. More than an ancient power. Here, she *was* Power. She was his lady, and he knew her with a visceral sense of destiny.

Without hesitation, without any thought at all beyond giving her thanks and the obeisance due a presence of undeniable importance, Sebastian fell to his knees before the tree, bowed his head, and waited to see what his lady wanted.

Lily shot a quick glance at Eve and caught the raised eyebrow, the shock on the goddess's face as Sebastian suddenly knelt before the massive tree and bowed his head.

Then Eve's eyes went wide and she knelt as well. Confused, Lily opened her senses to the tree. The blast of power almost sent her reeling.

She was on her knees beside Sebastian before she realized what had happened. He reached for her and grabbed her hand, and she realized he was holding on to Eve as well.

The three of them, kneeling to a huge tree that, for some reason, felt as if it held the answers to all questions, the power for all worlds.

Eve was the one to speak first. She raised her head and smiled at the towering tree, and her face literally glowed. "Blessed Mother. I have missed your touch. Please? Tell us what we must do to right what is wrong."

15

"Well, that could have gone a little better." Alex held Annie's hand as the two of them left her parents' house and walked toward the edge of the woods. He had no destination in mind beyond getting far away from her father's angry stare and cutting words, just slipping away from the compound to be alone with Annie. He wondered if Lily's cottage might be empty and then decided it was damned time for him to build his own house.

He'd need one when he took Annie as his mate, because there was no way he was ever giving her up, but he wished he knew what she was thinking. She'd locked everything down when her dad started in on all the reasons why Alex wasn't a suitable partner for her. She hadn't agreed with anything Tinker said, but she hadn't defended Alex, either.

Of course, she'd never let go of his hand the entire time they were at the house. That had to mean something. He glanced her way and said, "Your dad's never going to look beyond the fact I was a jerk when I was a pup."

Annie wrapped her hands around his arm and hugged him

against herself. "You were never a jerk. You were a pain in the butt for the adults at times, but never because you were a jerk."

He turned and raised his eyebrows. "Thank you. I think."

She punched his arm. "You know what I mean. You were a cutup and always thinking out of the box, but you weren't a bully, and you never, ever did anything to make anyone feel bad." She giggled, adding, "Though I imagine you gave the older generation a few extra gray hairs."

"My father said he never felt his age until I turned into an eagle and flew up into a tree out in the yard to get a kite that got caught in the branches. I was about six, and that was the first time he saw me shift, even though Lily and I had been shifting for months already." He chuckled softly. "I think that was about the same time Lily was taking her historic walk on the astral, meeting up with all the Chanku ancients. Goddess, but I hate to think what my kids will be like."

"I think that's the problem, you know." She stopped and gazed up at him, and Alex felt it like a punch to the gut. She was breathtaking and wonderful—and everything he'd ever wanted.

And he wanted those kids of his with her. No one else.

Unfortunately, her father had said and done just about everything he could to discourage Annie from loving him. "What? Beyond the fact Tinker would like to strangle me."

"Oh, he doesn't want to strangle you," she said, but her eyes twinkled. "He merely wants you to move far away, preferably to another country, until he can find what he considers a suitable mate for his poor, pathetic, not-so-bright daughter."

He looped his arms over her shoulders. "What daughter would that be? Because there's nothing pathetic about you, and you're one of the smartest women I know."

"Ya think?"

He shrugged. "Of course I do. You love me, don't you?"

She nodded, but there was no sense of laughter when she said, "Yes, Alex. I love you more than I can say. So much it's sort of scary, to have this much feeling about someone. It makes me feel afraid and vulnerable."

He took her hands in his. "But why? You have to know I love you. That I will do whatever it takes to convince your parents I'm the right man for you." He leaned close and kissed her. Her lips were full and soft and whispered against his, promising so much more. He lost himself in her taste, her textures, the fullness of her love. It wasn't easy to end the kiss, but he did.

"You do think I'm the right man, don't you?" *Dear Goddess . . .*

"Of course I do, but that doesn't make this any less terrifying."

"Because of what your dad said?"

She wrapped her arms around him and held him close, but she had a huge grin on her face. "Goddess, no. I hope you realize the only reason I didn't argue with him is because he wasn't in the mood to listen. I would have been wasting my breath, along with arguments I may need to use later." She laughed. "Alex, don't worry. He wants everyone to think he's big and scary, but my father is an absolute softy. He loves me and he worries, just as you will worry when we have our own young. Mom will talk him around. She loves you, Alex. She always has."

She paused a moment and glanced toward the dark forest. He heard her sigh, but she kept her gaze locked on the woods. "I'm afraid, Alex, because I never had this much to lose."

"I don't understand. You're certainly not going to lose me."

She shrugged. "Tell my neurotic brain that. You, me . . . us. This is something I've fantasized about from the time I was little. You loving me is the most wonderful, most terrifying thing that's ever happened to me."

He loved her so much he ached. He wanted to howl, to thank Eve for putting this woman in his sights, but all he said was, "Run with me, Annie."

They were at the edge of the forest near a well-beaten path. Someone had nailed hooks to a big pine where they could hang their clothing, and within minutes Alex had his jeans and shirt hanging beside Annie's shorts and tank top.

And damn, but he was hard even before their run. He wondered how that would translate to the usual sexual rush after their shift, but decided he'd just have to wait and find out.

Annie shifted and was off like a shot, her gray fur with the black tips rippling like burnished silver in the filtered sunlight. Alex followed close behind as she quickly slipped off the main trail and headed for a smaller track winding down through the lower valley. He wondered if it was a conscious choice, to run in the opposite direction from the Xenakis property, and applauded her thinking.

That was the last thing they needed, especially when his thoughts were all caught up in Annie and not particularly attuned to the world around them.

Normally, when he ran as a wolf, he was enthralled by his wolven senses. As a human he was gregarious and outgoing, but when he shifted, Alex had always preferred the solitude of the forest, even when running with packmates. He kept his thoughts within and used the time as a wolf to connect with those parts of him the world never saw. It was something he'd not grown tired of—the increased sensitivity to scent and sound, the change in visual input and the way his muscles worked, his tendons and sinews stretching, tightening, powering this four-legged form.

He could easily take almost any shape, but the wolf would always be his favorite, this powerful predator with the strength of the pack empowering his heart and soul. But last night he'd discovered he no longer cared to run as a lone wolf.

Running with Annie McClintock beat running alone all to hell and back. He wanted her. Not just for now, but forever, and damn her father for thinking he wasn't worthy. What man would love Annie more? Would fight harder to keep her safe? Would protect her and stand beside her for as long as they both should live?

His thoughts made him think of wedding vows, the words running over and over through his head as his big paws tore up the trail. He watched the gorgeous bitch who led him, caught in the graceful stretch of sinew and muscle as her body streaked along the narrow trail. And when she turned off the trail and cut through a thick swath of bracken ferns and low-lying shrubs, he knew exactly what she wanted.

It was the same thing he yearned for. No doubts. None.

He felt it in the determined glance she cast over her shoulder, in the ripe scent of her lust. She wanted him. Wanted him in the way of wolves, now. Today, beneath a bright summer's sun. It wasn't the full moon he'd envisioned for their mating, but it didn't matter. Annie mattered. What she wanted, when she wanted. As long as she wanted him, any time was perfect.

Sooner rather than later.

He burst through the undergrowth and saw her standing at full alert with one paw raised, her ears pricked forward. A brilliant shaft of sunlight filtering through thick alder trees bathed her in light as if she stood upon a stage. The soft song of a rushing creek fed by snowmelt was her accompaniment. Ferns covering the banks, thick and lush with new growth, created a perfect setting for the beautiful female waiting for him.

The words came to him then. The vow that had filled his mind as he ran, and he said them now, placing his heart in her hands, shivering inside with fear that she might change her mind.

I want you, Annie. Not just for now, but forever. No man can possibly love you more. No man will fight harder to keep you safe. No other will protect you and stand beside you, ready to give his life the way I would freely give mine. Anne Marie McClintock, I know this truth—you are my one, true mate. The one destined for me. The one I've searched for without realizing it was you all along. Take me as your partner, your lover, the one to give you children if we should be so blessed. I promise to stand beside you and keep you safe for as long we both shall live. I swear by our goddess, always to be there for you. Will you honor me by becoming my mate?

She stepped close to him, touched his nose with hers. *Alex, you have always been mine, deep in the most secret places of my heart. I have loved you and wanted you, have dreamed of walking by your side as your mate. You are the only man alive who can make my dreams come true. I would be honored to join with you. Here, now, with our goddess as our witness. I love you, Alexander Anton Aragat. I will be yours for all time.*

There were no words left to speak. He, a man who always had a glib comment or a sarcastic comeback, was speechless. He stared into Annie's sparkling amber eyes and felt a sense of wonder, of fate settling into place in a way he'd never before experienced.

This was as it was meant to be. Here. Now. Just the two of them making this life affirming, life altering decision. He brushed her shoulders with his paw, almost expecting her to run, to lead him on a merry chase before she allowed him to catch her, but she merely turned her back to him, tilted her head, and gazed steadily at him over her left shoulder.

No games, Alex. I've told you I love you, that I want you. I don't intend to run from you. Not now. Her soft laughter filtered through his mind. *That doesn't mean, however, that I won't give you a run for your money later, or that I will always agree with you. I am my mother's daughter, and she is a strong woman.*

Left unspoken was the truth, that if Lisa McClintock could

control her big mate, she must be one of the most powerful bitches in the entire pack. Tinker was a force of nature, and it was well known his mate was the true leader in that family unit.

Alex yipped and rubbed his muzzle over her back, loving her all the more. *I have a feeling I'm going to enjoy whatever battles we face, Annie.*

She'd actually fantasized about this moment, knowing it would only ever be fantasy because Alex loved Lily and the two would one day mate forever.

But Lily loved Sebastian, and Alex loved her, which was why this act, this perfect moment, took on a dreamlike quality, a living, waking dream with a man who had always been bigger than life in her imagination. Yet, in reality, she'd discovered that Alex was more than she'd expected, much better than her dreams.

He was a selfless, generous lover, funny and sweet and so caring that his love for her made her ache. Now, as his paw brushed her shoulder, as his teeth gently nipped the thick ruff of fur at her neck and then his powerful jaws clamped down and held her, she braced her legs and prepared for his weight.

Inside, her heart was singing, the feelings and words and a lifetime of yearning all tumbled together, and everything was Alex Aragat. He came down on her so carefully, easing his body gently over hers that she was unprepared for the strength of his thrust once he was in position. The sharp, quick slide of his wolven penis into her tight channel; the speed as he filled her deep, again as he withdrew and was back again, thrusting so fast this mating was unlike any sex she could imagine in human form.

Her mind wanted to dissect and compartmentalize everything that happened, but the wolf in her took control, her instincts so sharp and powerful that she gave into the act itself, the amazing act of mating in her wolven form.

And in doing so, she gave everything over to Alex.

She felt her climax building, rushing her toward completion. His front legs clasped her back and the sharp nails dug into her sides. He filled her, harder, deeper, with such pistonlike power her front legs collapsed and she went to her knees. Panic edged her conscious mind, a fear of this man she loved as his stronger body overpowered hers. His wolven cock suddenly swelled inside her and she knew this was the moment, this indescribable link when they tied and she accepted the mating bond.

They would be bound for all time.

For all time, Annie. You and me. For all time.

His voice calmed her as his thick knot filled her tight sheath and his thrusts slowed. She felt the steady, rhythmic pulse of his ejaculation, and something more. Something intrinsic to the Chanku mating as their minds found that perfect synchronicity and linked.

She didn't remember falling, but she and Alex lay together, bodies tied, eyes half lidded, as she fell deeper and deeper into his mind. Like a movie in highest definition showing every detail, she saw his first shift when he was barely five and listened while he agreed with Lily that no, this was probably not something they should share with their parents. Then she experienced his first sexual explorations with Lily, two bright and precocious kids on the cusp of their teen years, touching and learning with the innocence of the young.

She'd expected jealousy, yet felt none. Instead she felt honored to learn this about two people she loved without reservation, knowing their love was as constant and strong now as it had been when they were children—the love of true friends who were also lovers, yet not fated to love as mates.

His life spilled into hers, and she felt her life flowing into Alex. She knew he recognized how she'd always been there, on the periphery of everything he did, a silent yet steadfast admirer of a young man still finding his way.

She felt his hesitation when he learned of those long, lonely years when she'd studied in England, traveling all over Europe, meeting people, learning languages and customs, and yet always alone. A pack animal without her pack.

And, within the power of the link, he knew those languages she spoke with ease. Accepted the impossible and knew it was the magic of their kind, that what she knew, he would know. What he had mastered, Annie would share in full.

But all of it wasn't perfect. He saw how her visits home had grown farther apart. They'd been painful reminders that both she and Alex were growing older, both of them unmated, and yet the specter of his relationship with Lily was proof he would one day have his mate, and Annie was destined to go on alone.

Not anymore. Never alone again; never without Alex.

She had no idea how long they lay there in the dappled shadows. How long they shared memories, ideas, beliefs, and fears. Long after their bodies had relaxed and Alex had slipped free, they remained connected by their mating link. The bond was strong and true, and when Alex finally lifted his head and stared into Annie's eyes, they shifted as one, lying there naked in the lush grass, mesmerized by the sharing that had changed each of them forever.

"You're an amazing woman, Anne McClintock. A beautiful, intelligent, strong, amazing woman." He rolled over on top of her, supported himself on his elbows, and looked into her eyes as if he saw her for the first time.

Maybe he did, because she knew she'd never seen Alex like this. She hadn't understood the struggles he'd had finding his place within the pack. It wasn't easy, the eldest son of the über-alpha's second. So much expected of him at such a young age, when he'd only wanted to be a kid. And always the expectation that he and Lily would bond as mates, something they'd continued to deny. Then he'd grown and discovered he loved his work in research and development with Chanku Global Industries, but the job as pack liaison to the local sheriff's department—originally designed more for public relations than an actual position—meant his career had been put on the back burner once the murders of the young women had been linked to both wolves and humans.

The deaths frustrated and angered him, and he took each one as a personal assault. The attack on Annie last night had just about put him over the top. Making love to her this morning had been the finest moment he'd ever known, at least until they mated, and he loved her so much it made her want to weep.

"I want to make love to you, Annie. Just the two of us, together in the forest. Mates, the way we'll be for all time." He smiled and nuzzled her neck before kissing her in that terribly sensitive spot he'd discovered behind her ear. "I love the sound of that. Mates. Damn. I do love you. So very much."

She wrapped her arms around his neck and looked at that beloved face, and finally she believed. It wasn't merely a dream. It wasn't just a fantasy. This was Alex and he was real. She'd been inside his head, she'd felt the love in his heart, knew she was forever a part of his soul. The way he felt in her arms, in her heart, in her soul—all of it real. "Love me, Alex."

He bent and twirled his tongue around her taut nipple before drawing it into his mouth. She cried out and then whimpered, undone by that simple caress, but before she could get herself under control, he cupped her left breast in his palm and drew her right nipple between his lips.

Her hips writhed beneath his weight, and she was so aware of the heavy length of him, of that huge, hot erection lying against her belly—close, but not where she wanted him. She lifted her hips, trying her best to trap him, but he wouldn't allow it. Instead he kept up the steady kneading of her breast with his long, strong fingers, and the almost painful pressure around her nipple, using his lips, his tongue, and then his teeth.

The firm, steady pressure of sharp teeth on the taut peak left her sobbing. Sobbing and needing, so aroused she trembled.

She slipped into his mind, shocked by how easy it was to read him now that the mating bond was complete. She shared her frustration, her need, and her almost painful arousal, swamping his mind with her impressions until he was every bit as inflamed, as turned on as she.

His eyes were blazing when he tilted his hips and thrust into her, filling her in one quick drive that took her to the edge and beyond. She'd never come so fast, never felt such intense passion, never wanted as much as she wanted now, with Alex. All of it, the beauty and the pain, the struggles they faced. She wanted it all, and she wanted it with this man.

Her man.

Blinking slowly, she gazed into his dark eyes and read the passion there and in the harsh lines of his beautiful face. "I love you," she said, and it felt so good to say the words that she said them again. "I love you. I will always love you."

He nodded, but he didn't speak. Not aloud, not even in her mind. She realized his eyes were filled with tears and reached up to brush one from his cheek. "Alex?"

He drew a deep yet shaky breath. "This is more than I ever dreamed," he said. His voice was hoarse, strained with emotion. She frowned when he shook his head and rested his forehead against hers. "Don't tell Lily you made me cry. I'll never live it down."

"Never," she said, but her heart soared. "I wouldn't dream of blowing your cover."

He touched his forehead to hers. "We do need to tell your folks about us. Your dad's going to kill me."

She giggled. This was the man she was used to. "Actually, I think we should tell Anton. He can tell my dad."

Alex rolled off her, laughing. "That sounds like a plan, but it's the coward's way out." He lay on his back beside her, turned, and gazed at her. "You're thirty years old, Annie. I'm thirty-two. We're not pups anymore, and while I appreciate the fact that Chanku young seem to take longer to mature, we are adults. I don't intend to hide this from anyone, least of all your father. I love you. I'm so damned proud to be your mate, I want to scream it to the mountains." He stood and held a hand out to her. "And I fully intend to tell your father. In person."

Once she was standing, he kissed her forehead and chuckled softly. "But I'm not an idiot, either. I think what we need to do is ask your mom and dad to meet us at Anton and Keisha's. I want my parents there, too, on neutral ground. We'll tell them all at the same time, okay?"

Annie giggled. She couldn't help herself. "Brilliant. He wouldn't dare kill you with witnesses present."

"Exactly what I was thinking."

They shifted at precisely the same time, so in sync since the bonding that it was the most natural thing in the world to know what Alex was going to do next. He pulled her into his thoughts and contacted Anton first.

Annie and I would like to meet with our parents at your house tonight. Is that okay?

If you get here in the next ten minutes, you can sit down to dinner with them. Annie's parents just arrived, and yours will be here in a couple of minutes.

Alex wanted to laugh out loud. *You know, don't you? How do you do that?*

Pack alpha secret, and no, I don't know, but I'm guessing you and Annie have mated, and if so, you have my congratulations.

Thank you.

Annie added her thanks. *We want to tell our parents at the same time,* she said.

With witnesses, so Tinker won't kill me.

Anton's laughter wasn't unexpected. *The only witnesses will be your parents, Keisha, and me. Lily and Sebastian aren't back from their visit with Eve on the astral. Come quickly. I expect this will be one of our more interesting dinner parties.*

Annie glanced at Alex and caught the twinkle in her mate's eyes. She was afraid their alpha might just be right.

Alex sat beside his father with Tinker on the far side of Stefan at Anton's bar while the alpha poured drinks for all of them. Tinker hadn't said much during dinner, especially when the women had been all over the two of them with congratulations, hugs, and kisses.

Now the four women—Keisha, Xandi, Lisa, and Annie— had headed off to town to shop for something special for Annie to wear when their mating was announced to the pack.

Alex didn't like the fact they'd left the compound, especially since it was already after seven. Not with Aldo Xenakis back in town and rogue wolves about, but he figured he'd better get used to deferring to what his woman wanted—to a point. He took the cognac Anton handed him and caught his father's steady gaze. "Congratulations, Alex. I think you've made a brilliant choice." His dad held his glass out in a casual toast.

Alex touched his glass to Stefan's. "Thank you. She's pretty amazing, Dad." Then he glanced at Tinker. "I do love your daughter, Tink. I promise I'll be good to her, and I'll do whatever it takes to make her happy. Just knowing she loves me is the best thing that's ever happened to me."

"Damned straight you'll be good to her." He practically growled, but at least he smiled when he said it. Then he touched his glass to Alex's.

Anton held up his glass. "My very best to both of you, Alex. Though, because of you, my wife has once again proved both your father and me wrong."

Stefan chuckled and took a sip of his cognac. "I know. Include Xandi in that, too. She's said all along that you and Annie would make a better pairing than you and Lily. How come we were the last ones to see this coming?"

Tinker shook his head and shot a grin at Alex. "Well, I sure as hell missed out on everything, but Lisa always says I'm the last to figure stuff out. So, what's the plan now, son?"

Alex silently cringed at the unspoken challenge in that question. He swallowed down the short shot of Hennessy and set the glass on the bar. "The plan right now is to follow the women to town." He stood up and shoved the bar stool back under the bar. "I know that Keisha, Lisa, and Xandi are a formidable team, but a couple of rogues tried to capture us last night, and I don't feel comfortable with the women going into Kalispell without backup."

Tinker studied him with a surprising show of respect. Then he nodded slowly, finished his drink, and set the glass on the bar. "Do you want company?"

"Yes, sir, I do. Dad? Anton? Interested in an evening shopping trip in town?"

Anton's lip curled up in a grin. "The girls won't like it."

Alex looked him directly in the eye. No submission at all. Not this time. "Does that really matter?"

Anton shook his head and clapped Alex on the shoulder. "Not a bit. C'mon. We'll take the Rover."

Anton handed the keys to Alex and then rode shotgun. He wanted to sit where he could watch him, see how he continued to handle the situation, and he didn't want to be distracted by either the need to drive or by sitting next to Stefan.

Besides, Stefan needed a little time to bond with Tinker. They were now forever linked through their children, and in spite of his inability to see this one coming, Anton had a good feeling about Alex and Annie as a pair.

They were going to add a strong dynamic to the pack. Alex was already impressing him with the confidence he'd shown today. He'd not only stood up to Tinker, but he'd not backed down in front of either his father or his pack alpha, which was a whole new side of Alex Aragat.

And, while Anton really hated admitting he'd been wrong all along, Lily and Sebastian were a much better match, just as Alex and Annie were absolutely perfect.

Alex floored it as soon as he hit the two-lane paved road that led to the highway, and the Rover practically flew. The women hadn't left until after the men gathered in the bar, so they couldn't be far ahead.

Alex? We probably shouldn't let them see us. You might want to slow down.

No. Alex flashed him a stark look. *They're in danger. I feel it. Annie's terrified but she can't mindspeak. Contact Keisha.*

Anton hit a blank wall where his wife's mind should be. "Stefan, Tink! Try and reach Lisa and Xandi. Ask them what's going on. Quickly. Alex, what's Annie saying?"

"Crap, Anton. Nothing. I think they've got her." Alex slammed his foot down on the gas, and the Rover leapt forward.

Anton swung around in his seat and looked at Stefan and Tink. Both men stared at the road ahead, but they were shaking their heads.

"Nothing, Anton." Stefan grabbed the back of Alex's seat. "What the fuck's going on?"

"Don't know. I can't reach Keisha. Alex got a quick sense of Annie's fear, then nothing. Tinker?"

The big guy raised his head. Tears rolled down his dark cheeks. "I heard Lisa scream Annie's name. Then nothing. Shit, Anton. Where the fuck are they?"

"Up ahead. I see the car. There. They're in the ditch." Alex swung the wheel to the right. Tinker leapt from the moving vehicle as Alex hit the brakes and parked over dark skid marks going off the road.

Anton, Stefan, and Alex reached the car as Tinker grabbed

hold of the crumpled passenger door and tore it completely off. He tossed the thing aside as if it weighed nothing and went straight for his mate in the backseat.

Keisha was slumped over the steering wheel. Xandi lay half on top of her, trapped in her seat belt. Lisa was curled against the shattered window behind the driver's seat, bleeding from a head wound.

There was no sign of Annie, but a chemical scent filled the air around the car.

Anton undid Xandi's seat belt and handed her limp body to Stefan. "Get them out of here. Quick. They've been gassed, but I don't know if it's poisonous or just something to knock them out." He freed Keisha, holding her close against his heart for a relieved prayer of thanks to the goddess. His mate still lived. He carried her to a small green area and laid her down.

Alex knelt to check his mother while his father and Tinker worked to free Lisa. "Dad? Mom's coming around." He stood and touched Anton's shoulder. "I'm going after Annie. If Aldo Xenakis is behind this, I think I know where they've taken her."

Kneeling beside his wife, Anton touched his fingers to her throat and found a strong pulse. Breathing a sigh of relief, he shot a quick glance at Alex. "Are you certain this is Xenakis's work?"

He'd never seen Alex like this—focused, determined, and absolutely furious. He seethed with anger that felt ready to blow, though it was anger locked under tight control.

Alex nodded. "I am. I recognize the scent of wolves, the same ones who attacked us last night. Lily said they're the same breed as the ones Xenakis uses as bodyguards."

Anton felt Keisha stir. Relief and a horrible, dark wave of anger swept over him. "Where do you want the pack to meet you?"

"The big oak, the one that's on the ridge between the Xenakis property and yours. Link with me when you can so we can coordinate once I get up there and see what the fuck that bastard has planned. It's easier to connect when you open the link."

Keisha groaned. Then she blinked rapidly and grabbed Anton's arm. "My love," she gasped, struggling to sit. Anton wrapped his arms around her and helped her up. "Anton. They've got Annie. That bastard Xenakis plans to sacrifice her for some spell he's planning. It's going to happen tonight."

16

"That's a first." Eve cocked her head to one side and stared toward the huge tree and the man kneeling beneath it.

"What is?" Lily settled herself comfortably on the grass. Her knees ached. They'd knelt before the Mother for a long time. At least it felt like a long time, though time itself on the astral was often a matter of interpretation.

"Being summarily dismissed by the Mother. Generally, her thoughts just end and she's gone from my *where.* Instead, you and I were sent away, but she's still here. Talking to Sebastian."

Lily chuckled. "Eve, you sound a bit disgruntled."

Eve smiled and shook her head. "I know, but trust me, Lily. I take this goddess gig seriously. And though Sebastian is certainly good-looking, he is still a man."

This time Lily let it go and laughed out loud. After so much stress over the past few weeks, it felt good to sit here on the astral with her dearest friend and relax—at least, relax as much as one could, knowing all hell was breaking loose at home. She focused once again on Sebastian and realized he looked even sexier on his knees, which opened her to all kinds of wicked thoughts. She glanced at Eve. "I wonder what she's saying to him."

Eve merely shrugged. "I don't know. I can't read the Mother's mind the way I can yours. I'm still surprised that he knows her. It's not like the Mother is a social being." Eve glanced at Lily and then focused once again on Sebastian. "It's a mystery to me, but something unusual must be happening." Then she sighed, reached into the air, and pulled out a tray of small open-faced sandwiches followed by two glasses of wine.

Lily took one of the crystal goblets and a sandwich and realized she was starving. Time had no meaning here, but her stomach seemed to think otherwise. She had no idea how long she and Eve had knelt in thrall to the Mother as the powerful spirit answered what questions she would before dismissing them to speak alone with Sebastian.

Long enough that they'd probably missed that beautiful rib roast her mom was fixing for dinner. Hopefully there'd be leftovers. Lily took a bite of one of Eve's sandwiches. "These are good. I didn't realize how hungry I was. How long have we been here?"

"A couple of hours, as time is counted on the astral, but I'm not really certain how much time has passed in your world. The Mother's visit can affect the way we experience time." She shrugged and nibbled on a sandwich. "There's nothing to be done about that. So what do we know now that we didn't know before?"

"That the wolves killing those girls aren't regular Chanku. They're the Berserkers of Norse legend, shifters who are more wolf than human. They're bloodthirsty, feral creatures who have, for some reason, aligned themselves with Aldo Xenakis. But the rapist is an unknown human, not one of the shifters."

Lily stared at her wineglass. "We have to suspect Aldo in the rapes, but why would he do something so awful? And if the

Berserkers work for him, he must be directing the murders for some reason. It just doesn't make sense, but at least we know why the rogue wolves haven't shown up on your Chanku radar." She flashed a sympathetic smile at Eve.

"I don't sense them at all," Eve said. "The fact there are very few Berserkers left—so few the Mother assumed they were all gone—and because they're closer to the wolf side of their being than the human side, they just don't register the way you do. Plus, they've historically kept more to themselves, their primary form is the wolf, and when they die, they die as wolves, not humans. It's frustrating, not to be able to sense them."

"Do you sense Sebastian?" Lily watched him, still kneeling beneath the tree.

Eve shook her head. "No. His magic is too strong. It hides his nature."

Nodding, still studying Sebastian, Lily wondered about the unknown rapist. She hated to think it was his father. Goddess, that was too awful to contemplate. She glanced at Eve. "We can thank the US government, or at least one of the more clandestine branches of the military, for rediscovering the Berserkers, I imagine. Maybe they were already soldiers, if fighting and killing are basic to their nature. But how did Aldo Xenakis get control of them?"

"I don't know. The Mother was aware of the tests and the fact some unusual Chanku had been discovered, but when they turned out to be so unpredictable and dangerous, she no longer sensed them and thought they'd all been destroyed."

Lily shuddered. "I hate that. Destroyed, like they were vicious animals."

Eve touched her hand. "Lily, in effect, that's exactly what they were. What they are. Creatures that are more feral than human, even when they take human form. Intelligent creatures with no sense of conscience. They were bred as a warrior class on the Chanku home world and were among the first to strike out on their own after landing on Earth."

"From the way the Mother described it, it sounds more like they were banished. As far as I know, none have turned up in the general population. Of course, very few regular Chanku have been found. I wonder why the rogues weren't discovered before now?"

This was so frustrating. The Mother had offered just enough information to make her crazy. If the rogue wolves were Chanku, even if they were of a more violent subspecies, some of them should have taken the nutrients among the general population. Those capsules had been made available to anyone who wanted to see if they carried the Chanku genes, and yet none of the newly discovered Chanku had been anything at all like the wolves that had attacked her and Sebastian or the ones that had gone after Annie and Alex. Those creatures were so much larger, their size alone would have been noted.

And how was it that Aldo Xenakis appeared to have at least half a dozen of the creatures under his command? Were these the only Berserkers in existence?

They'd asked, but the Mother hadn't answered. No, she'd wanted time with Sebastian. *Time alone with Sebastian.*

He still knelt, unmoving while in communion with the Mother. She was all-powerful, and yet she'd explained that she couldn't control what her creatures did, that their free will was stronger than her ability to affect their behavior.

Lily had a feeling she was really good at nudging things to go her way, though. And she wondered why the Mother had chosen to nudge Sebastian. "Sebastian learned to shift by drawing power from the spirit in a huge oak on a ridge that straddles the line between our property and his father's." She glanced at Eve. "He thought it was a dryad, but it sounds as if he's been talking with the Mother all along, if she's the lady of the oak he's told me about."

"That doesn't make sense." Eve shook her head and nibbled on another sandwich. "She's the Mother, the one over all people in all worlds. Why would she spend time with a single young wizard?"

Lily grinned and took another swallow of wine. "Well, he's a very sexy young wizard, and the Mother is female, after all."

Eve practically sputtered. "Oh, Lily," she said, holding her hand over her mouth. "That's got to be sacrilegious."

Lily rolled her eyes. "I *think* I'm teasing, Eve." She glanced toward Sebastian, saw him bow his head, and then slowly stand, as if his joints were stiff from being on his knees for so long. He smiled at Lily, paused, turned back to the tree, and stepped up close. He pressed his hand against the rough bark and then nodded, as if in conversation. Then he spun away and walked toward Eve and Lily.

Halfway to them, he stopped. The air shimmered. Lily's father practically exploded onto the astral.

"Lily! Sebastian, you have to come with me. Annie's been taken by the rogues. Alex is certain Aldo's behind it. If it's him, I'm going to need your magic to help me get her back."

Eve lunged to her feet. "I'll be with you. Call on me when you need my strength." She paused a moment, glanced toward the tree, and bowed her head. "Thank you," she whispered. "Lily, go now. Both of you go with your father. The Mother is staying close. She's promised to help where she can."

Lily grabbed Eve for a quick hug, took hold of Sebastian's arm with her right hand, and grabbed her father's with her left. No need of a portal when three mages combined their power.

With little more than a wink and a spell, they stepped back into the cavern beneath the house. Anton raced toward the exit tunnel. "Hurry!"

"Dad! What happened?" Lily ran after him, across the large

cavern, through the tunnel to the underground pantry, and up the stairs to the kitchen.

Sebastian pounded up the stairs behind her.

Anton didn't slow down a bit, but his thoughts filled Lily's head. When Sebastian grabbed her hand, she knew he heard as well. *Annie, Xandi, Lisa, and your mom were driving to town. They took Mom's car. It was rigged with a gas canister hidden inside. It exploded as they pulled off the driveway onto the main road.*

Is Mom okay?

Everyone is fine except for Annie. Mom was still driving, losing consciousness from the gas. The car went off the road, but she saw four huge men grab Annie and stuff her in a sack. She's sure they were Chanku, and she heard them talking about a sacrifice. Alex has gone to the oak that straddles the property line. He thinks Aldo plans to kill Annie there. If Aldo's using death magic, if he's recently killed, he could be stronger than all of us. I need your help. Sebastian? Are you willing to work against your father?

They'd reached the kitchen. Sebastian grabbed Anton's shoulder to stop him. Then he held out his hand. "I will back you in any way I can. You have my word on that."

Anton shook his outstretched hand. "Good. I figured we could count on you. Lily, I'll gather the pack in the big meadow. I hate to ask you to do this, but I want you and Sebastian to go up on the mountain. Alex is already there. He said it looks like they're setting up for some spell work, but he hasn't been able to connect with Annie yet. We can't do anything until we know where she is. Tinker and Stefan are with Alex. My plan is to use the pack to build energy for you and Sebastian to channel."

He grabbed Lily's shoulders and stared directly into her eyes, but he spoke aloud. "It would be easier if you and Sebastian were bonded, but even without that, the two of you are already more powerful than I can ever hope to be. Find a way to work together. Your combined magic along with what we can send to you should be much stronger than Aldo's."

Lily nodded, shocked her father would even mention bonding. Did he approve that strongly of Sebastian? She had no doubts. Not anymore. Even the Mother had given him a blessing of sorts, communing with him for so long.

She forced herself back to what her father was saying. The two of them had done this before, taking energy from the pack, working it between them. Together they could manipulate energy better than Anton could alone, but she'd never done it without him. Sebastian was a powerful mage, in some ways, even stronger than her father, though Sebastian's magic was instinctive. He lacked training, beyond what her dad had given him earlier today.

Would that be enough? One day's training to fight a wizard with a lifetime of dark magic behind him? It had to be, though she couldn't help but think how much stronger they would be were they to mate. But they couldn't. Not like this. Even the threat hanging over them wasn't worth forcing such a commitment on Sebastian.

But damn it all, what was Aldo Xenakis trying to do? She clutched Sebastian's arm and tugged him to face her. "Sebastian, what is your father's goal? Do you have any idea what he thinks he can gain by doing this? What will a human sacrifice do for him? He's got to be losing his mind, to think he can get away with this."

Sebastian just shook his head. "I have no idea, Lil. All I can think is, the man must be insane. He's always wanted more power, but this is beyond extreme. None of it makes sense."

"Crap. The timing does." Anton turned and raced down the hall toward the den with Lily and Sebastian right behind him. "Tonight's the full moon. Why didn't I realize how much greater the risk would be tonight?"

He paused in the doorway and glanced over his shoulder. "I notified the sheriff's department a while ago, told them there'd been a kidnapping of one of our pack, but that Alex was looking into it. They allow us to police ourselves whenever possible, and I don't want innocent deputies hurt. Your father's an unknown as far as how much power he's amassed with the killings, but I wanted you to know we're hoping to handle this on our own."

He ran his fingers through his hair, dislodging the tie holding it back from his face. Lily rarely saw him distraught.

"Hell." He shot a quick look at Sebastian. "I don't know anything at all about your father's magic. Blood magic, much less human sacrifice is way out of my league." He hit a switch on a large console next to his desk.

A map came up and lights went on all across the screen—the various households scattered around the property and beyond. He placed his hand on a sensor on a control panel at the bottom. His powerful voice sounded in Lily's mind, and she knew that every member of the pack, no matter how far away they might be, would hear his request.

Annie McClintock has been kidnapped. If you're able, please meet me in the meadow behind the main house. We need pack energy to defeat the one who has her. Be there by eleven tonight.

He swung around and took a quick glance out the window before focusing on Lily. "I wish I could go with you, but I believe I can better serve you here. Be careful." He turned to Sebastian. "Keep my daughter safe, and yourself as well. You're a good man, Sebastian Xenakis, and you are a powerful mage, but you are a man grown, not your father's son. Remember that."

Sebastian gave a short, sharp nod. "When's the moon going to be full and directly overhead?"

"At eleven thirty-five." Her dad ran his fingers over the

screen and drew up a schematic of the night sky. "It will pass over the top of the mountain southeast of the oak at approximately eleven eighteen, but it's not officially full until eleven thirty-five. If he's working blood magic, I imagine he'll time the climax of his spell accordingly." He glanced at the clock on the wall over the desk. "It's almost ten. It's a good half hour on four legs from here to the oak. Get something to eat. I think Mom left plenty of leftover roast in the refrigerator for you. It's cold, but you'll need fuel for what you have to do tonight."

He stopped, gazed steadily at Lily, and then drew her into a hug. "Damn, sweetheart. I hate sending you up there. I hate it."

"Dad? We'll be okay." She hugged him just as tight.

"I know you will, baby. I'm worried about you and worried sick about Annie and Alex. They mated today. They're bonded. If anything happens to either of them . . ."

"Oh, Goddess." She pulled away and stared at her father. His amber eyes glittered—tears of rage and compassion for a young man who was as much a son to him as either of his own boys. "I am so glad they've mated, but you're right. We have to go."

Her father suddenly looked away with the deep concentration that meant someone had contacted him. Lily grabbed Sebastian's hand and tried not to think of what Annie and Alex were going through right now. And Alex mated! She wanted to cheer, but at the same time, their new bond had to make this even harder for both Annie and Alex.

Sebastian wrapped an arm around her and held her close. Lily leaned against his side and hugged him back. "Let's go get something to eat. Dad's right. We need fuel. He'll tell us if he's learning something we need to know."

"Okay. Lily, we haven't had time to talk."

She tugged his hand, pulling him toward the kitchen. "About the Mother?"

He nodded. "She's the spirit of the tree. She's been giving me the power to shift, helping my magic, though until I can do it on my own, she can't be certain I'm Chanku."

"Even the Mother doesn't know?"

He shook his head. "No. And in my case, she said my magic is so strong that it affects her ability to read me. I need to keep taking the capsules. The nutrients will override my magic and allow me to shift naturally, if that's my heritage."

Anton caught up to them halfway to the kitchen. "Hurry. Eat something and get up on the ridge. That was Alex. He said there are twelve rogues up there now. He didn't expect that many, and there could be even more, but he's staying hidden. Tinker and Stefan are with him. There's no word yet from Annie. We're hoping she's merely unconscious and can't mind-speak. Hurry."

Sebastian felt as if they were doing a major disservice to Keisha's rib roast, but he and Lily cut huge slabs of the leftover beef and literally choked it down.

How could any woman look so beautiful, holding on to a bloody rib bone with both hands and gnawing at the rare meat still attached? He loved her. There was no doubt, not after this past day when he knew his life had forever changed. He'd not only made love with Lily, but traveled on the astral plane and communed with a goddess and a spirit even more powerful, and yet making love with Lily was still the most life-altering part of his day.

That and his connection with Alex. He'd filed that experience away for a time when he could truly analyze what had happened, but he hoped like hell it happened again. He'd never connected with another man like that—such a soul-deep sense of something so close to love it was almost scary. His emotions were all over the map, except when he thought of Lily.

Lily grounded him. She gave him hope and a sense of peace he'd never known before. So many changes in his life, all in just the last three days. Lily. Alex. Anton and Keisha. The goddess Eve. Meeting the spiritual Mother who presided over all of them, discovering she was the same spirit he'd known for these past months as the lady of the tree.

The spirit he'd felt so close to on the ridge above was so much more than a mere dryad. The Mother was a feminine spirit of absolute power.

Almost absolute power. She still couldn't tell him what he was. He spotted a jar of Anton's capsules on the kitchen counter and leaned his chair back far enough to reach for it. Lily raised her eyes to his when he popped two of the big green pills into his mouth and swallowed them down with a glass of water.

He shrugged. "Time's different on the astral, remember?" Then he chuckled as he grabbed his empty plate and carried it to the sink. "I felt like I was on my knees for at least two days."

Lily cleared her dishes as well, rinsed everything, and stuck the plates and utensils in the dishwasher while Sebastian wrapped up the roast and put it back in the refrigerator. When he turned around, she was watching him.

"What did you talk about?"

He shook his head. "*We* didn't talk. In fact, I didn't do any talking at all. She said there were things I would need to know and she would give them to me. I stayed on my knees in absolute silence, absorbing whatever it was she gave me. And no, I have no idea what I know now that I didn't before. It was really weird."

Stepping close, Lily pressed her fingers against his chest. "Trust her, Sebastian. She really does watch over us, usually through Eve, though. The Mother has never openly intervened before, at least not in any way we've known."

"I think she did some intervening today, though I have no idea how or what she did." He wiped his hands off on a paper towel and tossed it in the trash. "C'mon. We need to go. I want to get up to the ridge before anything happens to Annie. I can't imagine what Alex is going through. If he loves her as much as I love you . . ."

"Sebastian?" Lily paused and then turned. "Do you truly love me? Because I keep thinking about what Dad said, that mating could strengthen us even more."

He stepped close and wrapped his arms around her waist, and realized she still wore the yoga pants and crop top from this morning. So damned much had happened since they'd left her little cottage. "The mating bond? The permanent link you told me about?"

Lily nodded.

Sebastian wanted to shout to the heavens. Could she possibly love him enough to commit herself to him forever? But what if he wasn't Chanku? He said as much.

Lily shook her head. "If you're not Chanku, the bond won't work. But if you are, it's forever. Do you think you can love me that much, Sebastian? Enough to tie yourself to me for the rest of your life? And believe me, if you are Chanku, it's a long life."

"That's all I've thought about Lily. I said as much to the Mother. That's when she asked me to stay behind."

"Then she must approve. It's almost ten thirty. We need to go."

She paused and got that faraway look that told him she was communicating with someone. "I told Dad we're leaving. He said pack members are already showing up. Some of the bigger guys will meet us up on the ridge, but they're going through the caves and that takes a little longer. Unless your father has lookouts posted within the cave system, it will allow more of us to get to the site without detection."

"Good. But, Lily?"

She stopped in the doorway and looked over her shoulder,

and all he could think of was taking her as his mate. Not the reason why, that it would strengthen their magic, but because he loved her and he didn't want to ever risk losing her.

"What?"

"He's not my father. Not anymore. He's Aldo Xenakis, a crazy-sick bastard who needs to be taken down."

She flashed him a huge grin. "Gotcha. So . . . let's go take him down, okay?"

He followed her out onto the deck and stripped off his clothing as quickly as she removed hers. This time, he called directly on the Mother for the power to shift. He felt her energy pour through him, over him, and become a part of him. Within seconds they were both leaping off the deck and cutting across the big meadow. Wolves were arriving from all directions, and though he didn't know them, he sensed their common goal. Their power would be his tonight. More power than he'd ever wielded in his life.

He thought of his first attempts at magic, how he'd envied his father's magic and wanted that kind of power. How he'd considered the ethics of blood magic, found them wanting, and yet had skirted a fine edge before choosing good over evil. He'd come close, but he hadn't succumbed to the darkness, and it was Lily who had made him see the light.

Quite literally.

He couldn't help but think of what Lily had told him, how the power from a blood sacrifice was finite, that it was strong at first, but when it was gone, it was gone forever.

The power he and Lily would be working tonight was fueled by love. He saw it firsthand, here in this huge meadow bathed in the soft light shimmering from gaslight lamps along the deck stretching across the back of Anton Cheval's lovely home. Saw it in the dozens of wolves converging here as he and Lily raced beyond them and into the dark forest.

The sky glowed in the east where the moon would soon

crest the highest peaks, but for now, the two of them ran in darkness. Ran knowing Annie's life depended on their speed and their ability to work together.

He'd never felt stronger. Never known such a sense of purpose as they climbed the mountain, heading toward the huge oak where he'd first communed with the Mother, thinking her nothing more than a simple dryad, a tree nymph. She was so much more. Would she be there tonight? Would she be forced to bear witness to the murder of one of her beloved Chanku?

Not if he and Lily had anything to do about it.

They were almost to the ridge when Lily took a quick jog off the trail and raced through a thick tangle of bracken fern. He followed, trusting her. She knew these trails better than he ever could. She'd grown up here, hunted here, and made love here.

And then she was pausing in the quiet darkness, a shadow among shadows, yet still a perfect visual in amazing contrast through wolven eyes. Her ears perked forward. *Are you sure?*

Heart pounding, he stepped closer. *Here? Now?*

She blinked. A slow lowering of lashes over amber eyes. *Yes.*

Desire surged. Not the carnal lusts of a man knowing he was about to score, but an arousal of heart, mind, soul, and body, so deep, so pure, he trembled. *More certain than I've been of anything in my life. I love you, Lily, and we will bond. If not now, at another date, but you are mine. If the bond will help us save Annie, knowing we're going to do it anyway, I say we do it now. Ceremony isn't needed. Not for my promise to you. It will be as strong tonight as tomorrow. As strong tomorrow as an eternity from now.*

Agreed. I love you, Sebastian. And I pray to the goddess and the Mother that this bond is true, that you are the man I think you are. I believe you to be Chanku.

Chanku or not, Lily Milina Cheval, you are mine. You will

always be mine. I love you. Life would not be worth living without you. This bond will be true, and it will be forever.

There was no time for the romance he felt in his heart, for the words he wanted to say. These short vows they'd just made would have to suffice, but he had no doubt in his mind or his heart. No concern that this might not be the right choice.

It was the only choice, and he wanted it with all his heart.

Over the years, Lily had tried to imagine this moment with Alex, but she'd never been able to picture the two of them together, Alex mounting her as a wolf, bonding with her forever.

The whole idea just made both of them laugh.

She saw it so clearly with Sebastian. Knew in her heart that the ancient ones would agree this was a man who would meet her, challenge for challenge for the rest of their days.

But they had so little time, and as much as she loved him, she had to recognize that this was also a means to an end. Romance would come later, once Annie was safe. But when she glanced over her shoulder and caught the intent look in those unusual teal blue eyes of his, she knew he saw this moment, beyond their mating, as more than part of a plan to rescue Annie.

She had the strangest feeling Sebastian believed he was also rescuing himself. His paw brushed her shoulder, and she turned her back to him, raised her tail, and cocked it to one side. His powerful front legs grasped her back, and her legs shook beneath his weight. He was a huge wolf. Not as large as the rogues, but still big, and all she could think was the fact he was a fitting mate for the daughter of Anton Cheval.

She'd been raised like a princess. She knew she was far from royalty, but she'd been blessed by the goddess and by the Mother with exceptional abilities, with beauty and a powerful mind, and magic that had surpassed even her father's years ago.

And always, there had been love. Her parents, Alex, the rest of the pack. A life steeped in love, yet it paled beside what she felt for this man, from this man, a man who'd grown up without family, without the support of the pack.

He was an amazing individual. A strong and honorable man. She could only wonder how much more amazing he would be when he had the power of the pack behind him.

He tightened his grasp on her body, and she felt the first thrust of his wolven cock. She opened to him, ripe for invasion, for this feminine subjugation to the stronger male. She, a woman who had bowed her head to no man, felt him slide deep, felt the stretch of muscles never before tried. Without hesitation, she bowed her head, planted her paws, and braced herself to take him.

His rapid thrusts shot deep and hard, entirely unlike a human mating, yet all were sensations that felt perfect in this form. Understood and expected, yet entirely new—the thick slide of his sharp penis, then the fullness of his mating knot slipping past her vaginal lips, swelling deep inside.

Tying her to him. For now and with the grace of the goddess, forever.

She opened to him, anxious to see what he thought of this amazing experience, and their link clicked into place. Not a simple melding of minds, but something so powerful, so complete, it left her reeling.

She anchored herself in his brilliant mind, saw herself through Sebastian's eyes, and was astounded by the strength of his love, the depth of his feelings.

And she knew he saw the same in her. Knew so much more than she'd ever imagined. He was an open book to her—his fears, his hopes, and his desire to be what she needed. She saw his frustration over the father he'd hoped to find, and his disgust with the one he'd found. She realized his life had been one disappointment after another. Until now.

Now he saw his world as one filled with possibilities. He'd always had so much love to give, but there'd never been anyone there for him. Not even his mother who had lived in fear of the monster she'd married—so much fear, she'd been unable to love her only child as fully as he'd deserved.

Sebastian's memories, his history, his hopes and dreams and fears were Lily's, but with everything pouring into her mind, she held on to his love. Unblemished and pure, it was all for her.

Time seemed to stand still, but in the back of her mind was the knowledge that Annie needed them, that Alex waited for them, and after what felt like forever but probably lasted mere minutes, Lily slowly allowed her side of the link to fade.

Sebastian did the same, slipping out of her innermost thoughts, though the link didn't close entirely. They were truly bonded. Finally she understood what her parents had found with one another.

She'd never felt a link so close, had never known such a feeling of satisfaction, of pure, unadulterated love. Sebastian's love. She shifted, becoming human as quickly as Sebastian, and they lay there in the damp grass, staring at one another in the darkness.

A tiny sliver of moonlight reflected off his fascinating teal blue eyes, and the magnitude of their bonding was swamped by that stark reminder of the mission ahead of them. "The moon is rising over the ridge," she said.

Sebastian nodded. "We need to hurry."

She stood and gazed about her to get her bearings, but Sebastian was behind her, wrapping his big arms around her body, and kissing the side of her neck. "We have time. We're not that far from the site," he whispered. "Goddess, Lily. That was amazing. I was with you when you met the Ancient Ones. I know the Chanku history, just as they gave it to you. You have lived such an amazing life, it will take me months to assimilate all I've learned."

He kissed her lips, sliding softly over her mouth, and his

mind was open to hers, his thoughts cascading through her mind in a rainbow of images. His dreams for the two of them, for the children he hoped to have one day. His own family to love. "I'm so sorry we had to rush. I promise to make it up to you."

She turned in his arms and kissed him hard and fast before whispering against his lips. "You're damned right you'll make it up to me. We've got a job to do, but I'm holding you to your promise, big guy. I love you, and right now you know me better than I know myself. Just as I know you, but when it comes to this ridge, I think you're more familiar with the area than I am. What's next?"

"Link with Alex. Find out if he's heard from Annie. I'll concentrate on Aldo. But, Lily? Be careful. He's a dangerous man, and I don't know anything at all about the rogues, what kind of control he's got over them. They're not quite human, even when they look human."

She nodded and hugged him again. It was so hard not to touch him with the link still buzzing between them like an electrical charge, with arousal and desire and just plain old lust a living, breathing entity, but this was not the time. Then, just at the moment she prepared to shift, Alex's voice popped into her head.

Lily. I see her! Rogues are carrying Annie out. She's alive, but she's not in my head. I can't contact her. I don't know what . . . shit! They're tying her to the oak. Hurry, Lily. I don't think we have much time.

17

Thank the goddess they'd taken her out of that damned sack, though what they had planned for her couldn't be anything good. It was dark out, but Annie knew she was on the mountain not far from home. It smelled familiar, like home should smell, though the air was tainted with some kind of herbal stink, something she didn't recognize.

The only ones around were more of those huge men, and two of them were carrying her. One held her arms, the other her feet, and it didn't matter how much she tried to break out of their grasp, these jerks were strong. Annie fought them, anyway.

She'd tried shifting, but something blocked her so that she couldn't find her wolf. That had never happened before. Since the very first time she'd shifted, when she was just a little girl, her wolf had answered. She'd even tried other creatures. None had responded. It felt as if part of her had died.

She was naked, and while no one had raped her, they'd had their filthy hands all over her body, pinching and poking, leering at her and making stupid threats. She'd ignored them. One thing she'd learned from some of the older women in the pack—evil men could do terrible things to a woman's body, but they couldn't touch her soul.

These idiots hadn't even come close.

She knew Alex had to be nearby. Goddess, she'd been calling out to him for what felt like forever, but there'd been nothing. Where the sense of him had made up the brightest corners of her mind, there was nothing but darkness. He'd been a part of her since the moment he'd rescued her in town, and the feeling had only grown stronger since their mating.

Then just after those horrible men had stuffed her into a big sack, Alex had blinked out of her mind. He couldn't be dead. She'd know it if he were dead, wouldn't she? Their bond was new, but they were linked forever.

So where in the hell was he? When she couldn't get Alex, she'd tried to reach her father and Anton. Nothing. As powerful as Anton was, he should have answered. She'd never felt so totally cut off from the pack before.

She couldn't shift, couldn't mindspeak. She wanted to scream in frustration, but no sound came out. But she could still bite, damn it, and she twisted in the grasp of the guy holding her arms and bit down hard on his wrist.

He slammed her hard against the side of a huge tree. Stars exploded in her head, but she tasted blood and knew she'd hurt him.

"Shit. The fucking bitch bit me."

"Watch it. Don't damage the goods. Here. Stand her upright." An older man stepped into her line of sight. He was tall and dressed in a dark business suit, which was not what most people wore this high in the mountains.

For some reason, he looked familiar, though she knew she'd never met him. He ran his fingers over the side of her face, and the foulness of his touch scared the crap out of her. He felt evil, as if there were something terribly wrong about him. She shivered, instinctively drawing away.

"Good. Animals should be afraid of me." He held up a metal collar and tightened it around her neck. Even if she were able to shift, she couldn't now without strangling herself. He checked the clasp and then clamped some sort of metal restraints on her wrists while one of his men fastened the same things to her legs, just above her knees.

Then they lifted her up like a sack of potatoes and hung the restraints on hooks stuck in the thick bark of the tree. Her arms stretched over her head, and her legs were spread wide with her feet dangling against the rough bark. It scraped her back and buttocks, and her head was still spinning from getting knocked against the trunk, but she twisted against the restraints anyway, testing them.

Then she saw lights off in the distance and knew where she was. They'd hung her from the big oak that straddled the property between the Chanku land and their neighbor.

Sebastian's father. Shit. She'd heard people talking about him like he was some kind of crazy. This was not looking good, but it explained why he looked familiar.

He stood in front of her, smiling at her as if he was really proud of what he'd accomplished. She wanted to tell him what a piece of shit he was, but she couldn't talk.

Can't shift, can't talk, can't mindspeak.

Of course. He was a fucking wizard. It had to be some kind of spell blocking her. What other explanation could there be?

Alex might not have any idea where she was or who had her. If she couldn't link to him, it stood to reason he couldn't link to her. She'd been counting on that connection, but if she'd been magically blocked . . . damn.

She looked in all directions, but the fire burning just a few feet away cast everything beyond its glow in darkest night. She couldn't sense anyone nearby—not even the bastards who held her. How could Alex possibly find her if she was totally cut off? Her head fell forward; despair washed over her. She needed Alex. She'd always needed Alex, but dear Goddess, she really needed him now.

If his father hadn't knelt beside him in his human form with a restraining hand on his shoulder, Alex would probably be dead by now. He knew that with the same certainty that he realized men would die tonight.

Hopefully by his hand.

Poor Annie. She was so close and yet she might have been a million miles away. *The bastard's got to be blocking her.*

His dad squeezed his shoulder. *I asked Anton. He said it's possibly a warding spell, but instead of being used to protect Annie, it's acting like a shield, not allowing her to speak either verbally or mentally. It's got to be blocking her ability to shift, too. Otherwise, I'm sure Annie would have been going for throats, not merely wrists.*

My girl's a hell of a fighter. Tinker was less than ten feet away, concealed in heavy brush, and Alex sensed some sort of massive mental restraint holding the man in place. Anton? He didn't think his own dad was strong enough.

Those bastards will die tonight.

Oh, yeah. I'm with you, Tink. Help's on the way. I think Lily and Sebastian are close.

I'm here, Alex, Lily said. *Coming in behind you. Sebastian's trying to get closer to Aldo. Dad's got the pack together, and they're building up more energy for our magic.*

Then Anton was speaking. *Sebastian? Are you two there yet? Good. Look, we've got trouble. I just heard from the sheriff. There's been another murder—body of a young woman discovered on our land, down where it runs along the highway. Probably happened early this morning.*

Sebastian spoke. Calm, measured tones. *He'll be much stronger, even harder to stop.*

His control helped center Alex.

I know. Anton again, sounding calm and focused. Alex concentrated on his own focus as Anton continued.

Sebastian, be careful. We have to stop him tonight, before anyone else dies. Alex, I've confirmed my suspicions. Definitely a ward of some kind shielding Annie. I can't sense her at all, which means he's using some powerful magic. Blood magic from the death of that girl, I imagine. Sebastian? Lily? I'm holding pack energy. A lot of it. Link to me when you need it.

Thanks, Dad. And, Dad? Sebastian and I have mated.

There was a long silence. Then Anton again, sounding like a man fighting powerful emotions. *Good, sweetheart. Damn good. In fact, it's wonderful. Sebastian? You have an even greater responsibility to keep her safe.*

I've known that since the beginning. I won't let anything happen to those you love.

Alex glanced at his father and then felt Lily's chin on his back. *If Sebastian does anything stupid,* she said, *I will haunt him.*

I'll help.

Good.

The twelve rogues moved into position in a circle around the tree, six of them in human form, six as wolves. They stood just outside of the circle Aldo was scraping into the dirt.

He stood back and surveyed the circle and then stripped out of his clothing. One of the men, acting as an acolyte, slipped a black robe over Aldo's head and helped him tie the sash. Then he stepped back and joined the others around the tree.

Annie hung there, looking angry and frustrated and scared to death. Alex glanced over his shoulder at Lily. She shook her head. *Sebastian says he has an idea that should get Aldo to turn*

Annie free. Let's see what he'd got planned. Then we attack, but we wait until Annie is free. She's too vulnerable.

I know. And I don't know if we're strong enough to take them in a fight. He hadn't wanted to voice that concern. Not at all, but it was wrong to deny the truth. There were twelve huge rogue Chanku, and only eight of them, counting the three packmates who'd come up through the tunnels.

Everyone else was in the meadow channeling energy. He didn't trust magic. Not nearly as much as he trusted teeth and good old-fashioned fighting, but he forced himself to hold his position.

He wanted Annie to know they were here for her. That they'd be getting her away from the bastard who held her. Then, Goddess be blessed, Annie raised her head and looked right at Alex.

He gazed straight into her eyes and sent his love across the short distance, but he couldn't tell if she saw him or not. He could only wait to see what Lily and Sebastian had planned.

Sebastian linked privately with Lily. *We have to get Annie free of him. That has to come first. I'm going out there, but don't give yourself away. I want him to think I'm here alone.*

No, Sebastian. You can't. It's too dangerous.

I can, and I will be okay. I love you, Lily, and we have the power of the pack behind us. I can feel their strength.

Before Lily could say anything else, he shifted and strode out onto the moonlit ridge, but he pulled the power of the pack around him, and used their strength to mask his presence.

He felt it like a powerful drug, the energy from all those Chanku along with the added strength of the Mother thrumming in his veins. Even stronger was the power of Lily's love.

The moon was almost directly overhead—time was growing short. Moonlight caught him just outside the circle, and he dropped the glamour that had hidden him from view, standing there tall and proud, his naked body hard and pulsing with more power than he'd ever felt.

His skin glistened in the moonlight, his muscles practically quivered with power, and his cock rode high and hard against his belly. He felt as if all the elements waited for his call.

"Master! Behind you."

Aldo spun about when one rogue called out. He stood just inside the circle, still too close to Annie, but his eyes went wide as he realized who it was who challenged him.

"Son. I was hoping you'd stop by."

"Let her go." Sebastian folded his arms across his chest, and he knew he looked larger than life, that the magic flowed from him in waves of power.

Aldo took a short step back, obviously surprised. "Sebastian? Why, son, I had no idea." The man practically cackled as he stared at him, and Sebastian wondered what the old bastard was thinking.

Then he felt a surge of power from the pack, and he was there, in his father's mind, and the disgusting miasma coating the man's thoughts almost made him retch. But he knew. Suddenly Sebastian knew exactly what his father had planned.

He hoped like hell he hadn't made a terrible mistake. "Let her go, Aldo."

"What? You've always called me father. Have those foul creatures turned my only son against me?"

"There was no need for them to do anything. You are not my father. Not anymore. I want no part of you or your plans."

Aldo smiled, a hideous caricature of pleasure. "But they involve you, my beloved son. Why do you think you even exist? I fucked that bitch just to get you. Do you think I would have touched her otherwise? I knew about shapeshifters, even though they were still in hiding—documents I took from your mother. She'd gotten them when her older sister died. She was a lab technician who worked for a government official named

Milton Bosworth. It seems Bosworth had authorized secret experiments on a freak, a female who was part wolf. Do you know what fascinated me most about her? Tests showed she was practically immortal."

Sebastian. The authority in Anton's voice raised shivers along his spine. *Keep him talking. We're familiar with some of this information, but we need to know more.*

"What's your point, old man?"

"Interesting way to put it." Aldo's smile made his flesh crawl. "You'll never grow old. Did you know that? It's one of the things those Chanku bastards have over humans. You have it too. I want it. I want your power, and your immortality. I want your life force, son."

He stared at the one who had fathered him and felt ill. The man was truly insane. "Turn her loose. Now."

"I will. On one condition."

Sebastian glared at him. "Name it."

"That you take her place."

Lily cried out. *No, Sebastian. You can't. He'll kill you. I'm stronger than him.* "Set her free, first."

"How do I know you won't attack me? Why should I trust you?"

"Because I don't lie. And because I don't think you have the strength to fight my magic."

Aldo burst into laughter and glanced at the rogues behind him. "Set her free. The boy's got delusions of grandeur. He's never been stronger than me." He muttered something under his breath as two of the rogues went to Annie and unfastened her restraints.

Sebastian felt the power of the spell surround him. The connection linking him to Lily, to Anton, and the power of the pack flashed out like the blink of a light.

He stood before his father, his magic lying dead in his veins as Annie stumbled away from the tree. She reached for him as she passed, but energy from the wards sizzled and burned her hand. Stricken, she backed away.

Sebastian stood alone. The moon was almost directly overhead, and he felt the power of its brilliant reflection. As the rogues moved toward him, he raised his arms overhead and called out to the Mother, but there was no sound.

He couldn't let his father take him, but his legs refused to move, and he stood there, wondering if the pack would realize he was trapped within the same spell that had held Annie.

"Come, boy."

Like a mindless automaton, he followed Aldo toward the tree. He was vaguely aware of Annie stumbling away toward the woods, heading straight for Alex, closer to safety, but his goal had become the tree. He had to touch the bark, connect to the spirit that had guided him, and with that thought in mind, he found the strength to move beyond his father.

He felt the roots beneath his feet and drew the energy into his body. Reached out and touched the rough bark and the Mother answered his call. Her power rushed back into him, filling him with energy so pure, so powerful that his body glowed.

Brighter, as more power flowed into him. He felt the Mother, and the goddess Eve, and as Aldo's wards began to fail, the energy from the Chanku pack flew into him, and all of it was tempered by his love for Lily. He pressed himself against the trunk, drawing even more into himself. Wolves burst out of the surrounding forest, more than he'd realized were even nearby. The six massive rogue wolves leapt into battle, and the others still in human form drew guns. One grabbed Sebastian around the neck and pressed the barrel of a handgun to his temple.

"Don't kill him. Not this way." Aldo rushed the rogue and shoved the gun away. "He's mine. His energy is mine. His immortal spirit is mine."

He shoved Sebastian against the tree and strengthened the spell that was barely holding him, but that was exactly what Sebastian needed. The Mother was there, strong and giving, her energy passing through the bark, through the life-giving roots, filling Sebastian, drawing power from the rocks and the nearby stream, pulling it from the moon overhead, and sucking it out of Aldo Xenakis.

Sebastian felt his father's spell slough away like so much dead skin.

A fierce battle raged all around. All twelve of the rogue wolves had shifted, so that their numbers were almost evenly matched, but in size and strength the rogues had the edge.

Lily went down, a huge wolf at her throat, while Alex and his father fought off a pair who'd gone after Annie. Sebastian shoved Aldo, and the man stumbled, but then he pulled a long silver blade from the sleeve of his robe and rushed Sebastian.

Sebastian had barely a second to call on the Mother, to raise his hand to the nighttime sky and pull down the lightning. A single bolt of immense power and energy flashed out of the clear, moonlit sky.

A single bolt that struck Aldo Xenakis dead center in the middle of his chest. He'd not even fallen before the massive burst of energy grounded itself in Sebastian, standing his hair on end and sparking off his skin in crackling sparks of blue and gold.

Then it flashed from one rogue to another, too fast for the eye to follow so that only the afterimage burned into sensitive eyes told the story. Xenakis was dead before his body fell, a look of absolute disbelief on his face, that his son should have such power.

Before he hit the ground, lightning had speared each of the rogues. They died where they stood, falling so fast they made no sound. Unlike a dying Chanku shapeshifter who would return to human form, these creatures died as wolves, proof they were closer to their feral roots than the human side. Their bodies lay scattered across the ridge. Smoke drifted lazily from each, and the stench of ozone and burning hair and flesh polluted the air.

It was a small victory at a terrible cost. Sebastian didn't even glance at his father. Instead he leapt over the man's body, ran directly to Lily, and knelt beside her.

She lay in the torn dirt, still in her wolven form; her attacker sprawled beside her, dead. Lily's throat was torn and bleeding, but her eyes were open. As he knelt there, feeling helpless and afraid, Lily shifted, but she didn't try to speak. He carefully lifted her in his arms and held her against his chest.

Anton? We need help. Healers, now. Xenakis and the rogues are dead, but Lily's badly injured. I don't know how many others are hurt. Help us.

He felt a warm hand clasp his shoulder and glanced up. Anton stood beside him, covered in sweat and blood. "We're here. Adam, Logan, and Liana are working on the most seriously injured. Liana will be here to help Lily in just a few minutes."

He knelt beside Sebastian and took his daughter's hand. "Hell of a fight, sweetheart. I know it hurts, but the bastard missed the artery. Just hang on and think about this man you mated." He glanced at Sebastian and smiled. "I've never seen power like that before. You didn't draw it from the pack until the very end. Aldo had you blocked. Where did you get the power to call the lightning?"

"The goddess Eve was here. I felt her, but most came directly from the Mother." He glanced toward the tree. It was nothing more than an oak now. There was no sense of the spirit within. "She's always come when I've needed her. I just never realized what a tough old broad she was."

Oh, Sebastian. Lily's eyes actually sparkled. *Don't let Eve hear you say that.* Smiling even as he fought tears of relief, Sebastian held the woman he loved in his arms.

"Eve already heard that."

"Eve?" Sebastian watched as the goddess knelt beside Lily. "I sensed your spirit, but I didn't know you could physically leave the astral."

"Sometimes, when I'm needed." She brushed Lily's tangled hair back from her face and touched her fingers to the gaping wound on Lily's throat. "And it appears I am needed tonight."

The sun was high over the Rockies before they were able to return to the house. The sheriff's department had sent out their forensics team to collect samples from the dead wolves and to take Aldo Xenakis's body away, but Sebastian was still so wound up he doubted he'd ever sleep again.

The trip off the mountain had been slow, as he'd carried Lily the entire way down in his arms. He wasn't ready to turn his mate loose. Neither, it appeared, was Alex, who held Annie close against his chest. It was an unusual procession of naked men and woman along with a few wolves and a pair of snow leopards, but Sebastian realized it didn't seem as odd as it might have just a few days earlier.

His life continued to evolve.

He stopped by Lily's cottage and wrapped her in a beautiful copper-colored sarong, though she had to show him how to tie the knot. He found another pair of Alex's jogging shorts to wear.

"Does Alex actually go jogging?"

Lily just laughed and held out her arms. He picked her up and carried her through her mother's beautiful gardens, aware on some instinctual level which grasses he might want to nibble on. Then he carried Lily through the sliding glass door off the back deck and took her directly to Anton's den. Stefan, Alex,

Annie, and Keisha already sat in front of the bar. Alex's mom, Xandi, slept in one of the big overstuffed chairs, and Anton was behind the bar, opening a new bottle of Hennessy.

He nodded toward the leather couch, and Sebastian set Lily there. "I can sit at the bar, Sebastian."

"Humor me." He leaned over and kissed her. "You just got your throat torn out and almost killed by a rogue wolf." He trapped her between his extended arms and pressed a tender kiss against the healing marks before kissing her soundly.

She came out of the kiss with a dreamy expression on her face. "Okay. I guess."

"Thank you." He turned and walked over to the bar. Without a word, Anton handed him two snifters with healthy shots of cognac.

Then Anton did something totally out of character. He grabbed his own glass, walked out from behind the bar and across the room, and sat on the couch next to Lily. Sebastian took the other side, but he slung an arm over her shoulders. It was going to take a long time before he felt like turning her loose.

"I want to propose a toast," Anton said. His gaze slipped from Lily to Sebastian, and then settled on his daughter. "I always wondered how I would feel when my daughter took a mate. Would I be jealous that another male had her attention? Would I worry he wasn't strong enough to protect her? Would he be confident enough as a man to let her be the powerful woman she has always been? Lots of questions for a father to ponder as his daughter takes that huge step away from his protection."

He turned his gaze to Sebastian. "All of my worries, it appears, are for naught. You, Sebastian, have proven your strength, your honor, and your magical ability beyond all expectations. I welcome you as a member of our family and as a valued new member of the pack. To you, Sebastian Xenakis, and to my lovely daughter Lily. May you love long and love well, and always find laughter together."

He held his glass out. Lily tapped the rim with hers and then it was Sebastian's turn. "Thank you." He glanced toward the others still sitting at the bar, surprised at how the crowd had grown. "Thank you all, for giving me the family I've never had, and for trusting me with one of your most precious members."

He leaned close and kissed Lily, surprised when he tasted the salt of tears on her lips. He had to look away before his own spilled, and so he glanced again at the ones who'd joined the toast. The snow leopards, Mei and Oliver were here, along with others he was just getting to know. Adam and Liana, who had healed the injured with help from two pack members he'd not met before, Doc Logan and his mate, Jazzy Blue. Eve was still here, though he sensed her time on this plane was growing short. There were others he'd not seen before, and a threesome he hadn't met, though he recognized the men from tonight's battle.

The woman looked familiar on another level.

Anton waved her over. She walked across the room and stood in front of Sebastian. "It's good to meet you, Sebastian. I'm your cousin, Daci. Daciana Lupei. My mother and your mother were sisters." She held out her hand.

He stared at her for a moment in shock. Then he stood and pulled her into his arms. A cousin! There'd only ever been his mother, but hadn't Aldo said she had a sister? "Your mother was the lab assistant."

"That's right." Smiling broadly, the woman nodded. "She had an affair with Milton Bosworth, and I'm the result of the affair. I don't, however, claim my father."

Sebastian chuckled. "That seems to be going around."

The phone on Anton's desk rang. Keisha picked it up, listened for a few minutes, and then hung up. "That was the sheriff's department. Aldo has been linked by forensics to the rapes.

His wolves were responsible for the murders, at least of the young women up here. Since there's been no mention of them shifting and they died as wolves, it clears the Chanku entirely. Once the sheriff has Aldo's travel records and DNA from the victims down there, he says he expects he'll be able to link them to the killings in the Bay Area as well."

Alex slipped off his bar stool and grabbed Annie's hand. "That's good. I'm glad it's over." He turned and kissed Annie. "And I'm really glad I've got Annie."

Tinker stood and planted himself in front of Alex. "Son, I'm glad, too. I'm sorry I gave you such a hard time. I have to quit thinking of you as a ten-year-old bundle of hell-raising energy. I was really proud of you tonight. Both of you. I think you've both made a good match."

"Thanks, Tinker. I figure it's all about payback. One of these days, when Annie and I have pups of our own, they'll be your grandchildren. If they're anything like me, I imagine I'll be needing your experience then."

Tinker chuckled. "Here's hoping they take after their mother. For both your sakes."

Laughing, Alex tugged Annie along behind him. Almost to the door, they paused in front of Anton. "Any idea who the latest victim was?"

Anton nodded. "It was a girl you dated. Jennifer Martin. It turns out she worked for Aldo Xenakis. The guys who went after Annie in town that night were three of the rogues."

Alex sighed and slowly shook his head. "Interesting. I'm sorry about Jennifer, though if I'd known she worked for Aldo, a lot of things she said and did would have made more sense." He focused on Anton. "I think she was pumping me for information about the pack. I was careful not to tell her much, but I don't like feeling used."

Then he shot a teasing glance at Annie. "I just realized—no wonder those guys who hassled you in town were so big. Do you realize I flattened three rogues on my own to insure your honor?" He shot a grin at Tinker. "Your dad has to be nice to me now." He wrapped an arm around her neck and pulled her close. "Oh, Lil? Annie and I are taking the cottage tonight. Hope you don't mind."

Tinker growled softly, but Alex and Annie were both laughing as they left. Lily glared after them. "What about us?"

"We can stay here tonight." Sebastian leaned close and kissed her. "And since I'm Aldo Xenakis's only heir—something he loved to remind me of—I imagine we can do something with a twelve-room cabin on the five hundred thousand acres abutting your dad's property."

Lily turned and stared at him, wide-eyed. "Ya think?"

"And there's also the house in the city. It's over in the Sunset, not too far from your place in the Marina District. I have to admit, though, I like yours better."

Her smile lit up her entire face. "Me too."

He wondered if she was thinking of that sybaritic bathroom and remembering what they'd done there. He nodded. "We'll make a decision after a thorough cleansing of all the bad vibes around my father's properties. I don't want any essence of dark magic anywhere."

He stared at his glass of cognac and thought of all that had happened in such a short time, how much his life had changed. "We just might have to tear it down and build something new."

Anton wasn't sure what woke him, but he was a man who'd learned to listen to his instincts. He left his wife sleeping, slipped on a pair of worn sweatpants, and padded down the hallway.

He paused outside the room Lily and Sebastian had taken this morning. They'd not come out once during the day, though Keisha had delivered a couple of meals that hadn't been turned down.

He remembered days like that, staying in bed with his

beloved mate for hours on end. Making love, talking, learning one another.

He opened his senses and chuckled softly. Lily's sleeping mind was strongest, but it appeared Alex and Annie had joined them, just as Stefan and Xandi had so often spent the night with Keisha and him. As they still did.

Then he realized one mind was missing. He didn't sense Sebastian's thoughts, at least not here. Following a hunch, Anton walked back to the den and slipped through the door to the deck.

Sebastian was out there, wearing a pair of sweats that looked suspiciously like an old pair of Stefan's. He was leaning against the deck railing, staring out across the meadow.

Anton walked up beside Sebastian and rested his elbows on the railing. It was a full minute before Sebastian spoke.

"Remember that story in the news a couple years ago, the one where some doctor was cloning babies to harvest body parts?"

Anton nodded. "I do. It was terrible, but at least they were able to save the children, find them good homes."

"I remember being really disgusted by the whole thing, the ethics of it, the inhumanity, but I never really thought of the children's point of view. What it would feel like for them, when they got old enough to understand that their very existence was due to the fact that rich old men were willing to pay to grow them like a crop to harvest their parts. I wonder how that's going to affect them once they're old enough to understand what that means?"

"That's what Aldo did to you, isn't it?"

Sebastian nodded. "He knew my mother was a shapeshifter, knew she had the genetics to be nearly immortal, but he didn't understand enough about Chanku physiology to know how he could get that for himself, other than to get her with child, raise that child until he was sure he had a real Chanku shapeshifter, and then kill the child and take his life force."

"But your mother took you and ran."

Sebastian turned and looked at him. "Yep. She didn't know what he planned, but knew it couldn't be good. That's why she warned me against finding him. I should have listened to her."

Anton studied him a moment—the strong profile, the intelligence in those fascinating eyes—and then shook his head. "No. You did the right thing. If you hadn't found him, you wouldn't have stopped him. You stopped him tonight, son. You ended a reign of terror that law enforcement now believes has gone on for decades. They'll be following up on missing person reports for a long time, trying to figure out which ones might be linked to Aldo Xenakis. He's used death magic for years. That's what allowed him to become so powerful. Death magic gave him almost unlimited power. It didn't run out because he never stopped killing."

"How did he control the Berserkers? They followed him with such devotion. It makes no sense."

"I imagine it was a combination of magic, what he could offer them, and his natural charisma. He must have known about the military tests, the fact there were shapeshifters who were different from the rest of us, and when he discovered the strength of their bloodlust, their need to kill, he provided the victims and made sure they weren't discovered. Your father was a brilliant, charismatic man, I'll give him that, but he let his need for power corrupt him."

Sebastian turned away and stared toward the dark forest. "I saw things in his mind as he died. What he did to those young women. He used fear to increase the power of the magic. He'd rape them with the wolves all around, snarling and snapping at them until they were incoherent with terror. He fed off that. It made the magic stronger. Then, when he was done, he let the wolves tear them to pieces. They died so horribly, Anton. He stood there gloating, stealing their life force, watching them die in agony."

Sebastian shuddered, almost as if he tried to shake off his connection to the man who had fathered him. His struggle to maintain his composure was painful to watch, and when he finally turned and looked at Anton, he was hollow-eyed with the horror of what his father had done. "I'm afraid I'll live with those images forever."

Anton put his hands on the young man's shoulders and looked into eyes unlike any wolf he'd ever seen. Teal blue eyes, so troubled now, shadowed by terrible acts that would never be forgotten. Sometimes a man had to learn to live with evil deeds—horrible things that could not be altered—but that's where the strength of the pack came into play.

"What happened is over. You ended it, Sebastian. Without you, he would still be killing innocent young women. Think of the good you've done, the fact that your bravery and your magic have ended a nightmare. It's ended, now. It's part of the past."

Sebastian stared at the mountains bathed in moonlight. Just last night, he'd faced his own father on that mountain and had discovered strengths he'd never known he had. Anton wondered how that affected him, that experience with such power. Did he have his father's need for more?

"No," he said, smiling at Anton. "I seem to have come through last night's experience with more power than I ever imagined. Your thoughts are clear to me. I couldn't read you before unless you projected."

"How?"

"The lightning that killed him. I drew it down and it struck Aldo, but I felt the blast ground through me before it hit the Berserkers. My father had worked a spell that would take my life force and add it to his. Somehow it appears to have reversed when he died. I've got my father's magic, but not his darkness."

"Amazing. Does Lily know?"

"Not yet. I've only just figured it out myself. I can feel the power. It's not an easy melding, but I think it will settle down eventually." He turned to Anton then and smiled. "I'm going to need some training. Are you up to the job?"

"I think so." He felt the excitement growing. There hadn't been such a fascinating challenge in his life for much too long, and he loved the idea of the chance to get to know Sebastian better. The boy had spirit. He was smart and he obviously loved Lily. It was hard to find any fault with that.

"Lily's talking about taking a leave of absence, staying here until I learn more about being Chanku, about handling my magic. She wants me to get to know the pack, and for them to know me. Alex and Annie said they'd move into the Marina house for a while, take care of things for Lily at Cheval International." He chuckled, sounding more relaxed by the minute. "Personally, I think Alex wants time with Annie far from her father. I don't blame him. Tinker's got a scary side."

"Tinker works very hard to project that image, but Annie's right. He's a softie." Anton sensed Keisha awake and waiting for his return. He pushed himself away from the railing and clapped a hand on Sebastian's shoulder. "You are a son any man could be proud of. Welcome to the family, Sebastian."

"Thank you. I'll do my best not to disappoint you."

"Just don't ever disappoint Lily. She's the one who matters."

"Yes, sir."

He headed back to Keisha, feeling terribly pleased with the way things had worked out. He'd often wondered if Lily would find a man who could challenge her. It appeared she'd found exactly what she needed.

* * *

Sebastian wasn't certain how long he stood out there on the deck, leaning on the railing and watching the moon slide across the heavens, but he took the time to thank Eve, to honor the Mother with a prayer of thanks, and to think of all the changes in his life that had occurred over the past few days.

The biggest change wasn't the fact he was Chanku and could shift with merely a thought. It wasn't that his father was dead, by his hand, or that his magic was exponentially stronger than it had ever been before.

No, it was Lily. The woman waiting in the big bed with two others he was already growing to love. If there was any magic in this world, he was convinced it began and ended with Lily Cheval.

Smiling, he turned his back on the moonlight and the dark mountains and headed inside the house. Lily, Alex, and Annie were in there together. He'd left them sleeping, all curled together like a litter of pups, though Alex was the only one who'd been in his wolf form. He wondered what that felt like, spending an entire night as a wolf.

There was such a simple way to find out. He slipped out of his sweatpants, dropped them on an empty table, and shifted. Then, padding softly on his big paws, Sebastian Xenakis nudged open the door to the bedroom with his nose and leapt up on the bed. Alex grunted and moved aside, but Lily opened her arms and reached for him.

He lay down beside her and rested his chin on her breast. Her arms tightened around his neck, and he settled against her long, slim form, truly relaxed for the first time since he'd discovered his father's existence.

Lily's soft loving thoughts filled his mind, shoving the memories aside. It was time for new memories. Memories with the woman who'd sworn to love him for all time.

Turn the page for a special preview
of the second book in
Kate Douglas's brand-new series

DARK MOON

An Aphrodisia trade paperback coming soon!

1

December 21, 2008, Kalispell, Montana

Igmutaka, spirit guide, puma shapeshifter, and currently a very nervous man, stood at the foot of the birthing bed, hands raised in supplication to his gods and the woman's goddess. Tala Temple-Fuentes squatted amid the tangled sheets with her mate, Miguel Fuentes, a man who had long been Igmutaka's charge, supporting her gravid frame.

Her other mate clung to her hand, gazing at her with such love and so much intensity it was almost as if AJ Temple planned to push the babes out himself.

There were two. The male—the one created from the seed of the white man—would be a strong boy. AJ was a good man, and his son would grow to be a powerful warrior, an ideal sibling for the child Igmutaka waited to meet. The one who mattered to him most.

The girl child, the one born of Mik's seed, was to be the first female ever in Igmutaka's charge. Her father, like AJ, was a powerful Chanku shapeshifter, a good, strong man. Called Mik, he was the latest in the long line of Lakota Sioux warriors who had called on Igmutaka as their spirit guide.

Always Igmutaka had watched over the male progeny, but this child was different—not merely because of her gender.

He felt her strength, her power—the feminine power so different from that of the males he had guided. He'd been aware of this babe almost from the moment of conception. He'd known she was special, though he still didn't understand how or why.

He glanced up, aware the bedroom was filling quickly. Other females—shapeshifters all—coming to share the pain and the joy of the one who labored, using their minds and bodies to ease Tala as she pushed the babies from her womb. Men arrived, ready to share in the celebration of new members joining their pack, but also generously taking on Tala's pain.

It was all good. Igmutaka focused once again on the mother.

She grunted and strained. He had no time to think, no time to question why he should be the one who slipped his hands beneath her straining body and caught the babe amid a wash of fluids and blood, caught her in his big hands and stared into eyes that saw him in a way no one else had ever seen him before.

He held the squirming bundle of new life as his own impossibly long years flashed before him. Hers so new and fresh, his beginning so long ago that his childhood was lost to memory. He knew he must have started in a time long past, though not as a babe like this. No, he'd not been a helpless child, born of woman into an ancient world.

He'd been a puma cub. Born amid a litter of siblings, though he had no memory of that life.

He'd been spirit far too long.

He'd only taken on a physical body again in the past few years, running as a wild puma so that he could interact with the Chanku shapeshifters who had called him from the spirit world.

Then, mere weeks ago, he'd manifested as a human male for

the first time, the same male who stood here now, holding Tala and Mik's newborn daughter. A beautiful, dark-haired girl child who would one day grow to be a strong and beautiful woman.

Adam, one of their healers, cut the umbilical cord, separating the newborn from her mother. One of the women quickly wiped away the blood and afterbirth on the child he held as Tala delivered the second babe. Twins. A boy and a girl. Both strong, healthy babies.

Igmutaka bowed his head as he placed the newborn against her mother's breast. Bowed to the babe and to fate, to the woman this child would grow to be.

A woman Igmutaka knew would change his life for all time.

New Haven, Connecticut, thirty years later

Star Fuentes heard the soft tone that signaled her mother's call, checked the time, and realized she still had a few minutes before her date was due to arrive.

She took a sip of her wine, flipped on the cell, and smiled at her mom, a sixty-two-year-old woman who appeared to be in her late twenties. That was one of the wonderful things about being Chanku—aging slowed and practically stopped at the prime of life.

Tala's mates looked just as young—early thirties at most— both of them so damned good-looking it was hard for Star to think of them as her two dads. In reality, Mik was sixty-eight and AJ already seventy-two. As with all Chanku, each faced an unlimited life span with those same youthful bodies and minds.

Star quit woolgathering as Tala's broad grin and sparkling amber eyes chased away the discontent that had followed her like a cloud over the past weeks. "Hey, Mom. What's up?"

"You mean other than your fathers?"

Star slapped her hand over her mouth to keep from spewing wine on the small screen. "Too much information, ya know?"

Tala's laughter sent a shaft of homesickness through Star. She hadn't been home to Montana for much too long. She missed Mik, her biological father, and AJ, her mom's other mate. Hell, she even missed her damned spirit guide, but that was the last thing she'd ever admit.

"I just wondered when you were planning to come home." Tala's smile slipped. "I miss you, honey. You've been gone so long."

"I visited last Christmas." Short and not nearly enough time to reconnect with her mountain home. With her family. Her pack.

"You know that visit was much too brief, and you only let us talk you into it because it was your thirtieth birthday." Her mom sighed. "Don't you think it's time to come back? You're a pack animal at heart, Star." She laughed, and Star felt the sting of tears in her eyes. "You can only stay away for just so long. Even Jack misses you."

"Jack said that?" Star rolled her eyes. "Now that's hard to believe."

"You're not kidding. For your twin to admit something like that, well, it's downright scary." Then the smile slipped from Tala's lips, and she softly added, "It's been almost fourteen years, sweetheart."

Scrambling for yet another excuse, Star glanced at the stack of papers lying beside her computer. "I don't know, Mom. I'm thinking of applying for another doctoral program. I'll need to make the decision this week."

"Star, don't you think you have enough letters after your name? Don't you miss the pack? Miss your family?"

So much it hurt to even think about it, but she wasn't ready. Not yet. A brisk knock on the door caught her attention.

"Gotta go, Mom. My date's here, but I promise to think about it. I love you."

"I love you, too. The dads send their love. Sunny said to tell you hi."

"Thanks. Give her a big hug for me, and the dads, too. Bye, Mom."

"Star? Before you go, one last thing."

"What's that?"

"You can't hide from him forever, sweetheart. Some things are stronger than we are, and he's one of them. I love you."

A shiver raced along Star's spine as the screen went dark. In all the years she'd been away, her mother had never asked her to come home to stay, had never mentioned the real reason she'd chosen to live so far from the pack. Why now?

Besides, she wasn't hiding. Not really.

He knew where to find her.

Another knock brought Star to her feet and her womb clenched in what she knew was probably futile anticipation.

That was the problem with living among humans. Her Chanku libido ran circles around that of the average male. Fourteen years of less than satisfactory sex was probably reason enough to call it quits and head home, but damn it all, the risk was too great.

She'd gotten her spirit guide's promise to let her live life on her own terms while she was away at school. Of course, he probably hadn't figured she'd make a career out of getting an education, but she knew that once she returned, he'd be right back in her life.

Taking over her life.

She'd grown up with two fathers, a concerned mother, an overprotective twin brother, and a pack full of uncles and aunties watching out for her. None of them had threatened her independence the way Igmutaka managed with nothing more than a soft suggestion, a raised eyebrow, or the turn of a phrase.

Talk about frustrating. He protected her and guarded her against harm, which also meant protecting her from life in general. He'd also managed to keep all the eligible boys away at the same time, but that wasn't the worst part.

No, it was the fact he was absolutely beautiful, and she'd loved him. Loved him as only a young girl could love. Deeply, with all of her heart and soul. Tall and lean with smooth, bronzed skin, gorgeous green eyes, and thick, dark hair, he had an androgynous beauty that would make him look as striking if he'd been a woman, yet there was no doubting the masculinity of the man. Nope. No doubt at all.

Star practically whimpered as she drew his image close. So beautiful as a cougar, with a sinewy grace that carried over to his human form. He rarely showed himself to her as a man, yet his was the face that filled her dreams, her fantasies, and her lonely nights.

Except, he didn't feel the same way. Igmutaka was her spirit guide, fated to protect her, not to bed her. She'd loved him without reservation from the time she could remember—first as a father figure, and then when she'd realized he was still young and sexy and she was definitely growing older and interested—as a potential mate.

He'd treated her as something fragile. Untouchable, and while she knew he wasn't celibate, he'd certainly kept his charge—the one he called Mikaela Star—that way. She'd not lost her virginity with a man until she finally left home for college, though she still couldn't figure out what the big deal was.

She knew other Chanku women managed to have wonderful sex with humans, though they all eventually mated with Chanku, but she'd never once found satisfaction with a human male.

Not that she didn't keep trying, but since she'd rarely had the chance to have sex with another Chanku, and only on the rare occasions when one of the guys visited her in New Haven, she really had very little for comparison, goddess be damned.

She pushed Igmutaka and a lifetime of sexual frustration out of her mind and opened the door. Her date stood there, poised to knock a third time. He was tall and handsome, his smile as perfect as modern technology could make it.

And for the life of her, she couldn't remember his name.

"Are you ready?" he asked.

"As ready as I'll ever be." She flashed him a bright smile as she grabbed her bag and a soft wrap. At least as ready as she'd be with a man she hardly knew, but who, at least, wasn't her insufferable, sensual, pain-in-the-ass spirit guide.

Sunny Daye sprawled bonelessly over the long, lean body of her lover. He was gorgeous, absolutely spectacular in bed, and it just about broke her heart knowing he'd never satisfy that empty spot in her soul, the part of her crying out for a mate.

His long fingers stroked her left breast and then he playfully tapped her nipple. It tightened immediately, and she felt the touch between her legs as her womb rippled in response.

Supporting her upper body on her elbows, she raised her head and glared at him. Why in the hell couldn't he be the one? She'd known, though. Since the very first time he'd made love to her—the night he gently took her virginity so many years ago—that as much as she loved him, she couldn't love him *that way*. Still, the man could make magic when they came together. She sighed, flopped back on the mattress, and arched into his touch. "I hope you're planning to follow through with that."

Igmutaka gave her a long, lazy smile, reached down, and stroked his sizeable erection with one hand. "Have you ever known me not to follow through?"

She felt her anger sliding away. It wasn't his fault he was absolutely perfect, and at the same time, perfectly wrong. For her, at least. She knew the one he loved. Knew that, so far anyway, that love wasn't being returned. "Star's an idiot."

He grinned as he stroked a line from her throat to her pubes. "Mikaela Star is young. She has yet to discover her path. It will, of course, lead directly to me."

"You sound so sure." She laughed softly as his hands slid up her body and he stroked the sensitive skin beneath her breasts. "What if you're wrong? What if she chooses another?"

Lying beside her, he teased the nipple he'd tapped earlier, working it gently with his teeth and tongue for a moment before lifting his head. His lips were shiny—as slick and shiny as her nipple—and they parted on a soft smile. "Then I will kill the bastard."

Sunny laughed. Ig was not really a killer . . . was he?

He grinned at her. "I've not told many of this, but it was foretold when she was still in Tala's womb. I knew Mikaela Star was special when Tala carried her and we actually communicated before her birth. When Tala pushed her forth and she fell into my hands, I knew she was mine." He gazed at Sunny over the dark red nipple he'd so skillfully aroused. "One does not question a gift from the gods."

"I see." She moaned as he lowered his head and began working on the other breast. After only a moment of pure bliss, Ig raised his head again.

"You are a gift as well, Sunny. Not for me, though. Your man is out there. I sense him drawing close. You will know him soon." He tilted his head and frowned. "Very soon."

My man? Soon? Sunny shoved herself up on her elbows so quickly she knocked Igmutaka aside. "Where is he? Who is he? How do you know?"

Laughing, Ig rolled to his back. "I don't know the details. I just know he's coming." He sat up, and his look grew pensive as he shrugged those wide shoulders. "Just as I know that tonight Mikaela Star is with yet another young man, another lover who will disappoint her. Before long, she will accept that I am the one who loves her, that I am the only one who can make her happy."

The yearning in his voice was almost her undoing. Sunny ran her fingers through the thick hair tumbled across his forehead. "I know you're not my mate, Ig, but you've never disappointed me, and you always make me smile."

He leaned close and kissed her. Covered her small body once again with his much larger one. She arched beneath him, finding the broad head of his penis already pressing against her labia. With a slight tilt to her hips, she opened to him, felt the slick burn as he filled her, sliding that thick length all the way to the end of her vaginal sheath.

He was big and hard and fit her perfectly. He was funny and sweet, brave and powerful, and so beautiful he made her ache.

A perfect man.

Just not a perfect mate.

At least not for Sunny Daye.

After a really nice dinner, they'd ended up back at his apartment, which was a good thing, especially since Star still hadn't recalled his name. She finally spotted it on a framed diploma on the wall. Haydon. His name was Haydon Smith, and she remembered that she'd met him in one of the libraries on campus.

Another good thing about ending up at Haydon's apartment was that it was his place, not hers. She hated having to ask a man to leave after sex, but she had sex with a lot of guys, and she didn't want them hanging around afterward, especially when they never managed to leave her satisfied.

This guy hadn't even tried very hard, but he'd certainly managed to find his own satisfaction. More than once. Now he slept soundly, so she carefully lifted his arm off her breasts and slid out from beneath him. As she turned away to get out of the bed, that same arm snaked around her waist.

"Leaving, Star?"

Well, crap. "Uh, yeah. I need to get home." She glanced over her shoulder and realized he was wide awake, glaring at her for whatever reason.

"What if I don't want you to go yet?"

She shrugged her shoulders. "It's late. I had a good time, but I really have to leave."

His grasp around her waist tightened. He was a lot bigger than her, and he pulled her back across the bed and roughly nuzzled her neck. "Mmmmm. You smell good." He bit her earlobe hard enough for it to hurt, but she refused to react. He was really starting to piss her off.

"You know what the guys call you?" He tightened his hold around her waist. "The Ballbuster. Word is you can go all night and then walk away like it was nothing." His voice dropped to a low, threatening growl. "I haven't had all night yet, Star. You can walk away when I say you can walk. Not before."

Now this was a first. She tried to break free of his grasp, but he merely held on tighter. His breath was hot as he spoke directly into her ear. "I think you owe me the rest of the night, don't you, Star? That was a really expensive dinner."

She'd managed almost fourteen years of world travel, college, and grad school without guys acting anything but grateful after a night of sex. Plus, not a single man had ever guessed she wasn't human. Though the world knew shapeshifters existed among them, she'd chosen to guard her Chanku origins and keep her abilities secret from all but a select few on campus.

Maybe this jerk was a sign. Maybe Mom was right—it was time to go home. And she wasn't thinking of merely going back to her apartment.

She shifted. Even though the wolf came most naturally, she chose her cougar form, twisting her strong, sinuous body out of his grasp as her date suddenly screamed like a little girl and scrambled across the bed so fast he fell off the other side.

Star merely stretched out over the bed, hooked her claws deep into the mattress until the fabric ripped, hung her head over the edge, and stared at him. Eyes wide, he stared back at her. She stretched one broad paw toward him and further unsheathed her long, curved nails.

Babbling, he scrambled backward on all fours until he hit the wall, so she crouched on the edge of the mattress and raised her hindquarters as if to leap. Snarling, she let a bit of saliva drip from her open jaws and flexed her muscles.

An acrid stench filled her sensitive nostrils as a pool of urine stained the carpet between his legs. Star chuffed, which was the closest her puma could get to laughter, spun about on the bed, and shifted once more.

She didn't even look his way as she snagged her clothes off the floor and quickly dressed. Grabbing the door handle, she glanced over her shoulder. He was still sitting in a soggy, stinking heap on the floor across the room. She gave him her most disdainful look. "Don't ever pull that stunt on a woman again, or I will hunt you down."

Then she walked out of his room and headed back to her apartment.

Not quite the way she'd expected her night to end, but at least it hadn't been boring. And, if nothing else, it had helped make up her mind about the doctoral program.

Her mom was right. She had enough letters after her name, and she'd played the coward long enough. It was time to return to the pack, even if it meant finally having it out with her spirit guide. Igmutaka had been running her life for far too long—the fact she'd not felt comfortable returning home was proof she'd given him more control over her life than he deserved.

If he didn't love her, it was on him, and it was his loss, not hers, but it was time for Star to move forward.

It was early morning when she finally reached her own apartment—still much too early to call Montana. She showered, grabbed something to eat, and gave her folks until six before she finally called home. Her father answered, and she almost broke down and cried when his beautiful face flashed on the screen. There was something so elemental about him with his dark skin and strong Lakota Sioux and Hispanic features, an innate power that few men wore as well. Only Igmutaka came close. She missed her dad, missed her mom, and missed her other dad AJ just as much.

"What's up, sweetie? Mom said she talked to you last night. Is everything okay?"

She thought about that, and realized that yes, it was absolutely wonderful. Finally. "Everything's good, Dad. I've decided to come home, though not right away. I'm hoping for a chance to spend some time alone once I leave Connecticut. Is the cabin at Lassen free? I thought I'd go there for a week or so."

"We'll make sure it's available. When do you need it?"

She loved that about her parents. No questions. They just did what they could to make her life easier. "It's going to take me at least a week to get my stuff packed up and shipped, and another week to make the drive. If I can't get out of my lease, I'll have to sublet the apartment, but that shouldn't be a problem. It's a great location."

"It's going to be cold at the cabin. No one's been there for a while. I'll have it stocked for you. Will you be flying to California or driving?"

"Driving. And, Dad? Thank you. I love you."

"I love you, too, Mikaela Star. I've missed you. We've all missed you. Be safe. Come home to us as quickly as you can."